Betrayed

She took her hands from her face then and looked up at me, but I already knew who it was. I'd recognized her voice. And I also recognized what was happening to her. I forced myself to approach her calmly. She stared up at me. Her face was covered with tears.

'Come on, Aphrodite. You're having a vision. I need to get you to Neferet.'

'No!' she gasped. 'No! Don't take me to her. She won't listen to me. She – she doesn't believe me anymore.'

I remembered what Neferet had said earlier about Nyx withdrawing her gifts from Aphrodite. Why should I even mess with her at all? Who knew what was going on with Aphrodite? She was probably making some pathetic play for attention, and I didn't have time for this crap.

'Fine. Let's say I don't believe you either,' I told her. 'Stay here and have your vision or whatever. I have other things to worry about.' I turned to head into the stable, and her hand snaked out, grabbing my wrist.

'You have to stay!' she said through chattering teeth. Obviously, she was having difficulty talking. 'You have to hear the vision!'

'No, I do not.' I pried her vicelike fingers from my wrist. 'Whatever's going on, it's about you – not me. You deal with it.' This time when I turned I walked away more quickly.

But not quick enough. Her next words felt like she'd sliced them through me.

'You have to listen to me. If you don't your grandma will die.'

BY P. C. CAST AND KRISTIN CAST

The House of Night

MARKED

BETRAYED

CHOSEN

UNTAMED

HUNTED

TEMPTED

BURNED

AWAKENED

DESTINED

HIDDEN

The House of Night Novellas

DRAGON'S OATH

LENOBIA'S VOW

NEFERET'S CURSE

THE FLEDGLING HANDBOOK

A HOUSE of NIGHT novel

Betrayed

P.C. & KRISTIN CAST

www.atombooks.net

ATOM

First published in the United States in 2007 by St Martin's Press
First published in Great Britain in 2009 by Atom
This edition published in 2012 by Atom

A CIP catalogue record for this book
is available from the British Library.

ISBN 978-0-349001-13-5

Typeset in Granjon by Palimpsest Book Production Limited,
Falkirk, Stirlingshire
Printed and bound by CPI Group (UK) Ltd, Croydon CR0 4YY

Papers used by Atom are from well-managed forests
and other responsible sources.

MIX
Paper from
responsible sources
FSC® C104740

Atom
An imprint of
Little, Brown Book Group
100 Victoria Embankment
London EC4Y 0DY

An Hachette UK Company
www.hachette.co.uk

www.atombooks.net

We would like to dedicate this book to (Aunty) Sherry Rowland, friend and publicist. Thank you, Sher, for taking care of us. Even when we're high maintenance and annoying (and especially when you give us 'treaties'). We heart you very much.

Acknowledgments

As usual, we want to thank Dick L. Cast,
Dad/Grandpa, for knowing everything biological
and helping us with stuff.

Thank you to our amazing agent,
Meredith Bernstein, who came up with the
fabulous idea that began this series.

We would like to thank our St Martin's team,
Jennifer Weis and Stefanie Lindskog, for helping us
create such a wonderful series. In particular a big
WE HEART YOU to the talented artists
who designed such beautiful covers.

And we'd like to note a special acknowledgment
to Street Cats, a cat rescue and adoption service in Tulsa.
We support Street Cats (and actually adopted Nala
from them!) and appreciate their dedication to and
love for cats. Please visit their website at

www.streetcatstulsa.org for more information. If you're interested in giving to a pet rescue charity we promise that they are an excellent choice!
—P. C. & Kristin

I would like to send thanks out to my high school students who 1) beg to be put in these books and then killed off, 2) provide constant comedic fodder for me, 3) and will actually leave me alone sometimes so I can write.

NOW GO DO YOUR HOMEWORK.
Oh, and expect a quiz.
—Miss Cast

CHAPTER ONE

'NEW KID. CHECK IT OUT,' SHAUNEE SAID AS SHE SLID INTO the big boothlike bench we always claim as ours for every school meal served in the dining hall (translation: high-class school cafeteria).

'Tragic, Twin, just tragic.' Erin's voice totally echoed Shaunee's. She and Shaunee had some kind of psychic link that made them bizarrely similar, which is why we'd nicknamed them 'the Twins,' even though Shaunee is a café latte-colored Jamaican American from Connecticut and Erin is a blond-haired, blue-eyed white girl from Oklahoma.

'Thankfully, she's Sarah Freebird's roommate.' Damien

nodded toward the petite girl with seriously black hair who was showing the lost-looking new kid around the dining hall, his sharp, fashion-wise gaze checking out the two girls and their outfits – from shoes to earrings – in one fast glance. 'Clearly her fashion sense is better than Sarah's, despite the stress of being Marked and changing schools. Maybe she'll be able to help Sarah out with her unfortunate ugly shoe propensity.'

'Damien,' Shaunee said. '*Again* you are getting on my damn—'

'—last nerve with your unending vocab bullshit,' Erin finished for her.

Damien sniffed, looking offended and superior and gayer than he usually looked (even though he is definitely gay). 'If your vocabulary wasn't so abysmal you wouldn't have to carry a dictionary around with you to keep up with me.'

The Twins narrowed their eyes at him and sucked air to begin a new assault, which, thankfully, my roommate interrupted. In her thick Oklahoma accent, Stevie Rae twanged the two definitions as if she was giving clues for a spelling bee. 'Propensity – an often intense natural preference. Abysmal – absolutely horrible. There. Now would y'all quit bickering and be nice? You know it's almost time for parent visitation, and we shouldn't be acting like retards when our folks show up.'

'Ah, crap,' I said. 'I'd totally forgotten about parent visitation.'

Damien groaned and dropped his head down on the table, banging it not-so-gently. 'I'd totally forgotten, too.' The four of us gave him sympathetic looks. Damien's parents were cool with him being Marked, moving to the House of Night, and beginning the Change that would either turn him into a vampyre or, if his body rejected the transformation, kill him. They were not okay with him being gay.

At least Damien's parents were okay with something about him. My mom and her current husband – my step-loser, John Heffer – on the other hand, hated absolutely everything about me.

'My 'rentals aren't coming. They came last month. This month they're too busy.'

'Twin, once again we prove our twin-ness,' Erin said. 'My 'rentals sent me an e-mail. They aren't coming either 'cause of some Thanksgiving cruise they decided to take to Alaska with my Aunt Alane and Uncle Liar Lloyd. Whatever.' She shrugged – apparently as unbothered as Shaunee by her parents' absence.

'Hey, Damien, maybe your mama and daddy won't show either,' Stevie Rae said with a quick smile.

He sighed. 'They'll be here. It's my birthday month. They'll bring presents.'

'That doesn't sound so bad,' I said. 'You were talking about needing a new sketch pad.'

'They won't get me a sketch pad,' he said. 'Last year I asked for an easel. They got me camping supplies and a subscription to *Sports Illustrated*.'

'Eeesh!' said Shaunee and Erin together while Stevie Rae and I wrinkled our noses and made sympathetic noises.

Clearly wanting to change the subject, Damien turned to me. 'This'll be your parents' first visit. What're you expecting?'

'Nightmare,' I sighed. 'Total, absolute, and complete nightmare.'

'Zoey? I thought I'd bring my new roommate over to meet you. Diana, this is Zoey Redbird – the leader of the Dark Daughters.'

Glad to be diverted from having to talk about my own horrid parental issues, I looked up, smiling, at the sound of Sarah's tentative, nervous voice.

'Wow, it's really true!' the new girl blurted before I could even say hi. As per usual she was staring at my forehead and blushing bright red. 'I mean, uh . . . sorry. I didn't mean to be rude or anything . . .' she trailed off, looking miserable.

'That's okay. Yeah, it is true. My Mark is filled in and added to.' I kept my smile in place, trying to make her feel better, even though I truly hated that it seemed like I was the main attraction at a freak show. Again.

Thankfully, Stevie Rae chimed in before Diana's staring and my silence could get any more uncomfortable.

'Yeah, Z got that cool lacy spiral tattoo thing on her face and down along her shoulders when she saved her ex-boyfriend from some scary-assed vampyre ghosts,' Stevie Rae said cheerily.

'That's what Sarah told me,' Diana said tentatively. 'It just sounded so unbelievable that, well, I uh . . .'

'You didn't believe it?' Damien said helpfully.

'Yeah. Sorry,' she repeated, fidgeting and picking at her finger-nails.

'Hey, don't worry about it.' I worked up a fairly authentic smile. 'It seems pretty bizarre to me sometimes, and I was there.'

'And kicking butt,' Stevie Rae said.

I gave her my you-are-so-not-helping-me look, which she ignored. Yes, I might someday become their High Priestess, but I'm not exactly the boss of my friends.

'Anyway, this whole place can seem pretty strange at first. It gets better,' I told the new kid.

'Thanks,' she said with genuine warmth.

'Well, we better go so I can show Diana to where her fifth hour class will be,' Sarah said, and then she totally embarrassed me by getting all serious and formal and saluting me with the traditional vampyre sign of respect, closed fist over her heart and bowed head, before she left.

'I really hate it when they do that,' I muttered, picking at my salad.

'I think it's nice,' Stevie Rae said.

'You deserve to be shown respect,' Damien said in his school-teacher voice. 'You're the only third former ever to have been made leader of the Dark Daughters and the only fledgling or vampyre in history who has shown an affinity for all five of the elements.'

'Face it, Z,' Shaunee said around a bite of salad while she gestured at me with her fork.

'You're special.' Erin finished for her (as usual).

A third former is what the House of Night called freshmen – so a fourth former is a sophomore, et cetera. And, yes, I am the only third former to be made leader of the Dark Daughters. Lucky me.

'Speaking of the Dark Daughters,' Shaunee said. 'Have you decided what you want the new requirements for membership to be?'

I stifled the urge to shriek, *Hell no, I still can't believe I'm in charge of this thing!* Instead I just shook my head, and decided – with what I hoped was a stroke of brilliance – to put some of the pressure back on them.

'No, I don't know what the new requirements should be. Actually, I was hoping you guys would help me. So, do you have any ideas?'

As I suspected, all four of them got quiet. I opened my mouth to thank them very much for their muteness, but our High Priestess's commanding voice came over the school intercom. For a second I was happy about the interruption, and then I realized what she was saying and my stomach started to clench.

'Students and professors, please make your way to the reception hall. It is now time for this month's parent visits.'

Well, hell.

'Stevie Rae! Stevie Rae! Ohmygosh I have missed you!'

'Mama!' Stevie Rae cried and flew into the arms of a woman who looked just like her, only fifty pounds heavier and twenty-some years older.

Damien and I stood awkwardly just inside the reception hall, which was starting to fill up with uncomfortable-looking human parents, a few human siblings, a bunch of fledgling students, and several of our vampyre professors.

'Well, there're my parents,' Damien said with a sigh. 'Might as well get this over with. See ya.'

'See ya,' I mumbled and watched him join two totally ordinary people who were carrying a wrapped present. His mom gave him a quick hug and his dad shook his hand with exuberant masculinity. Damien looked pale and stressed.

I made my way over to the long, linen-draped table that ran the length of one wall. It was filled with expensive cheese and meat platters, desserts, coffee, tea, and wine. I'd been at the House of Night for a month, and it still was a little shocking to me that wine is served so readily here. Part of the reason they do is simple – the school is modeled after the European Houses of Night. Apparently, in Europe wine with meals is like tea or Coke with meals here – so no big deal. The other part is a genetic fact – vampyres don't get drunk – fledglings can barely get buzzed (at least on alcohol – blood, unfortunately, is a whole other issue). So wine literally is no big deal here, although I thought it would be interesting to check out how Oklahoma parents reacted to booze at school.

'Mama! You have to meet my roommate. Remember I told you about her? This is Zoey Redbird. Zoey this is my mama.'

'Hi, Mrs Johnson. It's good to meet you,' I said politely.

'Oh, Zoey! It is just so nice to meet you! And, *oh my!* Your Mark is as pretty as Stevie Rae said it was.' She surprised me with a soft mom hug and whispered, 'I'm glad you're taking care of my Stevie Rae. I worry about her.'

I squeezed her back and whispered, 'No problem, Mrs Johnson. Stevie Rae's my best friend.' And even though it was totally unrealistic, I suddenly wished my mom would hug me and worry about me like Mrs Johnson worried about her daughter.

'Mama, did you bring me any chocolate chip cookies?' Stevie Rae asked.

'Yes, baby, I did, but I just realized that I left them in the car.' Stevie Rae's mom twanged in an Okie accent that was identical to her daughter's. 'Why don't you come out with me and help me carry them inside. I made a little extra for your friends this time.' She smiled kindly at me. 'You're more than welcome to come on out with us, too, Zoey.'

'Zoey.'

I heard my voice spoken like a frozen echo of Mrs Johnson's warm kindness, and looked over her shoulder to see my mom and John coming into the hall. My heart fell into my stomach. She'd brought him. Why the hell couldn't she have come alone and let it be just her and me for a change? But I knew the answer to that. He would never allow it. And his not allowing it meant that she wouldn't do it. Period. End of subject. Since she'd married John Heffer my mom didn't have to worry about money. She lived in a gihugic house in a quiet suburban neighborhood. She volunteered for the PTA. She was majorly active in church. But during the past three years of her 'perfect' marriage she'd completely and utterly lost herself.

'Sorry, Mrs Johnson. I see my parents now, so I better go.'

'Oh, honey, I'd love to meet your mama and daddy.' And, like we were at any normal high school function, Mrs Johnson turned, smiling, to meet my parents.

Stevie Rae looked at me, and I looked at her. *Sorry*, I mouthed to her. I mean, I wasn't absolutely sure anything bad would happen, but with my step-loser closing the distance between us as if he were some testosterone-filled general leading a death march, I figured the odds were probably good for a nightmare scene.

Then my heart lifted way out of my stomach and everything suddenly got much, much better when my favorite person in the world stepped around John and held her arms out to me.

'Grandma!'

She enfolded me in her arms and the sweet scent of lavender that always moved with her, as if she carried a piece of her beautiful lavender farm everywhere she went.

'Oh, Zoeybird!' She held tight to me. 'I have missed you, *u-we-tsi-a-ge-ya*.'

I smiled through my tears, loving the sound of the familiar Cherokee word for daughter – it meant security and love and unconditional acceptance. Things I hadn't felt in my home for the past three years – things that before I'd come to the House of Night I'd only found at my grandma's farm.

'I've missed you, too, Grandma. I'm so glad you came!'

'You must be Zoey's grandmamma,' Mrs Johnson said when

we'd quit clinging to each other. 'It's so good to meet you. You have a fine girl here.'

Grandma smiled warmly and started to reply, but John interrupted in his usual I'm-so-superior voice.

'Well, actually, that would be *our* fine girl you would be complimenting.'

As if on a Stepford Wives cue, my mother finally managed to speak. 'Yes, we're Zoey's parents. I'm Linda Heffer. This is my husband, John, and my mother, Sylvia Red—' Then, in the middle of her oh-so-polite introductions, she bothered to actually look at me and her voice came to a breath-gulping halt midword.

I made my face smile, but it felt hot and hard, like it was poured plaster and had been sitting in the summer sun and would crack all to pieces if I wasn't careful.

'Hi, Mom.'

'For the love of God what have you done to that Mark?' Mom said the word *Mark* like she'd say the word cancer or pedophile.

'She saved the life of a young man and tapped into a Goddess-given affinity for the elements. In return Nyx has touched her with several unusual Marks for a fledgling,' Neferet said in her smooth musical voice as she walked into the middle of our awkward little group, hand extended directly to my step-loser. Neferet was what most adult vampyres are, stunningly perfect. She was tall, with long waves of dark auburn hair and brilliant, almond-shaped eyes an unusual shade of moss green. She moved with a grace and confidence that was clearly not human, and her skin was so spectacular that it looked like someone had turned a light on inside her. Today she was wearing a sleek, royal blue silk suit with silver spiral earrings (representing the path of the Goddess, but it's not like most parents knew that). A silver form of the Goddess with upraised hands was embroidered over her left breast, as it was over all the other professors' breasts. Her smile was dazzling. 'Mr Heffer, I am Neferet, High Priestess of the House of Night, although it might be easier if you would just think of me as you would any ordinary high school's principal. Thank you for coming to parent visitation night.'

I could tell that he took her hand automatically. I was sure he would have refused it if she hadn't caught him by surprise. She shook his hand quickly and then turned to my mom.

'Mrs Heffer, it is a pleasure to meet Zoey's mother. We are so pleased that she has joined the House of Night.'

'Well, uh, thank you!' my mom said, clearly disarmed by Neferet's beauty and charm.

When Neferet greeted my grandma, her smile widened and became more than just polite. I noticed that they shook hands in the traditional vampyre greeting style, grasping each other's forearms.

'Sylvia Redbird, it is always a pleasure to see you.'

'Neferet, it makes my heart glad to see you, too, and I thank you for honoring your oath to look after my granddaughter.'

'It is an oath that is not a burden to fulfill. Zoey is such a special girl.' Now Neferet's smile included me in its warmth. Then she turned to Stevie Rae and her mother. 'And this is Zoey's roommate, Stevie Rae Johnson, and her mother. I hear that the two of them are practically inseparable, and that even Zoey's cat has taken to Stevie Rae.'

'Yeah, it's true. She actually sat on my lap while we watched TV last night,' Stevie Rae said laughingly. 'And Nala doesn't like anyone except Zoey.'

'Cat? I don't remember anyone giving permission for Zoey to get a cat,' John said, making me want to retch. Like anyone except Grandma had bothered to talk to me for an entire month!

'You misunderstand, Mr Heffer, at the House of Night cats roam free. They choose their owners, not the other way around. Zoey didn't need permission when Nala chose her,' Neferet said smoothly.

John made a snorting noise, which I was relieved to see everyone ignored. Jeesh, he's such an ass.

'May I offer you some refreshment?' Neferet waved graciously at the table.

'Oh, golly! That reminds me of the cookies I left in the car. Stevie Rae and I were just on our way out there. It was really nice to meet y'all.' With a quick hug for me and a wave for everyone else, Stevie Rae and her mom escaped, leaving me there, even though I wished I were anywhere else.

I stayed close to Grandma, lacing my fingers through hers as we walked over to the refreshment table, thinking how much easier this would be if it was just she who had come to visit me. I snuck a look at my mom. A permanent frown seemed to have been painted on her face. She was looking around at the other kids, and hardly even glanced in my direction. *Why come at all?* I wanted to scream at her. *Why seem like you might actually care – might actually miss me – and then show so obviously that you don't?*

'Wine, Sylvia? Mr and Mrs Heffer?' Neferet offered.

'Thank you, red please,' Grandma said.

John's tight lips registered his displeasure. 'No. We don't drink.'

With a superhuman effort I didn't roll my eyes. Since when didn't he drink? I would bet the last fifty dollars in my savings account that there was a six-pack of beer in the fridge at home right now. And my mom used to drink red wine like Grandma. I even saw her throw Grandma a narrow-eyed, envious look as she sipped the rich wine Neferet had poured for her. But *no* they didn't drink. At least not in public. Hypocrites.

'So, you were saying that the addition to Zoey's Mark happened because she did something special?' Grandma squeezed my hand. 'She told me that she'd been made leader of the Dark Daughters, but she didn't tell me how exactly that happened.'

I felt myself tense up again. I really didn't want to deal with the scene it would cause if my mom and John found out that what had actually happened was that the ex-leader of the Dark Daughters had cast a circle on Halloween night (known at the House of Night as Samhain, the night the veil between our world and the world of spirits is thinnest), conjured some very scary vampyre spirits, and then lost control of them when my human ex-boyfriend, Heath, stumbled up looking for me. And I so didn't want anyone to *ever* mention what only a couple of people knew – that Heath was looking for me because I'd tasted his blood and he was fast becoming fixated on me, something humans do pretty easily when they get involved with vamps – even vamp fledglings, for that matter. So the then leader of the Dark Daughters, Aphrodite, totally lost control of the ghosts and they were going to eat Heath. Literally. Worse – they were also acting like they wanted to take a chomp out of the rest of us, too, including totally hot Erik Night, the vamp kid who I can happily report is definitely not my *ex*-boyfriend, but who I've sorta been dating this past month so he's my *almost*-boyfriend. Anyway, I had to do something, so with some help from Stevie Rae, Damien, and the Twins, I cast my own circle, tapping into the power of the five elements: wind, fire, water, earth, and spirit. Using my affinity for the elements, I managed to banish the ghosts back to wherever it is they live (or unlive?). When they were gone I had these new tattoos, a delicate collection of lacelike sapphire swirls that framed my face – totally unheard of for a mere fledgling to have – and matching Marks interspersed with cool runelike-looking symbols on my shoulders, something no fledgling or vamp has ever had. Then Aphrodite was exposed as the rotten-assed leader she was, causing Neferet to fire her and put me in her place. Consequently, I'm also in training to be a High Priestess of Nyx, the vampyre Goddess, who is Night personified.

None of that would go over well with ultra-religious, ultra-judgmental Mom and John.

'Well, there was a small accident. Zoey's quick thinking and bravery made sure no one got hurt, and at the same time she connected with a special affinity she has been given to draw energy from the five elements.' Neferet's smile was proud and I felt a wash of happiness at her approval. 'The tattooing is simply an outward sign of the favor she's found with the Goddess.'

'What you're saying is blasphemy.' John spoke in a tight, strained voice that managed to sound condescending and angry at the same time. 'You are putting her immortal soul in danger.'

Neferet turned her moss-colored eyes on him. She didn't look angry. Actually, she looked amused.

'You must be one of the Elders of the People of Faith.'

His birdlike chest swelled up. 'Well, yes, yes I am.'

'Then let us come to an understanding quickly, Mr Heffer. I would not think of coming into your home, or into your church, and belittling your beliefs, though I disagree profoundly with them. Now, I do not expect you to worship as I do. In truth, I would never even think to attempt to sway you to my beliefs, even though I have a deep and abiding commitment to my Goddess. So all I insist upon is that you show me the same courtesy I have already awarded you. When you are in my "home", you respect my beliefs.'

John's eyes had become mean little slits and I could see his jaw clenching and unclenching.

'Your way of life is sinful and wrong,' he said fiercely.

'Thus says a man who admits to worshipping a God who vilifies pleasure, relegates women to roles that are little more than servants and broodmares, though they are the backbone of your church, and seeks to control his worshippers through guilt and fear.' Neferet laughed softly, but the sound was humorless and the unspoken warning in it made the hair on my forearms prickle. 'Have a care for how you judge others; perhaps you should look to cleaning your own house, first.'

His face reddening, John sucked in a breath and opened his mouth for what I knew would be an ugly lecture on how right his beliefs are and how wrong everyone else's are, but before he could respond Neferet cut him off. She hadn't raised her voice, but it was suddenly filled with the power of a High Priestess and I shivered in fear, even though her wrath was not directed at me.

'You have two choices. You may visit the House of Night as its invited guest, which means you will respect our ways and keep your displeasure and judgment to yourself. Or you may leave and not return. Ever. *Decide now*.' The last two words washed against my skin and I had to force myself not to cringe. I noticed that my mom was staring with wide, glassy eyes at Neferet, her face pale as milk. John's face had gone the opposite color. His eyes were narrow and his cheeks were flushed a very unattractive red.

'Linda,' he said through his teeth. 'Let's go.' Then he looked at me with such disgust and hatred that I literally took a step back. I mean, I knew he didn't like me, but until that moment

I hadn't realized how much. 'This place is what you deserve. Your mother and I won't be back. You're on your own now.' He spun around and started for the door. My mom hesitated, and for a second I thought she might actually say something nice – like she was sorry about him – or that she missed me – or that I shouldn't worry, she'd be back no matter what he said.

'Zoey, I can't believe what you've gotten yourself into now.' She shook her head and, as usual, followed John's lead and left the room.

'Oh, sweetheart, I'm so sorry.' Grandma was there, instantly hugging me and whispering reassurance. 'I'll be back, my little bird. I promise. And I'm so proud of you!' She held me by my shoulders and smiled through her tears. 'Our Cherokee ancestors are proud of you, too. I can feel it. You have been touched by the Goddess, and you have the loyalty of good friends,' she glanced up at Neferet and added, 'and wise teachers. Someday you might even learn to forgive your mother. Until then remember that you are the daughter of my heart, *u-we-tsi-a-ge-ya*.' She kissed me. 'I must leave, too. I drove your little car here, and I will leave it for you, so I must ride back with them.' She handed me the keys to my vintage Bug. 'But remember always that I love you, Zoeybird.'

'I love you, too, Grandma,' I said, and kissed her back, hugging her hard and taking deep breaths of her scent like I could hold her in my lungs and exhale her slowly over the next month as I missed her.

'Bye, sweetheart. Call me when you get a chance.' She kissed me again and then left.

17

I watched her leave, and didn't realize I was crying until I felt the tears drip from my face onto my neck. I'd actually forgotten Neferet was still standing beside me, so I jumped a little in surprise when she handed me a tissue.

'I am sorry for that, Zoey,' she said quietly.

'I'm not.' I blew my nose and wiped my face before I looked at her. 'Thanks for standing up to him.'

'I did not mean to send your mother away, too.'

'You didn't. She chose to follow him. Just like she's been doing for over three years now.' I felt the hotness of tears threaten the back of my throat and spoke quickly, willing them away. 'She used to be different. It's stupid, I know, but I keep expecting her to turn back into what she was before. It never happens, though. It's like he's killed my mom and put a stranger in her body.'

Neferet put her arm around me. 'I like what your grandma said – that maybe someday you can find the ability to forgive your mother.'

I stared at the door the three of them had just disappeared through. 'That someday is far away.'

Neferet squeezed my shoulder sympathetically.

I looked up at her, so glad she was there with me, and I wished – for about the zillionth time – that she was my mom. Then I remembered what she had told me almost a month ago, that her mom had died when she was a little girl, and her dad had abused her, physically and mentally, until she had been saved by being Marked.

'Did you ever forgive your father?' I asked tentatively.

Neferet looked down at me and blinked several times, as if she were slowly coming back from a memory that had taken her far, far away. 'No. No I didn't ever forgive him, but when I think of him now it is as if I'm remembering someone else's life. The things he did to me he did to a human child, not a High Priestess and vampyre. And to a High Priestess and vampyre he, like most humans, is completely inconsequential.'

Her words sounded strong and sure, but as I looked into the depths of her beautiful green eyes I saw a flicker of something old and painful and definitely not forgotten, and wondered how honest she was being with herself . . .

CHAPTER TWO

I WAS INCREDIBLY RELIEVED WHEN NEFERET SAID THERE WAS no reason for me to stay in the reception hall. After the scene with my family I felt like everyone was staring at me. I was, after all, the girl with the freaky Marks *and* the nightmare family. I took the shortest way out of the reception hall – the sidewalk that led outside through the pretty little courtyard that the windows of the dining hall looked out onto.

It was a little after midnight, which was – yes – a totally weird time for a parent open house, but the school begins classes at 8:00 P.M., and finishes up at 3:00 A.M. On the surface it seemed to make more sense to have parent visitation begin at 8:00, or maybe even an hour or so before school started, but Neferet had explained to me that the point was that parents accept their child's Change, and understand that days and nights would forever be different for them. On my own I decided that another plus of making the time inconvenient is that it gave a lot of parents the excuse they needed not to come, without outright telling their kid, *Hey – I don't want anything to do with you now that you're turning into a bloodsucking monster*.

Too bad my parents hadn't taken that out.

I sighed and slowed down, taking my time following one of the winding paths through the courtyard. It was a cool, clear November night. The moon was almost full, and its bright silver light was a pretty contrast to the antique gaslights that illuminated the courtyard with their soft yellow glows. I could hear the fountain that sat in the middle of the garden, and I automatically changed direction so that I was heading toward it. Maybe the soothing tinkle of the water would help my stress level . . . and help me forget.

When I rounded the curve that led to the fountain I was walking slowly, and daydreaming a little about my new almost-boyfriend, the totally delicious Erik. He was away from the school for the yearly Shakespeare monologue competition. Naturally, he'd finished first at our school, and had advanced easily to the Houses of Night international competition. It was Thursday, and he'd only been gone since Monday, but I missed him like crazy and couldn't wait till Sunday when he was supposed to get back. Erik was the hottest guy at our school. Hell, Erik Night might be the hottest guy at any school. He was tall, dark, and handsome – like an old-time movie star (without the latent homosexual tendencies). He was also incredibly talented. Someday soon he was going to join the rank of other vamp movie stars like Matthew McConaughey, James Franco, Jake Gyllenhaal, and Hugh Jackman (who is totally gorgeous for an old guy). Plus, Erik was truly a nice guy – which only added to his hotness.

So I will admit to being preoccupied with visions of Erik as Tristan and me as Isolde (only our passionate love story would have a happy ending), and didn't notice that there were other people in the courtyard until a raised male voice shocked me with how mean and disgusted it sounded.

'You are one disappointment after another, Aphrodite!'

I froze. Aphrodite?

'It was bad enough that your getting Marked meant that you couldn't go to Chatham Hall, especially after everything I did to be sure you were accepted,' said a woman in a brittle, cold voice.

'Mother, I know. I said I was sorry.'

Okay, I should leave. I should turn around and walk quickly and quietly out of the courtyard. Aphrodite was probably my least favorite person at school. Actually, Aphrodite was probably my least favorite person anywhere, but purposefully listening in on what was clearly an ugly scene with her parents was just wrong wrong wrong.

So I tiptoed a few feet off the path where I could hide more easily behind a big ornamental bush *and* have a decent view of what was going on. Aphrodite was sitting on the stone bench closest to the fountain. Her parents were standing in front of her. Well, her mom was standing. Her dad was pacing.

Man, her parents were really pretty people. Her dad was tall and handsome. The kind of guy who kept in shape, kept all of his hair, and had really good teeth. He was dressed in a dark suit that looked like it cost a zillion dollars. He also looked weirdly familiar, and I was sure I'd seen him on TV or something. Her mom was totally gorgeous. I mean, Aphrodite was blond and perfect-looking, and her mom was an older, richly dressed, well-groomed version of her. Her sweater was obviously cashmere, and her pearls were long and real. Every time she gestured with her hands the gihugic pear-shaped diamond on her ring finger flashed a light as cold and beautiful as her voice.

'Have you forgotten that your father is the mayor of Tulsa?' Aphrodite's mom snapped viciously.

'No, no, of course not, Mother.'

Her mom didn't seem to hear her. 'Spinning a decent slant on the fact that you're here instead of on the East Coast preparing for Harvard was difficult enough, but we consoled ourselves with the fact that vampyres can attain money and power and success, and we expected you to excel in this' – she paused and grimaced distastefully – 'rather unusual venue. And now we hear that you're no longer leader of the Dark Daughters and have been ejected from High Priestess training, which makes you no different than any of the other riffraff at this wretched school.' Aphrodite's mother hesitated, as if she needed to calm herself before continuing. When she spoke again I had to strain to hear her hissing whisper. 'Your behavior is unacceptable.'

'As usual, you disappoint us,' her father repeated.

'You already said that, Dad,' Aphrodite said, sounding like her usual smart-ass self.

Like a striking snake, her mom slapped Aphrodite across her face, so hard that the crack of skin against skin made me jump and wince. I expected Aphrodite to leap off the bench and go after her mom's throat (please – we don't call her a hag from hell for nothing), but she didn't. She just pressed her own palm against her cheek and bowed her head.

'Do not cry. I've told you before, tears mean weakness. At least do this one thing right and don't cry,' her mom snapped.

Slowly Aphrodite raised her head and took her hand from her cheek. 'I didn't mean to disappoint you, Mother. I'm really sorry.'

'Saying you're sorry doesn't fix anything,' her mom said. 'What we want to know is what you're going to do about getting your position back.'

In the shadows I held my breath.

'I – I can't do anything about it,' Aphrodite said, sounding hopeless and suddenly very young. 'I messed up. Neferet caught me. She took the Dark Daughters away from me and gave them to someone else. I think she's even considering transferring me to a different House of Night completely.'

'We already know that!' Her mom raised her voice, clipping her words so that they seemed to be made of ice. 'We talked with Neferet before we saw you. She was going to transfer you to another school, but we interceded. You will remain at this school. We also tried to reason with her about giving you your position back after perhaps some period of restriction or detention.'

'Oh, Mother, you didn't?'

Aphrodite sounded horrified, and I couldn't blame her. I could only imagine the impression these cold, pretending-to-be-perfect parents made on our High Priestess. If Aphrodite had ever had even the slightest chance of getting back in Neferet's favor, her creepy parents had probably ruined it for her.

'Of course we did! Did you expect us to just sit by while you destroyed your future by becoming a vampyre nobody at some nondescript foreign House of Night?' her mom said.

'More than you already have,' her dad added.

'But it's not about me being on some kind of high school restriction,' Aphrodite said, obviously trying to control her frustration and reason with them. 'I messed up. Big time. That's bad enough, but there's a girl here whose powers are stronger than mine. Even if Neferet gets over being mad at me, she's not going to give me back the Dark Daughters.' Then Aphrodite said something that totally shocked me. 'The other girl is a better leader than I am. I realized that on Samhain. She deserves to be head of the Dark Daughters. I don't.'

Ohmygod. Did hell just freeze over?

Aphrodite's mom took a step closer to her and I flinched

25

with her, sure she was going to get smacked again. But her mother didn't hit her. She bent so that her beautiful face was staring right into her daughter's. From where I was standing they looked so similar that it was scary.

'Don't you *ever* say someone deserves something more than you. You're my daughter, and you will always deserve the best.' Then she straightened again and ran her hand through her perfect hair, even though I was pretty sure it wouldn't dare get messed up. 'We couldn't convince Neferet to give you back your position, so you're going to have to convince her.'

'But, Mother, I already told you—' she started, but her dad cut her off.

'Get the new girl out of the way, and Neferet will be more likely to give you back your position.'

'Ah, crap. 'The new girl' was me.

'Discredit her. Cause her to make mistakes, and then be sure it's someone else who tells Neferet about them and not you. It'll look better that way. Her mom spoke matter-of-factly, like she was talking about which outfit Aphrodite should wear tomorrow instead of plotting against me. Jeesh, talk about a hag from hell!

'And watch yourself. Your behavior has to be beyond reproach. Maybe you should be more forthcoming about your visions, at least for a while,' her father said.

'But you've told me for years to try to keep the visions to myself, that they are the source of my power.'

I could hardly believe what I was hearing! A month ago

Damien had told me that several of the kids thought that Aphrodite was trying to hide some of the visions from Neferet, but they thought it was because she hated humans – and Aphrodite's visions were always about a future tragedy where humans died. When she shared her visions with Neferet, the High Priestess was almost always able to stop the tragedy from happening and save lives. So Aphrodite purposefully keeping her visions to herself was one of the things that made me decide that I had to take her position as leader of the Dark Daughters. I'm not power hungry. I didn't really want the position. Hell, I still wasn't sure what to do with it. I'd just known that Aphrodite was bad news, and that I had to do something to stop her. Now I was hearing that some of the crap she'd been doing was because she let her hateful parents boss her around! Her mom and dad actually thought it was okay to keep quiet about information that could save lives. And her father was the mayor of Tulsa! (No wonder he looked familiar.) It was so bizarre it was making my head hurt.

'The visions aren't your *source* of power!' her dad was saying. 'Do you never listen? I said that your visions could be used to *gain* power for you because information is always power. The source of your visions is the Change that's taking place inside your body. It's genetics, that's all.'

'It's supposed to be a gift from the Goddess,' Aphrodite said softly.

Her mother's laugh was cold. 'Don't be stupid. If there was such a thing as a goddess, why would she grant *you* powers? You're just a ridiculous child, and one who is prone to making mistakes, as this last little escapade of yours has once again proven. So be smart for a change, Aphrodite. Use your visions to gain favor back, but act humble about it. You have to make Neferet believe that you're sorry.'

I almost didn't hear Aphrodite's whispered, 'I am sorry . . .'

'We'll expect much better news next month.'

'Yes, Mother.'

'Good, now walk us back to the reception hall so that we can mingle with the others.'

'Can I please stay here for a little while? I'm really not feeling very well.'

'Absolutely not. What would people say?' her mother said. 'Pull yourself together. You'll escort us back to the hall and you'll be gracious about it. Now.'

Aphrodite was slowly standing up from the bench, and heart beating so hard I was afraid it would give me away, I hurried back down the path till I came to the fork that would take me out of the courtyard. Then I practically ran from the garden.

I thought about what I'd overheard all the way back to the dorm. I believed that I had nightmare parents, but they were like *The Brady Bunch* mom and dad (hello – I watch Nickelodeon reruns like everyone else) compared to Aphrodite's hateful, power-freak parents. Much as I hated to admit it, what I saw tonight made me understand why Aphrodite acted like she did. I mean, what would I be like if I hadn't had Grandma Redbird to love me and support me and help me grow a backbone these past three years? And that was something else, too. My mom had been normal. Sure, she'd been stressed out and overworked, but she'd been normal for the first thirteen of my almost seventeen years of life. It was only after she married John that she changed. So I'd had a good mom and a fantastic grandma. What if I hadn't? What if all I'd ever known was how it had been for the past three years – me being an unwanted outsider in my own family?

I might have turned out like Aphrodite, and I might still be letting my parents control me because I was hoping desperately that I would be good enough, make them proud enough, so that someday they would really love me.

It made me see Aphrodite with totally new eyes, which I wasn't particularly thrilled about.

CHAPTER THREE

'YEAH, ZOEY, I UNDERSTAND WHAT YOU'RE SAYIN' AND ALL, but hello! Part of what you overheard was that Aphrodite is gonna try to set you up so that she can get you kicked out of the Dark Daughter leadership, so don't go feeling too darn sorry for her,' Stevie Rae said.

'I know – I know. I'm not getting all warm and fuzzy about her. I'm just saying that after overhearing her with her psycho parents I understand why she is like she is.'

We were walking to first hour. Well, actually, Stevie Rae and I were practically running to first hour. As usual, we were almost late. I knew I shouldn't have had that second bowl of Count Chocula.

Stevie Rae rolled her eyes. 'And you say I'm too nice.'

'I'm not being nice. I'm being understanding. But understanding doesn't change the fact that Aphrodite acts like a hag bitch from hell.'

Stevie Rae made a snorting noise and shook her head, causing her blond curls to bounce like she was a little girl. Her short cut was odd at the House of Night where everyone, even most of the guys, had ridiculously long, thick hair. Okay, my hair has always been long, but still – it was really weird when I first got here and was bombarded with hair hair hair. Now it made perfect sense. Part of the physical Change that happens as we become vampyres is that our hair and nails grow abnormally fast. After a little practice, you can tell what year a fledgling is without checking the crest on her jacket. Vampyres looked different than humans (not bad different – just different), so it's only logical that as a fledgling passes through more and more of the Change her body looks different, too.

'Zoey, you're so not paying attention.'

'Huh?'

'I said, don't let your guard down about Aphrodite. Yes, she has nightmare parents. Yes, they're controlling and manipulating her. Whatever. She's still hateful and mean and vindictive. Watch out for her.'

'Hey, don't worry. I will.'

'Okay, good. I'll see you third hour.'

'See ya,' I called to her back. Jeesh, she was such a worrier.

I hurried into class and had just taken my seat in the desk next to Damien, who raised an eyebrow at me and said, 'Another two-bowl morning?' when the bell rang and Neferet swept into the room.

Okay, I know it's bordering on weird (or maybe queer is the better word choice) to continually notice how gorgeous a woman is when you're a woman, too, but Neferet is so damn beautiful that it's like she has the ability to focus all the light in the room on herself. She was wearing a simple black dress and totally to die for black boots. She had on her silver Goddess path earrings and, as always, the silver embroidered Goddess rested over her heart. She didn't exactly look like the Goddess Nyx – who I swear I'd seen in a vision the day I was Marked – but she had the Goddess's aura of strength and confidence. I'll just admit it. I wanted to be her.

Today was unusual. Instead of lecturing for most of the hour (and, no, amazingly enough Neferet was never a boring lecturer) she gave us an essay assignment on the Gorgon, who we had been studying all week. We learned that actually she had not been a monster who turned men to stone with a glance. She had been a famous vampyre High Priestess whose Goddess-given gift was an affinity, or a special connection, for the earth, which is probably where the 'turn to stone' myth came from. I'm pretty sure if a vamp High Priestess got pissed enough and had a magical connection with the earth (stones *do* come from the earth), she could easily zap someone into granite. So today's assignment was to write an essay on human

myth and symbolism, and the meaning behind the fictional-
ization of the Gorgon's story.

But I was too restless to write. Plus, I had all weekend to
finish the essay. I was way more worried about the Dark
Daughters. The full moon was Sunday. I would be expected
to lead the ritual for the Dark Daughters. I realized everyone
was also expecting me to make an announcement about
changes I planned to make. Uh, I needed to have a clue about
those changes. Surprisingly, I did have an idea, but it definitely needed help.

I ignored Damien's curious look as I quickly gathered up
my notebook and went up to Neferet's desk.

'Problem, Zoey?' she asked.

'No. Uh, yes. Well, actually, if you would let me go to the
media center for the rest of the hour, my problem would probably go away.' I realized I was nervous. I'd only been at the
House of Night for a month, and I still wasn't sure about the
protocol for being excused from class. I mean, there were only
two kids in the entire month who'd gotten sick. And they'd
died. Both of them. Their bodies had rejected the Change,
one had happened right in front of me during Lit class. It
had been totally gross. But other than the occasional dying
kid students rarely missed class. Neferet was watching me,
and I remembered that she was an intuitive and she could
probably sense the ridiculous babble going on in my head. I
sighed. 'It's Dark Daughters stuff. I want to come up with
some new leadership ideas.'

She looked pleased. 'Anything I can help you with?'

'Probably, but I need to do some research and get my ideas straight first.'

'Very well, come to me when you're ready. And feel free to spend as much time in the media center as you need,' Neferet said.

I hesitated. 'Do I need a pass?'

She smiled. 'I am your mentor and I have given you permission, what more could you need?'

'Thanks,' I said, and hurried out of the classroom feeling stupid. I would be so glad when I'd been at the school long enough to know all the little inside rules. And, anyway, I don't know what I'd been so worried about. The halls were deserted. Unlike my old high school (South Intermediate High School in Broken Arrow, Oklahoma – which is a totally boring suburb of Tulsa) there were no Napoleon Complex, overly tanned vice principals with nothing better to do than to prowl the halls harassing kids. I slowed down and told myself to relax – jeesh, I'd been stressed out lately.

The library was in the front center area of the school in a cool multilevel room that had been built to mimic the turret of a castle, which fit in well with the theme of the rest of the school. The whole thing looked like something out of the past. That was probably one of the reasons it had attracted the attention of the vamps five years ago. Then it had been a stuck-up rich kids' prep school, but it had originally been built as a monastery for the Saint Augustine People of Faith monks. I remember that when I asked how the prep school had been talked into selling to the vamps Neferet had told me that they'd made them a deal they couldn't refuse. The memory of the dangerous tone her voice had taken still made my skin crawl.

'Me-eeh-uf-ow!'

I jumped and almost peed on myself. 'Nala! You scared the crap outta me!'

Unconcerned, my cat launched herself into my arms, and I had to juggle notebook, purse, and small (but chubby) orange cat. All the while Nala complained at me in her grumpy old lady cat voice. She adored me, and she'd definitely chosen me as her own, but that didn't mean that she was always pleasant. I shifted her, and pushed open the door to the media center.

Oh – what Neferet had told my stupid step-loser John had been the truth. Cats do roam free all over the school. They often followed 'their' kid to class. Nala, in particular, liked to find me several times a day. She'd insist I scratch her head, complain a little at me, and then take off and go do whatever cats did with their free time. (Plot world domination?)

'Do you need help with her?' the media specialist asked. I had only met her briefly during my orientation week, but I remembered her name was Sappho. (Uh, she wasn't the *real* Sappho – that vampyre poet had died like a thousand years ago – right now we were studying her work in Lit class.)

'No, Sappho, but thank you. Nala doesn't really like anyone except me.'

Sappho, a tiny dark-haired vamp whose tattoos were elaborate symbols Damien had told me were Greek alphabet glyphs, smiled fondly at Nala. 'Cats are such wonderfully interesting creatures, don't you think?'

I moved Nala to my other shoulder and she grumbled in my ear. 'They're definitely not dogs,' I said.

'Thank the Goddess for that!'

'Do you mind if I use one of the computers?' The media center was lined with row after row of books – thousands of them – but it also had a very cool, up-to-date computer lab.

'Of course, make yourself at home and feel free to call on me if you can't find what you need.'

'Thanks.'

I picked a computer that sat on a nice big desk and clicked into the internet. This was something else that was way different than my old school. Here there were no passwords and no internet filtering program that restricted sites. Here students were expected to show some sense and act right – and if they didn't it's not like the vamps, who were almost impossible to lie to, wouldn't find out. Just thinking about trying to lie to Neferet made my stomach hurt.

Focus and stop messing around. This is important.

Okay, so an idea had been milling around in my head. It was time to see if there was anything to it. I pulled up Google and typed in 'private preparatory schools.' Zillions came up. I started narrowing. I wanted exclusive and upper class (none of those stupid 'alternative academies' that were really just holding pens for future criminals – ugh). I also wanted old schools, ones that had been around for generations. I was looking for something that had passed the test of time.

I easily found Chatham Hall, which was the school Aphrodite's parents had thrown in her face. It was an exclusive East Coast prep school and, man, did it look stuck-up. I clicked out. Any place Aphrodite's freak parents approved of would not be something I wanted to use as a role model. I kept searching . . . Exeter . . . Andover . . . Taft . . . Miss Porter's (really – hee hee – that's the school's name) . . . Kent . . .

'Kent. I've heard that name before,' I told Nala, who had curled up on top of the desk so that she could watch me sleepily. I clicked into it. 'It's in Connecticut – that's why it's familiar. This is where Shaunee had been going when she was Marked.' I browsed through the site, curious to see where Shaunee had spent the first part of her freshman (or third former) year. It was a pretty school – there was no denying that. Stuck-up, sure, but there was something about it that seemed more welcoming than the other prep schools. Maybe it was just because I knew Shaunee. I kept going through the site – and suddenly sat up straighter. 'This is it,' I muttered to myself. 'This is the kind of stuff I need.'

I pulled out my pen and notebook paper and got busy taking notes. Lots of notes.

If Nala hadn't hissed a warning, I would have jumped out of my skin when a deep voice spoke behind me.

'You look completely engrossed in that.'

I glanced over my shoulder – and froze. Ohmygod.

'Sorry, I didn't mean to interrupt you. It was just so unusual to see a student writing feverishly in longhand, rather than pecking away at the computer keys, that I thought you might be writing poetry. You see, I prefer to write poetry longhand. The computer is just too impersonal.'

Stop being such a moron! Speak to him! My mind screamed at me. 'I – uh – I'm not writing poetry.' God, that was brilliant.

'Oh, well. Doesn't hurt to check. Nice talking with you.'

He smiled and started to turn away and my mouth finally managed to work a little more correctly. 'Uh, I think computers are impersonal, too. I've never really written poetry, but when I write something that's important to me I like to do it like this.' Totally dorklike, I held up my pen.

'Well, maybe you should try writing poetry. Sounds like you might have the soul of a poet.' He held out his hand. 'Usually about this time of day I come by and give Sappho a break. I'm not a full-time professor because I'm only here for one school year. I just teach two classes, so I have extra time. I'm Loren Blake, Vampyre Poet Laureate.'

I grasped his forearm in the traditional vampyre greeting, trying not to think about how warm his arm was, how strong he felt, and how alone we were in the empty media center.

'I know,' I said. Then I wanted to slit my throat. What an idiotic thing to say! 'What I mean is I know who you are. You're the first male Poet Laureate they've named in two hundred years.' I realized I was still grasping his arm and let go of him. 'I'm Zoey Redbird.'

His smile made my heart flop around inside my chest. 'I

know who you are, too.' His gorgeous eyes, so dark they looked black and bottomless, sparkled mischievously. 'You're the first fledgling to have a colored-in, expanded Mark, as well as the only vamp, fledgling or adult, to have an affinity for all five of the elements. It's nice to finally meet you face-to-face. Neferet's told me a lot about you.'

'She has?' I was mortified that my voice squeaked.

'Of course she has. She's incredibly proud of you.' He nodded at the empty seat beside me. 'I don't want to interrupt your work, but do you mind if I sit with you a little while?'

'Yeah, sure. I need a break. I think my butt's asleep.' Oh, God, just kill me now.

He laughed. 'Well then, would you like to stand while I sit?'

'No, I'll – uh – just shift my weight.' And then I'll hurl myself out the window.

'So, if it's not too personal, may I ask what you're working so diligently on?'

Okay, I needed to think and talk. Be normal. Forget that he was easily the most heart-stoppingly beautiful man I'd ever been near in my entire life. He's a professor at the school. Just another teacher. That's all. Yeah, right. Just another teacher who looked like every woman's dream of The Perfect Man. And I did mean Man. Erik was hot and handsome and very cool. Loren Blake was a whole other universe. A totally off-limits, impossibly sexy universe I was not allowed access to. As if he saw me as anything but a kid anyway. Please. I'm sixteen. Okay, almost seventeen, but still. He's probably at least twenty-one or something. He was just being nice. More than likely he wanted a closer look at my freaky Marks. He could be collecting research for a highly embarrassing poem about the—

'Zoey? If you don't want to tell me what you're working on, that's fine. I really didn't mean to bother you.'

'No! It's okay.' I drew a deep breath and got myself together. 'Sorry – guess I was still thinking about my research,' I lied, hoping that he was a young enough vamp that he didn't have the incredible lie detector powers the older profs had. I blundered quickly on. 'I want to change the Dark Daughters. I think it needs a foundation – some clear rules and guidelines. Not just to join, but once you're in there should be standards. You shouldn't be given a free pass to be as big a jerk as you want to be, and still get the privilege of being a Dark Daughter or Son.' I paused and I could feel my face getting hot and red. What the hell was I babbling on about? I must sound like the school idiot.

But instead of laughing at me or, worse, saying something patronizing and taking off, he seemed to be considering what I said.

'So what have you come up with?' he asked.

'Well, I like the way this private school called Kent runs their student leadership group. Look—' I clicked on the right link and read from the text. 'The Senior Council and Prefect System is an integral part of life at Kent. These students are chosen as leaders who vow to be role models and to manage all aspects of student life at Kent.' I used my pen to point at the computer screen. 'See, there are several different Prefects, and they are elected to each yearly Council by votes of the students and the faculty, but the final choice is made by the Headmaster – which would be Neferet – and the Senior Prefect.'

'Which would be you,' he said.

I could feel my face getting hot. Again. 'Yeah. It also says every May new Council members are "Tapped" as possible appointees for the next school year, and there's a big service held to celebrate.' I smiled, and said, more to myself than him, 'Sounds like a new ritual Nyx would approve of.' As I said the words I felt the rightness of them deep within me.

'I like it,' Loren said. 'I think it's a great idea.'

'Really? You're not just saying that?'

'There's something about me that you should know. I don't lie.'

I stared into his eyes. They seemed bottomless. He was sitting so close to me that I could feel the heat from his body, which made me suppress a shiver from a sudden rush of forbidden desire. 'Well, thanks then,' I said softly. Feeling suddenly bold, I continued. 'I want the Dark Daughters to stand for more than just a social group. I want them to set examples – do the right things. So I thought that each of us would have to swear to uphold five ideals representing the five elements.'

His brows went up. 'What did you have in mind?'

'The Dark Daughters and Sons should swear to be authentic

for air, faithful for fire, wise for water, empathetic for earth, and sincere for spirit.' I finished without looking at my notes. I already knew the five ideals by heart. So I watched his eyes instead. He didn't say anything for a moment. Then, slowly, he reached out and traced one finger over the fluid line of my tattoo. I wanted to tremble under his touch, but I couldn't move.

'Beautiful and intelligent and innocent,' he whispered. Then his incredible voice recited, '*The best part of beauty is that which no picture can express.*'

'So sorry to interrupt, but I really do need to check out the next three books in this series for Professor Anastasia.'

Aphrodite's voice broke the spell between Loren and me, as well as almost giving me a heart attack. Actually, Loren looked as shaken as I felt. He dropped his hand from my face and walked quickly to the checkout counter. I sat where I was like I'd grown to my chair, trying to look oh-so-busy scribbling more notes (which were actually, well, scribble). I heard Sappho come back in and take over checking out Aphrodite's books from Loren. I could hear him leaving, and almost as if I couldn't help it, I turned and looked at him. He was walking out the door and not paying the least bit of attention to me.

But Aphrodite was staring straight at me with a wicked smile curving her perfect lips.

Well, hell.

CHAPTER FOUR

I WANTED TO TELL STEVIE RAE ABOUT WHAT HAD HAPPENED with Loren, and about Aphrodite busting in on us, but I wasn't up to going into it in front of Damien and the Twins. Not that they weren't my friends, too, but I had hardly had time to process what had happened, and the thought of the three of them chattering like crazy about it made me cringe. Especially since the Twins had rearranged their school schedules to get into Loren's poetry elective, where they freely admitted they spent the entire hour every day just staring at him. They would totally lose their minds when I told them what had happened. (Plus, had anything happened? I mean, the guy had just touched my face.)

'What's wrong with you?' Stevie Rae asked.

The attention that the four of them had been focusing on trying to figure out if there was a hair in Erin's salad or if it was just one of those weird string things from a piece of celery shifted instantly to me.

'Nothin', I'm just thinking about the Full Moon Ritual Sunday.' I looked at my friends. They were watching me with eyes that said that they totally believed I'd come up with something and not make an ass out of myself. I wish I had their confidence in me.

'So what are you going to do? Have you decided?' Damien asked.

'I think so. Actually, what do you guys think of this idea . . .' I launched into the whole Council and Prefect idea, and realized about halfway through explaining it to them that it really was a pretty good plan. I finished with the five ideals that were each allied with an element.

No one said anything. I was just starting to worry when Stevie Rae threw her arm around me and hugged me hard.

'Oh, Zoey! You're going to be an awesome High Priestess.'

Damien was all misty-eyed and his voice cracked adorably. 'I feel like I'm in the court of a great queen.'

'Or you could just be a great queen,' Shaunee said.

'Her Majesty Damien . . . hee hee,' Erin said, giggling.

'Y'all . . .' Stevie Rae warned.

'Sorry,' the Twins said together.

'It was just so hard to resist,' Shaunee said. 'But seriously, we love the idea.'

'Yeah, sounds like an excellent way to keep the hags out,' Erin said.

'Well, that's another thing I needed to talk to you guys about.' I took a deep breath. 'I think seven is a good number for the Council. That way it's a decent size, and it's impossible to have a tie vote.' They nodded. 'So, everything I've been reading – not just about the Dark Daughters, but about student leadership groups in general – says that the Council members are upperclassmen. Actually the Senior Prefect, which would be me, is a, well, senior, and not a freshman.'

'I like the title third former better. It sounds older,' Damien said.

'Whatever we call it, it's still abnormal that we're so young. Which means we need two older kids on the Council with us.'

There was a pause, and then Damien said, 'I nominate Erik Night.'

Shaunee rolled her eyes.

Erin said, 'Okay, how many times do we have to explain this to you – the boy is not on your team. He likes breasts and vaginas, not penises and anu—'

'Stop!' I absolutely did not want to get off on this subject. 'I think Erik Night is a good choice, and *not* because he likes me or, well . . .'

'Girl parts?' Stevie Rae offered.

'Yes, girl parts versus boy parts. I think he has the qualities we're looking for. He's talented, well liked, and he's really a good guy.'

'And he's totally drop dead . . .' Erin said.

'. . . gorgeous,' Shaunee finished.

'It's true; he is. But we're absolutely not basing membership on appearance.'

Shaunee and Erin frowned, but didn't argue with me. They're actually not real shallow; they're just kinda shallow.

I drew a deep breath. 'And I think the seventh member of the Council needs to be one of the seniors who was part of Aphrodite's inside group. That is, if one of them petitions to join our Council.'

This time there was no bedazzled silence. Erin and Shaunee, as usual, spoke at the same time.

'One of the hags from hell!'

'No f-ing way!'

Damien spoke while the Twins were taking breaths so they could shriek again. 'I don't see how that could be a good idea.'

Stevie Rae just looked upset and picked at her lip.

I held up my hand, and was pleased (and surprised) when they actually shut up.

'I didn't take over the Dark Daughters to start a war at school. I took over because Aphrodite was a bully, and she had to be stopped. Now that I'm in charge I want the Dark Daughters to be a group kids are honored to belong to. And I don't mean just a little select clique of kids, like when Aphrodite was the leader. The Dark Daughters and Sons should be hard to get into and it should be select. But not because only the current leader's friends have a chance to get in. I want the Dark Daughters and Sons to be something everyone is proud of, and I think by allowing one of the old group on my Council I'll be sending the right message.'

'Or you'll be letting a viper into our midst,' Damien said quietly.

'Correct me if I'm wrong, Damien, but aren't snakes closely allied with Nyx?' I spoke quickly, following the intuitive feeling that was prompting me. 'Haven't they gotten a bad reputation because historically they've been symbols of female power, and men wanted to take that power away from women and make it something disgusting and scary instead?'

'No, you're right,' he said reluctantly, 'but that doesn't mean letting one of Aphrodite's gang into our Council is a good idea.'

'See, that's the point. I don't want it to just be *our* Council. I want it to be something that becomes a tradition with the school. Something that lasts beyond us.'

'So you mean if any of us don't make it through the Change, founding this new kind of Dark Daughters will be like we've lived on,' Stevie Rae said, and I could see that she'd captured the interest of the rest of them.

'That's exactly what I meant – even though I don't think I realized it until this second,' I said in a rush.

'Well, I like that part of it, even though I have no intention of drowning in my own bloody lungs,' Erin said.

'Of course you won't, Twin. It's a much too unattractive way to die.'

'I don't want to even think about not making it through the Change,' Damien said, 'but if – if something awful were to happen to me, I would want something about me to live on here at the school.'

'Could we have plaques?' Stevie Rae asked, and I noticed she was suddenly looking unusually pale.

'Plaques?' I had no clue what she was talking about.

'Yeah. I think we should have a plaque or something that records the names of the . . . the . . . what did you call them?'

'Prefects,' Damien said.

'Yeah, Prefects. The plaque, or whatever, could have the names of each year's Prefect Council, and it'll be displayed for ever and ever.'

'Yeah,' said Shaunee, warming to the idea. 'But not just a plaque. We need something cooler than just a plain old plaque.'

'Something that's unique – like us,' Erin said.

'Handprints,' Damien said.

'Huh?' I asked.

'Our handprints are unique. What if we made cement casts of each of our handprints, then signed our names below them,' Damien said.

'Like the stars do in Hollywood!' Stevie Rae said.

Okay, it seemed kinda cheesy, which meant I couldn't help but like it. The idea was like us – unique – cool – and bordering on tacky.

'I think handprints are an excellent idea. And you know where the perfect place for them is?' They looked at me with bright, happy eyes, their worry about one of Aphrodite's friends joining us, as well as the pretty much constant fear of sudden death we all carried around with us, temporarily forgotten. 'The courtyard is the perfect place.'

The bell rang, calling us back to class. I asked Stevie Rae to tell our Spanish teacher, Profesora Garmy, that I had gone to see Neferet, so I'd be late. I really wanted to tell her about my ideas while they were still fresh in my mind. It wouldn't take long – I'd just give her a basic outline and see if she liked the direction I was heading. Maybe . . . maybe I'd even ask her to come to the Full Moon Ritual Sunday, and be there when I announced the new selection process for membership to the Dark Daughters and Sons. I was thinking about how nervous I'd be if Neferet was there, watching me cast a circle and lead my own ritual, and was telling myself sternly that I'd have to get rid of my nerves . . . that it was the best thing for the Dark Daughters if Neferet was there showing her support of my new ideas and—

'But that's what I saw!' Aphrodite's voice, carrying from the cracked door of Neferet's classroom, jarred my thoughts and made me stop short. She sounded awful – totally upset and maybe even scared.

'If your sight is no better than that, then perhaps it's time you quit sharing what you see with others.' Neferet's voice was ice, terrifying, cold, and hard.

'But, Neferet, you asked! All I did was tell you what I saw.'

What was Aphrodite talking about? Ah, hell. Could she have run to Neferet about seeing Loren touch my face? I looked around the deserted hall. I should get out of here, but no damn way I was going to leave if that hag was talking about me – even if it seemed Neferet wasn't believing anything she was saying. So instead of leaving (like a smart girl), I walked quickly and quietly into the shadowed corner near the partially opened door. And then, thinking fast, I took off one of my silver hoop earrings and tossed it into the corner. I come and go from Neferet's classroom a lot – it's not beyond all reason that I'd be looking for a lost earring outside her door.

'You know what I want you to do?' Neferet's words were so filled with anger and power that I could feel them crawl across my skin. 'I want you to learn to not speak of things that are *questionable*.' She drew the word out. Was she talking about gossiping about Loren and me?

'I – I just wanted you to know.' Aphrodite had started crying, and she choked the words between sobs. 'I th-thought there might be something you could do to stop it.'

'Perhaps it would be wiser for you to think that because of your selfish actions in the past, Nyx is withholding her power from you because you are no longer in her favor and that what you are now seeing are false images.'

I'd never heard the kind of cruelty that filled Neferet's voice. It didn't even sound like her, and it scared me in a way that was hard for me to define. The day I'd been Marked, I'd had an accident before I got to the House of Night. When I was unconscious I'd had an out-of-body experience, which ended with me meeting Nyx. The Goddess told me that she had special plans for me, and then she kissed my forehead.

When I woke up my Mark had been filled in. I had a powerful connection with the elements (although I didn't realize that till much later), and I also had a weird new gut feeling that sometimes told me to say or do certain things – and sometimes told me very clearly to keep my mouth shut. Right now my gut feeling was telling me that Neferet's anger was all wrong, even if it was in response to Aphrodite's malicious gossip about me.

'Please don't say that, Neferet!' Aphrodite sobbed. 'Please don't tell me that Nyx has rejected me!'

'I don't have to tell you anything. Search within your soul. What is it telling you?'

If Neferet had spoken the words gently, they might have been nothing more than a wise teacher, or priestess, giving someone who was troubled some direction – as in look inside yourself to find, and fix, the problem. But Neferet's voice was cold and sneering and cruel.

'It's – it's telling me that I've – I've, uh, made m-mistakes, but not that the Goddess hates me.'

Aphrodite was crying so much that she was getting harder and harder to understand.

'Then you should look closer.'

Aphrodite's sobs were wrenching. I couldn't listen anymore. Leaving my earring, I followed my gut and got the hell out of there.

CHAPTER FIVE

MY STOMACH HURT ALL THROUGH THE REST OF SPANISH class, so much so that I even figured out how to ask Profe Garmy, '*puedo ir al bano*,' and spent so much time in the bathroom that Stevie Rae followed me in there asking what was wrong.

I know I was worrying the hell out of her – I mean, if a fledgling starts looking sick, that tends to mean that she's dying. And I'm positive I looked awful. I told Stevie Rae that I was getting my period and the cramps were killing me – although not literally. She didn't seem convinced.

I was incredibly glad to get to my last class of the week,

Equestrian Studies. Not only did I love the class, but it always calmed me. This week I'd graduated to actually cantering Persephone, the horse that Lenobia (no prof title for her, she said the name of the ancient vampyre queen was title enough) had assigned to me the first week of class, and practiced changing leads. I worked with the beautiful mare until both of us were sweating and my stomach felt a little better, then I took my time cooling her off and grooming her, not caring that the bell had signaled the end of the school day a good half an hour before I emerged from her stall. I went to the immaculately kept tack room to put away the curry combs, and was surprised to see Lenobia sitting on a chair outside the door. She was rubbing saddle soap into what looked like an already spotlessly clean English saddle.

Lenobia was striking-looking, even for a vampyre. She had amazing hair that reached her waist and was so blond it was almost white. Her eyes were a weird color of gray, like a stormy sky. She was tiny, and carried herself like a prima ballerina. Her tattoo was an intricate series of knots entwining around her face – within the sapphire design horses plunged and reared.

'Horses can help us work through our problems,' she said without looking up from the saddle.

I wasn't sure what to say. I liked Lenobia. Okay, when I started her class she had scared me; she was tough and sarcastic, but after I got to know her (and proved I understood horses were not just big dogs), I'd come to appreciate her wit and her no-nonsense attitude. Actually, next to Neferet, she was my favorite teacher, but she and I hadn't ever talked about anything except horses. So, hesitantly, I finally said, 'Persephone makes me feel calm, even when I don't feel calm. Does that make any sense?'

She looked up at me then, her gray eyes shadowed with concern. 'It makes perfect sense.' She paused, and then added, 'You've been given many responsibilities in a very short amount of time, Zoey.'

'I don't really mind,' I assured her. 'I mean, being leader of the Dark Daughters is an honor.'

'Often things that bring us the most honor can also bring us the most problems.' She paused again and maybe I was imagining it, but she seemed to be trying to decide whether to say more or not. Then she drew her already straight spine up even straighter and continued. 'Neferet is your mentor, and it is only right that you go to her with your confidences, but sometimes High Priestesses can be difficult to talk with. I want you to know that you can come to me – about anything.'

I blinked in surprise. 'Thank you, Lenobia.'

'I'll put these up for you. Run along. I'm sure your friends are wondering what has happened to you.' She smiled and reached out to take the curry combs from me. 'And feel free to come by the barn to visit Persephone anytime. I have often found that grooming a horse can somehow make the world seem less complex.'

'Thank you,' I said again.

As I left the barn I could swear that I heard her call softly after me something that sounded a lot like *May Nyx bless and watch over you.* But that was just too weird. Of course, it was also too weird that she had said I could talk to her. Fledglings formed special bonds with their mentors – and I had an extra-special mentor in the High Priestess of the school. Sure, we liked the other vamps, but if a kid had a problem she couldn't solve on her own, the kid took that problem to his or her mentor. Always.

The walk from the stables to the dorm wasn't a long one, but I took my time, trying to stretch out the sense of peace working with Persephone had given me. I meandered off the sidewalk a little, heading toward the old trees that lined the eastern side of the thick wall surrounding the school grounds. It was almost four o'clock (A. M., of course), and the deepness of the night was beautiful lit by the fat setting moon.

I'd forgotten how much I loved walking out here by the school wall. Actually, I'd avoided coming out here for the past month. Ever since I'd seen – or thought I'd seen – the two ghosts.

'*Mee-uf-ow!*'

'Crap, Nala! Don't scare me like that.' My heart was beating like crazy as I lifted my cat into my arms and petted her while she complained at me. 'Hello – you could have been a ghost.' Nala peered at me and then sneezed right in my face, which I took as her comment on the possibility of her being a ghost.

Okay, the first 'sighting' might have been a ghost. I'd been out here the day after Elizabeth had died last month. She'd been the first of two fledgling deaths to shake the school. Well, more accurately, to shake *me*. As fledglings who could – any of us – drop dead at any time during the four years it took the physiological Change from human to vampyre to happen within our bodies, the school expected us to deal with death as just another fact of fledgling life. Say a prayer or two for the dead kid. Light a candle. Whatever. Just get over it and go on with your business.

It still seemed wrong to me, but maybe that was because I was only a month into the Change and still more used to being human than vamp, or even fledgling.

I sighed and scratched Nala's ears. Anyway, the night after Elizabeth's death I'd caught a glimpse of something that I thought was Elizabeth. Or her ghost, 'cause she was definitely dead. So it was no more than a glimpse, and Stevie Rae and I had discussed it without really deciding what was up with it. The truth was that we knew all too well that ghosts existed – the ones Aphrodite had conjured a month ago had almost killed my human ex-boyfriend. So I might very well have seen Elizabeth's newly freed spirit. Of course I might also have caught a glimpse of a fledgling and, because it had been night and I'd only been here for a few days and had, in those few days, gone through all sorts of unbelievable crap, I might have imagined the whole thing.

I came to the wall and turned to my right, meandering along it in the direction that would eventually lead me near the rec hall, and then, in turn, the girls' dorm.

'But the second sighting definitely wasn't my imagination.

Right, Nala?' The cat's answer was to burrow her face into the corner of my neck and purr like a lawn mower. I snuggled her, glad she'd followed me. Just thinking about the second ghost still freaked me out. Like now, Nala had been with me. (The similarity made me glance nervously around and step up my meandering.) It had not been long after the second kid had drowned in his own lung tissue and bled out right in front of my Lit class. I shuddered, remembering how awful it had been – especially because of my gross attraction to his blood. Anyway, I'd watched Elliott die. Then later that day Nala and I had run into him (almost literally) not far from where we were right now. I'd thought he was another ghost. At first. Then he'd tried to attack me, and Nala (precious kitten) had launched herself at him, which had made him leap over the twenty-foot wall and disappear into the night, leaving Nala and me totally freaked out. Especially after I noticed that my cat had blood all over her paws. *The ghost's blood.* Which made no damn sense.

But I hadn't mentioned this second sighting to anyone. Not my best friend and roommate Stevie Rae, not my mentor and High Priestess Neferet, not my totally delicious new boyfriend, Erik. No one. I'd meant to. But then all the stuff had happened with Aphrodite ... I'd taken over the Dark Daughters ... started dating Erik ... been extremely busy with school ... blah, blah, one thing led to another and here I was a month later and I hadn't said anything to anyone. Just thinking about telling someone now sounded lame in my own mind. *Hey, Stevie Rae/Neferet/Damien/Twins/Erik, I saw the specter of*

Elliott last month after he'd died and he'd been really scary and when he tried to attack me Nala made him bleed. Oh, and his blood smelled all wrong. Believe me. I'm way into good-smelling blood (just another freakish thing about me, most fledglings have no bloodlust). Just thought I'd mention it.

Yeah, right. They'd probably want to send me to the vamp equivalent of a shrink, and oh, boy, wouldn't that help me to instill confidence in the masses as the new leader of the Dark Daughters? Not hardly.

Plus, the more time passed, the easier it was for me to convince myself that maybe I'd imagined some of the Elliott encounter. Maybe it hadn't been Elliott (or his ghost or whatever). I didn't know every single one of the fledglings here. There could be another kid who had ugly, bushy red hair and pudgy, too white skin. Sure, I hadn't seen that kid again, but still. And about the weird-smelling blood. Well, maybe some fledglings had weird-smelling blood. Like I could possibly be an expert in one month? Also both 'ghosts' had glowing red eyes. What had that been about?

The whole thing was giving me a headache.

Ignoring the jumpy, spooky feeling this entire chain of thought was causing, I started to turn resolutely from the wall (and from the subject of ghosts and such) when a movement caught at the corner of my eye. I froze. It was a shape. A body. It was *some*body. The person was standing under the enormous old oak I'd found Nala in last month. His or her back was to me, and he or she was leaning against the tree, head bowed.

Good. It hasn't seen me. I didn't want to know who or what it was. The truth was that I already had enough stress in my life. I didn't need the addition of ghosts of any type. (And, I promised myself, this time I was going to tell Neferet about the weirdly bleeding ghosts that hung out by the school's wall. She was older. She could deal with the stress.) Heart pounding so loud that I swear the sound of it was drowning out Nala's purr, I slowly and quietly started backing away, telling myself firmly that I was never going to walk out here in the middle of the night alone again. Ever. What was I, mentally impaired? Why couldn't I learn the first, or even the second time?

Then my foot came down squarely in the middle of a dry branch. *Crack!* I gasped. Nala grumbled a very loud complaint (I was inadvertently squashing her to my bosom). The head of the figure under the tree snapped up and it turned around. I tensed to get ready to either scream and run from a red-eyed malevolent ghost, or to scream and fight a red-eyed malevolent ghost. Either way a scream would definitely be involved, so I sucked in air and—

'Zoey? Is that you?'

The voice was deep, sexy, and already familiar. 'Loren?'

'What are you doing out here?'

He made no move to come closer to me, so out of pure awkward fidgeting I grinned as if I hadn't been scared poo-less just seconds ago, shrugged nonchalantly, and joined him under the tree. 'Hi,' I said, trying to sound grown. Then I remembered that he'd asked me a question and I was glad that it was dark enough that my blush wasn't totally obvious. 'Oh, I was walking back from the stables and Nala and I decided to take a long-cut.' A long-cut? Had I really said that?

I thought he'd looked tense when I'd walked up to him, but this made him laugh and his completely gorgeous face relaxed. 'A long-cut, huh? Hello again, Nala.' He scratched the top of her head and she rudely, but typically, grumbled at him and then leaped neatly from my arms to the ground, shook herself, and still grumbling, padded delicately away.

'Sorry. She's not very sociable.'

He smiled. 'Don't worry about it. My cat, Wolverine, reminds me of a grumpy old man.'

'Wolverine?' I raised my eyebrows.

His gorgeous smile went all crooked and boylike and, unbelievably, it made him even more handsome. 'Yeah, Wolverine. He chose me as his when I was a third former. That was the year I was completely into the *X-Men*.'

'That name could account for why he's so grumpy.'

'Well, it could have been worse. The year before I couldn't stop watching *Spider-Man*. He came within an inch of being Spidey or Peter Parker.'

'Clearly, you're a great burden for your cat to bear.'

'Wolverine would most definitely agree with you!' He laughed again and I tried hard not to let his overwhelming hotness make me giggle hysterically like a pre-teen at a boy band concert. I was, for the moment, actually *flirting with him! Remain calm. Don't say or do anything idiotic.*

'So, what are you doing way out here?' I asked, ignoring my mind babble.

'Writing haiku.' He lifted his hand and I noticed for the first time that he was holding one of those cool, ultra-expensive leather-bound writer's journals. 'I find inspiration being out here, alone, in the hours before dawn.'

'Oh, gosh! I'm sorry. I didn't mean to interrupt you. I'll just say bye and leave you alone.' I waved (like a dork) and started to turn away, but he caught my wrist with his free hand.

'You don't have to go. I find inspiration in more things than being out here alone.'

His hand was warm against my wrist and I wondered if he could feel my pulse jump.

'Well, I don't want to bother you.'

'Don't worry about that. You're not bothering me.' He squeezed my wrist before (sadly) letting it go.

'Okay, so. Haiku.' His touch had left me ridiculously flustered and I tried to regain my facade of good sense. 'That's Asian poetry with a set meter count, right?'

His smile made me ever so glad I'd actually paid attention in Mrs Wienecke's English class last year during the poetry unit.

'That's right. I prefer the five-seven-five format.' He paused and his smile changed. Something about it made my stomach do a little fluttery thing, and his dark, beautiful eyes locked on mine. 'Speaking of inspiration – you could help me out.'

'Sure, I'd be happy to,' I said, glad I didn't sound as breathless as I felt.

Still looking into my eyes, he lifted his hand so that it brushed my shoulder. 'Nyx has Marked you there.'

It didn't sound like a question, but I nodded. 'Yes.'

'I would like to see it. If it wouldn't make you too uncomfortable.'

His voice shivered through me. Logic was telling me that he was only asking to see my tattoos because of how freakishly different they are, and that he was in no way coming on to me. To him I must seem nothing more than a child – a kid – a fledgling with weird Marks and unusual powers. That's what logic was telling me. But his eyes, his voice, the way his hand was still caressing my shoulder – those things were telling me something completely different.

'I'll show it to you.'

I was wearing my favorite jacket – black suede and cut to fit me perfectly. Under it I had on a deep purple tank. (Yes, it's the end of November, but I don't feel the cold like I did before I was Marked. None of us do.) I started to shrug out of the jacket.

'Here, let me help you.'

He was standing very close to me, in front and to the side. He reached up with his right hand, caught the collar of my jacket with his fingers, and slid it over and down my shoulder so that it pooled around my elbows.

Loren should be looking at my partially bare shoulder, gawking at the tattoos there that not one other fledgling or vampyre that I knew of had ever had. But he wasn't. He was still staring into my eyes. And suddenly something happened within me. I stopped feeling like a goofy, jittery, dorky teenage girl. The look in his eyes touched the woman inside me, awakening her, and as this new me stirred I found a calm confidence in myself that I had rarely known before. Slowly, I reached up and pushed the small strap of my ribbed cotton tank over my shoulder so that it joined my half-discarded jacket. Then, still meeting his eyes, I swept my long hair out of the way, lifted my chin, and turned my body slightly, giving him a clear view of the back of my shoulder, which was now completely bare except for the slim line of my black bra.

He continued to meet my gaze for several more seconds, and I could feel the cool breath of the night air and the caress of the nearly full moon on the exposed skin of my breast and shoulder and back. Very deliberately, Loren moved even closer to me, holding my upper arm while he looked at the back of my shoulder.

'It's incredible.' His voice was so low it was almost a whisper. I felt his fingertip lightly trace the labyrinthlike spiral pattern that was, except for the exotic-looking runes interspersed around the spirals, much like my facial Mark. 'I've never seen anything like this. It's as if you're an ancient priestess who has materialized in our time. How blessed we are to have you, Zoey Redbird.'

He said my name like a prayer. His voice mixed with his touch made me shiver as goose bumps lifted on my skin.

'I'm sorry. You must be cold.' Gently, but quickly, Loren pulled up my tank strap and my jacket.

'I wasn't shivering because I was cold.' I heard myself say

the words, and couldn't decide if I should be proud of myself or shocked at my boldness.

> *'Cream and silk as one*
> *How I long to taste and touch*
> *The moon watches us.'*

His eyes never left mine as he recited the poem. His voice, which was usually so practiced, so perfect, had gone all deep and rough, like he was having a hard time speaking. As if his voice had the ability to heat me, I was so flushed that I could feel my blood pounding fiery rivers through my body. My thighs tingled and it was hard to catch my breath. *If he kisses me I might explode*. The thought shocked me into speaking. 'Did you write that just now?' This time my voice sounded as breathless as I felt.

He shook his head slightly, a smile barely touching his lips. 'No. It was written centuries ago by an ancient Japanese poet about how his lover looked naked under the full moon.'

'It's beautiful,' I said.

'You're beautiful,' he said, and cupped my cheek in his hand. 'And tonight you have been my inspiration. Thank you.'

I could feel myself leaning into him, and I swear his body responded. I may not be highly experienced. And, hell yes, I'm still a virgin. But I'm not an utter moron (most of the time). I know when a guy is into me. And this guy – for that moment – was definitely into me. I covered his hand with

my own, and forgetting about everything, including Erik and
the fact that Loren was an adult vamp and I was a fledgling,
I willed him to kiss me, willed him to touch me more. We
stared at each other. We were both breathing hard. Then,
within the space of an instant, his eyes flickered and changed
from dark and intimate to dark and distant. He dropped his
hand from my face and moved a step back. I felt his with-
drawal like an icy wind.

'It was nice to see you, Zoey. And thanks again for allowing
me to look at your Mark.' His smile was polite and proper.
He gave me a little nod that was almost a formal bow, and
then he walked away.

I didn't know whether I should scream in frustration, cry
in embarrassment, or growl and be pissed. Frowning and
muttering to myself, I ignored the fact that my hands were
shaking and marched back to the dorm. This was definitely
an I-need-my-best-friend emergency.

CHAPTER SIX

STILL MUMBLING TO MYSELF ABOUT MEN AND MIXED messages, I entered the front room of the dorm and wasn't surprised to see Stevie Rae and the Twins clustered together watching one of the TVs. Clearly, they'd been waiting for me. I felt an incredible wash of relief. I didn't want the whole world (translation – the Twins and/or Damien) to know what had just happened, but I was going to tell Stevie Rae every single, tiny, juicy detail about Loren – and let her help me figure out what the hell all of it meant.

'Uh, Stevie Rae, I'm clueless about our, uh, Soc paper that's due Monday. Maybe you could help me with it. I mean, it

won't take too long and—' I started, but Stevie Rae interrupted me without taking her eyes from the TV.

'Wait, Z, come here. You gotta see this.' She motioned me
over to the TV. The Twins' eyes were glued to the screen, too.

I frowned when I noticed how tense they all looked, causing
the subject of Loren to (temporarily) slide from my mind.
'What's going on?' They were watching a rebroadcast of the
local Fox 23 evening news. Chera Kimiko, the anchor, was
talking and some familiar pictures of Woodward Park were
flashing on the screen. 'It's hard to believe that Chera isn't a
vamp. She is abnormally gorgeous,' I said automatically.

'Shush and listen to what she's saying,' Stevie Rae said.

Continuing to be surprised by how weird they were acting,
I shushed and listened.

'So, to repeat our lead story tonight – the search continues for
Union High School teenager Chris Ford. The seventeen-year-old
disappeared yesterday after football practice.' The picture on the
screen was a shot of Chris in his football uniform. I let out a
little yelp as the name and face registered.

'Hey – I know him!'

'That's why I called you over here,' Stevie Rae said.

'Search parties are combing the area around Utica Square and
Woodward Park, which is where he was last seen.'

'That's really close to here,' I said.

'Shush!' Shaunee said.

'We know!' Erin said.

'So far there are no leads as to why he was in the Woodward
Park area. Chris's mother said she didn't even know her son knew

67

the way to Woodward Park, she's never known him to go there before. Mrs Ford also said that she expected him home right after football practice. He has now been missing for more than twenty-four hours. If anyone has any information that might help the police locate Chris, please call Crime Stoppers. You may remain anonymous.'

Chera went on to another story and everyone unfroze.

'So, you know him?' Shaunee asked.

'Yeah, but not real well. I mean, he's one of Union's star running backs and when I was kinda sorta dating Heath – you guys know he's Broken Arrow's quarterback?'

They nodded impatiently.

'Well, he used to drag me to parties with him, and all the football jocks knew each other, so Chris and his cousin Brad were at a bunch of them. Rumor has it they've graduated from getting trashed on cheap beer to getting trashed on cheap beer while they pass around nasty joints.' I looked at Shaunee, who had been showing an unusual amount of interest in the newscast. 'And before you ask, yes, he is as cute in real life as he was in his picture.'

'Damn shame when something bad happens to a cute brother,' Shaunee said, shaking her head sadly.

'Damn shame when something happens to any cute guy – no matter what color, Twin,' Erin said. 'We shouldn't discriminate. Cuteness is cuteness.'

'You're right, as usual, Twin.'

'I don't like marijuana,' Stevie Rae piped in. 'It smells bad. I tried it once and it made me cough my head off and burned my throat. Plus I got some of the weed in my mouth. It was just nasty.'

'We don't do ugly,' Shaunee said.

'Yeah, and pot's ugly. Plus it makes you eat for no good reason. It's a shame the hottie football players are into that,' Erin said.

'Makes them less hottie,' Shaunee said.

'Okay, hottie-ness and pot are not really the point,' I said. 'I have a bad feeling about this whole disappearance thing.'

'Oh, no,' Stevie Rae said.

'Well shit,' Shaunee said.

'I really hate it when she gets one of those feelings,' Erin said.

All any of us could talk about was Chris's disappearance and how bizarre it was that he had last been seen so close to the House of Night. In comparison to a kid being missing, my little drama-trauma with Loren seemed insignificant. I mean, I still wanted to tell at least Stevie Rae about it, but I couldn't seem to concentrate enough on anything but the sucking black feeling that had filled me since I'd seen the news.

Chris is dead. I didn't want to believe it. I didn't want to know it. But everything inside me said that the kid would be found, but he'd be found dead.

We met Damien in the dining hall, and everyone's conversation was centered around Chris and theories about his disappearance, which ranged from the Twins' insistence that 'the hottie probably had a fight with his parental units and he's off drinking cheap beer somewhere' to Damien's firm belief that he might have discovered homosexual tendencies and had taken off for New York City to fulfill his dream of being a gay model.

I didn't have a theory. All I had was a terrible feeling, which I wasn't willing to talk about.

Naturally, I couldn't eat. My stomach was killing me. Again.

'You're picking at your excellent food,' Damien said.

'I'm just not hungry.'

'That's what you said at lunch.'

'Okay, well, I'm saying it again!' I snapped, and was instantly sorry when Damien looked hurt and frowned down at his yummy bowl of Vietnamese noodle salad called Bun Cha Gio. The Twins raised one eyebrow each at me, and then went back to focusing on using chopsticks correctly. Stevie Rae just stared at me, silent worry clear on her face.

'Here. I found this. I have a feeling it's yours.'

Aphrodite dropped the silver hoop beside my plate. I looked up at her perfect face. It was weirdly expressionless, as was her voice.

'So, is it yours?'

I reached up automatically and touched its mate, which was still in my ear. I'd forgotten all about that I'd dropped the damn thing so that I could pretend to find it while I eavesdropped on Aphrodite and Neferet. Crap. 'Yes. Thank you.'

'Don't mention it. Guess you're not the only one who has *feelings* about things, huh?'

She turned and walked out of the dining hall through the

glass doors and into the courtyard. Even though she was carrying a tray with her uneaten dinner on it, she didn't even pause to look at the table where her friends sat. I noticed that they glanced up as she passed, but then they looked hastily away. None of them met her eyes. Aphrodite ate outside in the dimly lit courtyard where she'd been eating for most of the past month. Alone.

'Okay, she is just weird,' Shaunee said.

'Yeah, weird as in psycho bitch from hell,' Erin said.

'Her own friends won't have anything to do with her,' I said.

'Stop feeling sorry for her!' Stevie Rae said, sounding uncharacteristically pissed off. 'She's trouble, can't you see that?'

'I didn't say she wasn't,' I said. 'I just commented that even her friends have turned their backs on her.'

'Did we miss something?' Shaunee asked.

'What's going on with you and Aphrodite?' Damien asked me.

I opened my mouth to tell them about what I'd overheard earlier, and was silenced by Neferet's smooth, 'Zoey, I hope you don't mind if I pull you away from your friends tonight.'

I looked slowly up at her, almost scared about what I might see. I mean, last time I heard her voice she had sounded incredibly hateful and cold. My eyes lifted to hers. They were moss green and beautiful and her kind smile was just starting to look worried.

'Zoey? Is something wrong?'

'No! I'm sorry. My mind was wandering.'

'I'd like you to have dinner with me tonight.'

'Oh, sure. Of course. No problem; I'd like that.' I realized I was babbling, but there didn't seem to be anything I could do about it. I hoped it would eventually stop. Kinda like how you can't have diarrhea forever – it eventually has to stop.

'Good.' She smiled at my four friends. 'I need to borrow Zoey, but I will return her soon.'

The four of them gave her hero-worshiping grins and quick assurances that they were cool with whatever.

I know it's ridiculous, but their easy release of me made me feel abandoned and insecure. But that's stupid. Neferet is my mentor, and High Priestess of Nyx. She's one of the good guys.

So why was my stomach clenching as I followed her out of the dining hall?

I glanced over my shoulder at my group. They were already talking away. Damien was holding up his chopsticks, obviously giving the Twins another lesson in how to maneuver them. Stevie Rae was demonstrating for him. I felt eyes on me and looked from them to the wall of glass that separated the dining area and the courtyard. Sitting alone in the night, Aphrodite was watching me with an expression that might almost be pity.

CHAPTER SEVEN

THE VAMPS' DINING HALL WASN'T A CAFETERIA. IT WAS A very cool room that was directly above the students' dining hall. It, too, had a wall of arched windows. Wrought-iron tables and chairs were set up on the balcony that overlooked the courtyard below. The rest of the room was tastefully and expensively decorated with a variety of different size tables and even a few booths made of dark cherry-wood. There were no trays here and no serve-yourself buffets. Linens, china, and crystal were set tastefully on the tables, and long, thin white tapers burned happily in crystal holders. There were a few professors eating in quiet couples or small groups. They nodded at Neferet respectfully and smiled quick welcomes to me before going back to their meals.

I tried to gawk at what they were eating without being too obvious, but all I saw was the same Vietnamese salad we'd been eating downstairs, and some fancy-looking spring rolls. There wasn't one sign of raw meat or anything that resembled blood (well, except for the red wine). And, of course, I really didn't need to bother about gawking. If they'd been feasting on bloody whatever I would have smelled it. I was intimately familiar with the delicious scent of blood . . .

'Would the cool night bother you if we sat outside on the balcony?' Neferet asked.

'No, I don't think so. I don't feel the cold like I used to.' I smiled brightly at her, reminding myself severely that she's an intuitive and she was probably 'hearing' pieces of the stupid stuff cascading through my mind.

'Good, I prefer dining on the balcony in all seasons.' She led me through the doors to a table already set for two. A server magically appeared – obviously a vampyre by her filled-in Mark and the series of slim tattoos that framed her heart-shaped face, but she looked really young. 'Yes, bring me the Bun Cha Gio and a pitcher of the same red wine I had last night.' She paused, and then with a secret smile to me added, 'And please bring Zoey a glass of any brown pop we have, so long as it isn't diet.'

'Thank you,' I told her.

'Just try not to drink too much of that stuff. It's really not good for you.' She winked at me, making her admonishment a little joke.

I grinned at her, happy that she remembered what I like, and I started to feel more relaxed. This was Neferet – our High Priestess. She was my mentor and my friend and in the month I'd been here she'd never been anything but kind to me. Yes, she'd sounded scary as hell when I overheard her with Aphrodite, but Neferet was a powerful Priestess, and as Stevie Rae kept reminding me, Aphrodite was a selfish bully who deserved to be in trouble. Hell! She'd probably been gossiping about me.

'Feeling better?' Neferet said.

I met her eyes. She was studying me carefully.

'Yeah, I am.'

'When I heard about the missing human teenager I began to worry about you. This Chris Ford was a friend of yours, wasn't he?'

Nothing she said should surprise me. Neferet was incredibly smart and gifted by the Goddess. Add to that the weird sixth sense all the vamps had, and more than likely she knew literally everything (or at least everything important). It had probably been easy-peasy for her to know that I'd had my own intuitive feeling about Chris's disappearance.

'Well, he wasn't really a friend of mine. We've been at some of the same parties, but I don't really like to party, so I didn't know him that well.'

'But something about his disappearance has upset you.'

I nodded. 'It's just a feeling I have. It's silly. He probably had a fight with his parents and his dad grounded him or something like that, so he took off. More than likely he's already home.'

'If you really believed that you wouldn't still feel so worried.' Neferet waited until the server finished giving us our drinks and food before she said more. 'Humans believe that adult vampyres are all psychic. The truth is that though many of us do have a gift for precognition or clairvoyance, the vast majority of our people have simply learned to listen to their intuition – which is something most humans have been fright- ened out of doing.' Her tone was much like it was in her classroom, and I listened to her eagerly while we ate. 'Think about it, Zoey. You're a good student – I'm sure you remember from your history classes what has historically happened to humans, especially female humans, when they pay too much attention to their intuition and begin "hearing voices in their head" or even foreseeing the future.'

'They were usually thought of as in league with the devil, or whatnot, depending on what time it was in history. Bottom line was they caught hell for it.' Then I blushed because I'd said the H word in front of a teacher, but she didn't seem to care, she was just nodding in agreement with me.

'Yes, exactly. They even attacked holy people, like their Joan of Arc. So you see that humans have learned to silence their instincts. Vampyres, on the other hand, have learned to listen and listen well to them. In the past, when humans attempted to hunt and destroy our kind, it was all that saved many of our foremothers' and forefathers' lives.'

76

I shivered, not liking to think about how tough it must have been to be a vampyre a hundred or so years ago.

'Oh, you don't need to worry, Zoeybird.' Neferet smiled. Hearing my grandma's nickname for me made me smile, too. 'The Burning Times will never come again. We may not be revered as we were in ancient days, but never again will humans be able to hunt and destroy us.' For a moment her green eyes flashed dangerously. I took a big drink of my brown pop, not wanting to meet those scary eyes. When she continued, she sounded like herself again – all hint of danger was gone from her voice and she was just my mentor and friend. 'So, what all this means is that I want you to be sure that you listen to your instincts. If you get bad feelings about a situation or about someone, pay attention to it. And, of course, if you need to talk with me, you may come to me at any time.'

'Thanks, Neferet, that means a lot to me.'

She waved away my thanks. 'That's what it means to be a mentor and a High Priestess – two roles I fully expect you to take on someday.'

When she talked about my future and me being a High Priestess, I always got a funny feeling. It was made up partially of hope and excitement, and partially of abject fear.

'Actually, I was surprised that you didn't come see me today after you finished in the library. Did you not decide on a new direction for the Dark Daughters?'

'Oh, uh, yeah. I did.' I forced myself not to think about the library and my encounter with Loren, and the east wall and my second encounter with him . . . No way did I want Neferet and her intuition picking up anything about . . . well . . . *him*.

'I sense your hesitation, Zoey. Would you rather not share what you've decided with me?'

'Oh, no! I mean, yes. Actually, I did come by your room, but you were . . .' I looked up quickly, remembering the scene I'd overheard. Her eyes seemed to see into my soul. I swallowed hard. 'You were busy with Aphrodite. So I left.'

'Oh, I see. Now your nervousness around me makes much more sense.' Neferet sighed sadly. 'Aphrodite . . . she has become a problem. It really is a pity. As I said on Samhain when I realized how far wrong she'd gone, I feel partially responsible for her behavior and her transformation into the dark creature she has become. I knew she was selfish, even when she first joined our school. I should have stepped in sooner and taken a firmer hand with her.' Neferet's gaze caught mine. 'How much did you overhear today?'

A warning skittered down my spine. 'Not very much,' I said quickly. 'Aphrodite was crying really hard. I heard you tell her to look within. I knew you wouldn't want to be interrupted.' I stopped, careful not to say specifically that that was *all* I had heard – careful not to lie outright. And I didn't look away from her sharp eyes.

Neferet sighed again and sipped her wine. 'I would not normally talk about one fledging to another, but this is a unique case. You know that Aphrodite's Goddess-given affinity was to be able to foresee disastrous events?'

I nodded, noting the past tense she used when she mentioned Aphrodite's ability.

'Well, it seems that Aphrodite's behavior has caused Nyx to withdraw her gift. It's something that is highly unusual. Once the Goddess touches someone, she rarely revokes what she has given.' Neferet shrugged sadly. 'But who can know the mind of the Great Goddess of Night?'

'It must be awful for Aphrodite,' I said, more thinking aloud than really meaning to comment.

'I appreciate your compassion, but I did not tell you this so that you would pity Aphrodite. Rather, I tell you so that you know to be on your guard. Aphrodite's visions are no longer valid. She might say or do things that are disturbing. As leader of the Dark Daughters, it will be your responsibility to be certain that she does not upset the delicate balance of harmony among the fledglings. Of course we encourage you to work out problems among yourselves. You are much more than human teenagers, and we expect more from you, but feel free to come to me if Aphrodite's behavior becomes too' – she paused, like she was considering the next word carefully – 'erratic.'

'I will,' I said, my stomach beginning to hurt again.

'Good! Now, why don't you tell me the plans you've made for your reign as leader of the Dark Daughters.'

I put Aphrodite out of my mind and outlined my new plans for the Prefect Council and the Dark Daughters. Neferet listened attentively and was openly impressed by my research and what she called a 'logical reorganization.'

'So, what you want from me is to lead the faculty in voting on the two new Prefects, because I agree with you that you and your four friends have more than proven your worth and are already an excellent working Council.'

'Yes. The Council wants to nominate Erik Night for the first of the two open positions.'

Neferet nodded her head. 'Erik is a wise choice. He's popular with the fledglings, and he has an excellent future before him. Who did you have in mind for the last position?'

'Here's where my Council and I disagree. I think we need another upperclassman, and I also think that person should be one who belonged to Aphrodite's inner circle.' Neferet raised her brows in surprise. 'Well, including a friend of hers reinforces what I've said all along, that I didn't come into this because I'm power crazy and set out to steal what was Aphrodite's or anything stupid like that. I just wanted to do the right thing. I didn't want to start some kind of silly clique war. If one of her friends is on my Council, then the rest of them might understand that it's not about me getting over on her – it's about something more important than that.'

Neferet considered for what seemed like forever. Finally she said, 'You know that even her friends have turned from her.'

'I realized that today in the dining hall.'

'Then what is the point of putting an ex-friend of hers on your Council?'

'I'm not convinced they are ex-friends. People act different in private than they do in public.'

'Again, I agree with you. I already made the announcement to the faculty that Sunday the Dark Daughters and Sons will convene a special Full Moon Ritual and meeting. I would expect that the vast majority of the old members will attend – if for no other reason than curiosity about your powers.'

I gulped and nodded. I was already way too aware that I was the main attraction in a freak show.

'Sunday is the right time for you to tell the Dark Daughters about your new vision for it. Announce that there is one spot left on your Council, and that it must be filled by a sixth former. You and I will look over the applications and decide who is the best fit.'

I frowned. 'But I don't want it to just be our choice. I want the faculty to vote, as well as the student body.'

'They will,' she said smoothly. 'Then we will decide.'

I wanted to say more, but her green eyes had gone cold; I'm not ashamed to admit that that scared me. So instead of arguing with her (which was totally impossible) I went down a different road (as my grandma would say).

'I also want the Dark Daughters to get involved with a community charity.'

This time Neferet's brows totally disappeared into her hairline.

'You mean community as in the human community?'

'I do.'

'You think they will welcome your help? They shun us. They abhor us. They are afraid of us.'

'Maybe that's because they don't know us,' I said. 'Maybe

if we acted like part of Tulsa, we'd get treated like part of Tulsa.'

'Have you read about the Greenwood riots in the 1920s? Those African-American humans were part of Tulsa, and Tulsa destroyed them.'

'It's not 1920 anymore,' I said. It was hard to meet her eyes, but I knew, deep inside, that I was doing the right thing. 'Neferet, my intuition is telling me this is something I must do.'

I watched her expression soften. 'And I did tell you to follow your intuition, didn't I?'

I nodded.

'What charity will you choose to get involved with – providing they actually allow you to help them?'

'Oh, I think they'll let us help them. I've decided to contact Street Cats – the cat rescue charity.'

Neferet threw back her head and laughed.

CHAPTER EIGHT

I WAS ALREADY OUT OF THE DINING HALL AND HEADING TO the dorm when I realized that I hadn't said anything to Neferet about the ghosts, but no way did I want to go back upstairs and start that subject. The conversation I'd already had with Neferet had completely exhausted me, and despite the beautiful dining room with its great view and its crystal and linen, I'd been eager to get out of there. I wanted to go back to the dorm and tell Stevie Rae about the whole Loren thing and then do nothing but veg out and watch bad reruns on TV and try to forget (at least for one night) that I had a terrible premonition about Chris's disappearance and that I was A

Big Deal now and in charge of the most important student group at the school. Whatever. I just wanted to be me for a while. As I'd told Neferet, Chris was probably safely at home already. And there was plenty of time for everything else. Tomorrow I'd write down an outline of what I was going to say to the Dark Daughters on Sunday. I guess I'd also have to work on a Full Moon Ritual ... my first real public circle casting and formal ritual. My stomach started to gurgle. I ignored it.

I was halfway to the dorm when I remembered that I also had an essay due Monday for Vamp Soc. Sure, Neferet had excused me from most of the third former work in that class so I could focus on reading ahead in the higher level Soc text, but I'd been trying really hard to be 'normal' (Whatever that was – hello – I'm a teenager and a fledgling vampyre. How could any of that be normal?), which meant I made sure I turned in papers when the rest of the class did. So I hurriedly backtracked to my homeroom class, where my locker and all of my books were kept. It was also Neferet's room, but I'd just left her having wine with several of the other profs upstairs. For a change I didn't have any worries about over-hearing something awful.

As usual, the door was unlocked. Why have locks when you had vamp intuition to scare the bejeezus out of kids instead? The room was dark, but that didn't matter. I'd only been Marked one month, but already I saw just as well with the lights off as with them on. Actually, better. Bright lights hurt my eyes – sunlight was almost unbearable.

I hesitated as I opened my locker, realizing that I hadn't seen the sun in almost a month. I hadn't even thought about it till now. Huh. Weird.

I was considering the bizarreness of my new life when I noticed the piece of paper that had been taped to the inside shelf of my locker. It fluttered in the temporary breeze I'd created by opening the door. My hand lifted to calm it, and I felt a jolt of shock when I realized what it was.

Poetry.

Or, more accurately, a poem. It was short and written in a bold, attractive cursive. I read it and reread it, registering specifically what it was. Haiku.

Ancient Queen awake
A chrysalis not yet formed
Will your wings unfold?

I let my fingers brush the words. I knew who had written it. There was only one logical answer. My heart squeezed as I whispered his name, 'Loren . . .'

'I'm serious, Stevie Rae. If I tell you, you have to swear you won't say anything to anyone. And when I say *anyone* I especially mean Damien and the Twins.'

'Dang, Zoey, you can trust me. I said I swear. What do you want me to do, open a vein?'

I didn't say anything.

'Zoey, you really can trust me. Promise.'

I studied my best friend's face. I needed to talk to someone – someone who was not a vamp. I searched inside myself, to the core of what Neferet would call my intuition. It felt right to confide in Stevie Rae. It felt safe.

'Sorry. I know I can trust you. I'm just . . . I don't know.' I shook my head, frustrated by my own confusion. 'Okay, weird stuff has happened today.'

'You mean more than the normal weirdness that goes on around here?'

'Yeah. Loren Blake came into the library today while I was there. He was the first person I talked to about the Prefect Council idea and my new ideas for the Dark Daughters.'

'Loren Blake? As in the most gorgeous vamp any of us have ever seen? Ohmygoodness. I better sit down.' Stevie Rae collapsed on her bed.

'That's who I mean.'

'I can't believe you haven't said anything about this until now. You must have been dying.'

'Well, that's not all. He . . . uh . . . touched me. And more than once. Okay, actually I saw him more than once today. Alone. And I think he wrote me a poem.'

'What!'

'Yeah, at first I was sure it was perfectly innocent and I was imagining anything else. In the library we just talked about the ideas I had for the Dark Daughters. I didn't think it meant anything. But, well, he touched my Mark.'

'Which one?' Stevie Rae asked. Her eyes were huge and round and she looked like she was going to explode.

'The one on my face. That time.'

'What do you mean *that time!*'

'Well, after I got done with brushing Persephone I wasn't in any hurry to get back to the dorm. So I went for a walk over by the east wall. Loren was there.'

'Ohmydearsweetlord. What happened?'

'I think we flirted.'

'You think!'

'We were laughing and smiling at each other.'

'Sounds like flirting to me. God, he is so totally gorgeous.'

'Tell me about it. When he smiles at me I can hardly breathe. And get this – *he recited a poem to me*,' I said. 'It was a haiku a man wrote about looking at his naked lover in the moonlight.'

'You have got to be kidding!' Stevie Rae started fanning herself with her hand. 'Get to the touching part.'

I took a deep breath. 'It was really confusing. Everything was going really well. Like I said, we were laughing and talking. Then he said he was out there by himself because that's how he gets inspired to write haiku—'

'Which is insanely romantic!'

I nodded and continued. 'I know. Anyway, I told him I hadn't meant to mess up his inspiration and bother him, and he said that more things inspired him than just the night. And he asked me if *I'd* be his inspiration.'

'Holy shit.'

'Exactly what I thought.'

'Naturally you said you'd be happy to inspire him.'

'Naturally,' I said.

'And . . .' Stevie Rae prompted eagerly.

'And he asked to see my Mark. The one on my shoulders and back.'

'He did not.'

'He did.'

'Man, I would have peeled off my shirt faster than you can say Bubba loves trucks!'

I laughed. 'Well, I didn't take my shirt off, but I slid my jacket down. Actually, he helped me.'

'Are you telling me Loren Blake, Vampyre Poet Laureate and hottest f-ing male on two feet, helped you off with your jacket like an old-time gentleman?'

'Yeah. Like this.' I demonstrated by pushing my jacket down around my elbows. 'And then I don't exactly know what came over me, but all of a sudden I wasn't all nervous and stupid-acting. I took the strap of my tank off for him. Like this.' I pushed my tank strap down, exposing my back and shoulder and a good part of my breast (relieved all over again that I had on my good black bra). 'That's when he touched me. Again.'

'Where?'

'He traced the pattern of my Mark on my back and shoulder. He told me that I look like an ancient vampyre queen and recited the poem to me.'

'Holy shit,' Stevie Rae said again.

I plopped down on my bed facing her and sighed, pulling the strap of my tank back up. 'Yeah, it was amazing for a little while. I was sure we connected. Really connected. I think he almost kissed me. Actually, I know he wanted to. And then, out of nowhere, he changed. He got all polite and formal and thanked me for showing him my Mark and then he walked away.'

'Well, that's no big surprise.'

'It sure as hell was to me. I mean, one second he was staring into my eyes and sending major signals that he wanted me and the next – nothing.'

'Zoey, you're a student. He's a teacher. This is a vamp school and a whole different world from life at a normal high school, but some things don't change. Students are off-limits to teachers.'

I chewed at my lip. 'He's only a part-time, temporary teacher.'

Stevie Rae rolled her eyes. 'As if that matters.'

'That's not all that happened. I just found this poem in my locker.' I handed her the piece of paper with the haiku on it.

Stevie Rae sucked air. 'Ohmygood*ness*. This is so romantic I could die. How? How did he touch the Mark on your back?'

'Jeesh, how do you think? With his finger. He traced the pattern.' I swear I could still feel the heat of that touch.

'He recited a love poem to you, touched your Mark, and then wrote a poem for you . . .' She sighed dreamily. 'It's like you're Romeo and Juliet with the whole forbidden lovers thing.' In the middle of fanning herself dramatically she stopped and sat straight up again. 'Ah oh, what about Erik?'

'What do you mean, what about Erik?'

'He's your boyfriend, Zoey.'

'Not officially,' I said sheepishly.

'Well, shoot, what does the kid have to do to make it "official"? Get down on one knee? It's been pretty obvious this past month that y'all are dating.'

'I know,' I said miserably.

'So do you like Loren more than you like Erik?'

'No! Yes. Oh, hell, I don't know. It's like Loren's in a whole other world. And it's not like he and I can really date, or whatever.' But I wasn't so sure about the whatever. Could Loren and I see each other secretly? Did I want to?

As if she could read my thoughts Stevie Rae said, 'You could sneak around and see Loren.'

'This is ridiculous. He probably doesn't even feel like that about me.' But even as I said the words I remembered the heat of his body and the desire in his dark eyes.

'What if he does, Z?' Stevie Rae was studying me carefully. 'You know, you're different than the rest of us. No one has ever been Marked like you before. No one has ever had an affinity for each of the five elements. Maybe the same rules don't apply to you.'

My gut clenched. Since I'd arrived at the House of Night I had been struggling to fit in. All I really wanted was to make this new place my home – to have friends I considered family. I didn't want to be different and I didn't want to play by different rules. I shook my head and said through clenched teeth, 'I don't want it to be like this, Stevie Rae. I just want to be normal.'

'I know,' Stevie Rae said softly. 'But you *are* different. Everyone knows that. Plus, don't you want Loren to like you?'

I sighed. 'I'm not sure what I want, except that I know I *don't* want anyone to find out about Loren and me.'

'My lips are sealed.' Stevie Rae, little Okie dork that she is, pantomimed zipping her lips closed and throwing the key away over her shoulder. 'No one's gonna get a word from me,' she mumbled through half-sealed lips.

'Hell! That reminds me, Aphrodite saw Loren touching me.'

'That hag followed you out to the wall!' Stevie Rae squeaked.

'No no no. No one saw us out there. Aphrodite walked into the media center when he was touching my face.'

'Ah, crap.'

'Ah, crap, is right. And there's more. Remember when I missed part of Spanish 'cause I wanted to talk to Neferet? I didn't talk to her. I got to her class and the door was cracked, so I could overhear what was going on inside. Aphrodite was in there.'

'That bitch was telling on you!'

'I'm not sure. I only heard a little of what they were saying.'

'I'll bet you were totally freaked when Neferet pulled you out of the dining hall to eat with her.'

'Totally,' I agreed.

'No wonder you looked so sick. Jeesh, it all makes sense now.' Then her eyes got even bigger. 'Did Aphrodite get you in trouble with Neferet?'

'No. When Neferet talked to me tonight she said that Aphrodite's visions are false because Nyx has withdrawn her gift. So whatever Aphrodite told her, Neferet didn't believe.'

'Good.' Stevie Rae looked like she'd like to break Aphrodite in half.

'No, not good. Neferet's reaction was too harsh. She made Aphrodite sob. Seriously, Stevie Rae, Aphrodite was destroyed by what Neferet said to her. Plus, Neferet didn't even sound like herself.'

'Zoey, I cannot believe we're going over this again. You've got to quit feeling sorry for Aphrodite.'

'Stevie Rae, you're not getting the point. This isn't about Aphrodite, it's about Neferet. She was cruel. Even if Aphrodite was ratting me out and exaggerating what she saw, Neferet's response was wrong. And I'm getting a bad feeling about it.'

'You're getting a bad feeling about Neferet?'

'Yes ... no ... I don't know. It's not just Neferet. It's like it's a mixture of stuff – everything coming down at once. Chris ... Loren ... Aphrodite ... Neferet ... something's off, Stevie Rae.' She looked confused, and I realized she needed an Okie analogy to get it. 'You know how it feels right before a tornado hits? I mean when the sky's still clear, but the wind's starting to cool off and change direction. You know some-thing's coming, but you don't always know what. That's how things feel to me right now.'

'Like a storm's comin'?'

'Yep. A big one.'

'So you want me to ... ?'

'Help me be a storm watcher.'

'I can do that.'

'Thanks.'

'But first can we be movie watchers? Damien just ordered *Moulin Rouge* from Netflix. He's bringing it over, and the Twins managed to get their hands on some honest-to-God real chips and non-fat-free dip.' She glanced at her Elvis clock. 'They're probably downstairs right now pissed because they've been waiting for us.'

I loved the fact that I could unload what felt like earth-shattering stuff to Stevie Rae and one second she could be 'ohmygoodness-ing' and the next talking about something as simple as movies and chips. She made me feel normal and grounded and like everything wasn't so overwhelming and confusing. I smiled at her. '*Moulin Rouge?* Doesn't that have Ewan McGregor in it?'

'Definitely. I hope we get to see his butt.'

'You talked me into it. Let's go. And remember—'

'Jeesh! I know I know. Don't say anything about any of this to anyone.' She paused and waggled her brows. 'So just let me say it one more time. *Loren Blake has the hots for you!*'

'Are you done now?'

'Yeah.' She grinned mischievously.

'I hope someone brought me some brown pop.'

'You know, Z, you're weird about your brown pop.'

'Whatever, Miss Lucky Charms,' I said, pushing her out the door.

'Hey, Lucky Charms are good for you.'

'Really? So, tell me, what are marshmallows – a fruit or a vegetable?'

'Both. They're unique – like me.'

I was laughing at silly Stevie Rae and feeling better than I had all day when we trotted down the stairs and into the front area of the dorm. The Twins and Damien had staked out one of the big flat-screen TVs, and they waved us over. I could see Stevie Rae had been right, they were munching on real Doritos and dipping them in full-fatted green onion dip (it sounds gross, but it's really yummy). My good feeling got even better when Damien handed me a big glass of brown pop.

'Took you guys long enough,' he said, scooting over so that we could sit by him on the couch. The Twins, naturally, had commandeered two identically big chairs they'd pulled over by the couch.

'Sorry,' Stevie Rae said, and then added with a grin at Erin, 'I had to have a bowel movement.'

'Excellent use of proper descriptions, Stevie Rae,' Erin said, looking pleased.

'Ugh, just put in the movie,' Damien said.

'Hang on, I have the remote,' Erin said.

'Wait!' I told her right before she clicked play. The volume had been turned down, but I could see Fox News 23's Chera Kimiko. Her face looked sad and serious as she talked earnestly into the camera. At the bottom of the screen ran the blurb *body of teenager found*. 'Turn up the volume.' Shaunee clicked off the mute.

'Repeating our lead story this morning: the body of the missing Union running back, Chris Ford, was discovered by two kayakers late Friday afternoon. The body had become snagged in the rocks and sand barges used to dam the Twenty-first Street area of the Arkansas River to create the new recreational rapids. Sources tell us that the teenager died of loss of blood associated with multiple lacerations, and that he might have been mauled by a large animal. We'll have more on that for you after the official medical examiner's report is released.'

My stomach, which had finally settled down and was acting normal, clenched. I felt my body go cold. But the bad news wasn't over. Chera's beautiful brown eyes looked earnestly into the camera as she continued.

'On the heels of this tragic news comes the report of another Union football player who has been listed as missing.' The screen flashed a picture of another cute guy in Union's traditional red and white football uniform. *'Brad Higeons was last seen after school Friday at the Starbucks at Utica Square where he was posting pictures of Chris. Brad was not only Chris's teammate, he was also his cousin.'*

'Ohmygoodness! The Union football team is dropping like flies,' Stevie Rae said. She glanced at me and I saw her eyes widen. 'Zoey, are you okay? You don't look so good.'

'I knew him, too.'

'That's weird,' Damien said.

'The two of them were always at parties together. Everyone knew them because they're cousins, even though Chris is black and Brad is white.'

'Makes perfect sense to me,' Shaunee said.

'Ditto, Twin,' Erin said.

I could barely hear them through the buzzing in my ears.
'I . . . I need to go for a walk.'

'I'll go with you,' Stevie Rae said.

'No, you stay here and watch the movie. I just – I just need to get some air.'

'Are you sure?'

'Positive. I won't be gone long. I'll be back in time to see Ewan's butt.' Even though I could almost feel the worried look Stevie Rae was giving my back (and hear the Twins arguing with Damien about whether they would actually see Ewan's butt), I rushed out of the dorm and into the cool November night.

Blindly, I turned away from the main school building, instinctively moving in the opposite direction from anywhere I'd run into people. I forced myself to keep moving and to breathe. *What the hell was wrong with me?* My chest felt tight and my stomach was so sick I had to keep swallowing hard so I wouldn't puke. The buzzing in my ears seemed to be better, but there was no relief from the anxiety that had settled over me like a shroud. Everything inside me was screaming, *Something's not right! Something's not right! Something's not right!*

As I walked I gradually noticed that the night, which had been clear, with a sky full of stars helping the almost full moon to illuminate its thick darkness, suddenly had clouded up. The soft, cool breeze had turned cold, causing dry leaves to shower down around me, mixing the smells of earth and wind with the darkness . . . somehow this soothed me and the tumult of disjointed thoughts and anxiety lifted enough for me to actually think.

I headed to the stables. Lenobia had said that I could groom Persephone whenever I needed to think and be alone. I definitely needed that, and having a direction to go – an actual destination – was one small good thing in the midst of my internal chaos.

The stables were just ahead, sprawling long and low, and my breath had started to come a little easier when I heard the sound. At first I didn't know what it was. It was too muffled – too odd. Then I thought that it might be Nala. It was like her to follow me and complain at me in her weird old lady cat voice until I stopped and picked her up. I looked around and called 'Kitty-kitty' softly.

The sound got more distinct, but it wasn't a cat, I could tell that. A movement close to the barn caught my eye, and I saw that a shape was slumped on the bench near the front doors. There was only one gaslight there, and it was right beside the doors. The bench was just outside the edge of the pool of flickering yellow light.

It moved again, and I could tell that the shape must be a person . . . or fledgling . . . or vampyre. It was sitting, but kinda hunched over, almost folded in on itself. The sound started again. This close I could hear that it was a weird wailing – like whoever was sitting there was in pain.

Naturally, I wanted to run in the opposite direction, but I couldn't. It wouldn't be right. Plus, I *felt* it – the knowledge within me that I could not leave. That whatever was happening on the bench was something I had to face.

I took a deep breath and approached the bench.

'Uh, are you okay?'

'*No!*' The word was an eerie, whispering explosion of sound.

'Can – can I help you?' I asked, trying to peer into the shadows and see who was sitting there. I thought I could see light-colored hair, and maybe hands covering a face . . .

'The water! The water is so cold and deep. Can't get out . . . can't get out.'

She took her hands from her face then and looked up at me, but I already knew who it was. I'd recognized her voice. And I also recognized what was happening to her. I forced myself to approach her calmly. She stared up at me. Her face was covered with tears.

'Come on, Aphrodite. You're having a vision. I need to get you to Neferet.'

'No!' she gasped. 'No! Don't take me to her. She won't listen to me. She – she doesn't believe me any more.'

I remembered what Neferet had said earlier about Nyx withdrawing her gifts from Aphrodite. Why should I even mess with her at all? Who knew what was going on with Aphrodite? She was probably making some pathetic play for attention, and I didn't have time for this crap.

'Fine. Let's say I don't believe you either,' I told her. 'Stay here and have your vision or whatever. I have other things to worry about.' I turned to head into the stable, and her hand snaked out, grabbing my wrist.

'You have to stay!' she said through chattering teeth. Obviously, she was having difficulty talking. 'You have to hear the vision!'

'No, I do not.' I pried her vicelike fingers from my wrist. 'Whatever's going on, it's about you – not me. You deal with it.' This time when I turned I walked away more quickly.

But not quick enough. Her next words felt like she'd sliced them through me.

'You have to listen to me. If you don't your grandma will die.'

CHAPTER NINE

'WHAT IN THE HELL ARE YOU TALKING ABOUT!' I ROUNDED on her.

She was gasping in weird little panting breaths, and her eyes were starting to flutter. Even in the darkness I could see the whites in them beginning to show. I grabbed her shoulders and shook her.

'Tell me what you see!'

Clearly trying to control herself she nodded with a jerky little movement. 'I will,' she panted. 'Just stay with me.'

I sat beside her on the bench and let her grab my hand, not caring that she was squeezing so hard it felt like she was going to break something – not caring that she was my enemy and someone I'd never trust – not caring about anything except the fact that Grandma might be in trouble.

'I'm not going anywhere,' I said grimly. Then I remembered how Neferet had prompted her. 'Tell me what you see, Aphrodite.'

'Water! It's awful . . . so brown and so cold. It's all confusion . . . can't – can't get the door of the Saturn open . . .'

I felt a horrible jolt. Grandma has a Saturn! She bought it because it was one of those ultra-safe cars that were supposed to be able to survive anything.

'But where's the car, Aphrodite? What water is it in?'

'Arkansas River,' she panted. 'The bridge – it collapsed.' Aphrodite sobbed, sounding terrified. 'I saw the car in front of me fall and hit the barge. It's on fire! Those little boys . . . the ones who were trying to get truck drivers to honk as they passed . . . they're in the car.'

I swallowed hard. 'Okay, what bridge? When?'

Aphrodite's whole body suddenly tensed. 'I can't get out! I can't get out! The water, it's . . .' She made a horrible noise that I swear sounded like she was being choked, and then she slumped back against the bench, her hand going limp in mine.

'Aphrodite!' I shook her. 'You have to wake up. You have to tell me more about what you saw!'

Slowly, her eyelids moved. This time I didn't see the whites of her rolled back eyeballs, and when she opened them they looked like normal eyes. Aphrodite abruptly let go of my hand

and shakily pushed her hair out of her face. I noticed it was damp, and that she was covered with sweat. She blinked a couple more times before meeting my eyes. Her gaze was steady, but I couldn't read anything except exhaustion in her expression or her voice.

'Good, you stayed,' she said.

'Tell me what you saw. What happened to my grandma?'

'The bridge her car's on collapses and she crashes into the river and drowns,' she said flatly.

'No. No, that won't happen. Tell me what bridge. When. How. I'll stop it.'

Aphrodite's lips curled up in the hint of a smile. 'Oh, you mean you suddenly believe my visions?'

Fear for Grandma was like a boiling pain inside me. I grabbed her arm and stood up, pulling her up with me. 'Let's go.'

She tried to jerk away from me, but she was too weak, I held on to her easily. 'Where?'

'To Neferet, of course. She'll figure this crap out, and you'll damn sure talk to her.'

'No!' she almost screamed. 'I won't tell her. I swear I won't. No matter what, I'll say I don't remember anything except water and a bridge.'

'Neferet will get this out of you.'

'No she won't! She'll be able to tell that I'm lying, that I'm hiding something, but she won't be able to tell what. If you take me to her, your grandma will die.'

I felt so sick I'd started to tremble. 'What do you want,

Aphrodite? Do you want to be leader of the Dark Daughters again? Fine. Take it back. Just tell me about my grandma.'

A look of raw pain passed over Aphrodite's pale face. 'You can't give it back to me, Neferet has to.'

'Then what do you want?'

'I just want you to listen to me so that you know that Nyx hasn't abandoned me. I want you to believe that my visions are still real.' She stared into my eyes. Her voice was low and strained. 'And I want you to owe me. Someday you're going to be a powerful High Priestess, more powerful even than Neferet. Someday I may need protection, and that's when you owing me will come in handy.'

I wanted to say that there was no way I could protect her from Neferet. Not now – maybe not ever. And I wouldn't want to. Aphrodite was messed up, and I'd already witnessed how selfish and hateful she could be. I didn't want to owe her; I didn't want anything to do with her.

I also didn't have any choice.

'Fine. I won't take you to Neferet. Now what did you see?'

'First give me your word that you owe me. And remember, this isn't an empty human promise. When vampyres give their word – be they fledgling or adult – it is binding.'

'If you tell me how to save my grandma I give you my word that I will owe you a favor.'

'Of my choice,' she said slyly.

'Yeah, whatever.'

'You have to say it to complete the oath.'

'If you tell me how to save my grandma I give you my word that I will owe you a favor of your choice.'

'So it is spoken; so it shall be done,' she whispered. Her voice sent chills up my back, which I ignored.

'Tell me.'

'I have to sit down first,' she said. Suddenly shaky again, she collapsed onto the bench.

I sat beside her and waited impatiently while she collected herself. When she started to talk I felt the stark horror of what she was saying pass through me, and I knew deep within my soul that what she was telling was a true vision. If Nyx was pissed at Aphrodite, the Goddess wasn't showing it tonight.

'This afternoon your grandma will be on the Muskogee Turnpike on her way to Tulsa.' She paused and cocked her head to the side, like she was listening in the wind for something. 'Your birthday's next month. She's coming into town to get you a present.'

I felt a jolt of surprise. Aphrodite was right. My birthday was in December – I had a sucky December twenty-fourth birthday, so I never got to really celebrate it. Everyone always wanted to mush it in with Christmas. Even last year, when I was turning sixteen and I should have had a big, cool party, I didn't get to do anything special. It was really annoying . . . I shook myself. Now was not the time to get lost in my life-long birthday complaint.

'Okay, so she's coming into town this afternoon, and what happens?'

Aphrodite narrowed her eyes, like she was trying to see out into the darkness. 'It's weird. I can usually tell exactly why these accidents happen – like a plane doesn't work or whatever, but this time I was so tuned in to your grandma, that I'm not sure why the bridge breaks.' She glanced at me. 'That might be because this is the first vision I've ever had where someone I recognize dies. It threw me off.'

'She's not going to die,' I said firmly.

'Then she can't be on that bridge. I remember the clock on her car's dashboard said three fifteen, so I'm sure it happens in the afternoon.'

Automatically, I glanced at my watch – 6:10 A.M. It'd be light in the next hour (and I should be going to bed), which meant that Grandma would be waking up. I knew her schedule. She woke up around dawn and went for a walk in the soft morning light. Then she came back to her cozy cabin and had a light breakfast before beginning whatever work needed to be seen to on her lavender farm. I'd call her and tell her to stay home, that she shouldn't even take a chance on driving anywhere today. She'd be safe; I'd make sure of it. Then another thought tickled at my mind. I looked at Aphrodite.

'But what about the other people? I remember you said something about some kids in the car in front of you, and that car crashed and caught on fire.'

'Yeah.'

I frowned at her. 'Yeah, what?'

'Yeah, I was watching from your grandma's point of view

and I saw a bunch of other cars crashing around me. It happened fast, though, so I couldn't really tell how many.'

She didn't say anything else, and I shook my head in disgust. 'What about saving them? You said little boys died!'

Aphrodite shrugged. 'I told you my vision was confusing. I couldn't tell exactly where it was, and the only reason I knew when is because I saw the date and time on your grandma's dash.'

'So you're just going to let the rest of those people die?'

'What do you care? Your grandma's going to be okay.'

'You make me sick, Aphrodite. Do you care about anyone but yourself?'

'Whatever, Zoey. Like you're so perfect? I didn't hear you caring about anyone else except your grandma.'

'Of course I was worried about her the most! I love her! But I don't want anyone else to die, either. And no one else is going to if I have anything to say about it. So, you need to figure out some way to let me know which bridge we're talking about.'

'I already told you – it's on the Muskogee Turnpike. I can't tell which one.'

'Think harder! What else did you see?'

She sighed and closed her eyes. I watched her face as her brow wrinkled and she seemed to cringe. With her eyes still closed she said, 'Wait, no. It's not on the turnpike. I saw a sign. It's the I-40 bridge over the Arkansas River – the one that's right off the turnpike near Webber's Falls.' Then she opened her eyes. 'You know when and where. I can't tell you much more. I think some kind of flat boat, like a barge, hits the bridge, but that's all I know. I didn't see anything to identify the boat. So, how are you going to stop it?'

'I don't know, but I will,' I muttered.

'Well, while you're thinking about how to save the world, I'm going to go back to the dorm and do my nails. Raggedy nails are something I consider tragic.'

'You know, having crappy parents isn't an excuse to be heartless,' I said. She'd turned away and I saw her pause. Her back got really straight and when she looked over her shoulder at me I could see that her eyes were narrowed in anger.

'What would you know about it?'

'About your parents? Not much except that they're controlling and your mom's a nightmare. About screwed-up parents in general? Plenty. I've been living with pain-in-the-ass parent issues since my mom remarried three years ago. It sucks, but it's not an excuse to be a bitch.'

'Try eighteen years of a lot more than just "pain-in-the-ass parent issues" and maybe you'll start to get something about it. Until then, you don't know shit.' Then, like the old Aphrodite I knew and couldn't stand, she flipped her hair and stalked away, wiggling her narrow butt like I cared.

'Issues. The girl has major issues.' I sat down on the bench and began rummaging through my purse for my cell phone, glad I carried it around with me even though I'd been forced to keep it on silent, without even vibrate on. The reason could be summed up in one word – Heath. He was my human almost-ex-boyfriend, and since he and my definitely ex-best friend, Kayla, had tried to 'break me out' (that's actually what they'd said – morons) of the House of Night, Heath had been way over the top on his obsession level for me. Of course, that wasn't really his fault. I was the one who had tasted his blood and started the whole Imprint thing with him, but still. Anyway, even though his messages had dwindled down from like a zillion (meaning twenty or so) a day, to two or three, I still didn't feel like leaving my phone on and being bothered by him. And, sure enough, when I flipped it open there were two missed calls, both from Heath. No messages, though, so hopefully he's demonstrating the ability to learn.

Grandma sounded sleepy when she answered the phone, but as soon as she realized it was me she perked up.

'Oh, Zoeybird! It's so nice to wake up to your voice,' she said.

I smiled into the phone. 'I miss you, Grandma.'

'I miss you, too, sweetheart.'

'Grandma, the reason I called is kinda weird, but you're just going to have to trust me.'

'Of course I trust you,' she replied without hesitation. She's so different than my mom that sometimes I wonder how they could be related.

'Okay, later today you're planning on coming into Tulsa to do some shopping, right?'

There was a brief pause, and then she laughed. 'I guess it's going to be hard to keep birthday surprises from my vampyre granddaughter.'

'I need you to promise me something, Grandma. Promise that you won't go anywhere today. Don't get in your car. Don't drive anywhere. Just stay home and relax.'

'What's this about, Zoey?'

I hesitated, not sure how to tell her. Then with her life-long ability to understand me, she said softly, 'Remember, you can tell me anything, Zoeybird. I'll believe you.'

I hadn't realized that I'd been holding my breath until that instant. On my let out breath I said, 'The bridge on I-40 that goes over the Arkansas River by Webber's Falls is going to collapse. You were supposed to be on it, and you would have died.' I said the last part softly, almost whispering.

'Oh! Oh, my! I'd better sit down.'

'Grandma, are you okay?'

'I suppose I am now, but I wouldn't be if you hadn't warned me, which is why I'm feeling light-headed.' She must have picked up a magazine or something because I could hear her fanning herself. 'How did you find out about this? Are you having visions?'

'No, not me. It's Aphrodite.'

'The girl who used to be leader of the Dark Daughters? I didn't think you two were friends.'

I snorted. 'We're not. Definitely not. But I found her having a vision and she told me what she saw.'

'And you trust this girl?'

'No way, but I do trust her power, and I saw her, Grandma. It was like she was there, with you. It was awful. She saw you crash, and those little kids die . . .' I had to stop and breathe. The truth had suddenly caught up with me: my grandma could have died today.

'Wait, there were more people in the crash?'

'Yeah, when the bridge collapses a bunch of cars go into the river.'

'But what about the other people?'

'I'm going to take care of that, too. You just stay home.'

'Shouldn't I go to the bridge and try to stop them?'

'No! Stay away from there. I'll make sure no one gets hurt – I promise. But I have to know that you're safe,' I said.

'Okay, sweetheart. I believe you. You don't have to worry about me. I'll be safe and sound at home. You take care of whatever you need to do, and if you need me, call. Anytime.'

'Thanks, Grandma. I love you.'

'I love you, too, *u-we-tsi-a-ge-ya*.'

After I hung up I spent a little while just sitting there, willing myself to stop shaking, but only a little while. A plan was already brewing in my head, and I didn't have time to freak out. I needed to get busy.

CHAPTER TEN

'SO WHY CAN'T WE TELL NEFERET ABOUT THIS MESS? ALL she'd have to do is make a few calls, like she did last month when Aphrodite had a vision about that plane going down at the Denver airport,' Damien said, careful to keep his voice low. I'd hurried back to the dorm, huddled my group together, and given them the short version of Aphrodite's vision.

'She made me promise I wouldn't go to Neferet. The two of them are having some kind of weird fight.'

'It's about time Neferet started seeing her as the bitch she is,' Stevie Rae said.

'Hateful cow,' Shaunee said.

111

'Hag from hell,' Erin agreed.

'Yeah, well, what she is doesn't really matter. It's her visions and the people who are in danger of dying that matter,' I said.

'I heard that her visions aren't really believable anymore because Nyx has withdrawn her favor from Aphrodite,' Damien said. 'Maybe that's why she made you promise not to go to Neferet, because this is all something she made up and she wants you to freak out and do something that will either embarrass you and make you look bad, or get you in trouble.'

'I'd think that too if I hadn't watched her having the vision. She wasn't faking it, I'm sure of that.'

'But is she telling you the whole truth?' Stevie Rae asked.

I thought about that for a second. Aphrodite had already admitted to me that she could withhold parts of her visions from Neferet. What made me think she wasn't doing that with me, too? Then I remembered the whiteness of her face, the way she had gripped my hand, and the fear in her voice as she joined my grandma in her death. I shivered.

'She was telling me the truth,' I said. 'You guys will just have to trust that my intuition is right.' I looked at my four friends. None of them were happy about this, but I knew that each of them trusted me and that I could count on them. 'So, here's the deal, I've already called my grandma. She won't be on that bridge, but a bunch of other people will. We need to figure out a way to save those other people.'

'Aphrodite said that a bargelike boat hit the bridge causing it to collapse?' Damien asked.

I nodded.

'Well, you could pretend to be Neferet and do what she does, call whoever's in charge of the barge and tell them one of your students has had a vision of a tragedy. People listen to Neferet; they're scared not to. It's a well-known fact that her information has saved lots of human lives.'

'I already thought about that, but it won't work because Aphrodite didn't see the boat clearly. She wasn't even sure it was a barge. So I have no way of knowing how to even begin contacting anyone about stopping it. And I can't pretend to be Neferet. It feels way wrong. I mean, talk about asking to get in trouble. You can't tell me that whoever I call won't call back with some kind of follow-up report to Neferet. Then all hell would break loose.'

'Ugly scene,' Shaunee said.

'Yeah, Neferet would find out that the hag had another vision, so your promise to keep it quiet would be broken,' Erin said.

'Okay, so stopping the boat is out, and pretending to be Neferet is out. That leaves closing the bridge as our only option,' Damien said.

'That's what I thought, too,' I said.

'Bomb threat!' Stevie Rae said suddenly. We all looked at her.

'Huh?' Erin asked.

'Explain,' Shaunee said.

'We call whoever those freaks who make bomb threats call.'

'That could actually work,' said Damien. 'When there's a bomb threat in a building they always evacuate it. So it figures that if there's a bomb threat about a bridge, the bridge will be closed, at least until they find out the bomb threat is fake.'

'If I call from my cell phone they won't be able to tell who I am, will they?' I asked.

'Oh, please,' Damien said, shaking his head like I was a total moron. 'Of course they can trace cell phones. This isn't the nineties.'

'Then what do I do?'

'You can still use a cell. It just has to be a disposable one,' Damien explained.

'You mean like a disposable camera?'

'Where have you been?' Shaunee asked.

'Who doesn't know about disposable cells?' Erin said.

'I don't,' Stevie Rae said.

'Exactly,' the Twins said together.

'Here' – Damien pulled a big dorky looking Nokia out of his pocket – 'use mine.'

'Why do you have a disposable?' I studied the phone. It looked fairly normal.

'I got it after my parents freaked about me being gay. Until I was Marked and came here it felt like they were grounding me for life from life. I mean, not that I really expected them to lock me in a closet somewhere, but it's good to be prepared. Since then I've made sure I always have one.'

None of us knew what to say. It really sucked that Damien's parents were so psycho about him being gay.

'Thanks, Damien,' I finally said.

'No problem. When you're done making the call be sure you turn it off and then give it back to me. I'll destroy it.'

'Okay.'

'And be sure you tell them that the bomb's planted under the waterline. That way they'll have to close the bridge long enough for them to send in divers to check it out.'

I nodded. 'Good idea. I'll tell them that the bomb's going to explode at three fifteen, which is the exact time Aphrodite saw on my grandma's dashboard clock when she crashed.'

'I don't know how long these things take, but you should probably call about two thirty, that sounds like enough time for them to get out there and close the bridge, but not so much that they'll have time to figure out it's a fake threat, and let cars back on the bridge too soon,' Stevie Rae said.

'Uh, guys,' Shaunee said. 'Who are you gonna call?'

'Hell, I don't know.' I was feeling the stress settle around my shoulders and knew I was going to have a major headache very soon.

'Google it,' Erin said.

'No,' Damien said quickly. 'We don't want any kind of computer trail. You just need to call the local branch of the FBI. That'll be in the phone book. They'll do whatever it is they do when freaks call.'

'Like track them down and put them in jail for the rest of eternity,' I muttered gloomily.

'No, they're not going to catch you. You're not leaving any

kind of a trail. They'll have no reason to think it's any of us. Call at about two thirty. Tell them you've planted a bomb under the bridge because . . .' Damien hesitated.

'Because of pollution!' Stevie Rae chirped.

'Pollution?' Shaunee said.

'I don't think it should be because of pollution. I think it should be because you're sick and tired of government interference in the private sector's lives,' Erin said.

I just blinked at her. What the hell did she just say?

'Excellent point, Twin,' Shaunee said.

Erin grinned. 'I sounded just like my dad when I said that. He'd be proud. Well, not about the pretending to blow up a bridge part, but the other stuff, yeah.'

'We understand, Twin,' Shaunee said.

'I still like saying that it's because you're tired of pollution. Pollution's a real problem,' Stevie Rae said stubbornly.

'Okay, how about I say it's because of government interference *and* pollution in our rivers? That'll be the reason the bomb's on a bridge.' They looked at me with blank expressions. I sighed. 'Because of pollution in the river.'

'*Ohhh*,' they said.

'We'd make dorky terrorists,' Stevie Rae said with a giggle.

'I think that's actually a good thing,' Damien said.

'So we're in agreement? I call the FBI, and we all keep our mouths shut about Aphrodite's vision.'

They nodded.

'Good. Okay. Guess I'll find a phone book and look up the number for the FBI, and then—'

A movement caught at the corner of my vision, and I glanced up to see Neferet escorting two men in suits into the dorm. Everyone went instantly silent, and I heard a whisper of '*They're human* . . .' begin to buzz through the room. Then I didn't have time to think or to listen, because it was obvious that Neferet and the two human men were walking directly over to me.

'Ah, Zoey, there you are.' Neferet smiled at me with her usual warmth. 'These gentlemen need to speak with you. I believe we can step into the library. This shouldn't take more than a moment.' Neferet regally gestured for the suits and me to follow her as she swept from the big main room (with everyone gawking openmouthed at us) to the little side room we called the dorm library, but was actually more of a computer room with some comfortable chairs and a few shelves filled with paperbacks. There were only two girls at the row of computers, and with a quick command Neferet got rid of them. They scurried out and she closed the door behind them, then she turned to face us. I glanced at the clock over the computer. It was 7:06 A.M. on Saturday morning. What was going on?

'Zoey, this is Detective Marx' – she pointed at the taller of the two men – 'and Detective Martin from the homicide division of the Tulsa Police Department. They wanted to ask you a few questions about the human boy who was killed.'

'Okay,' I said, wondering what kind of questions they could possibly want to ask me. Hell, I didn't know anything. I hadn't even known him that well.

'Miss Montgomery,' Detective Marx began, but he was cut neatly off by Neferet.

'Redbird,' she said.

'Ma'am?'

'Zoey legally changed her last name to Redbird when she became an emancipated minor upon entrance to our school last month. All of our students are legally emancipated. We find it helpful with the unique nature of our school.'

The cop gave a short nod. I couldn't tell whether he was annoyed or not, but I guessed by the way he kept looking at Neferet the answer was not.

'Miss Redbird,' he continued, 'we have received information that you are acquainted with Chris Ford and Brad Higeons. Is this true?'

'Yeah, I mean yes,' I hastily corrected. Clearly this wasn't a good time to sound like a silly teenager. 'I know . . . well, *knew* both of them.'

'What do you mean by *knew*?' Detective Martin, the shorter cop, said sharply.

'Well, I mean that I don't hang out with human teenagers anymore, but even before I was Marked I didn't see Chris or Brad much.' I wondered what he was so uptight about, and then I realized that because Chris was dead and Brad was missing that my talking about them in the past tense probably sounded really bad.

'When was the last time you saw the two boys?' Marx asked.

I chewed my lip, trying to remember. 'Not for months – since the beginning of football season, and then I just went to maybe two or three parties and they were there, too.'

'So you weren't with either boy?'

I frowned. 'No. I was kinda dating the Broken Arrow quarterback. That's the only reason I knew any of those Union guys.' I smiled, trying to lighten things up. 'People think Union players hate BA players. It's not really true. Most of them grew up together. A bunch of them are still friends.'

'Miss Redbird, you've been at the House of Night for how long?' the short cop asked as if I hadn't tried to be pleasant.

'Zoey has been with us for almost exactly one month,' Neferet answered for me.

'And in that month did either Chris or Brad visit you here?'

Totally surprised, I said, 'No!'

'Are you saying no human teenagers have visited you here at all?' Martin fired the question quickly.

Caught off guard I sputtered like a moron and I'm sure looked completely guilty. Thankfully, Neferet saved me.

'Two friends of Zoey's did see her during her first week here, although I do not believe you'd call it an official visit,' she said with a smooth, adult smile aimed at the detectives that clearly said *kids will be kids*. Then she nodded encouragement at me. 'Go ahead and tell them about your two friends who thought it'd be fun to scale our walls.'

Neferet's green eyes locked on mine. I'd told her all about Heath and Kayla climbing the wall with the ridiculous idea of busting me out. Or at least that had been Heath's idea. Kayla, my *ex*-best friend, had just wanted me to see that she'd staked a claim on Heath. I'd told Neferet all of that, and more. How I'd kinda accidentally tasted Heath's blood – until Kayla had caught me and totally lost her mind. Staring into Neferet's eyes I knew as sure as if she'd said the words aloud that I was to keep the little blood-tasting incident to myself, which was more than okay with me.

'There really wasn't much to it, and it was a whole month ago. Kayla and Heath thought they'd sneak in and bust me out.' I paused to shake my head like I thought they were totally crazy, and the tall cop jumped in with, 'Kayla and Heath who?'

'Kayla Robinson and Heath Luck,' I said. (Yeah, Heath's last name really is Luck, but the only thing he was particularly lucky about is not getting picked up DUI.) 'Anyway, Heath is kinda slow sometimes, and Kayla, well, Kayla's really good at shoes and hair, but not so good at common sense. So they hadn't really thought out the whole "Hey, she's turning into a vampyre and if she leaves the House of Night she'll die" issue. So I explained to them that not only did I not want to leave, I *couldn't* leave. And that was about it.'

'Nothing unusual happened when you saw your friends?'

'You mean when I went back to the dorm?'

'No. Let me rephrase the question. Nothing unusual happened when you saw Kayla and Heath?' Martin said.

I swallowed. 'No.' Which wasn't actually a lie. Apparently it's not unusual for fledglings to experience a vampyre's blood-lust. I shouldn't so early in my Change, but my Mark shouldn't be filled in and I shouldn't have the added decorative tattooing of an adult vamp either. Not to mention the fact that no other fledgling or vamp had ever been Marked on the shoulder and back like I had. Okay, I'm not exactly a normal fledgling.

'You didn't cut the boy and drink his blood?' The short cop's voice was like ice.

'No!' I cried.

'Are you accusing Zoey of something?' Neferet said, stepping closer to me.

'No, ma'am. We're simply questioning her to try and get a clearer idea of the dynamics of the friends of Chris Ford and Brad Higeons. There are several aspects of the case that are rather unusual and . . .' The short cop rambled on and on while my mind raced.

What was going on? I hadn't cut Heath; I'd scratched him. And I hadn't done it on purpose. And 'drinking' his blood wasn't exactly what I'd done – it was more like I lapped it up. But how the hell did they know anything about it? Heath wasn't very bright, but I didn't think he'd run around telling people (especially not detective people) that the chick he had the hots for drank blood. No. Heath wouldn't have said anything, but—

And I knew why they were asking me questions.

'There's something you should know about Kayla Robinson,' I said suddenly, interrupting the short cop's boring tirade. 'She saw me kiss Heath. Well, actually *Heath* kissed *me*. She likes Heath.' I looked from one cop to the other. 'You know, she really *likes* Heath, as in wants to date him now that I'm out of the way. So when she saw him kiss me she got pissed and started yelling at me. Okay, I admit I didn't act very mature. I got pissed back at her. I mean, it's just wrong when your best friend goes after your boyfriend. Anyway' – I fidgeted, like I was embarrassed to admit what I was telling them – 'I said some mean stuff to Kayla that scared her. She freaked out and left.'

'What kind of mean stuff?' Detective Marx asked.

I sighed. 'Something like if she didn't go away I'd fly off the wall and suck her blood.'

'Zoey!' Neferet's voice was sharp. 'You know that's inappropriate. We have enough problems with image without you frightening human teenagers on purpose. Little wonder the poor child spoke to the police.'

'I know. I'm really sorry.' Even though I understood Neferet was playing along with me, I still had to work at not cringing away from the power in her voice. I glanced up at the detectives. Both of them were staring at Neferet with wide, startled eyes. Huh. So, up until then she'd only shown them her gorgeous public face. They had no idea what kind of power they were dealing with.

'And you haven't seen either teenager since then?' the tall cop asked after an uncomfortable pause.

'Only once more, and then it was just Heath alone, during our Samhain Ritual.'

'Excuse me, your what?'

'Samhain is the ancient name for a night you would probably best know as Halloween,' Neferet explained. She was back to stunningly beautiful and kind, and I could understand why the cops looked confused, but they returned her smile as if they had no choice. Knowing Neferet's powers – they might not. 'Go on, Zoey,' she told me.

'Well, there were a bunch of us and we were having a ritual. Kinda like a church service outside,' I explained. Okay, it was *nothing* like a church service outside, but no way was I going to explain circle-casting and calling the spirits of carnivorous dead vamps to a couple human cops. I glanced at Neferet. She nodded encouragement. I drew a deep breath and mentally edited the past as I talked. I knew it really didn't matter what I said. Heath didn't remember anything about that night – the night he'd almost been killed by the ghosts of ancient vampyres. Neferet had made sure that his memory had been totally and permanently blocked. All he knew was that he'd found me with a bunch of other kids and then passed out. 'Anyway, Heath snuck into the ritual. It was really embarrassing, especially since . . . well . . . he was totally wasted.'

'Heath was drunk?' Marx asked.

I nodded. 'Yes, he was drunk. I don't want to get him in any trouble, though.' I'd already decided not to mention Heath's unfortunate, and hopefully temporary, experimentation with pot.

'He's not in trouble.'

'Good. I mean, he's not my boyfriend but he's basically a good guy.'

'Don't worry about it, Miss Redbird, just tell us what happened.'

'Nothing really. He crashed our ritual, and it was embarrassing. I told him to go home and not come back, that we were through. He made a fool out of himself and then passed out. We left him there, and that was it.'

'You haven't seen him since?'

'No.'

'Have you heard from him in any way?'

'Yeah, he calls way too much and leaves annoying messages on my cell. But that's getting better,' I added hastily. I really didn't want to get him into trouble. 'I think he's finally getting it that we're through.'

The tall cop finished taking some notes, and then he reached into his pocket and pulled out a plastic bag that had something in it.

'And how about this, Miss Redbird? Have you ever seen this before?'

He handed me the bag and I realized what was in it. It was a silver pendant on a long black velvet ribbon. The pendant was in the shape of two crescent moons back-to-back against a full moon encrusted with garnets. It was the symbol of the triple Goddess – mother, maiden, and crone. I had one just like it because it was the necklace that the leader of the Dark Daughters wore.

CHAPTER ELEVEN

'WHERE DID YOU GET THIS?' NEFERET ASKED. I COULD TELL she was trying to keep her voice under control, but there was a powerful, angry edge to it that was impossible to hide.

'This necklace was found near Chris Ford's body.'

My mouth opened, but I couldn't seem to say anything. I knew my face had gone pale, and my stomach clenched painfully.

'Do you recognize the necklace, Miss Redbird?' Detective Marx repeated his question.

I swallowed and cleared my throat. 'Yes. It's the leadership pendant of the Dark Daughters.'

'Dark Daughters?'

'The Dark Daughters and Sons is an exclusive school organization, made up of our finest students,' Neferet said.

'And you belong to this organization?' he asked.

'I'm its leader.'

'So you wouldn't mind showing us your necklace?'

'I – I don't have it with me. It's in my room.' Shock was making my head feel woozy.

'Gentlemen, are you accusing Zoey of something?' Neferet said. Her voice was quiet, but the thread of outraged anger that ran through it brushed against my skin, causing my flesh to prickle and rise. I could see from the nervous glance the detectives shared that they felt it, too.

'Ma'am, we're simply questioning her.'

'How did he die?' My voice was faint, but it sounded abnormally loud in the tense silence that surrounded Neferet.

'From multiple lacerations and loss of blood,' Marx said.

'Someone cut him with a switchblade or something?' On the news they'd said that Chris had been mauled by an animal, so I already knew the answer to the question, but I felt compelled to ask.

Marx shook his head. 'The wounds were like nothing a knife would leave. They were more like animal scratches and bites.'

'His body was almost entirely drained of blood,' Martin added.

'And you're here because this appears to be a vampyre attack,' Neferet said grimly.

'We're here looking for answers, ma'am,' Marx said.

'Then I suggest you do a blood alcohol content test on the human boy. Just from the little I know about the group of teenagers the boy had as friends, they are habitual drunks. He probably got intoxicated and fell into the river. The lacerations were more than likely made by rocks, or perhaps even animals. It's not uncommon for coyotes to be found along the river, even within Tulsa city limits,' Neferet said.

'Yes, ma'am. Tests are being performed on the body. Even drained of blood, it will still tell us many things.'

'Good. I'm sure one of the many things it will tell you is that the human boy was drunk, perhaps even high. I think you should look to more reasonable causes for this death than a vampyre attack. Now, I assume you're done here?'

'One more question, Miss Redbird,' Detective Marx asked me without looking at Neferet. 'Where were you Thursday between eight and ten o'clock?'

'In the evening?' I asked.

'Yes.'

'I was at school. Here. In class.'

Martin gave me a blank look. 'School? At that time?'

'Perhaps you should do your own homework before questioning my students. Classes at the House of Night begin at 8:00 P.M. and go till 3:00 A.M. Vampyres have long preferred the night.' The dangerous edge was still in Neferet's voice. 'Zoey was in class when the boy died. *Now* are we finished?'

'For the time being we are finished with Miss Redbird.'

Marx flipped a couple pages back in the little notebook he'd been writing in before he added, 'We do need to speak with Loren Blake.'

I tried not to react to Loren's name, but I know my body jumped and I felt my face heat up.

'I'm sorry, Loren left yesterday before dawn on the school's private jet. He has gone to our East Coast school to support our students who are in the final round of our international Shakespearean monologue contest. But I can certainly give him a message to call you when he returns Sunday,' Neferet said while she walked toward the door, clearly dismissing the two men.

But Marx hadn't moved. He was still watching me. Slowly he reached into his inside jacket pocket and pulled out a business card. Handing it to me he said, 'If you think of anything – anything at all – that you believe might help us find who did this to Chris, call me.' Then he nodded at Neferet. 'Thank you for your time, ma'am. We'll be back Sunday to talk with Mr Blake.'

'I'll see you out,' Neferet said. She squeezed my shoulder, and breezed by the two detectives, leading them from the room.

I sat there trying to collect my tumbling thoughts. Neferet had lied, and not just by omission about me drinking Heath's blood and Heath almost getting killed during the Samhain ritual. She'd lied about Loren. He hadn't left the school yesterday before dawn. At dawn he'd been at the east wall with me.

I clutched my hands together to try to keep them from shaking.

I didn't get to sleep until almost 10:00 (as in the A.M.). Damien, the Twins, and Stevie Rae wanted to know everything about the detectives' visit, and telling them was cool with me. I thought going back over the details might give me a clue about what the hell was going on. I was wrong. No one could figure out why a Dark Daughters' leadership necklace had been with a human kid's dead body. Yes, I checked and mine was still safely in my jewelry box. Erin, Shaunee, and Stevie Rae all thought that somehow Aphrodite was behind the cops getting the necklace and maybe even the killing. Damien and I weren't so sure. Aphrodite couldn't stand humans, but to me that didn't equate to kidnapping and killing a very built football player who couldn't exactly be hidden in her lovely Coach purse. She definitely didn't hang out with humans. And, yes, she used to have a Dark Daughters' leadership necklace, but Neferet had taken it from her and given it to me the night I became the leader of the Dark Daughters and Sons.

Besides the mystery of the necklace, all we could figure was that 'Stank Bitch Kayla' (as the Twins called her) had basically told the cops that I was the killer because she was jealous that Heath was still crazy about me. Obviously the cops didn't have any real suspects if they rushed over here on the word of a jealous teenager. Of course my friends didn't know anything about the blood-drinking issue. I still couldn't bring myself to tell them that I drank (lapped, whatever) Heath's blood. So I'd given them the same edited version I'd told the detectives. The only people who knew the real story about the blood thing (besides Heath and Stank Bitch Kayla) were Neferet and Erik. I'd told Neferet, and Erik had found me right after I'd had the big scene with Heath, so he knew the truth. Speaking of – I suddenly wanted Erik to hurry and get back to school. I'd been so busy lately that I hadn't actually had time to miss him, or at least I hadn't until today when I wished that there was someone who wasn't High Priestess I could talk to about what was going on.

Sunday, I reminded myself as I tried to fall asleep. Erik would be back Sunday. The same day Loren would be back. (No, I wouldn't think about the stuff that might be going on between Loren and me, and how that was part of the 'busyness' that had kept me from missing Erik.) And why the hell did the detectives need to talk to Loren anyway? None of us could figure that out.

I sighed and tried to relax. I really hated needing to fall asleep and not being able to. But I couldn't shut off my mind. Not only was the Chris Ford/Brad Higeons mess going round and round in my head, but pretty soon I'd have to call the FBI and pretend to be a terrorist. Add to that the fact that I'd hardly thought about the circle I needed to cast and the Full Moon Ritual I was supposed to lead, and it was no wonder I had a horrible tension headache.

I glanced at the alarm clock. It was 10:30 A.M. Four more hours before I needed to get up and call the FBI, and then try to figure out how to get through the day while I waited to hear news about the bridge accident (hopefully that it was averted), and news about the Higeons kid being found (hopefully alive), and tried to figure out how I'd lead the Full Moon Ritual (hopefully without totally embarrassing myself).

Stevie Rae, who I swear could fall asleep standing on her head in the middle of a blizzard, snored softly across the room. Nala was curled up beside my head on my pillow. Even she'd stopped complaining at me and was breathing deeply with her weird cat snores. I worried briefly if I should have her checked out for allergies. She did sneeze an awful lot. But I decided I was just obsessively adding to my stress level. The cat was as fat as a Butterball turkey. I mean, her tummy looked like she had a pouch and could hide a herd of baby kangaroos in there. That's probably why she wheezed. Carrying around all that cat fat couldn't be easy.

I closed my eyes and started counting sheep. Literally. It was supposed to work. Right? So I made up a field in my head with a gate and had cute fuzzy white sheep start jumping over the gate. (I think that's the proper way to count sleep sheep. Sleep sheep . . . hee hee.) After sheep number 56 the numbers started to blur in my mind and I finally slipped into a fitful dream where I noticed the sheep were wearing Union's red and white football uniform. They had a shepherdess directing them over the gate they were jumping (which now looked like a mini-goalpost). My dreaming self was floating gently above the sheep scene like I was a superhero. I couldn't see the shepherdess's face, but even from the back I could tell she was tall and beautiful. Her auburn hair was waist length. As if she could feel me watching, she turned toward me and her moss green eyes looked up at me. I grinned. Of course Neferet was in charge, even if it was just a dream. I waved at her, but instead of responding, Neferet's eyes narrowed dangerously and she suddenly spun around. Snarling like a wild animal, she grabbed a football-playing sheep, lifted it, and in one practiced motion slashed its throat with her abnormally strong, talonlike fingernails, burying her face in the animal's bleeding throat. My dreaming self was horrified as well as freakishly drawn to what Neferet was doing. I wanted to look away, but I couldn't . . . wouldn't . . . then the sheep's body began to shimmer, like heat waves rising from a boiling pot. I blinked and it wasn't a sheep anymore. It was Chris Ford, and his dead eyes were wide open, set and staring at me accusingly.

I gasped in horror and tore my gaze from his blood, meaning to look away from the gory dream scene, but my vision got trapped because it was no longer Neferet who was feeding at Chris's throat. It was Loren Blake, and his eyes were smiling up at me over the river of red. I couldn't look away. I stared and stared and . . .

My dreaming body shivered as a familiar voice drifted in the air around me. At first the whisper was so soft I couldn't hear it, but as Loren drank the last drop of Chris's blood the words became audible as well as visible. They danced in the air around me with a silver light that was as familiar as the voice.

132

. . . Remember, darkness does not always equate to evil, just as light does not always bring good.

My eyelids jerked open and I sat up, breathing hard. Feeling shaky and slightly sick to my stomach, I looked at my clock: 12:30. I stifled a groan. I'd only slept for two hours. No wonder I felt so crappy. Quietly I went into the bathroom I shared with Stevie Rae to splash water on my face and try to wash away my grogginess. Too bad washing away the awful foreboding feeling the bizarre dream had given me wasn't as easy.

No way was I going to be able to sleep now. I walked listlessly over to our heavily curtained window and peeked out. It was a gray day. Low clouds obscured the sun and a light, constant drizzle made everything look blurred. It matched my mood perfectly, and it also made the daylight bearable. How long had it been since I'd gone outside during the day anyway? I thought about it and realized that I hadn't seen more than an occasional dawn in a good month. I shivered. And suddenly I couldn't stay inside for another instant. It felt claustrophobic, tomblike, *coffinlike*.

I went into the bathroom and opened the little glass jar that held the concealer that completely covered fledgling tattoos. When I'd first arrived at the House of Night I'd had a mini-panic attack when I'd realized that until I entered the school grounds, I'd never seen a fledgling. I mean ever. Naturally, I thought that meant that the vamps kept fledglings locked inside the walls of the school for four years. It didn't take long to find out the truth: fledglings had quite a bit of freedom, but if they chose to go outside the school walls they needed to follow two very important rules. First, they had to cover their Mark and not wear anything that bore any of the distinctive class insignias.

Second (and, to me, most important), once a fledgling entered the House of Night, he or she must stay in close proximity with adult vamps. The Change from human to vampyre was a bizarre and complex one – not even today's cutting-edge science completely understood it. But one thing was certain about the Change, if a fledgling was cut off from contact with adult vampyres, the process escalated and the teenager died. Every time. So, we could leave the school for shopping and whatnot, but if we stayed away from the vamps for more than a few hours our bodies would begin the rejection process and we'd die. It was no wonder that before I'd been Marked I thought I'd never seen a fledgling. I probably had, but (a) he/she/they had had all Marks covered, and (b) he/she/they understood that they couldn't just loiter about like typical teenagers. They'd been there, but they'd just been busy and disguised.

The reason for the disguise made sense, too. It wasn't about wanting to hide amid humans and spy or whatever ridiculous things humans would assume. The truth was that humans and vampyres coexisted in an uneasy state of peace. Broadcasting that fledglings actually left the school and went shopping and to the movies like normal kids was asking for trouble and exaggeration. I could just imagine what people like my horrid step-loser would say. Probably that vamp teenagers were hanging out in gangs, engaging in all sorts of sinful juvenile delinquent behavior. He was such an ass. But he wouldn't be the only human adult who freaked. Clearly the vamp rules made sense.

Resolutely, I stared, patting the concealer on the sapphire Marks that told the world what I was. It was amazing how well the stuff covered up Marks. As my darkened-in crescent moon disappeared, along with the small network of blue spirals that framed my eyes, I watched the old Zoey reappear and wasn't quite sure how I felt about her. Okay, I knew there'd been a lot more changed within me than a few tattoos could represent, but the absence of Nyx's Mark was shocking. It gave me a weird, unexpected sense of loss.

Looking back, I should have listened to my internal hesitation, scrubbed my face, grabbed a good book, and gone directly back to bed.

Instead, I whispered, 'You look really young,' to my reflection, and pulled on my jeans and a black sweater. Then I rummaged (quietly – if I woke up Stevie Rae or Nala no way would I get out of there alone) through my dresser drawers until I found my old *Borg Invasion 4D* hoodie and put it on, along with my comfy black Pumas, and with my OSU trucker's hat securely on my head and my cool Maui Jim sunglasses I was ready. Before I could (wisely) change my mind, I grabbed my purse and tiptoed out of the room.

No one was in the main room of the dorm. I opened the door and took a deep breath to steady myself before I walked outside. The whole vampyres-burst-into-flames-if-sun-touches-them thing was a ridiculous lie, but it is true that daylight causes adult vamps pain. As a fledgling who was weirdly 'advanced' in the Change process, it's definitely uncomfortable for me, but I gritted my teeth and stepped out into the drizzle.

The campus looked totally deserted. It was weird not to pass one student or vamp all along the sidewalk that wound around behind the main building (which still reminded me of a castle) to the parking lot. My vintage 1966 VW Bug was easy to find amid the slick, expensive cars the vamps preferred. Its dependable engine sputtered for only a second, then it turned over and hummed like it was brand-new.

I tapped the garage door opener-like keypad that Neferet had given me after Grandma had brought my car to me. The wrought-iron gate to the school swung open silently.

Despite the fact that even the weak, foggy daylight bothered my eyes and made my skin feel twitchy, my mood lightened as soon as I was outside the school gates. It's not that I hated the House of Night or anything like that. Actually, the school and my friends there had become my home and family. It was just that today I needed something more. I needed to feel normal again – normal as in pre-Marked Zoey, when my biggest worry was geometry class and the only 'power' I had was the eerie ability to find cute shoes on sale.

Actually, shopping sounded like a good idea. Utica Square was less than a mile down the street from the House of Night, and I loved the American Eagle store there. My wardrobe had, tragically, become overstocked in dark colors like purple, black, and navy since I'd been Marked. A bright red sweater was exactly what I needed.

I parked in the less used lot behind the row of stores that American Eagle sat in the middle of. The trees in this lot were bigger, so I liked the shade, along with the fact that there were fewer people in the back lot. I know my reflection showed a normal teenage kid, but inside I was still Marked, and more than a little nervous about my first daylight trip into my old world.

Not that I expected to run into anyone I knew. I was the one my high school friends had called 'weird' and 'out there' because I liked to shop in the chic midtown stores versus the loud, boring, food court-smelling mall. Grandma Redbird was responsible for my out-of-the-ordinary tastes. She used to call it 'field-tripping' when she'd take me all over Tulsa on fun day trips. No way was I going to run into Kayla and the Broken Arrow crowd at Utica, and pretty soon the familiar smells and sights of American Eagle were working their retail magic on me. By the time I paid for the totally cute red knit sweater my stomach had quit hurting, and despite the fact that it was the middle of the day and I was sleep-deprived, my headache was gone, too.

But I was starving. There was a Starbucks across the street from American Eagle. It was on the corner that framed a pretty, shady courtyard in the middle of the square. With the wet, dreary day I would bet no one would be sitting at the little iron tables on the wide, tree-lined sidewalk. I could get a yummy cappuccino, one of their mega-big blueberry muffins, a copy of the *Tulsa World*, and sit outside and pretend like I was a college kid.

It seemed like a seriously good plan. I was totally right — there was no one sitting in the outside tables, and I snagged the one closest to the big magnolia tree and set about putting the proper amount of raw sugar in my cappuccino as I nibbled at my mountain-sized muffin.

I don't remember when I first felt his presence. It started subtly, like a weird itch under my skin. I moved restlessly in my chair, trying to concentrate on the movie page and thinking that maybe I could talk Erik into checking out the latest chick flick next weekend . . . But I couldn't pay attention to the movie reviews. The annoying, under-my-skin feeling wouldn't go away. Completely irritated I glanced up and froze.

Heath was standing under a streetlight not fifteen feet away from me.

CHAPTER TWELVE

HEATH WAS TAPING SOME KIND OF FLYER TO THE LIGHT POST. I could see his face clearly and it surprised me how handsome he looked. Okay, sure, I'd known him since third grade and watched him go from cute to gawky to cute to hot, but I'd never seen this look on him. His face was set in grim, non-smiling lines that made him appear much older than eighteen. It was like I was catching a glimpse of the man he would turn into – and it was a nice glimpse. He was tall and blond, with high cheekbones and a really strong chin. Even from that distance I could see the thick eyelashes that were surprisingly dark, and knew the gentle brown eyes they framed.

And then, as if he could feel my gaze, his eyes slid from the light post and locked on me. I watched his body go completely still, and then a shudder ran through it, as if someone had blown freezing air across his skin.

I should have gotten up and retreated into Starbucks, where it was busy with clusters of people talking and laughing, and where it would be impossible for Heath and me to really be alone. But I didn't. I just sat there as he dropped the flyers. They fluttered around the sidewalk like dying birds as he walked quickly over to me. He stood across the little table without saying anything for what seemed like forever. I didn't know what to do, especially because I was unexpectedly nervous. Finally I couldn't stand the intense silence any longer.

'Hi, Heath.'

His body jerked like someone had just jumped out from behind a door and scared the crap right outta him.

'Shit!' The word left his mouth in a rush of air. 'You're really here!'

I frowned at him. He'd never been exactly brilliant, but even for him this sounded pretty dumb. 'Of course I'm here. What did you think I was, a ghost?'

He dropped into the chair across from me as if his legs wouldn't hold him anymore. 'Yes. No. I dunno. It's just that I see you a lot and you're never really there. I thought this was just another one of those times.'

'Heath, what are you talking about?' I narrowed my eyes and sniffed in his direction. 'Are you drunk?'

He shook his head.

'High?'

'No. I haven't had a drink in a month. I quit smoking then, too.'

The words sounded simple, but I blinked and felt like I was trying to reason through mind mud. 'You quit drinking?'

'And smoking. I quit it all. That's one of the reasons I've been calling you so much. I wanted you to know that I've changed.'

I really didn't know what to say. 'Oh, well. I'm, uh, glad.' I know I sounded like a moron, but the way Heath's eyes were focused on me was almost a physical thing. And there was something else. I could smell him. It wasn't a cologne smell, or a sweaty guy smell. It was a deep, seductive scent that reminded me of heat and moonlight and sexy dreams. It was coming from his pores and it made me want to scoot my chair around the table so that I could be closer to him.

'Why didn't you return any of my calls? You didn't even text me back.'

I blinked, trying to block the attraction I was feeling for him and think clearly. 'Heath, there's no point. There can't be anything between you and me,' I said reasonably.

'You know there's already something between us.'

I shook my head and opened my mouth to explain to him how wrong he was, but he interrupted me.

'Your Mark! It's gone.'

I hated his excited tone, and automatically snapped back, 'You're wrong *again*. My Mark's not gone. It's just covered so the stupid humans around here won't freak out.' I ignored the hurt look that seemed to take all the adultness out of his face and turn him back into that cute boy I used to be so crazy about. 'Heath,' I softened my voice. 'My Mark will never go away. I'm either going to Change into a vampyre, or I'm going to die in the next three years. Those are my only two choices. I'll never be like I was. It can never be like it used to be between us.' I paused, and then added gently, 'I'm sorry.'

'Zo, I get that. What I don't get is why any of that has to end things between us.'

'Heath, things had ended between us before I was Marked, remember?' I said, exasperated.

Instead of his usual cocky comeback he kept looking into my eyes, and utterly sober and serious, said, 'That's because I was acting like a jerk. You hated that I was getting drunk and high. And you were right. I was messing up. I've stopped that. Now I'm focusing on football and my grades so that I can get into OSU.' He gave me the adorable, little-boy smile that's been melting my heart since third grade. 'That's where my girlfriend will be going, too. She's gonna be a vet. A vampyre vet.'

'Heath – I—' I hesitated, working hard to swallow back the huge lump that was suddenly burning my throat and making me want to cry. 'I don't know if being a vet is still what I want to do, and even if it is, that doesn't mean you and I can be together.'

'You're seeing someone else.' He didn't sound mad, he just sounded extremely sad. 'I don't remember much from that night. I've tried, but whenever I think too hard about it, everything gets all jumbled up into one nightmare that doesn't make any sense and I get a really bad headache.'

I sat very still. I knew he was talking about the Samhain Ritual he'd followed me to where Aphrodite had lost control of vampyre ghosts. Heath had almost been killed. Erik had been there, and as Neferet had said then, he had proven himself a warrior when he'd stayed by Heath's side and fought the specters, giving me time to cast my own circle and send the ghosts back to wherever it is they'd slithered away from. The last time I'd seen Heath he'd been unconscious and bleeding from multiple lacerations. Neferet had assured me that she would heal his wounds and fog his memory. Clearly, the fog had grown thin.

'Heath, don't think about that night. It's over and done with and better if—'

'You were there with someone,' he interrupted me. 'Are you going out with him?'

I sighed. 'Yes.'

'Give me a chance to get you back, Zo.'

I shook my head, even though his words tugged at my heart. 'No, Heath, it's impossible.'

'Why?' He slid his hand across the table and put it on top of mine. 'I don't care about the vampyre stuff. You're still Zoey. The same Zoey I've known forever. The Zoey who was the first girl I ever kissed. The Zoey who knows me better than anyone else on this earth. The Zoey I dream about every night.'

His scent drifted up to me from his hand, hot and delicious, and I could feel his pulse thumping against my fingers. I didn't want to tell him, but I had to. I looked him straight in the eyes and said, 'The reason you're not over me is because when I tasted your blood that time on the school wall I started to Imprint with you. So you want me because that's what happens when a vampyre, or apparently some fledglings, drink blood from a human victim. Neferet, our High Priestess, says that you haven't Imprinted all the way with me, and if I just stay away from you it'll fade and you'll be normal again and forget about me, so that's what I've been doing.' I finished in a rush. I knew he'd probably freak out and call me a monster or something, but I really hadn't had a choice, and now that he knew he could put all of this in perspective and—

His laughter interrupted my mental tirade. He'd thrown back his head and was laughing with typical Heath exuberance, and the familiar, sweet, silly sound of it made it really hard for me not to smile at him.

'What?' I said, trying to frown.

'Oh, Zo, you crack me up.' He squeezed my hand. 'I've been crazy about you since I was eight. Like that had anything to do with you sucking my blood?'

'Heath, believe me, we've started to Imprint.'

'I'm cool with that.' He grinned at me.

'Will you also be cool with me outliving you by several hundred years?'

Dorklike, he wagged his eyebrows at me. 'I can think of worse things than having a hot, young vampyre chic when I'm, like, fifty.'

I rolled my eyes. He was such a guy. 'Heath, it's not that simple. There're a lot of things to consider.'

His thumb traced a circular pattern over the top of my hand. 'You always did make things too complicated. There's you and me. That's all we need to consider.'

'That's not all there is, Heath.' A thought came to me and I lifted my brows and gave him a pretend-innocent smile. 'Speaking of, how's my ex-best friend Kayla?'

Totally unaffected, he shrugged. 'I dunno. I hardly ever see her anymore.'

'Why not?' That was weird. Even if he wasn't dating Kayla, they'd hung out in the same group for years, we all had.

'It's not the same. I don't like the stuff she says.' He wouldn't look at me.

'About me?'

He nodded.

'What has she been saying?' I couldn't decide if I was more hurt or pissed.

'Just stuff.' He still wouldn't look at me.

I narrowed my eyes with realization. 'She thinks I had something to do with Chris.'

He moved his shoulders restlessly. 'Not you, or at least she doesn't say you. She thinks it's vampyres, though, but so do a lot of people.'

'Do you?' I asked softly.

His eyes shot back to mine. 'No way! But something bad's happening. Someone's kidnapping football players. That's why I was here today. I'm taping up flyers with Brad's picture on

145

them. Maybe someone will remember him being dragged away or something.'

'I'm sorry about Chris.' I laced my fingers through his. 'I know you guys were friends.'

'It sucks. I can't believe he's dead.' He swallowed hard, and I knew he was trying not to cry. 'I think Brad's dead, too.'

I thought he was, too, but I couldn't say it out loud. 'Maybe not. Maybe they'll find him.'

'Yeah, maybe. Hey, Chris's funeral is Monday. Would you go with me?'

'I can't, Heath. Do you know what would happen if a fledgling showed up at the funeral of a kid people think was killed by a vampyre?'

'I guess it would be bad.'

'Yes, it would be. And that's what I've been trying to make you see. You and me together – we'd have to deal with issues like that all the time.'

'Not when we're out of school, Zo. Then you could wear that cover-up stuff you have on your face now, and no one would even know.'

What he was saying probably should have pissed me off, but he was so serious, so sure that if I slapped a little concealer on my tattoos everything could go back to the way it was. And I couldn't be mad because I understood his wanting it. Wasn't that what I was doing there? Hadn't I been trying to relive part of my old life?

But this wasn't me anymore, and deep within me I didn't

really want it to be. I liked the new Zoey, even if saying good-bye to the old Zoey wasn't only hard, it was a little sad, too.

'Heath, I don't want to cover my Mark. That wouldn't be who I am.' I drew a deep breath and continued. 'I've been Marked specially by our Goddess, and Nyx has given me some unusual powers. It would be impossible for me to pretend to be the human Zoey again, even if I wanted to. And, Heath, I don't want to.'

His eyes searched my face. 'Okay. We'll do it your way and say to hell with people who don't like it.'

'That's not my way, Heath. I don't—'

'Wait, you don't have to say anything right now. Just think about it. We can meet here again in a few days.' He grinned. 'I'll even come at night.'

It was a lot harder than I'd imagined to tell Heath that I'd never see him again. Actually, I hadn't imagined that I would have to have this talk with him. I'd thought we were over. Sitting here with him now felt weird – part normal, part impossible. Which actually described our relationship pretty well. I sighed and glanced down at our joined hands, and caught a look at my watch.

'Oh, shit!' I pulled my hand from his and grabbed my purse and my American Eagle bag. It was 2:15. I had to make that damn call to the FBI in fifteen minutes. 'I gotta go, Heath. I'm really late for something at school. I'll – I'll call you later.' I started to hurry away and wasn't really surprised that he came with me.

'No,' he interrupted when I started to tell him to go away. 'I'm walking you to your car.'

I didn't argue with him. I knew that tone. As goofy and exasperating as Heath could be, his daddy had raised him right. Since third grade he'd been a gentleman, opening doors for me and carrying my schoolbooks, even when his friends called him a pussy-whipped dork. Walking me to my car was just part of what Heath did. Period.

My VW was sitting all alone under a big tree, just like when I'd parked it. As usual, he reached past me and opened my door. I couldn't help smiling at him. I mean, there was a reason I'd liked the kid for all these years – he really was sweet.

'Thanks, Heath,' I said, and slid into the driver's seat. I was going to roll down the window and say bye to him, but he was already moving around the car and in about two seconds he was sitting in the passenger's seat grinning at me. 'Uh, you can't come with me,' I told him. 'And I'm in a hurry, so I can't give you a ride anywhere.'

'I know. I don't need a ride. I have my truck.'

'Okay, well. Then bye. I'll call you later.'

He didn't move.

'Heath, you have to—'

'I have to show you something, Zo.'

'Can you show me quickly?' I didn't want to be mean to him, but I really had to get back to the school and make that call. Why the hell hadn't I put Damien's disposable phone in my purse? I tapped the steering wheel impatiently while Heath put his hand in his jeans pocket and felt around for something.

'There it is. I started carrying this around a couple weeks ago, just in case.' He pulled something that was about an inch long and flat out of his pocket. It was wrapped in what looked like folded cardboard.

'Heath, really. I gotta go and you . . .' My words faded as the breath left my body. He'd unwrapped the little thing. The blade caught the dim light and glittered seductively. I tried to speak, but my mouth had gone dry.

'I want you to drink my blood, Zoey,' he said simply.

A shiver of terrible longing broke over my body. I was gripping the steering wheel with both hands to keep them from shaking . . . or reaching out and taking the razor blade and slicing it into his warm, sweet skin so that his delicious blood would drip and drip and . . .

'No!' I shouted, hating the way the power in my voice made him cringe. I swallowed and got control of myself. 'Just put it away and get out of my car, Heath.'

'I'm not scared, Zo.'

'I am!' I almost sobbed.

'You don't have to be afraid. It's just you and me, like it's always been.'

'You don't know what you're doing, Heath.' I couldn't even look at him. I was scared if I did I wouldn't be able to keep saying no.

'Yes I do. You drank some of my blood that night. It was . . . it was incredible. I haven't been able to stop thinking about it.'

149

I wanted to scream with frustration. I hadn't been able to stop thinking about it, either, no matter how hard I tried. But I couldn't tell him that. I wouldn't tell him that. Instead, I finally looked at him and forced my hands to relax. Just thinking about drinking his blood made my skin feel tight and hot. 'I want you to go, Heath. This isn't right.'

'I don't care about what people think is right, Zoey. I love you.'

And before I could stop him, he lifted the razor blade and drew it down the side of his neck. Fascinated, I watched a thin line of scarlet spring up against the white of his skin.

Then the smell hit me – rich and dark and seductive. Like chocolate, only sweeter and wilder. In seconds the little car was thick with it. It drew me like nothing I'd ever experienced before. It wasn't just that I wanted to taste it. I needed to taste it. *I had to taste it*.

I hadn't even realized that I'd moved until Heath spoke, but suddenly I was leaning across the small space between our seats as his blood drew me to him.

'Yes. I want you to do it, Zoey.' Heath's voice sounded deep and rough, like he was having a hard time controlling his breathing.

'I – I want to taste it, Heath.'

'I know, baby. Go ahead,' he whispered.

I couldn't stop myself. My tongue flicked out and licked the blood from his neck.

CHAPTER THIRTEEN

THE TASTE EXPLODED IN MY MOUTH. AS MY SALIVA TOUCHED the shallow wound his blood began to flow more quickly, and with a moan that I hardly recognized as my own, I opened my mouth and pressed my lips to his skin, licking up the delicious scarlet line. I felt Heath's arms go around me as mine wrapped around his shoulders so that I could hold him more firmly against my mouth. His head fell back and I heard him groan 'yes.' One of his hands cupped my butt and the other one went under my sweater to squeeze my breast.

His touch only made it better. Heat slammed through my body, setting me on fire. Like someone else was in control of my movements, my hand slid from Heath's shoulder, down his chest, to rub over the hard lump that was in the front of his jeans. I sucked on his neck. Rational thought flew from my mind. All I could do was feel and taste and touch. Somewhere in the depths of my mind I knew I was reacting on a level that was almost animalistic in its need and ferocity, but I didn't care. I wanted Heath. I wanted him like I'd never wanted anything in my life.

'Oh, God, Zo, *yes*,' he gasped and his hips started to thrust in time with my hand.

Someone banged on the passenger's side window. 'Hey! Y'all can't make-out here!'

The man's voice jolted through me, shattering the heat that had been building inside me. I caught a glimpse of a security guard's uniform, and started to lurch away from Heath, but he tucked my head down into the side of his neck and turned his body so that the guard, who was obviously standing right outside the passenger's door, couldn't see me very well, and so that the blood that was dripping steadily from Heath's neck was completely hidden.

'Did you kids hear me!' the guy bellowed. 'Get out of here before I take your names and call your parents.'

'No problem, sir,' Heath yelled good-naturedly. Amazingly, he sounded perfectly normal, if a little breathless. 'We're leaving.'

'You better. I'm watching you two. Damn teenagers . . .' he grumbled as he stomped away.

'Okay, he's far enough away now that he can't see the blood,' Heath said as he relaxed his hold on me.

Instantly I jerked back, pressing myself against the door, as far away from Heath as I could get. With shaking hands I zipped open my purse and fished out a Kleenex, handing it to him without touching him. 'Press this against your neck so that it'll stop bleeding.'

He did as I said.

I rolled down my window, clutched my hands together, and breathed deeply of the fresh air, trying to block the scent of Heath's body and Heath's blood from my mind.

'Zoey, look at me.'

'I can't, Heath.' I swallowed down the tears that burned in the back of my throat. 'Please just leave.'

'Not until you look at me and listen to what I have to tell you.'

I turned my head and looked at him. 'How the hell can you be so calm and normal-sounding?'

He was still pressing the Kleenex against his neck. His face was flushed and his hair was messed up. He smiled at me, and I didn't think I'd ever seen anyone look so absolutely adorable.

'Easy, Zo. Making-out with you is totally normal for me. You've been driving me crazy for years.'

I'd had the whole I'm-not-ready-to-have-sex-with-you-yet conversation with him when I was fifteen and he was almost seventeen. He'd said then that he understood and was willing to wait – of course that didn't mean that we didn't do some heavy making-out – but what had just happened in the car had been different. It was hotter, rawer. I knew that if I allowed myself to continue seeing him I wouldn't be a virgin much longer, and not because Heath would pressure me into it. It would be because I couldn't control my bloodlust. The thought scared me almost as much as it fascinated me. I closed my eyes and rubbed my forehead. I was getting a headache. Again.

'Does your neck hurt?' I asked, peeking up at him through my fingers like I was watching a stupid slasher movie.

'Nope. I'm fine, Zo. You didn't hurt me at all.' He reached over and pulled my hand from my face. 'Everything'll be okay. Stop worrying so much.'

I wanted to believe him. And, I suddenly realized, I also wanted to see him again. I sighed. 'I'll try. But I really do have to go. I can't be late getting back to school.'

He took my hand in his. I could feel the pulse of his blood, and knew it was beating in time with my own heart, like he and I had somehow become internally synchronized. 'Promise me you'll call me,' he said.

'I promise.'

'And you'll meet me here again this week.'

'I don't know when I can get away. During the week it's going to be hard for me.'

I expected him to argue with me, but he just nodded and squeezed my hand. 'Okay, I get that. Living twenty-four seven at school is probably a pain in the ass. How about this: Friday we're playing Jenks at home. Could you meet me at Starbucks after the game?'

'Maybe.'

'Will you try?'

'Yes.'

He grinned and leaned over to give me a quick kiss. 'That's my Zo! I'll see you Friday.' He got out of the car and before he closed the door bent down and said, 'I love ya, Zo.'

As I drove away I could see him in my rearview mirror. He was standing in the middle of the parking lot, Kleenex still pressed to his neck, waving bye at me.

'You have no clue what you're doing, Zoey Redbird,' I said aloud to myself as the gray sky opened and poured cold rain over everything.

It was 2:35 when I tiptoed back into our room. The fact that I was short on time was actually good. It didn't give me a chance to overthink what I had to do. Stevie Rae and Nala were still sound asleep. Actually, Nala had abandoned my empty bed and was curled up beside Stevie Rae's head on her pillow, which made me smile. (The cat was a notorious pillow hog.) Quietly I opened the top drawer on my computer desk and grabbed Damien's disposable phone, along with the slip of paper I'd scribbled the FBI's number on, and then went into the bathroom.

I took a couple deep, calming breaths, remembering Damien's advice: Keep it short. Sound a little angry, and kinda semi-crazy, but don't sound like a teenager. I dialed the number. When an official-sounding man answered, 'Federal Bureau of Investigation. How may I help you?' I pitched my voice low and sharp, cutting off my words like I had to be careful to hold myself back because of the dam of hatred that was built up behind them (which is how Erin, with her suddenly and bizarrely unexpected political knowledge, described how I should pretend to feel). 'I want to report a bomb.' I kept talking, not giving him time to interrupt me, but speaking slowly and clearly because I knew I was being recorded. 'My group, Nature's Jihad (Shaunee came up with our name), planted it just below the waterline on one of the pylons (a word Damien had come up with) of the bridge that crosses the Arkansas River on I–40 near Webber's Falls. It's set to go off at 1515 (using military time was another brilliant idea of Damien's). We're taking full responsibility for this act of civil disobedience (more Erin input, although she said terrorism is not actually civil disobedience, it's . . . well . . . terrorism, which is definitely different) protesting the U.S. government's interference in our lives and pollution in America's rivers. Be warned that this is only our first strike!' I hung up. Then I quickly flipped the scrap of paper over and punched in the phone number on the other side of it.

'Fox News Tulsa!' said the perky woman.

This part was actually my idea. I figured if I called a local news station we would have a better chance of having the threat reported quickly on the local news, and then we could keep an eye on the news and maybe even know when (or if) our attempt to get the bridge closed had been successful. I took another deep breath and then launched into the rest of the plan.

'A terrorist group known as Nature's Jihad has called the

FBI with information that they've planted a bomb on the I–40 bridge over the Arkansas River by Webber's Falls. It's set to explode at three fifteen today.' I made the mistake of pausing for a fraction of a second, and the woman, who was suddenly not so perky-sounding, said, 'Who are you, ma'am, and where did you get this information?'

'Down with government intervention and pollution and up with the power of the people!' I yelled and then hung up. Immediately I pressed the power off button. Then my knees wouldn't hold me up any longer and I collapsed onto the closed toilet lid. I'd done it. I'd really done it.

Two soft knocks sounded against the bathroom door, followed by Stevie Rae's soft Oklahoma twang.

'Zoey? Are you okay?'

'Yeah,' I said faintly. I forced myself to stand up and go to the door. I opened it to see Stevie Rae's rumpled face peering up at me like a sleepy, countrified rabbit.

'Did ya call 'em?' she whispered.

'Yeah, and you don't have to whisper. It's just you and me.' Nala yawned and made a grumpy *mee-uf-ow* at me from the middle of Stevie Rae's pillow. 'And Nala.'

'What happened? Did they say anything?'

'Not after the "hello FBI" part. Damien said I shouldn't give them a chance to talk, remember?'

'Did you tell them that we're Nature's Jihad?'

'Stevie Rae. We're *not* Nature's Jihad. We're just pretending to be.'

'Well, I heard you yelling the down with the government

and pollution thing, so I thought . . . maybe . . . actually I dunno what I thought. I guess I just got caught up in the moment.'

I rolled my eyes. 'Stevie Rae, I was just acting. The news lady asked me who I was and I guess I kinda freaked. And, yes, I told them everything we said I should. I just hope it works.' I pulled off my hoodie and hung it on the back of a chair to dry.

Stevie Rae suddenly registered that my hair was wet and my Mark was covered, something I'd totally forgotten about in my hurry to make the phone calls. Hell.

'Did you go somewhere?'

'Yeah,' I said reluctantly. 'I couldn't sleep, so I went to the American Eagle at Utica and bought a new sweater.' I pointed at the soggy American Eagle bag I'd tossed in the corner.

'You should have woken me up. I would have gone with you.'

If she hadn't sounded so hurt I would have had more time to think about just exactly how much I was going to tell her about Heath before I blurted, 'I ran into my ex-boyfriend.'

'Ohmygood*ness*! Tell me everything.' She plopped down on her bed, eyes shining. Nala grumbled and jumped from her pillow to mine. I got a towel and started to dry my hair.

'I was at Starbucks. He was taping up flyers with Brad's picture on them.'

'And? What happened when he saw you?'

'We talked.'

She rolled her eyes. 'Come on – what else?'

'He's quit drinking and getting high.'

'Wow, that's major. Isn't his drinking and smoking why you quit seeing him to begin with?'

'Yeah.'

'Hey, what about Stank Kayla and him?'

'Heath says he's not seeing her because of the crap she's talking about vampyres.'

'See! We were right about her being the reason those cops were here asking stuff about you,' Stevie Rae said.

'Seems like it.'

Stevie Rae was watching me way too closely. 'You still like him, don't you?'

'It's not that simple.'

'Well, actually, part of it is that simple. I mean, if you don't like him, that's pretty much it. You won't see him again. Simple,' Stevie Rae said logically.

'I still like him,' I admitted.

'I knew it!' She did a little bed bounce. 'Man, you have like a zillion guys, Z. What are you gonna do?'

'I have not got one clue,' I said miserably.

'Erik comes back from the Shakespeare competition tomorrow.'

'I know. Neferet said that Loren went to support Erik and the rest of the kids from here, so that means he'll be back with them tomorrow, too. And I told Heath I'd go out with him Friday after the game.'

'Are you going to tell Erik about him?'

'I dunno.'

'Do you like Heath more than Erik?'

'I dunno.'

'What about Loren?'

'Stevie Rae, I do not know.' I rubbed at the headache that seemed to have firmly attached itself to me. 'Can we just not talk about it for a while – at least until I get a little of this figured out.'

'Okay. Let's go.' She grabbed my arm.

'Where?' I blinked at her, totally confused. She'd gone from Heath to Erik to Loren and then to let's go way too fast.

'You need your Count Chocula fix, and I need my Lucky Charms. And we both need to watch CNN and the local news.'

I started to shuffle to the door. Nala stretched, meowed grumpily, and then reluctantly followed me. Stevie Rae shook her head at both of us.

'Come on you two. Everything will seem better after you've had your Count Chocula.'

'And brown pop,' I said.

Stevie Rae screwed up her face like she just sucked a lemon. 'For breakfast?'

'I have a feeling it's a brown-pop-for-breakfast kind of day.'

CHAPTER FOURTEEN

THANKFULLY, WE DIDN'T HAVE TO WAIT LONG BEFORE WE heard something. Stevie Rae, the Twins, and I were watching *The Dr Phil Show* and at exactly 3:10 (Stevie Rae and I were on our second bowls of cereal and I was on my third brown pop) Fox News broke into the program with a Special Report.

'This is Chera Kimiko with breaking news. We have learned that shortly after two thirty this afternoon the Oklahoma branch of the FBI received a bomb threat from a terrorist group calling themselves Nature's Jihad. Fox News has discovered that the group claimed to have planted a bomb on the I–40 Arkansas River bridge

not far from Webber's Falls. Let's go live to Hannah Downs for an update.'

The four of us sat very still as we watched the camera shot take in the young reporter who was standing in front of a normal-looking highway bridge. Well, it was normal-looking except for the hordes of uniformed men who were swarming around it. I breathed a relieved sigh. The bridge was definitely closed.

'Thank you, Chera. As you can see the entire bridge has been closed by the FBI and local police, including Tulsa's ATF team. They're doing a thorough search for the alleged bomb.'

'Hannah, have they found anything yet?' Chera asked.

'It's too early to tell, Chera. They just launched the FBI boats.'

'Thank you, Hannah.' The camera went back to the newsroom.

'We'll keep you updated on this breaking story when we have more information on the alleged bomb, or on this new terrorist group. Until then, Fox returns you to . . .'

'A bomb threat. That was smart.'

The words were spoken so softly and I was so focused on the TV that it took a second for Aphrodite's voice to register with me. When it did I looked up quickly. She was standing to my right, just a little behind the couch Stevie Rae and I were sitting on. I expected her face to be settled in its usual haughty sneer, so I was surprised when she nodded slightly, almost respectfully, at me.

'What do you want?' Stevie Rae's voice was uncharacteristically sharp, and I noticed that several girls who had been busy in their own little TV-watching groups up until then stopped what they were doing to look our way. By Aphrodite's instant change in expression, she noticed it, too.

'From an ex-refrigerator? Nothing!' she sneered.

I felt Stevie Rae stiffen beside me at the slur. I knew she hated the reminder that she had allowed Aphrodite and her inner group of Dark Daughters to use her blood in the ritual that had gone so totally wrong last month. Being used as a 'refrigerator' was not a good thing – and being called one was an insult.

'Hey, hag bitch from hell,' Shaunee said in a sweet, friendly tone. 'That reminds us, seems the new Dark Daughters inner group—'

'Which would so be us and not you and your skanky friends,' Erin inserted.

'. . . Has an opening for a new refrigerator for the ritual tomorrow,' Shaunee continued smoothly.

'Yeah, and since you're not shit anymore, the only way you'll get into the ritual is as that night's snack,' Erin said. 'Are you here to apply for the job?'

'If you are, sorry. There's no telling where you've been and we don't like nasty,' Shaunee said.

'Bite me, bitch,' Aphrodite snapped.

'Not even if you begged,' Shaunee said.

'Ya ho,' Erin finished.

Stevie Rae just sat there, looking pale and upset. I wanted to knock all their heads together.

'Okay, stop.' They all shut up. I looked at Aphrodite.

'Don't ever call Stevie Rae a refrigerator again.' Then I turned to the Twins. 'Fledglings being used during our rituals is one of the things I'm doing away with, so we won't need a kid to act as our sacrifice. Which means no one is going to be a snack.' Okay, I hadn't actually yelled at the Twins, but they gave me identical looks of hurt and shock. I sighed. 'We're all on the same side here,' I said quietly, making sure my voice didn't carry to the obviously listening kids in the room. 'So it would be nice if we could lose some of the bickering.'

'Don't kid yourself. We're not on the same side – not even close.' Then, with a laugh that was more like a snarl, she stalked off.

I watched her leave and just before she went out the front door she glanced back at me, met my eyes, and winked.

What was that about? She'd looked almost playful, like we were friends and just kidding around. But that wasn't possible. Was it?

'She gives me the creeps,' Stevie Rae said.

'Aphrodite has issues,' I said, and the three of them looked at me like I'd just said Hitler really hadn't been that bad. 'You guys, I really want the new Dark Daughters to be a group that brings people together, not one that's stuck-up and so exclusive that only a few from a chosen clique can join.' They just stared at me. 'It was her warning that saved my grandma and several other people today.'

'She only told you because she wants something from you. She's hateful, Zoey. Don't ever think she's not,' Erin said.

'Please do not tell me that you're thinking of letting her back into the Dark Daughters,' Stevie Rae said.

I shook my head. 'No. And even if I wanted to, which I *don't*,' I added quickly, 'according to my own new rules she doesn't qualify for membership. A Dark Daughter or Son has to uphold our ideals by her or his behavior.'

Shaunee snorted. 'No damn way that hag knows how to be authentic, faithful, wise, earnest, and sincere about anything except her own hateful plans.'

'For world dominance,' Erin added.

'And don't think they're exaggerating,' Stevie Rae told me.

'Stevie Rae, she is not my friend. I just . . . I dunno . . .' I floundered, trying to put the instinct that so often whispered to me and goaded me to do, or not to do, things into words. 'I guess I really do feel sorry for her sometimes. And I also think I understand her a little. Aphrodite just wants to be accepted, but she goes about it all wrong. She thinks manipulation and lies mixed with control can force people to like her. It's what she saw at home, and that's what made her like she is now.'

'Sorry, Zoey, but that's bullshit,' Shaunee said. 'She's way too old to be acting a fool because she has a screwed-up mommy.'

'Please. Just please with the blame-my-mommy-'cause-I'm-a-bitch crap,' Erin said.

'Not to be mean or anything, but you have a screwed-up mama, too, Zoey, and you didn't let her, or your step-loser of a dad, mess you up,' Stevie Rae said. 'And Damien has a mama who doesn't like him anymore because he's gay.'

'Yeah, and he didn't turn into a hateful slut hag,' Shaunee said. 'Actually, he's the opposite. He's like . . . he's like . . .' She paused, looking to Erin for help. 'Twin, what's the Julie Andrews character's name in *The Sound of Music*?'

'Maria. And you're right, Twin. Damien is like that goody-goody nun. He needs to loosen up some or he's never gonna get any.'

'I cannot believe you guys are discussing my love life,' Damien said.

We all jumped guiltily and muttered, *'Sorry.'*

He shook his head while Stevie Rae and I scooted over so he could sit beside us. 'And I'll have you know I don't just want to "get some" as you guys so nastily put it. I want a lasting relationship with someone I really care about, and I'm willing to wait for that.'

'Ja, fräulein,' Shaunee whispered.

'Maria,' Erin muttered.

Stevie Rae tried to hide her giggle in a cough.

Damien narrowed his eyes at the three of them. I decided that was my cue to talk.

'It worked,' I said quietly. 'They closed the bridge.' I pulled his cell phone out of my pocket and gave it back to him. He checked to make sure it was off and nodded.

'I know, I saw the news and came right over.' Damien glanced at the digital clock on the DVD player that sat in the entertainment center with the TV, then he grinned at me. 'It's three twenty. We did it.'

The five of us smiled at each other. It's true; I was relieved, but I still had a nagging worried feeling I couldn't seem to get rid of that was more than just the stress about Heath. Maybe I needed a fourth brown pop.

'Okay, well, that's taken care of. So why are we sitting around here talking about my love life?' Damien said.

'Or lack thereof,' Shaunee whispered to Erin, who tried unsuccessfully (with Stevie Rae) not to laugh.

Ignoring them, Damien stood up and looked at me. 'Well, let's go.'

'Huh?'

He rolled his eyes heavenward and shook his head. 'Must I do everything? You have a ritual to perform tomorrow, which means we have a rec hall to transform. Did you think Aphrodite was going to volunteer to get things set up for you?'

'I guess I hadn't thought about it.' Like I'd had time?

'Well, think about it now.' He yanked on my hand and pulled me to my feet. 'We have work to do.'

I grabbed my brown pop and we all followed the Damien whirlwind out into a very cold, cloudy Saturday afternoon. The rain had stopped, but the clouds were even darker.

'Looks like snow,' I said, squinting up at the slate-colored sky.

'Oh, man, I wish. I'd love some snow!' Stevie Rae twirled around with her arms outstretched, looking like a little girl.

'Move to Connecticut. You'll have more snow than you can stand. It gets pretty damn tiresome after months and months of cold and wet. Please. It's why we northeasterners are so grumpy,' Shaunee said pleasantly.

167

'I don't care what you say. You can't ruin it for me. Snow is magic. I think it makes the earth look like it has a fluffy white blanket pulled over it.' She spread her arms wide and yelled, 'I want it to snow!'

'Yeah, well, I want those four-hundred-fifty-dollar embroidered vintage jeans I saw in the new Victoria's Secret catalog,' Erin said. 'Which proves we can't always have what we want, snow or cool jeans.'

'*Oooh*, Twin, maybe they'll go on sale. Those jeans are just too damn cute to give up on.'

'So why don't you just take your favorite pair of jeans and see if you can reproduce the pattern yourself? It can't be that hard, you know,' Damien said logically (and very gayly).

I was opening my mouth to agree with Damien when the first snowflake plopped on my forehead. 'Hey, Stevie Rae, your wish came true. It's snowing.'

Stevie Rae squealed happily. 'Yeah! Snow harder and harder!'

And she definitely got her wish. By the time we made it to the rec hall, fat, quarter-sized flakes of snow were covering everything. I had to admit that Stevie Rae was right. The snow was like a magic blanket on the earth. It turned everything soft and white, and even Shaunee (from grumpy, snowbound Connecticut) was laughing and trying to catch flakes with her tongue.

We were all giggling when we went into the rec hall. There were several kids inside. Some were playing pool, others were playing video games on the old-fashioned-looking arcade machines. Our laughing and brushing off snow made several of them stop what they were doing and pull back the thick black curtains that shielded the big room from daylight.

'Yep!' Stevie Rae yelled the obvious. 'It's snowing!'

I just smiled and made my way toward the little kitchen area in the back of the building, with Damien, the Twins, and snow-crazed Stevie Rae following me. I knew there was a storage room off the kitchen, and inside was the stuff the Dark Daughters kept there for their rituals. Might as well get started setting things up, and I might as well pretend like I knew what the hell I was doing.

I heard the door open and then close behind me, and was surprised by Neferet's voice.

'The snow is quite beautiful, isn't it?'

The kids standing around the windows answered Neferet with respectful yeses. I was surprised to feel a hint of annoyance, which I instantly squelched, as I stopped and turned to go back to greet my mentor. Like baby ducks, my gang followed me.

'Zoey, good. I'm glad I found you here.' Neferet spoke with such obvious affection for me that the annoyance I'd felt at her interruption vanished. Neferet was more than my mentor. She was like a mother to me, and it was selfish of me to be irritated that she had come looking for me.

'Hi, Neferet,' I said warmly. 'We were just getting ready to set up the room for tomorrow night's ritual.'

'Excellent! That's one thing I wanted to see you about. If you need anything for the ritual, please don't hesitate to ask.

And I definitely will be here tomorrow night, but don't worry' – she smiled at me again – 'I won't stay for the entire ritual – just long enough to show my support for your vision for the Dark Daughters. Then I'll leave the Daughters and Sons in your very capable hands.'

'Thank you, Neferet,' I said.

'Now, the second reason I wanted to find you and your friends' – she shared her brilliant smile with my group – 'was that I wanted to introduce our newest student to you.' She motioned, and a kid I hadn't noticed till then stepped slowly forward. He was cute, in a studious kind of a way, with tousled sandy blond hair and really pretty blue eyes. Clearly he was one of those geeky kids who is a dork, but a likable dork with potential (translation: he bathes and brushes his teeth, plus has good skin and hair and doesn't dress like a total loser). 'I'd like all of you to meet Jack Twist. Jack, this is my fledgling, Zoey Redbird, leader of the Dark Daughters, and her friends and Prefect Council members, Erin Bates, Shaunee Cole, Stevie Rae Johnson, and Damien Maslin.' Neferet gestured to each of them in turn, and there were 'hi's said all around. The new kid looked a little nervous and pale, but other than that he had a nice smile and didn't seem socially inept or anything like that. I was just wondering why Neferet had looked for me to introduce the kid to when she went on to explain.

'Jack is a poet and a writer, and Loren Blake is going to be his mentor, but Loren won't be back from his trip east until tomorrow. Jack is also going to be Erik Night's roommate. As you are all aware, Erik is away from school until tomorrow, too. So I thought it would be nice if the five of you would show Jack around and be sure he feels welcome and gets settled in today.'

'Of course, we'd be happy to,' I said without hesitation. It was never fun to be the new kid.

'Damien, you can show Jack to his and Erik's room, can't you?'

'Sure, no problem,' Damien said.

'I knew I could count on Zoey's friends.' Neferet's smile was incredible. It seemed to light the room by itself and it made me suddenly intensely proud that all of the other kids were standing around watching Neferet show such obvious favor for us. 'Remember, if you need anything for tomorrow, just let me know. Oh, because it's your first ritual I asked the kitchen to prepare something special for you and the Dark Daughters and Sons as a treat afterward. It should be a lovely celebration for you, Zoey.'

I was overwhelmed by her thoughtfulness, and couldn't help but compare it to the cold, unconcerned way my mom treated me. Hell, the truth was my mom didn't actually care enough to treat me like anything anymore. I'd only seen her that one time in a whole month, and after the stupid scene her loser husband had caused with Neferet, it looked like I wouldn't be seeing her again soon. Like I cared? No. Not when I had good friends and a mentor like Neferet to be there for me.

'I really appreciate this, Neferet,' I said, swallowing hard around the lump of emotion that had built in my throat.

'It's my pleasure and the least I can do for my fledgling's first Full Moon Ritual as leader of the Dark Daughters.' She gave me a quick hug, and then left the room, nodding kindly to the kids who spoke to her and saluted her respectfully.

'Wow,' Jack said. 'She's really amazing.'

'She sure is,' I said. Then I grinned at my friends (and the new kid). 'So, ready to get to work now? We have lots of stuff to clear out of here.' I saw poor Jack looking totally clueless. 'Damien, you better give Jack a quick catch-up lesson in vamp rituals so he doesn't feel so lost.' I started to walk back toward the kitchen (again), and heard Damien start his little professor act, beginning with the facts about the Full Moon Ritual.

'Uh, Zoey, can we help you?'

I glanced over my shoulder. Drew Partain, a short, athletic kid I recognized because he and I were in the same fencing class (he's an incredible fencer – as good as Damien, and that's saying something), was standing with a group of guys near the wall of black-shrouded windows. He smiled at me, but I noticed he kept checking out Stevie Rae. 'There's a lot of stuff to be pulled around. I know because the guys and I used to help Aphrodite get the room ready.'

'Huh,' I heard Shaunee say under her breath. Before Erin could add to the sarcastic sound, I said, 'Yeah, we could use your help.' And then I tested them. 'Except my ritual is going to be different. Damien can show you what I mean.' I waited for the disdainful looks and the sarcasm that the jocklike guys tended to throw at Damien and the few other openly gay kids

172

at the school, but Drew just shrugged and said, 'Cool with me. Just tell us what to do.' He grinned and winked at Stevie Rae, who giggled and blushed.

'Damien, they're all yours,' I said.

'I'm sure hell is freezing over somewhere,' Damien whispered, barely moving his lips. Then, in his regular voice he said, 'Well, the first thing Zoey didn't like is that it looks like a morgue in here with all of the arcade machines pushed to the walls and covered with that black fabric. So let's see if we can move most of them into the kitchen and the hall.' Drew's group started to work alongside Damien and the new kid, and Damien returned to his mini-lesson.

'We'll get the candles and pull the table out here,' I told the guys, and motioned for the Twins and Stevie Rae to follow me.

'Damien has died and gone straight to gay boy heaven,' Shaunee said as soon as we were out of earshot.

'Hey, it's about time those kids stopped acting like ignorant rednecks and behaved like they have some sense,' I said.

'She doesn't mean that, even though we agree with you,' Erin said. 'She means little Mr Jack the cute-gay-new-kid Twist.'

'Now why in the world would you think he's gay?' Stevie Rae asked.

'Stevie Rae, I swear you have got to broaden your horizons, girl,' Shaunee said.

'Okay, I'm lost, too. Why do you think Jack's gay?' I asked.

Shaunee and Erin shared a long-suffering look, then Erin

explained. 'Jack Twist is yummy Jake Gyllenhaal's totally gay cowboy character from *Brokeback Mountain*.'

'And just please! Anyone who chooses that name and who looks all geeky cute like that is totally, completely playing for Damien's team.'

'Huh,' I said.

'Well, I'll be,' Stevie Rae said. 'You know, I never did see that movie. It didn't come to the Cinema 8 in Henrietta.'

'You don't say?' Shaunee said.

'Please. I'm so shocked,' Erin said.

'Well, Stevie Rae. I do believe it's time for a DVD showing of that excellent flick,' Shaunee said.

'Do guys kiss in it?'

'Deliciously,' Shaunee and Erin said together.

I tried, but failed miserably not to laugh at the look on Stevie Rae's face.

CHAPTER FIFTEEN

WE WERE ALMOST FINISHED SETTING UP THE ROOM WHEN someone flipped on the nightly news on the big-screen TV we did have to leave in the main room. The five of us shared quick looks – what they were calling 'the bomb hoax by Nature's Jihad' was the lead story. Even though I knew my call couldn't be traced, and I'd watched Damien 'accidentally' drop and then totally step on and smash his disposable phone, I only breathed marginally easier when Chera Kimiko repeated that so far the police had no leads about the identity of the terrorist group.

In a related Arkansas River story Fox News reported that

this evening Samuel Johnson, captain of a river transport barge, had a heart attack while piloting the barge. It was a 'lucky coincidence' for him that river traffic had been halted and that police and paramedics were so close by. His life had been saved, and there had been no damage done to any other barges or bridges.

'That was it!' Damien said. 'He had a heart attack and ran the barge into the bridge.'

I nodded numbly. 'And that proves that Aphrodite's vision was true.'

'Not that that's good news,' Stevie Rae said.

'I think it is,' I said. 'As long as Aphrodite lets us know about her visions, at least we can take them seriously.'

Damien shook his head. 'There has to be a reason Neferet believes Nyx has withdrawn her gift from Aphrodite. It's too bad we can't tell her about this, then maybe she'd explain what's going on, or maybe even change her mind about Aphrodite.'

'No, I gave my word I wouldn't say anything.'

'If Aphrodite was really changing from hag to nonhag, she'd go to Neferet herself,' Shaunee said.

'Maybe you should talk to her about that,' Erin said.

Stevie Rae made a rude noise.

I rolled my eyes at Stevie Rae, but she didn't notice because Drew had grinned his way up to us and she was too busy blushing to pay attention to me.

'How's it look, Zoey?' he asked without taking his eyes from Stevie Rae.

Like you've got a thing for my roommate, is what I wanted to say, but I thought he was kinda cute and Stevie Rae's blush clearly said she thought so too, so I decided against mortifying her.

'Looks good,' I said.

'Doesn't look too bad from here, either,' Shaunee said, giving Drew a look up and down.

'Ditto, Twin,' Erin said, waggling her eyebrows at Drew.

The boy didn't notice either of the Twins. Seems all he noticed was Stevie Rae.

'I'm starving,' he said.

'Me, too,' Stevie Rae said.

'So, how about getting something to eat?' Drew asked her.

'Okay,' Stevie Rae said quickly, and then she seemed to remember we were all standing there watching her, and her face got even pinker. 'Gosh, it is dinnertime. We better all go get something.' With a nervous little gesture, she ran her fingers through her short curls and called across the room to Damien, who was thoroughly engrossed in a conversation with Jack. (From what I had overheard they were both into the same kind of books and were debating which of the Harry Potters was really the best. Clearly, they were dorkishly alike.) 'Damien, we're gonna go eat. Are you and Jack hungry?'

Jack and Damien exchanged a look, and then Damien called back, 'Yeah, we're coming.'

'Okeydokey,' Stevie Rae said, still grinning at Drew. 'I guess we're all hungry.'

Shaunee sighed, and started for the door. 'Just please. The

young love hormones in this room are enough to give me a headache.'

'I feel like I'm stuck in a *Lifetime* movie. Wait for me, Twin,' Erin said.

'Why are the Twins so cynical about love?' I asked Damien as he and Jack crossed the room to join us.

'They're not. They're just mad that the last few guys they've gone out with have bored them,' Damien said.

As a group, we went outside into the magic of a snowy November evening. The flakes had changed and were smaller, but they were still coming down steadily, making the House of Night look even more mysterious and castlelike than usual.

'Yeah, the Twins are hard on guys. It's like they double-time them,' Stevie Rae said. I noticed she was walking really close to Drew and that occasionally their arms brushed together.

I heard a bunch of muttered agreement noises from the guys who had been helping us drag furniture around the rec room. And I imagined it would be intimidating for any guy (vamp or human) to try to date one of the Twins.

'Do you remember when Thor asked Erin out?' said one of Drew's friends, whose name I think was Keith.

'Yeah, she called him a lemur. You know, like the moronic lemurs in that Disney movie,' Stevie Rae said, laughing.

'And Walter went out with Shaunee a total of two and a half dates. Then, right in the middle of Starbucks, she called him a Pentium 3 processor,' Damien said.

I gave him a totally clueless look.

'Z, we're up to Pentium 5 processors now.'

'Oh.'

'Erin still calls him Slowest McSlowenstein whenever she sees him,' Stevie Rae said.

'Clearly it's going to take a couple of really special guys to date the Twins,' I said.

'I think there's someone for everyone,' Jack said suddenly. We all turned to him and he blushed. Before any of the kids could snicker at him I spoke up, 'I agree with Jack.' *But figuring out which someone is the one for you is the hard part*, I added silently to myself.

'Totally!' Stevie Rae said with her usual perky optimism.

'Absolutely,' Damien said, winking at me. I grinned back at him.

'Hey!' Shaunee stepped out from behind a tree. 'What are you guys talking about?'

'Your nonexistent love life!' Damien called cheerfully.

'Really?' she said.

'Really,' Damien said.

'How about you talk about how cold and wet you are instead?' Shaunee said.

Damien frowned. 'Huh? I'm not.'

Erin popped out from around the other side of the tree, snowball in hand. 'You will be!' she yelled, throwing it and hitting Damien smack in the middle of his chest.

Of course the snowball war was on. Kids squealed and ran for cover while they scooped up handfuls of new snow and took aim at Shaunee and Erin. I started to back away.

'I told you snow was great!' Stevie Rae said.

'Well, let's just hope for a blizzard then,' Damien yelled, taking aim at Erin. 'Lots of wind and snow. Totally the best for snowball fights!' He let fly, but Erin was too quick and jumped for cover just in time to miss being plastered right in the head.

'Where are you going, Z?' Stevie Rae called from behind an ornamental shrub. I noticed Drew was right beside her, firing cover shots at Shaunee.

'To the media center – have to work on the words for the ritual tomorrow, so I'll grab something to eat back at the dorm when I get done.' I kept backing away more and more quickly. 'Hate to miss all the fun, but . . .' and I retreated inside the closest door, slamming it behind me just in time for it to catch the *plop plop plop* of three snowballs against its ancient wood.

I hadn't just been making an excuse to get out of the snowball war. I actually had been planning to ditch dinner and spend a few hours in the media center. Tomorrow I'd have to cast a circle and lead a ritual that might be as ancient as the moon itself.

I didn't know what the hell I was doing.

Okay, sure. I'd cast one circle with my friends a month ago as a little experiment to see if I really had an affinity for the elements, or if I'd been delusional. Until I felt the power of wind, fire, water, earth, and spirit rush through me and my friends witnessed it, too, I would have bet on the side of delusional. Not that I'm totally cynical or anything, but please.

180

Just please (as the Twins would say). Being able to tap into the power of the five elements was pretty bizarre. I mean, my life wasn't an X-Men movie (although I'd definitely like to spend some quality time with Wolverine).

The media center was predictably empty; it was, after all, Saturday night. Only total dorks spent Saturday night in the media center. Yes, I knew all too well what that made me. I'd already decided where to start my research. I pulled up the card catalogue on the computer and searched for old spell and ritual books, ignoring any that had recent publication dates. I was particularly drawn to one titled *Mystical Rites of the Crystal Moon* by Fiona. I vaguely recognized her name as one of the Vamp Poet Laureates from the early 1800s (there was a cool picture of her in our dorm). I scribbled down the Dewey Decimal Number for the book and found it up on an obscure shelf, dusty and lonely. I thought it was an excellent sign that it was one of those old leather-bound tomes. I wanted foundation and tradition so that under my leadership the Dark Daughters would know something more than Aphrodite's way too modern (and ho-ish) influence.

I opened my notebook and got out my favorite pen, which made me think about what Loren had said about preferring to write his poetry by hand rather than on a computer . . . and made me think about Loren touching my face . . . and my back . . . and the connection that had sizzled between us. I smiled and felt my cheeks get warm, and then realized I was sitting there grinning and blushing like a retard about a guy who was too old for me, *and* a vampyre. Both things made me really nervous (as well they should). I mean, he was totally gorgeous, but he was twenty-something. A real adult who knew all the vampyre secrets about bloodlust and, well, lust in general. Which, unfortunately, only made him more delicious, especially after my brief but very nasty bloodsucking make-out scene with Heath.

I tapped my pen against the blank notebook page. Okay, I'd been kissing and messing around a little with Erik some during the past month. Yes, I liked it. No, it hadn't gone very far. One reason was that despite recent evidence to the contrary, I didn't *usually* act like a slut. Another reason was that I was still way too aware that I'd accidentally watched Aphrodite, Erik's very ex-girlfriend, on her knees in front of him trying to give him a blowjob, and I didn't want there to be any confusion on Erik's part that I was definitely not a stank slut like Aphrodite the Ho. (I ignored the memory of my rubbing the bulge in Heath's pants.) So, I was definitely attracted to Erik, who everyone thought was my official boyfriend, even though we hadn't done much about that attraction.

My mind shifted to Loren. Outside in the moonlight with my skin bared to him Loren had made me feel like a woman – not an inexperienced, nervous girl, which is how I tended to feel around Erik. But when I'd seen the desire in Loren's eyes I'd felt beautiful and powerful and very, very sexy. And, yes, I had to admit to myself that I liked that feeling.

And how the hell did Heath fit into all of this? I felt different about Heath than I did about Erik or Loren. Heath and I had history. We'd known each other since we were kids, and we'd been dating, on and off, for the past couple years. I'd always been attracted to Heath, and we'd done some serious making-out, but he'd never turned me on before like he did when he cut his neck and I'd drunk his blood.

I shivered and automatically licked my lips. Just thinking about it made me feel hot and horrified at the same time. I definitely wanted to see him again. But was that because I still cared about him, or was it just because of the intense bloodlust I felt for him?

I had no idea.

True, I'd liked Heath for years. He was kinda dopey sometimes, but usually in a sweet way. He treated me right, and I liked to hang out with him – at least those things had been true before he'd started boozing it up and getting high. Then his dopiness had turned into stupidity, and I hadn't really trusted him anymore. But he said he'd quit all that, so did that mean he was back to the guy I used to like so much? And if so, what the hell was I supposed to do about (1) Erik, (2) Loren, (3) the fact that drinking Heath's blood was totally against the House of Night rules, and (4) I was definitely going to drink more of his blood.

My sigh sounded suspiciously like a sob. I really needed someone to talk to.

Neferet? No way. I wasn't about to tell an adult vamp about Loren. I knew I should admit that I'd been drinking Heath's blood (again – sigh) and had probably intensified the Imprint between us. But I couldn't. At least not yet. I know it was selfish, but I didn't want to be in trouble with her while I was still trying to settle into the Dark Daughters' leadership.

Stevie Rae? She was my best friend, and I wanted to tell her, but if I was going to *really* talk to her then that meant I'd have to admit to drinking Heath's blood. Twice. And how much I wanted to drink it again. How could that not freak her out? It freaked *me* out. I couldn't stand to think about my best friend looking at me like I was a monster. Plus, I didn't think she'd understand – not really.

I couldn't tell Grandma. She would definitely not like the fact that Loren was twenty-something. And I couldn't imagine talking to her about the lust part of bloodlust.

Ironically, I realized who the one person was who would not be freaked about the blood, and would definitely understand about the lust and such – Aphrodite. And, oddly enough, part of me wanted to talk to her, especially after discovering her visions were still true. I had a *feeling* about Aphrodite that was telling me there was a lot more to what was going on with her than the fact that she could definitely be a hateful bitch. She'd pissed off Neferet – that much was obvious. But Neferet had told Aphrodite, in cold, hateful words, that Nyx had withdrawn her favor from her, and she'd made it clear to me (and practically the entire school) that Aphrodite's visions were false. But I had proof that they weren't. It gave me a scared, skin-crawly feeling, but I was beginning to wonder how much I could actually trust Neferet.

Forcing my thoughts back to the media center and the

research I had to do, I opened the old ritual book, and a slip of paper fluttered out of it. I picked up the paper, thinking some kid had left her notes in it, and froze. My name was printed at the top in elegant handwriting I definitely recognized.

For Zoey

Alluring Priestess.
Night can't cloak your scarlet dream.
Accept Desire's call.

The words of the poem sent a shiver through me. What the hell? How had anyone, let alone Loren who was supposed to be on the East Coast, known I'd look in that book!

My hand was shaking, so I put the paper down and slowly reread the poem. If I pushed aside the fact that it was incredibly romantic that the Vamp Poet Laureate was writing me poetry and read the poem without being totally blown away by how sexy it was, I realized something as disturbing as the haiku being here in the first place. *Night can't cloak your scarlet dream*. Was I going absolutely crazy, or does that line sound like Loren knows I've been drinking blood? And suddenly the poem felt wrong . . . dangerous . . . like a warning that wasn't actually a warning, and I started to wonder about the poet. What if Loren hadn't written it? What if it was Aphrodite? I had overheard her talking to her parents. She was supposed to be getting me kicked out as the Dark

P. C. Cast and Kristin Cast

Daughters' leader. Could this tie into her plan? (Jeesh, 'her plan.' I was starting to sound like a bad comic book.)

Okay, Aphrodite had seen me with Loren, but how could she know about the haiku? Also, how would Aphrodite know that I'd be back in the media center looking at this particular old book? That sounded more like some weird piece of psychic info an adult vamp would have – although I didn't have a clue how. I mean, I hadn't even known I'd choose the book until a few minutes ago.

Nala jumped up on the computer desk, scaring the bejeezus out of me. She complained and rubbed against me.

'Okay, okay. I'll get to work.' But as I searched through the old book for traditional rituals and spells my mind kept circling around and around the poem and the uneasy feeling that seemed to have permanently lodged itself beneath my breastbone.

CHAPTER SIXTEEN

I WAS CARRYING NALA OUT OF THE MEDIA CENTER — THE cat had been so sound asleep that she hadn't even bothered to complain at me when I picked her up. I checked the clock as I left the room, and couldn't believe that several hours had passed. No wonder my butt was asleep and my neck was so stiff. But being temporarily uncomfortable didn't really matter because I'd actually figured out what I was going to do for the Full Moon Ritual. It was a huge weight lifted from my mind. I was still nervous, and didn't spend too much time considering the fact that when I performed the ritual I'd be doing so in front of a bunch of kids, the majority of whom were probably not thrilled that I had taken over leadership from their buddy Aphrodite. I just needed to stay focused on the ritual itself, and remember the amazing feelings that filled me whenever I invoked the five elements. The rest would work itself out. Hopefully.

I pushed open the heavy front door of the school and walked out into a different world. It was snowing steadily, and must have been for the entire time I was in the media center. The school grounds were completely blanketed by a comforter of downy white. The wind had whipped up and visibility was terrible. The gaslights that marked the obscured path were not much more than glowing pinpoints of yellow against the white darkness. I probably should have gone back in the building and made my way along the school's hall toward the dorm, staying inside for as long as I could, and then making a quick run from the far side of the school to the girls' dorm, but I really didn't want to. I thought about how right Stevie Rae had been. Snow really was magical. It changed the world, made it quieter, softer, more mysterious. As a fledgling, I already had quite a bit of an adult vampyre's natural protection against the cold, which used to creep me out. I mean, it made me think of cold, dead creatures who existed by drinking the blood of the living – totally gruesome, even if I was bizarrely drawn to the thought. Now I knew more about what I was becoming, so I understood that my protection against the cold was more about a heightened metabolism than about being undead. Vampyres aren't dead. They're just Changed. It was humans who liked to fuel the scary myth of the walking dead, which I was beginning to find more than slightly annoying. Anyway, I really enjoyed being able to walk around in a blizzard without feeling like I was going to freeze. Nala burrowed herself against me, purring loudly when I wrapped my arms around her protectively. The snow muffled my steps and it seemed for that moment that I was alone in a world where black and white had mixed together to form a unique color just for me.

I'd only walked a few steps when I sighed and would have popped myself in the forehead if my arms hadn't been filled with my cat. I needed to go by the school spells and rituals store and get some eucalyptus. From what I'd read in the old ritual book, eucalyptus was associated with healing, protection, and purification – three things I thought were important to evoke during my first ritual as leader of the Dark Daughters. I supposed I could get the eucalyptus tomorrow, but I was going to need it knotted into a rope as part of the spell I planned to cast, and . . . well . . . it was probably smart that I practiced so I didn't drop anything during the spell or, worse, suddenly discover that eucalyptus wasn't as flexible as I'd expected and it fell to pieces when I tried to knot it and then I'd turn bright red and want to crawl under the rec hall and curl up in a fetal position crying . . .

I shoved that lovely picture from my mind, turned around, and began to trudge back to the main building. That's when I saw the shape. It caught my eye because it didn't belong – and not just because it was unusual that another fledgling was silly enough to be out walking in the snowstorm. What struck me as weird was that the person, because it definitely wasn't a cat or a bush, wasn't walking on the sidewalk. He was heading in the general direction of the rec hall, but was cutting across the far lawn. I stopped and squinted against the falling snow. The person was wearing a long, dark cloak with a hood pulled up like a cowl.

An urge to follow him hit me with such strength that I gasped. Almost as if I had no will of my own, I stepped off the sidewalk and hurried after the mysterious person, who had just reached the edge of the tree line that grew along the outside wall.

My eyes widened. The instant the figure entered the shadows, whoever it was, he or she, began moving with inhuman speed, cloak billowing behind them wildly in the snow-filled wind so that the figure appeared to have wings. Red? Did I see scarlet flashes against glimpses of white skin? Snow stung my eyes and my vision blurred, but I held Nala tighter to me and kicked into a fast jog, even though I could tell that I was being led to the area of the east wall that held the trapdoor. The same place I'd seen the other two ghosts or specters or whatever. The place that I'd told myself I really didn't want to go again, at least not alone.

Yes, I should have turned to my left and marched directly to the dorm. Naturally, I didn't.

My heart was thudding like crazy and Nala was grumbling in my ear when I entered the tree line and continued to rush along the wall, all the time thinking how absolutely insane it was for me to be out here chasing what was at best some kid who was trying to sneak away from the school, and at worst a seriously scary ghost.

I'd lost sight of the person, but I knew I was getting close to the trapdoor, so I slowed down, automatically staying within the deepest shadows and moving from tree to tree. It was snowing even harder now, and Nala and I were covered in white and I was actually starting to feel chilled. *What am I doing out here?* No matter what my gut was telling me, my mind was saying that I was acting crazy and that I needed to get myself (and my shivering cat) back to the dorm. This was really none of my business. Maybe one of the teachers was checking the . . . I dunno . . . the grounds to make sure some moronic fledgling (like me) wasn't wandering around out in the storm.

Or maybe someone had just snuck on the school grounds after brutally killing Chris Ford and abducting Brad Higeons, and now they were sneaking off again, and if I confronted him/her I'd be murdered, too.

Yeah, right. Talk about an overactive imagination.

Then I heard the voices.

I slowed way down, practically tiptoeing forward until I finally saw them. There were two figures standing by the open trapdoor. I blinked hard, trying to see more clearly through the curtain of falling white. The person closest to the door was the one I'd been following, and now that he wasn't running (at a ridiculous speed) I could see that he stood weirdly, crouched down with a hunched-back posture. I shifted my attention to the other figure, and I felt the chill that had been brushing my skin with the snow sink into my soul. It was Neferet.

She looked mysterious, and powerful with her auburn hair flying around her and the snow covering the long black dress she was wearing. She was facing me, so I could see that her expression was stern, almost angry, and she was speaking intently to the cloaked person, using her hands expressively. Silently, I moved closer, glad I had on a dark outfit so that I blended well with the shadows near the wall. From this new position pieces of what Neferet was saying drifted to me on the snow-filled wind.

'. . . have more care with what you do! I will not . . .' I listened intently, trying to hear through the wailing wind, and realized that the breeze was bringing me more than just Neferet's words. I could smell something, even over the crisp scent of falling snow. It was a dry, moldy smell, weirdly out of place in this cold, wet night. '. . . much too dangerous,' Neferet was saying. 'Obey or . . .' I lost the rest of the sentence, and then she paused. The cloaked figure responded with a weird, grunting sound that was more animal than human.

Nala, who had been curled up under my chin and seemed to have fallen asleep, again, suddenly whipped her head around. I ducked even farther behind the trunk of the tree in whose shadow I was hiding as Nala began to growl.

'Shhh,' I whispered to her and tried to pet her into being calm. She quieted, but I could feel that the fur on her back had lifted and her eyes were narrowed to angry slits as she stared at the cloaked person.

'You promised!'

The guttural sound of the mystery man's voice had my skin crawling. I peeked out from behind the tree in time to see Neferet raise her hand as if she was going to strike him. He cowered back against the wall, causing the hood to fall from his face, and my stomach clenched so hard I thought I might throw up.

It was Elliott. The dead kid whose 'ghost' had attacked Nala and me last month.

Neferet didn't hit him. Instead she gestured violently at the open trapdoor. She'd raised her voice, so everything she said carried to me over the wind.

'You may not have any more! The time is not right. You cannot understand such things, and you may not question me. Now leave here. If you disobey me again you will feel my wrath, and the wrath of a goddess is terrible to behold.'

Elliott cringed away from Neferet. 'Yes, Goddess,' he whimpered.

It was him; I knew it was. Even though his voice was rough I recognized it. Somehow Elliott had not died, and he had not Changed into an adult vampyre. He was something else. Something terrible.

Even as I thought how disgusting he was, Neferet's expression softened. 'I do not wish to be angry with my children. You know that you are my greatest joys.'

Revolted, I watched as Neferet moved forward and caressed Elliott's face. His eyes began to glow the color of old blood, and even from a distance I could see that his entire body was trembling. Elliott had been a short, pudgy, unattractive kid with too white skin and carrot red hair that was habitually frizzed out. He was still all those things, but now his pale cheeks were gaunt and his body was hunched, as if it had curled in on itself. So Neferet had to bend down to kiss his lips. Totally grossed out, I heard Elliott moan in pleasure. She straightened and laughed. It was a dark, seductive sound.

'Please, Goddess!' Elliott whimpered.

'You know you don't deserve it.'

'Please, Goddess!' he repeated. His body was shivering violently.

'Very well, but remember. What a goddess gives, she can also take away.'

Unable to stop watching, I saw Neferet lift her arm and brush back her sleeve. Then she ran her fingernail up her forearm, leaving a slender scarlet line that immediately began to bead with blood. I felt the draw of her blood. When she held out her arm, offering it to Elliott, I pressed against the rough bark of the tree, forcing myself to stay still and hidden as he fell to his knees before her and, while he made feral grunts and moans, began to suck Neferet's blood. I tore my eyes from him to look at Neferet. She'd thrown her head back and her lips were parted as if having the grotesque Elliott creature suck the blood from her arm was a sexual experience.

Deep within me I felt an answering desire. I wanted to slice open someone's skin and . . .

No! I ducked completely behind the tree. I would not become a monster. I would not be a freak. I couldn't let this thing control me. Slowly and silently I started back the way I'd come, refusing to look at the two of them again.

CHAPTER SEVENTEEN

I WAS STILL FEELING SHAKY, CONFUSED, AND MORE THAN A little sick to my stomach when I finally got to the dorm. Clusters of damp kids pooled around the main room watching TV and drinking hot chocolate. I grabbed a towel from a stack by the door and joined Stevie Rae, the Twins, and Damien sitting around our favorite TV watching *Project Runway*, and started drying a grumbling Nala. Stevie Rae didn't realize I was being uncharacteristically quiet. She was too busy gushing about how the snowball fight I'd avoided earlier had morphed into a major battle after dinner that had raged until someone had thrown a snowball that had hit one of the windows of Dragon's office. Dragon was what everyone called the fencing professor, and he was not a vamp any fledgling would want to piss off.

'Dragon ended the snow war.' Stevie Rae giggled. 'But it was real fun until then.'

'Yeah, Z, you missed one hellacious wicked fight,' Erin said.

'We knocked the crap outta Damien and his boyfriend,' Shaunee said.

'He's not my boyfriend!' Damien said, but his little smile seemed to add an unspoken 'yet' to the end of the sentence.

'What . . .'

'. . . ever,' said the Twins.

'I think he's cute,' Stevie Rae said.

'Me, too,' Damien said, turning adorably pink.

'What do you think of him, Zoey?' Stevie Rae asked.

I blinked at Stevie Rae. It was like I was inside a fishbowl in the middle of a typhoon, and everyone else was on the outside cluelessly enjoying lovely weather.

'Is everything okay, Zoey?' Damien said.

'Damien, can you get me some eucalyptus?' I said abruptly.

'Eucalyptus?'

I nodded. 'Yeah, some strands of it, and some sage, too. I need both for the ritual tomorrow.'

'Yeah, no problem,' Damien said, watching me entirely too closely.

'Did you get the ritual all figured out, Z?' Stevie Rae asked.

'I think so.' I paused and took a long breath. Then I met

Damien's questioning gaze steadily. 'Damien, has there ever been a case of a fledgling who seemed to have died, but later was found alive?'

To his credit, Damien didn't freak or ask me if I had gone insane. I could feel that the Twins and Stevie Rae were staring at me like I'd just announced I was going to be on *Girls Gone Wild: Vamp Edition*, but I ignored them and kept focused on Damien. We all knew he spent hours studying, and he remembered everything he read. If any of us would know the answer to my bizarre question, it would be him.

'When a fledgling's body starts rejecting the Change there is no stopping it. That's clear in all the books. It's also what Neferet has told us. Zoey,' I'd never heard him sound so serious. 'What is wrong?'

'Please, please, please tell me you're not feeling sick!' Stevie Rae practically sobbed.

'No! It's nothing like that,' I said quickly. 'I'm fine. I promise.'

'What's going on?' Shaunee said.

'You're scaring us,' Erin said.

'I don't mean to,' I told them. 'Okay, this is coming out all wrong, but I think I saw that Elliott kid.'

'Huh!' 'What!' the Twins said together.

'I don't understand,' Damien said. 'Elliott died last month.'

Stevie Rae's eyes suddenly widened. 'Like Elizabeth!' she said. Before I could say anything, she blurted, in one long, breathless sentence, 'Last month Zoey thought she saw

Elizabeth's ghost out by the east wall but we didn't say anything 'cause we didn't want to scare y'all.'

I opened my mouth to explain about Elliott – and Neferet. And shut it again. I should have realized before I'd said one word to any of them that I absolutely could not tell them about Neferet. Vampyres were all intuitive to some degree. High Priestess Neferet was amazingly intuitive. So much so that she often seemed to be able to read actual thoughts. No way could my four friends walk around school knowing that I'd seen her letting some kind of disgusting undead Elliott creature suck her blood without Neferet knowing everything in their freaked-out minds.

What I'd witnessed tonight I would have to keep completely to myself.

'Zoey?' Stevie Rae put her hand on my arm. 'You can tell us.'

I smiled at her and wished with all my heart that I could.

'I did think I saw Elizabeth's ghost last month. And tonight I think I saw Elliott's,' I finally said.

Damien frowned. 'If you saw ghosts why did you ask me about fledglings recovering from rejecting the Change?'

I looked my friend in the eye and lied my ass off. 'Because it seemed easier to believe than I was seeing ghosts – or at least it did until I said it. Then it sounded crazy.'

'Seeing a ghost would have freaked me right out,' Shaunee said.

Erin nodded enthusiastic agreement.

'Was it like with Elizabeth?' Stevie Rae asked.

At least this I didn't have to lie about. 'No. He seemed more real, but I saw them both in the same place, over by the east wall, and both of their eyes glowed a weird red color.'

Shaunee shivered.

'I'm sure as shit staying away from the spooky east wall,' Erin said.

Damien, always the scholar, tapped his chin like a professor. 'Zoey, maybe you have yet another affinity. Maybe you can see dead fledglings.'

I would have thought this was a possibility, even though it was a gross one, if I hadn't seen the supposed ghost, solid and totally real, drinking my mentor's blood. Still, it was a good theory, and an excellent way to keep Damien busy. 'You might be right,' I said.

'Ugh,' Stevie Rae said. 'I hope not.'

'Me, too. But could you do some research on it for me, Damien?'

'Of course. I'll also check out any references to hauntings by fledglings.'

'Thanks, I appreciate that.'

'You know, I do think I remember reading something in an old Greek history text about vampyre spirits that restlessly prowl the ancient tombs of . . .'

I shut out Damien's lecture, glad that Stevie Rae and the Twins were more involved with listening to his ghost stories than asking me more specific questions. I hated lying to them, especially since I really would have liked to have told them everything. What I saw had truly frightened me. How the hell was I going to face Neferet again?

Nala rubbed her face against mine and then settled down in my lap. I stared at the TV and petted her while Damien droned on and on about old vamp ghosts. And then I realized what I was seeing and lunged across Stevie Rae for the remote that was sitting on the lamp table beside her, causing Nala to *mee-uf-ow* snort! in annoyance and jump from my lap. I didn't even take time to soothe her, but quickly turned up the volume.

It was Chera Kimiko again on a repeat of the evening news' lead story.

'The body of the second Union High School teenager, Brad Higeons, was found by museum security guards this evening in the stream that runs along the Philbrook Museum grounds. The cause of death is not being officially reported at this time, but sources have told Fox News that the boy died of blood loss through multiple lacerations.'

'No . . .' I felt my head shaking back and forth. There was a terrible ringing in my ears.

'That's the stream we crossed over when we went to the yard of the Philbrook for the Samhain Ritual last month,' Stevie Rae said.

'It's just down the street from here,' Shaunee said.

'The Dark Daughters used to sneak out there all the time for rituals,' Erin said.

Then Damien said what we were all thinking. 'Someone is trying to make it look like vampyres are killing human kids.'

'Maybe they are.' I hadn't actually meant to speak my thought aloud, and pressed my lips closed, immediately sorry I'd let that slip.

'Why would you say that, Zoey?' Stevie Rae sounded utterly shocked.

'I – I don't know. I didn't really mean it,' I stuttered, not sure what I really meant or why I'd said it.

'You're freaked, that's all,' Erin said.

'Of course you are. You knew both those kids,' Shaunee added. 'And on top of all of this, you saw a damn ghost today.'

Damien was studying me again. 'Did you have a feeling about Brad before you heard he was dead, Zoey?' he asked quietly.

'Yes. No.' I sighed. 'I thought he was dead as soon as I heard he'd been taken,' I admitted.

'Did any specifics come with the feeling? Do you know anything more?' Damien said.

As if Damien's questions had prodded them from my memory, the snatches of words that I'd heard Neferet speak replayed in my mind: . . . *much too dangerous . . . You may not have any more . . . You cannot understand . . . You may not question me . . .* I felt a terrible chill that had nothing to do with the snowstorm outside. 'Nothing specific came with the feeling. I have to go to my room,' I said, suddenly unable to look at any of them. I hated lying, and doubted I could keep it up if I stayed with them much longer. 'I have to finish up the words for the ritual tomorrow,' I said lamely. 'And I didn't get much sleep last night. I'm really tired.'

'Okay, no problem. We understand,' Damien said.

They were all so obviously worried about me that I could barely meet their eyes. 'Thanks, guys,' I mumbled as I left the room. I was halfway up the stairs when Stevie Rae caught up with me.

'Do you mind if I come back to the room now, too? I have a really bad headache. I really just want to go to sleep. I won't bug you while you study or anything.'

'No, I don't mind,' I said quickly. I glanced at her. She did look kinda pale. Stevie Rae was so sensitive that even though she didn't know Chris or Brad, their deaths were clearly upsetting her. Add to that my announcement about ghosts, and the poor kid probably was scared to death. I put my arm around her and gave her a squeeze as we came to our door. 'Hey, everything's gonna be okay.'

'Yeah, I know. I'm just tired.' She grinned up at me, but she didn't sound as perky as usual.

We didn't say much while we put on our pajamas. Nala scooted in through the cat door, jumped up on my bed, and was asleep almost as fast as Stevie Rae, which was a relief to me because I didn't have to pretend to be writing words to a ritual I'd already finished. There was something else I had to do, and I didn't want to explain any part of it to anyone, not even my best friend.

CHAPTER EIGHTEEN

MY VAMPYRE SOCIOLOGY 415 TEXT WAS EXACTLY WHERE I left it in the bookshelf over my computer desk. It was a senior or, as they're called here, sixth former level book. Neferet had given it to me shortly after I'd arrived when it was obvious that the Change going on within my body was happening at a different rate than what went on with normal fledglings. She'd wanted to pull me out of my third former Soc class and move me into the upper level section of Soc, but I'd managed to talk her out of it, saying that I was already different enough, I didn't need anything else to make me more of a freak to the rest of the kids here.

Our compromise was that I would go through the 415 level text, chapter by chapter, and ask her questions along the way.

Okay, well, I'd meant to do that, but what with one thing and another (taking over the Dark Daughters, dating Erik, regular schoolwork, and whatnot), I'd done little more than glance at the book on my shelf.

With a sigh that sounded almost as tired as I felt, I took the book to bed and propped myself up on a mound of pillows. Despite the horrible events of the day, I had to struggle to keep my eyes open as I turned to the index and found what I was looking for: bloodlust.

There were a whole string of page numbers after the word, so I marked the place in the index, wearily flipped to the first page listed, and started reading. At first it was stuff I'd already figured out for myself: as a fledgling gets farther into the Change, she develops a taste for blood. Blood drinking goes from being something abhorrent to something delicious. By the time a fledgling is well advanced in the Change process, she can detect the scent of blood from a distance. Because of changes in metabolism, drugs and alcohol have increasingly less effect on fledglings, and as this effect dissipates, they will find that the effects of drinking blood correspondingly increase.

'No kidding,' I said under my breath. Even drinking fledgling blood mixed in wine had given me an incredible buzz. Drinking Heath's blood had been like fire exploding deliciously inside me. I flipped ahead in the reading. I already knew all the stuff about blood being yummy. Then my eye caught a new heading, and I stopped at that page.

SEXUALITY AND BLOODLUST

Though the frequency of need differs depending upon age, sex, and general strength of the vampyre, adults must periodically feed on human blood to remain healthy and sane. It is, therefore, logical that evolution, and our beloved Goddess, Nyx, have insured the blood drinking process is a pleasurable one, both for the vampyre and the human donor. As we have already learned, vampyre saliva acts as an anticoagulant for human blood. Vampyre saliva also secretes endorphins during blood drinking, which stimulate the pleasure zones of the brain, human and vampyre, and can actually simulate orgasm.

I blinked and rubbed a hand across my face. Well, hell! No wonder I'd had such a slutty reaction to Heath. Being turned on while I drank blood was programmed into my Changing genes. Fascinated, I kept reading.

The older the vampyre, the more endorphins are released during blood drinking, and the more intense the experience of pleasure for vampyre and human.

Vampyres have speculated for centuries that the ecstasy of blood drinking is the key reason humans have vilified our race. Humans feel threatened by our ability to bring them such intense pleasure during an act they consider dangerous and abhorrent, so they have labeled us as predators. The truth, of course, is that vampyres can control their bloodlust, so there is little physical danger to human donors. The danger lies in the Imprint that often occurs during the ritual of blood drinking.

Completely engrossed, I hurried on to the next section.

IMPRINTING

An Imprint between vampyre and human does not occur every time a vampyre feeds. Many studies have been performed to try to determine exactly why some humans Imprint and some do not, but though there are several determining factors, such as emotional attachment, relationship between the human and the vampyre pre-Change, age, sexual orientation, and frequency of blood drinking, there is no way to predict with certainty whether a human will Imprint with a vampyre.

The text went on to talk about how vampyres should take care when drinking from a live donor, versus getting blood from blood banks, which are highly secretive businesses very few humans are aware exist at all (apparently those few humans are extremely well paid for their silence). The Soc book definitely frowned on drinking blood from humans and there were lots of warnings about how dangerous it is to Imprint a human, how not only is the human now emotionally bound to the vampyre, but the vamp is tied to the human, too. This made me sit up straighter. With a sick feeling in my stomach I read about how once the Imprint is in place a vamp can feel the human's emotions, and in some cases can actually call and/or track the human. There the text went off on a tangent about how Bram Stoker had actually been Imprinted by a vamp High Priestess, but that he had not understood her commitment to Nyx had to come before their tie, and in a fit of jealous anger had betrayed her by exaggerating the negative aspects of an Imprint in his infamous book, *Dracula*.

'Huh. I had no idea,' I said. Ironically, *Dracula* had been one of my favorite books since I read it when I was thirteen. I skimmed through the rest of the section until I came to a part that had me chewing my lip as I slowly read it.

FLEDGLING – VAMPYRE IMPRINTING

As discussed in the previous chapter, due to the possibility of Imprint, fledglings are prohibited from drinking the blood of human donors, but they may experiment with each other. It has been proven that fledglings cannot Imprint one another. However, it is possible for an adult vampyre to Imprint a fledgling. This leads to emotional and physical complications once the fledgling completes the Change that are often not beneficial for either vampyre; therefore, blood drinking between fledgling and adult vampyre is strictly prohibited.

I shook my head, appalled all over again by the blood drinking I'd witnessed between Neferet and Elliott. Setting aside the whole issue of Elliott being dead, which still confused the hell outta me, Neferet was a powerful High Priestess. No damn way should she be letting a fledgling drink from her (even a dead one).

There was a chapter about breaking Imprints, which I started reading, but it was just too depressing. Apparently it involved the aid of a powerful High Priestess, a lot of physical pain, especially on the part of the human, and even then the human and the vampyre had to be careful to stay away from each other or the Imprint could reestablish.

I suddenly felt overwhelmingly weary. How long had it been since I'd really slept? More than a day. I glanced at my alarm clock. It was 6:10 A.M. It would be getting light soon. Feeling stiff and old I got up and put the book back on the shelf. Then I pulled open one side of the heavy curtains that completely covered the one large window in our room and blocked out all light from the outside. It was still snowing, and in the hesitant light of predawn the world looked innocent and dreamy. It was hard to imagine that such horrible things as teenagers being killed and dead fledglings being reanimated could have happened out there. I closed my eyes and leaned my head against the cool windowpane. I didn't want to think of either of those things right now. I was too tired . . . too confused . . . too unable to come up with the answers that I needed.

My sleepy mind wandered. I wanted to lie down, but the cool window felt good against my forehead. Erik would be getting back later that day. The thought gave me equal pangs of pleasure and of guilt, which, of course, made me think of Heath.

I'd probably Imprinted him. The thought scared me, but it also drew me. Would it be so awful to be emotionally and physically tied to a sober Heath? Before I'd met Erik (or Loren) my answer would most definitely have been no, it wouldn't be awful. Now it wasn't the awfulness that I was worried about. It was the fact that I'd have to hide the relationship from everyone. *Of course I could lie* . . . the thought drifted like poison smoke through my overstressed mind. *Neferet and even Erik knew that I'd been put in a situation a month ago where I drank Heath's blood – before I knew anything about bloodlust and Imprinting. I could pretend like I'd Imprinted him then. I'd already mentioned the possibility to Neferet. Maybe I could figure out a way to keep seeing both Heath and Erik* . . .

I knew my thoughts were wrong. I knew that seeing both of them was dishonest to both Erik and Heath, but I was so torn! I was really starting to care about Erik, plus he lived in my world and understood issues like the Change and embracing a totally new way of life. Thinking about breaking up with him made my heart hurt.

But thinking about never seeing Heath again, never tasting his blood again . . . that made me feel like I was having a panic attack. I sighed again. If this was bad for me, it was probably a zillion times worse for Heath. After all, it'd been a month since I'd seen him, and all that time he'd been carrying around a razor blade in his pocket just on the outside chance he might run into me. He'd stopped drinking and smoking because of what had happened between us. And he'd been eager to cut himself and let me drink his blood. Remembering, I shivered, and not because of the coolness of the window I was still pressing my forehead against. Desire made me shiver. The Soc textbook had described the reasons behind bloodlust in logical, dispassionate words that didn't begin to represent the truth of it.

Drinking Heath's blood was an incredible turn on. Something I wanted to do again and again. Soon. Now, actually. I bit my lip to keep from moaning as I thought about Heath – the hardness of his body and the incredible taste of his blood.

And suddenly it was as if a part of my mind lifted, like a string thrown out of a big ball of yarn. I could feel that piece of me searching . . . hunting . . . tracking . . . until it burst into a dark room and hovered above a bed. I sucked in my breath. Heath!

He was lying flat on his back. His blond hair was tousled, making him look like a little boy. Okay, anyone would think the kid was totally cute. I mean, vamps were known for being stunningly beautiful and gorgeously handsome, and even a vamp would have to admit that Heath scored high on their own scale of good-looking.

As if he could sense my presence, he stirred in his sleep, turning his head and restlessly kicking off the sheet that covered him. He was naked except for a pair of blue boxers that had fat little green frogs all over them. The sight of them made me smile. But the smile froze on my face when I noticed that I could now see the thin pink line that ran down the side of his neck.

That was where he'd cut himself with the razor blade and where I'd sucked his blood. I could almost taste it again – the heat and the dark richness of it, like melted chocolate, only a zillion times better.

Unable to stop myself, I moaned, and at the same instant Heath moaned in his sleep.

211

'Zoey . . .' he muttered dreamily, and shifted restlessly again.

'Oh, Heath,' I whispered. 'I don't know what to do about us.' I knew what I *wanted* to do all too well. I wanted to ignore my exhaustion, get in my car, drive directly to Heath's house, sneak in the window of his bedroom (it's not like I hadn't done that before), open the freshly closed cut in his neck, and let his sweet blood flood my mouth while I pressed my body against his and made love for the first time in my life.

'Zoey!' This time Heath's eyes were fluttering open. He moaned again and his hand moved down to the hard lump in his pants and he began to—

My eyes sprang open and I was back in my dorm room with my forehead pressed against the window, breathing entirely too heavily.

My cell phone bleeped with the tone that said I had a text message. My hands were shaking as I flipped it open and read: I felt u here. Promise you'll meet me Friday.

I took a deep breath and answered Heath with two words that made my stomach flutter with excitement: I promise.

I closed the phone and turned it off. Then, forcing away the image of Heath with the unhealed cut on his neck, warm and desirable, obviously wanting me as much as I wanted him, I moved from the window and climbed into bed. Incredibly, my clock told me it was now 8:27 A.M. I'd been standing by the window for more than two hours! No wonder my body felt so stiff and crappy. I made a mental note to look up more info about Imprinting and the connection between the human and the vamp next time I was in the media center (which had better be soon). Before I turned off the little table lamp I glanced over at Stevie Rae. She was curled up on her side and her back was to me, but her deep breathing told me that she was definitely still asleep. Well, at least my friends didn't know what a bloodlust-filled, hornie freak I was turning into.

I wanted Heath.

I needed Erik.

I was intrigued by Loren.

I had no damn idea what I was going to do about the mess that my life had become.

I smushed my pillow into a ball. I was so tired I felt like someone had drugged me, but my mind still wouldn't shut itself off. When I woke up I'd see Erik again and probably Loren. I'd have to face Neferet. I'd perform my first ritual in front of a group of kids who would probably be happy to see me fail, or at least embarrass myself miserably, and there was always the possibility that both would happen. Then there was the weirdness of knowing that I'd seen what could only be Elliott's ghost behaving in a very unghostlike way. Not to mention another human teenager was dead and it was looking more and more as if a vamp had something to do with it.

I closed my eyes and told my body to relax and my mind to concentrate on something pleasant, like ... like ... how pretty the snow was ...

Slowly, exhaustion took over and I finally, gratefully, fell into a deep sleep.

CHAPTER NINETEEN

SOMEONE BANGING ON THE DOOR PULLED ME AWAKE FROM a dream about cat-shaped snowflakes.

'Zoey! Stevie Rae! You're gonna be late!' Shaunee's voice sounded muffled but urgent through the door, like an annoying alarm covered up by a towel.

'Okay, okay, I'm coming,' I called as I tried to struggle out of my covers while Nala complained loudly. I glanced at my alarm clock, which I hadn't bothered to set. I mean, it wasn't like it was a school day and I usually didn't sleep more than eight or nine hours at a time and—

'Hell!' I blinked. Sure enough, the time was 9:59 P.M. I'd

slept more than twelve hours? I stumbled to the door, pausing to shake Stevie Rae's leg.

'Mumph,' she muttered sleepily.

I cracked the door. Shaunee was glaring at me.

'Please with the sleeping all damn day! You two have got to stop staying up late if you can't get up. Erik's going to be performing in half an hour.'

'Ah, hell!' I rubbed my face, trying to force myself awake. 'I forgot all about that.'

Shaunee rolled her eyes. 'You better hurry up and get dressed. And slap some serious makeup on that pale face and do something about your nappy hair. Boyfriend's been looking all over for you.'

'Okay, okay. Crap! I'm coming. Will you and Erin—'

Shaunee put up her hand, cutting me off. 'Please. We've already got you covered. Erin's in the auditorium saving front row seats as we speak.'

'Is that you, Mama? I don't wanna go to school today . . .' Stevie Rae mumbled, clearly not awake.

Shaunee snorted.

'We'll hurry. You guys just save those seats for us.' I slammed the door shut and hurried over to Stevie Rae. 'Wake up!' I shook her shoulder. She squinted and frowned up at me.

'Huh?'

'Stevie Rae, it's ten o'clock. P.M. We slept forever and now we're so late it's ridiculous.'

'Huh?'

215

'Just wake the hell up!' I snapped, taking out my frustration that I'd overslept on her.

'Wha—' She looked blearily at the clock, and that seemed to finally get through to her. 'Ohmygood*ness*! We're late.'

I rolled my eyes. 'That's what I've been trying to tell you. I'm gonna throw on something and work on my hair and makeup. You better jump in the shower. You look terrible.'

''Kay.' She staggered into the bathroom.

I yanked on a pair of jeans and a black sweater, and then got to work on my hair and makeup. I could not believe I'd totally blown off the fact that Erik was performing the Shakespearian monologue he'd taken to the competition. Actually, I hadn't even worried about how he'd placed, which was definitely not good girlfriend etiquette. Of course it wasn't like I didn't have other things on my mind, but still. Everyone thought I was the lucky girl who had caught Erik after he'd escaped from Aphrodite's nasty spiderweb (and by web I mean crotch). Hell, *I* thought I was lucky to have him, something that had been hard to remember when I was sucking Heath's blood and flirting with Loren.

'Sorry about oversleeping, Z.' Stevie Rae came out of the bathroom in a gush of steamy air, towel-drying her short, blond curls. She was dressed a lot like I was, and she must still be half asleep because she looked pale and tired. She gave a huge yawn and stretched like a cat.

'No, it's my fault.' I felt bad for the way I'd jumped on her before. 'I should have known with how little I've been sleeping that I needed to set my alarm.' I guess it shouldn't have been

216

a surprise that Stevie Rae hadn't gotten much sleep lately, either. We are best friends and she definitely knows when I'm overstressed. We probably both needed a good, long, comalike sleep.

'I'll be ready in just a sec. I'm just gonna put on some mascara and gloss. My hair will dry in like two minutes anyway,' Stevie Rae said.

We were out of there in five minutes. No time for breakfast, we bolted out of the dorm and practically ran to the auditorium. We made it to seats Erin had saved for us just as the lights flicked on and off, announcing that there were two minutes before the program began, and for people to take their seats.

'Erik stayed out here waiting for you until just a second ago,' Damien said. I was glad to see he was sitting beside Jack. The two really did make a cute couple.

'Is he mad?' I asked.

'I'd say confused is a better description,' Shaunee said.

'Or worried. He looked worried, too,' Erin added.

I sighed. 'Did you not tell him that I'd overslept?'

'Hence the reason my Twin said he looked worried,' Shaunee said.

'I filled him in on the deaths of the two friends of yours. Erik understands it's been hard on you, and that's why he looked worried,' Damien said, frowning at Shaunee and Erin.

'I'm just sayin', Z, Erik is too hot to be stood up,' Erin said.

'Ditto, Twin,' Shaunee said.

'I did *not*—' I sputtered, but the lights going out cut me off.

The drama teacher, Professor Nolan, came out onstage and spent a while explaining the importance of actors being trained in the classics, and talking about how prestigious the Shakespeare monologue contest is for vamps around the world. She reminded us that each of the twenty-five House of Night campuses worldwide send their five strongest competitors, which meant there were a total of 125 talented fledglings who competed against one another.

'Jeesh, I had no idea Erik had to go up against so many kids,' I whispered to Stevie Rae.

'Erik probably kicked butt. He's awesome,' Stevie Rae whispered back. Then she yawned again and coughed.

I frowned at her. She looked like crap. How could she still be tired?

'Sorry.' She smiled sheepishly. 'I gotta frog in my throat.'

'Shhh!' the Twins hissed together.

I turned my attention back to Prof Nolan.

'The results of the competition have been sealed until today, when all of the students have returned to their home schools. I will announce the placings of each of our five finalists as I introduce them. Each will perform their competition monologue. I cannot begin to tell you how proud we are of our team. Every one of them did an exceptional job.' Prof Nolan beamed. Then she went on to introduce the first performer, who was a kid named Kaci Crump. She was a fourth former who I didn't know very well because around the dorm she was kinda shy and quiet, even though she seemed nice. I didn't think she was a member of the Dark Daughters, and

I made a mental note to send her an invitation to join. Prof Nolan announced that Kaci had placed fifty-second in the competition with her rendition of Beatrice's monologue from *Much Ado About Nothing*.

I thought she was good, but was blown away by the next kid, Cassie Kramme, a fifth former who'd placed twenty-fifth overall. She performed Portia's famous speech from *The Merchant of Venice* that begins, 'The quality of mercy is not strained . . .' I recognized it because I'd chosen it as the monologue I memorized my freshman year at SIHS. Uh, Cassie's acting definitely would have kicked my ass. I didn't think she was a member of the Dark Daughters, either. Huh. Seems Aphrodite hadn't wanted much competition in the way of other drama queens. Big surprise.

The next performer was a kid I knew because he was a friend of Erik's. Cole Clifton was tall, blond, and totally cute. He'd finished twenty-second with his rendition of Romeo's 'But soft, what light through yonder window breaks . . .' speech. Okay, he was good. Really, really good. I heard Shaunee and Erin (especially Shaunee) making lots of appreciative noises, and the clapping was furious from them when he finished. Hum . . . I'd have to talk to Erik about fixing Shaunee up with Cole. In my opinion more white boys should date women of color. It was good for expanding their horizons (especially true in Oklahoma white boys).

Speaking of women of color – the next performer was Deino. She was a drop-dead mixed girl with to-die-for hair and skin the color of vanilla latte. She was also one of Aphrodite's inner circle, or she used to be. I'd been introduced to her at Aphrodite's Full Moon Ritual. Deino was one of Aphrodite's three best friends. They'd renamed themselves after the mythological sisters of the Gorgon and Scylla: Deino, Enyo, Pemphredo. Translated, the names mean Terrible, Warlike, and Wasp.

The names definitely fit. They were three hateful, selfish bitches who had run out on Aphrodite during the Samhain Ritual and, as far as I could tell, hadn't spoken to her since. Okay, Aphrodite had messed up, and she was definitely haggish, but I could mess up and be a total hag and I don't think Stevie Rae, the Twins, or Damien would turn their backs on me. Get pissed at me – yep, definitely. Tell me I'd lost my mind – of course. But run out on me – no way.

Professor Nolan introduced Deino, saying that she'd finished an amazing eleventh overall, and then Deino began Cleopatra's death scene monologue. I had to admit that she was good. Really good. Watching her I was so dazzled by her talent that I started to wonder how much of her hateful haggishness had been because of Aphrodite's influence. Since I'd taken over the Dark Daughters none of Aphrodite's close friends had caused any kind of problems. Actually, now that I thought about it, I realized that Terrible, Warlike, and Wasp had been keeping a pretty low profile. Huh. Well, I'd said that I wanted to include one of Aphrodite's old inner circle in my new Prefect Council. Maybe Deino would be the right choice. I could ask Erik about her. With Aphrodite out of power I could give Deino a chance (as well as sincerely wish her name wasn't so disturbing).

I was still considering how to go about telling my friends (who were also my fellow Prefects) that I was thinking about asking Terrible to join our Council when Professor Nolan returned to the stage and waited for the audience to quiet down. When she started speaking her eyes were shining with excitement and she seemed ready to burst. I felt a little thrill run through me. Erik had finished in the top ten!

'Erik Night is our final performer. He has been an incredible talent since the day he was Marked three years ago. I am proud to be his teacher and his mentor,' she said, beaming. 'Please give him the hero's welcome he deserves for placing *first* in the International Shakespearian Monologue Competition!'

The auditorium exploded as Erik strode, smiling, onto the stage. I could hardly breathe. How could I have forgotten how utterly gorgeous he is? Tall – taller than Cole even – he had black hair that did that adorable Superman curl thing, and eyes so brilliant blue they were like staring into the summer sky. Like the other performers, he was dressed all in black, with the fifth former insignia of Nyx's golden chariot pulling a trail of stars over his left breast as the only break in the dark color scheme. And, let me tell you, he made black look good.

He walked to center stage, stopped, smiled directly (and obviously) into my eyes, and winked at me. He was so damn hot I thought I would die. Then he bowed his head and when he raised it he wasn't eighteen-year-old Erik Night, vampyre fledgling, fifth former at the House of Night, anymore. Somehow, right in front of our eyes, he had become a Moorish warrior who was trying to explain to a room full of doubters

how a Venetian princess had fallen in love with him, and he
with her.

> *'Her father lov'd me; oft invited me;*
> *Still question'd me the story of my life*
> *From year to year, the battles, sieges, fortunes*
> *That I have pass'd.'*

I couldn't take my eyes from him, and neither could anyone
else in the room as he transformed into Othello. I also couldn't
help but compare him to Heath. In his own way, Heath was
as successful and talented as Erik. He was Broken Arrow's
star quarterback, with a bright collegiate and maybe even
pro football career in front of him. Heath was a leader. Erik
was a leader. I'd grown up watching Heath play ball, had
been proud of him, and had cheered for him. But I had never
been awed by his talent like I was awed by Erik. And the
only time Heath had ever made me feel like I couldn't breathe
was when he sliced into his skin and offered his blood to me.

Erik paused in his monologue, and moved forward until
he was standing at the edge of the stage, so close that if I
stood I could reach up and touch him. Then he looked into
my eyes and completed Othello's speech *to me*, as though I
was the absent Desdemona he spoke of:

> *'She wish'd she had not heard it, yet she wish'd*
> *That heaven had made her such a man; she thank'd me,*
> *And bade me, if I had a friend that lov'd her,*

I should but teach him how to tell my story,
And that would woo her. Upon this hint I spake:
She lov'd me for the dangers I had pass'd,
And I lov'd her that she did pity them.'

Erik touched his fingers to his lips, then held his hand out to me as if to offer me his formal kiss, and then pressed those fingers over his heart and bowed his head. The audience erupted into cheers and a standing ovation. Stevie Rae stood cheering next to me, wiping her eyes and laughing.

'That was so romantic I almost peed my pants,' she yelled.

'Me, too!' I laughed.

And then Professor Nolan was back onstage, closing the performance and directing everyone to the wine and cheese reception set up in the lobby.

'Come on, Z,' Erin said, grabbing one of my hands.

'Yeah, we're staying with you 'cause that friend of Erik's that played Romeo is insanely hot,' Shaunee said as she grabbed my other hand. The Twins started hauling me through the crowd, shouldering us past the slow-moving kids like mini-tugboats. I looked helplessly back at Damien and Stevie Rae. Clearly they were going to have to catch up on their own. The Twins were a force beyond even my control.

We popped from the bottled-up crowd trying to exit the auditorium like three corks coming to the surface. And suddenly there Erik was, just entering the lobby from the side actors' entrance. Our eyes met and he instantly stopped talking to Cole and headed straight to me.

'Mmm, mmm, mmm. He is so totally *fiiiine*,' Shaunee murmured.

'As usual, we're in complete agreement, Twin,' Erin sighed dreamily.

I couldn't do anything but stand there and smile like a moron as Erik reached us. With a very naughty sparkle in his eyes he took my hand, kissed it, and then made a sweeping bow and proclaimed in his actor's voice that carried all around the room, 'Hello, my sweet Desdemona.'

I felt my cheeks getting really hot, and I actually giggled. He was just pulling me into a warm, but very proper-for-public-consumption hug when I heard a familiar hateful laugh. Aphrodite, looking amazing in a short black skirt, stiletto boots, and a slinky sweater, was laughing as she walked (actually, she twitched more than she walked – I mean, the girl could seriously shake her butt) past us. Over Erik's shoulder I met her eyes and, in a silky voice that would have sounded friendly had it not been coming from her mouth, said, 'If he's calling you Desdemona, then I suggest you be careful. If it even looked like you're cheating on him he'll strangle you in your bed. But you'd never cheat on him, would you?' Then she flipped her long, blond, perfect hair and twitched away.

No one said anything for a second, then the Twins, at the same time, said, 'Issues. She has issues,' and everyone laughed.

Everyone but me. All I could think about was the fact that she'd seen Loren and me in the media center, and that it definitely could have looked like I was cheating on Erik. Was she warning me that she was going to tell Erik? Okay, I wasn't worried about him strangling me in my bed, but would he believe her? Also, Aphrodite's all-too-perfect appearance reminded me that I was wearing wrinkled jeans and a hastily thrown-on sweater. My hair and makeup had definitely looked better. Actually, I think I still might have pillow marks on my cheek.

'Don't let her get to you,' Erik said gently.

I looked up at him. He was holding my hand and smiling down at me. I mentally shook myself. 'Don't worry, she's not,' I said brightly. 'Anyway, who cares about her? You won the competition! That's amazing, Erik. I'm so proud of you!' I hugged him again, loving his clean smell and how his height made me feel small and delicate. Then our little pocket of privacy was gone as more and more people poured out of the auditorium.

'Erik, it's so cool you won!' Erin said. 'But it's not like we're surprised. You definitely kick ass onstage.'

'Totally. And so does boyfriend over there.' Shaunee jerked her chin in Cole's direction. 'He is one fine Romeo.'

Erik grinned. 'I'll tell him you said so.'

'You can also tell him that if he wants a little brown sugar in his Juliet he need look no farther than right here.' She pointed at herself and shimmied her hips.

'Twin, if Juliet had been black I do not believe things would have come to such a shitty end between her and Romeo. I mean, we would have shown more sense than drinking that sleeping potion crap and going through all that drama just because of some unfortunate parental issues.'

'Exactly,' Shaunee said.

None of us stated the obvious – that Erin, with her blond hair and blue eyes, was definitely NOT BLACK. We were too used to her and Shaunee being twinlike to question the weirdness of it.

'Erik, you were amazing!' Damien rushed up with Jack following close behind.

'Congratulations,' Jack said shyly, but with definite enthusiasm.

Erik smiled at them. 'Thanks, guys. Hey, Jack. I was too nervous before the performance to say that I'm glad you're here. It'll be nice to have a roommate.'

Jack's cute face lit up, and I squeezed Erik's hand. This was one reason why I liked him so much. Besides being gorgeous and talented, Erik was an authentically nice guy. There were a lot of guys in his position (ridiculously popular) who would have either ignored this little third former roommate or, worse, been visibly pissed that they'd have to share a room with a 'fag'. Erik wasn't like that at all, and I couldn't help but compare him to Heath, who would probably have been freaked that he had to room with a gay kid. Not that Heath was hateful or anything like that, but he was a typical teenage Okie boy, which tended to mean narrow-minded homophobe. Which made me realize that I'd never asked Erik where he was from. Jeesh, I was a crappy girlfriend.

'Did you hear me, Zoey?'

'Huh?' Damien's question shut off my inner babbling, but no, I hadn't heard him.

'Hello! Earth to Zoey! I asked if you realized what time it was. And are you remembering the Full Moon Ritual starts at midnight?'

I looked at the wall clock. 'Ah, hell!' It was 11:05. I still needed to change my clothes and then get to the rec hall, light the circle candles, make sure the five candles for the elements were in place, and check on the Goddess's table. 'Erik, I'm so sorry, but I have to leave. There are a million things to do before the ritual starts.' I made eye contact with each of my four friends. 'You guys have to come with me.' They nodded like bobble-headed dolls. I turned back to Erik. 'You're coming to the ritual, aren't you?'

'Yeah. And that reminds me. I got you something in New York. Hang on for just a sec, and I'll go get it.'

He hurried back through the actors' entrance to the auditorium.

'I swear he is too damn good to be true,' Erin said.

'Let's hope his friend is just like him,' Shaunee said, sending Cole a flirty smile from across the room, which I noticed he returned.

'Damien, did you get the eucalyptus and sage for me?' I was already feeling nervous. Hell! I should have eaten. My stomach was an empty cavern just waiting to clench up on me.

'Don't worry, Z. I got the eucalyptus and I even braided it together with the sage for you,' Damien said.

'Everything will be perfect, you'll see,' Stevie Rae said.

'Yeah, you don't need to be nervous,' Shaunee said.

'We'll be right there with you,' Erin finished.

I smiled at them, incredibly glad they were my friends. And then Erik was back. He handed me the big white box he was carrying. I hesitated before tearing into it and Shaunee said, 'Z, if you don't open it I will.'

'Damn right,' Erin said.

Eagerly, I slid off the decorative string that held it shut, opened the lid, and gasped (along with everyone else who was standing close enough to see). Inside the box pooled the most beautiful dress I'd ever seen. It was black, but woven into the material were metallic specks of silver, so that wherever the light touched, it glittered and sparkled like shooting stars against the night sky.

'Erik, this is beautiful.' I sounded choked because I was trying really hard not to make a fool out of myself and burst into happy tears.

'I wanted you to have something special for your first ritual as leader of the Dark Daughters,' he said.

We hugged again before my friends and I had to rush out and head to the rec hall. I clutched the dress to my chest and tried not to think about the fact that while Erik was buying me an amazingly cool present I had been either sucking Heath's blood or flirting with Loren. And while I tried not to think about that, I also tried to ignore the guilty voice inside my head that kept saying, over and over, *You don't deserve him . . . you don't deserve him . . . you don't deserve him . . .*

CHAPTER TWENTY

'Shaunee, Erin, and Stevie Rae – you guys start lighting the white candles. Damien, if you place the colored candles for the elements in their positions I'll be sure that everything's set for Nyx's table.'

'Easy—' Shaunee said.

'Peasy,' Erin chimed in.

'Japanesy,' Stevie Rae added, making the Twins give her mirror eye rolls.

'Are the element candles still in the supply room?' Damien asked.

'Yep,' I called as I headed to the kitchen. I was glad I'd

already put together a big tray of fresh fruits, cheeses, and meats for Nyx's table. I just needed to retrieve it and the bottle of wine from the refrigerator, and arrange the bounty neatly on the table placed in the center of the large circle made of white candles. The table already had an ornate goblet on it, as well as a beautiful statue of the Goddess, a long, elegant lighter, and the purple candle that would represent spirit, the last element I would call to the circle. The table symbolized the richness of the blessings Nyx has given her children, vampyres and fledglings. I liked setting up the Goddess's table. It made me feel calm, something that I especially needed tonight. I arranged the food and wine, and went over and over in my mind the words of the ritual I was going to use in – I glanced at the clock and felt my stomach tighten – in fifteen minutes. Fledglings were already starting to come into the rec hall, but they were being pretty subdued and hanging out in the corners of the large room in clusters while they watched the Twins and Stevie Rae light the white candles that would form the circumference of the circle. Maybe I wasn't the only one nervous about tonight. It was a big change to have me lead the Dark Daughters. Aphrodite had been leader for the past two years, and in that time the group had become a cliquish, snobby club where fledglings who weren't part of the 'in' crowd were used and made fun of.

Well, things were changing tonight.

I glanced at my friends. We'd all hurried to change our clothes before coming to the rec hall, and everyone had chosen to wear solid black to keep with the theme of the amazing dress Erik had given me. I glanced down at myself for the zillionth time. The dress was simple, but perfect. It had a round neckline that was low, but not as low as ho-ish Aphrodite's ritual dresses had been. It was long-sleeved and hugged my body to the waist, from there down it swirled gracefully to the floor. The silver specks that covered it glimmered in the candlelight whenever I moved. What also glittered whenever I moved was the necklace that dangled from the silver chain around my neck. Each Dark Daughter and Son had a similar necklace, with two exceptions – my triple moons were encrusted with garnets, and mine was the only necklace that had been found with the body of a dead human teenager. Okay, it wasn't exactly *my* necklace that had been found. It was one like mine. Just like mine.

No. I wouldn't think about negative things tonight. I would only concentrate on positives, and on preparing myself to lead my first public circle-casting and ritual. Damien returned to the main room with a big tray on which he balanced the four candles that represented each element: yellow for air, red for fire, blue for water, and green for earth. I already had my purple spirit candle on Nyx's table. I smiled and thought how great my friends looked, dressed chicly in black with their silver Dark Daughters' necklaces. Stevie Rae had already taken her place at the northernmost part of the circle where earth should be. Damien handed her the green candle. I just happened to be watching them, so there was no mistaking what I saw. As Stevie Rae touched the candle, her eyes widened and she let out a weird sound that was a cross between a scream and a gasp. Damien had taken such a hasty step back that he had to clutch at the other candles to keep them from tumbling off the tray.

'Did you feel it?' Stevie Rae's voice sounded weird, hushed yet amplified.

Damien looked shaky, but he nodded and said, 'Yeah, and I smelled it, too.'

Then they both turned to look at me.

'Uh, Zoey, could you come here for a second?' Damien asked. He sounded normal again, and had I not been watching what had happened between the two of them I would have thought nothing more was going on than maybe they needed help with the candles.

But I had been watching, which is why I didn't yell from the center of the circle and ask what they wanted. Instead I hurried over to them and kept my voice low. 'What's going on?'

'Tell her,' Damien said to Stevie Rae.

Still looking wide-eyed, startled, and more than a little pale, Stevie Rae said, 'Can't you smell it?'

I frowned. 'Smell it? What are—' And then I did smell it – freshly cut hay, honeysuckle, and something else that I swear reminded me of newly plowed dirt in my grandma's lavender fields.

'I do,' I said hesitantly, feeling thoroughly confused. 'But I didn't call earth into the circle.' My affinity, or power, given to me by Nyx was the ability to materialize the five elements. Even after a month, I wasn't exactly sure what all that power encompassed, but one thing I did know was that when I cast a circle and called each element to it, all of them manifested very physically. The wind whipped around me when I called air. Fire made my skin glow with heat (and, quite frankly, made me sweat). I could feel the coolness of the sea when I evoked water. And when I called earth to the circle I smelled earthy things and even felt grass under my feet (even when I was wearing shoes, which was truly weird).

But, as I'd said, I hadn't begun casting the circle, so I hadn't called any of the elements, yet Stevie Rae, Damien, and I were clearly smelling earth smells.

Then Damien sucked air and his face split into a huge grin. 'Stevie Rae has an affinity for earth!'

'Huh?' I said brilliantly.

'No way,' Stevie Rae said.

'Try this,' Damien went on, his excitement growing by the second. 'Close your eyes, Stevie Rae, and think about the earth.' He looked at me. 'Don't *you* think about it.'

''Kay,' I said quickly. His excitement was contagious. It would be fantastic if Stevie Rae had an earth affinity. Having an elemental affinity was a powerful gift from Nyx, and I would definitely love it if my best friend had been blessed like that from our Goddess.

'Okay.' Stevie Rae sounded breathless, but she closed her eyes.

'What's happening?' Erin said.

'Why's she have her eyes closed?' Shaunee said. Then she sniffed the air. 'And why does it smell like hay over there?

Stevie Rae, I swear if you're trying out some kind of bumpkin perfume I might have to smack you.'

'Shhh!' Damien put his finger to his lips and shushed her. 'We think Stevie Rae might have developed an earth affinity.'

Shaunee blinked. 'Nuh uh!'

'Huh,' Erin said.

'I can *not* concentrate with y'all talking,' Stevie Rae said, opening her eyes to glare at the Twins.

'Sorry,' they muttered.

'Try again,' I encouraged her.

She nodded. Then she closed her eyes and screwed her forehead up in concentration while she thought about the earth. I did *not* think about it, which was actually pretty hard because within a couple of seconds the air was filled with the smells of freshly mowed grass, and flowers, and I could even hear birds chirping like crazy and—

'Ohmygod! Stevie Rae has an affinity for earth!' I blurted.

Stevie Rae's eyes sprang open and she covered her mouth with both of her hands, looking shocked and thrilled.

'Stevie Rae, that's amazing!' Damien said, and in seconds all of us were congratulating and hugging her while she giggled through happy tears.

Then it happened. I had one of my *feelings*. And this time it was (thankfully) a good one.

'Damien, Shaunee, Erin – I want you guys to take your places in the circle.' They gave me questioning looks, but must have recognized the tone of my voice because they instantly did what I told them to do. I wasn't exactly the boss of them, but my friends respected that I was in training to someday be their High Priestess, so they obediently walked to the place in the circle that I had assigned to each of them weeks ago when it had only been the five of us, and I was casting a circle to try to figure out if I really had a Goddess-given affinity, or if I just had very little sense and an overactive imagination.

As they took their places I looked around at the kids who were already in the rec hall. I definitely needed outside help. Then Erik walked into the room with Jack, and I grinned and motioned them over to me.

'What's up, Z? You look like you're going to explode,' Erik said, and then he lowered his voice, and for my ears alone added, 'And you look as hot in that dress as I thought you would.'

'Thanks, I love it!' I did a quick little twirl that was partially flirting with Erik, and partially pure happiness at what I was almost sure was getting ready to happen. 'Jack, would you please go over to Damien and get the tray of candles he's holding and bring them back here to the middle of the circle?'

'Yep,' Jack said and scampered off to do as I asked. Okay, he didn't actually scamper, but he was very perky.

'What's going on?' Erik asked.

'You'll see.' I grinned, barely able to suppress my excitement.

When Jack was back with the candles I put the tray on Nyx's table. I concentrated for a second, and decided my instincts were telling me fire would be the right choice. Then

I picked up the red candle and handed it to Erik. 'Okay, I need you to take this candle over to Shaunee.'

Erik wrinkled his forehead. 'Just take it over to her?'

'Yeah. Hand it to her and then pay attention.'

'To what?'

'I'd rather not say.'

He shrugged and gave me a look that said that even though he might think I was hot he also might think that I had lost my mind, but he did as I asked and walked over to where Shaunee was standing in the southernmost part of the circle – the area from which I called the element fire. He stopped in front of her. Shaunee looked around him at me.

'Take the candle from him,' I called across the circle to her, concentrating on how cute Erik looked so that I wouldn't be thinking about fire at all.

Shaunee shrugged. 'Okay,' she said.

She took the red candle from Erik. I was watching her closely, but I hadn't needed to. What happened was so obvious that several of the kids standing around the outside of the circle gasped along with Shaunee. The instant her hand touched the candle there was a *whoosh* noise. Her long, black hair began to lift and crackle as if it was filled with static electricity, and her beautiful chocolate skin glowed as if she had been lit from within.

'I knew it!' I cried, practically jumping up and down with excitement.

Shaunee looked up from her glowing body to meet my eyes. 'I'm doing this, aren't I?'

'You are!'

'I have an affinity for fire!'

'Yes, you do!' I yelled happily.

I heard lots of oohs and ahhs from the ever-increasing crowd, but I didn't have time for them right now. Following my gut feeling I motioned for Erik to come back to the center of the circle, which he did with a huge grin on his face.

'That may be the coolest thing I've ever seen,' he said.

'Just wait. If I'm right, and I think I am, there's more.' I gave him the blue candle. 'Now take this one to Erin.'

'Your wish is my command,' he said with an old-time flourish. If anyone else bowed like that in public they would have looked like an utter dork. Erik looked like an utter hottie – part gentleman, part bad boy pirate. I was thinking about how yummy Erik was when Erin and Shaunee let out twin squeals of happiness at almost the same instant.

'Look at the floor!' Erin was pointing to the tile floor of the rec hall. In a circular area around her the tile floor was rippling and it appeared to be lapping against feet, even though nothing was actually getting wet, making it seem that Erin was standing in the middle of the ghost of an ocean shore. Then she looked up at me with shimmering blue eyes. 'Oh, Z! Water is my affinity!'

I grinned at her. 'Yes, it is!'

Erik hurried back to me. This time I didn't have to prompt him to pick up the yellow candle.

'Damien, right?' he said.

'Totally right.'

237

He headed to Damien, who was fidgeting at the easternmost part of the circle where the element air should manifest. Erik offered the yellow candle to Damien. Damien didn't touch it. Instead, he peered around Erik to me. The boy looked scared to death.

'It's okay, go ahead and take it,' I told him.

'Are you sure it's going to be okay?' He glanced nervously around at what was now a large crowd of fledglings watching him expectantly.

I knew what was wrong. Damien was afraid he would fail, that he would be left out of the magic that was happening to the girls. In Soc class I'd learned that it was unusual for a gift as strong as an affinity for an element to be given to a male. Nyx gifted men with exceptional strength, and their affinities usually had to do with the physical, like Dragon, our fencing instructor, had been gifted with exceptional quickness and visual accuracy. Air was definitely a female affinity, and it would be nothing short of incredible for Nyx to gift Damien with an air affinity. But I had a calm, happy feeling deep inside me. I nodded at Damien and tried to telegraph confidence to him. 'I'm sure. Go on. I'll be busy thinking about how cute Erik is while you're calling air to you,' I said.

As Erik grinned over his shoulder at me Damien drew a deep breath, and looking a lot like he thought he was grabbing on to a live bomb, he took the candle from Erik.

'Superb! Glorious! Wondrous!' Damien made use of his large vocabulary while his brown hair lifted and his clothes flapped crazily in the sudden wind that surrounded him.

When he looked at me again happy tears were running down his cheeks. 'Nyx has given me a gift. *Me*,' he enunciated carefully, and I knew what he was saying in that one word – that he realized Nyx found him worthy even though his parents didn't, and even though much of his life people had made fun of him because he liked guys. I had to blink hard to keep from bawling like a baby.

'Yes, you,' I said firmly.

'Your friends are spectacular, Zoey.' Neferet's voice carried above the excited noise of the kids who were now converging on the four newly discovered talents.

The High Priestess was standing just inside the entrance to the rec hall, and I wondered how long she'd been there. I could see that there were a few professors with her, but they were in the shadow of the doorway and it was difficult to make out exactly who they were. *Okay. You can do this. You can face her*. I swallowed hard and forced my thoughts to focus on my friends and the miracles that had just happened to them.

'Yes, my friends are spectacular!' I agreed enthusiastically.

Neferet nodded. 'It is only right that Nyx, in her wisdom, has thought to gift you, a fledgling who has such unusual powers, with a group of friends who are also blessed with impressive powers of their own.' She dramatically swept out her arms. 'I prophesy that this group of fledglings will make history. Never before has so much been given to so many at the same time and place.' Her smile included all of us and she truly looked like a loving mother. I would have been as taken in as everyone else by her warmth and beauty if it hadn't been for the glimpse I got of the thin red line of a newly healing cut that marred her forearm. I shivered and forced my eyes and my thoughts from the evidence that what I'd witnessed had definitely not been a figment of my imagination.

Good thing, too, because Neferet had turned her attention to me.

'Zoey, I believe this is the perfect time to announce your blueprint for the new Dark Daughters and Sons.' I opened my mouth to start explaining what I had in mind (even though I hadn't planned on announcing the changes I wanted to make until *after* I'd cast the ritualistic circle and given the 'old' membership some tangible proof that I actually had been gifted by Nyx), but no one paid any attention to me. Everyone's attention was riveted on Neferet as she strode out into the room and stood not far from Shaunee so that my friend's manifestation of fire lit up the High Priestess like a spotlight made of flame. In the same powerful, alluring voice she used during rituals, Neferet spoke. Only this time she was using *my* words – *my* ideas.

'It is time the Dark Daughters had a foundation. It has been decided that Zoey Redbird will begin an era and a new tradition with her leadership. She will form a Prefect Council, made up of seven fledglings, of which she will be Head Prefect. The other members of the Council will be Shaunee Cole, Erin Bates, Stevie Rae Johnson, Damien Maslin, and Erik Night. There will be one more Prefect chosen from

Aphrodite's old Inner Circle to represent my wish for unity among the fledglings.'

Her wish? I ground my teeth together and tried to find my happy place while Neferet paused to let the general sounds of celebration die (which included the Twins, Stevie Rae, Damien, Erik, and Jack, cheering their brains out). Jeesh. She was making it seem like *she* was responsible for ideas I'd sweated over for weeks!

'The Prefect Council will be responsible for the workings of the new Dark Daughters and Sons, which includes being certain that from this day forth all members exemplify the following ideas: they should be authentic for air; they should be faithful for fire; they should be wise for water; they should be empathetic for earth; and they should be sincere for spirit. If a Dark Daughter or Son fails to uphold these new ideals, it will be the job of the Prefect Council to decide upon a penalty, which could include expulsion from the group.' She paused again, and I observed how serious and attentive everyone was, which was the exact reaction I had hoped for when I made this announcement during the actual Full Moon Ritual. 'I have also decided that it would behoove our fledglings to become more involved with the surrounding community. After all, ignorance breeds fear and hatred. So I want the Dark Daughters and Sons to begin working with a local charity. After much consideration I decided that the perfect organization would be Street Cats, the rescue charity for homeless cats.'

There was good-humored laughter at this, which was the

reaction Neferet had had when I'd told her *my* decision to have the Dark Daughters involved in that particular charity. I could not believe Neferet was taking credit for everything that I had told her that night at dinner.

'I will leave you now. This is Zoey's ritual, and I am simply here to show my heartfelt support for my talented fledgling.' She gave me a kind smile, which I made myself return. 'But first I have a gift for the new Prefect Council.' She clapped her hands together and five male vampyres I'd never seen before emerged from the shadows of the entryway. They were each carrying what looked like thick, rectangular tiles that must have been about a foot square and a couple of inches thick. They placed them at the floor by her feet and they disappeared back out the door. I stared at the things. They were a creamy color and looked like they might be wet. I had no clue what they were. Neferet's laughter bubbled around us, making me grind my teeth together. Did no one else think she sounded totally patronizing?

'Zoey, I'm shocked you don't recognize your own idea!'

'I – no. I don't know what they are,' I said.

'They're squares of wet cement. I remembered that you told me you wanted each of the members of the Prefect Council to have an imprint of his or her handprints made so that the fledgling's handprint will be preserved forever. Tonight six of the seven members of the new Council can do that.'

I blinked at her. Great. She was finally giving me credit for something, and it was Damien's idea. 'Thank you for the present,' I said, and then added quickly, 'And it was Damien's idea to make handprints, not mine.'

Her smile was blinding, and when she turned it on Damien I didn't have to look at him to know that he practically wriggled with pleasure. 'And what a lovely idea it was, too, Damien.' Then she addressed the entire room again. 'I am pleased that Nyx has gifted this group so fully. And I say blessed be to all of you, good night!' She dropped to the floor in a graceful curtsy. Then, to the cheers of the fledglings, she rose and made a skirt-flowing, magnificent exit.

Which left me standing in the middle of an un-cast circle feeling like I was all dressed up with nowhere to go.

CHAPTER TWENTY-ONE

IT TOOK FOREVER TO GET EVERYONE SETTLED DOWN AND IN place for the ritual to begin, especially because I couldn't show how I was really feeling – which was pissed. Not only would no one understand, but also no one would believe what I was beginning to see: that there was something dark and wrong about Neferet. And why should anyone understand or believe me? I was, after all, just a kid. No matter what powers Nyx had given me I was totally not in the same league with a High Priestess. Besides that, no one except me had witnessed the little puzzle pieces that were fitting together to create such a terrible picture.

Aphrodite would understand and believe me. I hated that the thought was true.

'Zoey, just let me know whenever you're ready and I'll start the music,' Jack called from the back corner of the rec hall where all the audio equipment was kept. Apparently the new kid was a genius with electronics, so I'd instantly drafted him to run the music for the ritual.

'Okay, just a sec. How about I nod at you when I'm ready?'

'Fine with me!' he said with a grin.

I backed up a few feet, realizing that, ironically, I was now standing almost exactly where Neferet had stood not long before. I tried to clear my mind of all the confusion and negatives that were swirling in it. My eyes traveled around the circle. There was a fairly large group of kids present – actually more than I had expected to show. They had quieted down, though there was still a general air of excitement in the room. The white candles in their tall glass containers illuminated the circle in a clean, bright light. I could see my four friends standing in their positions, waiting expectantly for me to begin the ritual. I focused on them and the wonderful gifts they had been given, and got ready to nod at Jack.

'I thought I'd volunteer my services to you.'

Loren's deep voice had me jumping and making an un-attractive little squeaking noise. He was standing behind me in the entranceway.

'Crap, Loren! You scared me so bad I almost peed on myself!' I blurted before I had time to control my dorky mouth. But I was telling the truth, Loren had me clutching my pearls in a total freak-out.

Apparently he didn't mind my inability to control my mouth. He gave me a long, slow, sexy smile. 'I thought you knew I was here.'

'No. I was a little distracted.'

'Stressed, I bet.' He touched my arm in a gesture that probably looked innocent. You know, friendly and professorially supportive. But felt like a caress, a really warm caress. His widening smile made me wonder about his vamp intuitiveness. If he could read any part of my mind I would just die. 'Well, I'm here to help you with that stress.'

Was he kidding? Just the sight of him made me lose my mind. Stress-free around Loren Blake? Not hardly.

'Really? How are you going to do that?' I asked with just a hint of a flirty smile, very aware that the entire room was watching us and that the entire room included my boyfriend.

'I'll do for you what I do for Neferet.'

The silence stretched between us as my mind wallowed around in the gutter wondering just exactly what he did for Neferet. Thankfully, he didn't let me wallow too long.

'Every High Priestess has a poet who recites ancient verse to evoke the presence of the Muse as she enters into her rituals. Today, I'm offering to recite for a very special High Priestess in training. Plus I believe there are some misconceptions that need to be cleared up.'

He crossed his fist over his heart in a gesture of respect people often used when they greeted Neferet. Unlike a cool, confident High Priestess, and very much like a dork, I just stood there staring at him. I mean, I didn't have a clue what he was talking about. Misconceptions? As in someone might believe I know what the hell I'm doing?

'But I will need your permission,' he continued. 'I wouldn't want to intrude upon your ritual.'

'Oh, no!' Then I realized what he must think my silence and then my blurted *oh, no* meant, and I got hold of myself. 'What I mean is that no, you definitely aren't intruding, and yes, I accept your offer. Graciously,' I added, wondering how I had ever felt grown and sexy around this man.

His smile made me want to melt in a pool at his feet. 'Excellent. Whenever you're ready, just give me the word and I'll begin your introduction.' He glanced over to where Jack was gawking at us. 'Mind if I have words with your assistant about the slight alteration in your plans?'

'No,' I said, feeling utterly surreal. As Loren walked past me his arm brushed mine intimately. Was I imagining the flirting that was going on between us? I looked at the circle and saw that everyone was staring at me. Reluctantly, I found Erik where he was standing beside Stevie Rae. He smiled at me and winked. Okay, it didn't seem like Erik had noticed anything wrong in Loren's behavior toward me. I glanced at Shaunee and Erin. They were following Loren with hungry eyes. They must have felt me looking at them, because they both managed to pull their gazes from Loren's butt. They waggled their eyebrows at me and grinned. They, too, were acting completely normal.

It was just me who was being weird about Loren.

'Get yourself together!' I hissed at myself under my breath. *Concentrate . . . concentrate . . . concentrate . . .*

'Zoey, I'm ready when you are.' Loren had moved back beside me.

I drew a deep, calming breath and lifted my head. 'I'm ready.'

His dark eyes held mine. 'Remember, trust your instincts. Nyx speaks to the hearts of her priestesses.' Then he walked a few paces into the room.

'It is a night for joy!' Loren's voice was not just deep and expressive, it was also commanding. He had the same ability Erik did to captivate a room using only his voice. Everyone instantly was silent, waiting eagerly for his next words. 'But you should know that the joy of this night isn't found only in the gifts Nyx has so visibly allowed to manifest here. Some of tonight's joy was born two nights ago when your new leader was deciding upon the future she wanted for the Dark Daughters and Sons.'

I felt a little start of surprise. I didn't know if anyone else really got what he was saying – that *I*, and not Neferet, had come up with the new standards for the Dark Daughters, but I appreciated his attempt to set things right.

'In celebration of Zoey Redbird, and her new vision for the Dark Daughters, I am honored to open her first ritual as your Head Prefect and High Priestess trainee with a classic poem about joy being newly born that was written by my namesake, the vampyre poet William Blake.' Loren looked back at me and mouthed, *You're on!* then he nodded to Jack, who hurriedly turned to the audio equipment.

The magical sounds of Enya's orchestral song 'Aldebaran' filled the room. I swallowed down the last of my nervousness, and began walking forward, tracing a path around the outside of the circle, like I'd watched both Neferet and Aphrodite do in the rituals they'd led. As they had, I moved in time with the music, making little impromptu turns and dance moves. I'd been really freaked out about this part of the ritual – I mean, I'm not clumsy, but I'm also not Ms Cheerleader/Pom Squad. Thankfully, it was lots easier than I'd imagined it to be. I'd chosen this particular music because of its beautiful, lilting beat, and also because I'd Googled Aldebaran and found out it was a giant star – and I thought music that celebrated the night sky was appropriate for tonight. It was a good choice, because it seemed as if the music was carrying me, moving my body gracefully around the room and overcoming my initial nerves and awkwardness. When Loren's voice began reciting the poem, he, too, echoed the cadence of the music, just like my body was, and it felt like we were making magic together.

"'I have no name,
I am but two days old.'
What shall I call thee?
'I happy am,
Joy is my name.'
Sweet joy befall thee!'

The words of the poem thrilled me. And as I moved toward the center of the circle I felt like I was literally personifying the emotion.

'Pretty joy!
Sweet joy but two days old,
Sweet joy I call thee;
Thou dost smile . . .'

Echoing the words of the poem, I smiled, loving the sense of magic and mystery that seemed to fill the room along with the music and Loren's voice.

'I sing the while—
Sweet joy befall thee.'

Somehow Loren timed it perfectly, and his poem concluded as I reached Nyx's table at the middle of the circle. I was only a little breathless as I smiled around the circle and said, 'Welcome to the first Full Moon Ritual for the new Dark Daughters and Sons!'

'Merry meet!' everyone responded automatically.

Without giving myself an opportunity to hesitate, I picked up the ornate ritualistic lighter and moved purposefully to stand before Damien. Air was the first element called when casting a circle, as well as the last to leave it when the circle was closed. I could feel Damien's excitement and expectation as if they were a physical force.

I smiled at him, swallowed hard to clear the dryness in my throat. When I spoke I tried to project my voice like Neferet. I'm not sure how good of a job I did. Let's just say I was glad that the circle was a relatively small one and the room was quiet.

'I call the element air first to our circle, and I ask that it guard us with winds of insight. Come to me, air!'

I touched the lighter to Damien's candle and it flared to life, even though he and I were suddenly standing in the middle of a very obvious whirlwind that lifted our hair and sang playfully within the full skirt of my beautiful dress. Damien laughed and whispered, 'Sorry, it's all so new to me that it's hard for me not to be a little overexuberant.'

'I understand completely,' I whispered back to him. Then I turned to my right and continued around the circle to Shaunee, who was looking unusually serious, like she was getting ready to take a math test. 'Relax,' I whispered, trying not to move my lips.

She nodded jerkily, still looking scared to death.

'I call the element of fire to our circle and ask that it burn brilliantly here with the light of might and passion, bringing both to guard and aid us. Come to me, fire!'

I started to touch the end of my lighter to the red candle Shaunee held, but before I could get it there the wick burst into a flickering white light that lifted up well past the lip of the glass jar holding it.

'Oopsie,' Shaunee mumbled.

I had to bite my cheek to keep from laughing, and I moved

quickly on to my right to where Erin was waiting with the blue candle clutched before her like it was a bird that would fly away if she didn't keep hold of it.

'I call water to this circle and ask that you guard us with your oceans of mystery and majesty, and nurture us as your rain does the grass and trees. Come to me, water!'

I lit Erin's blue candle, and it was the weirdest thing. I swear it was like I was suddenly transported to the shores of a lake. I could smell the water and feel it cool against my skin, even though I knew I was standing in the middle of a room and absolutely could not be anywhere near water.

'Guess I should tone it down a little,' Erin said softly.

'Nah,' I whispered. Then I headed to Stevie Rae. I thought she looked kinda pale, but she had a big grin on her face when I moved into the space in front of her.

'I'm ready!' she said, so loud the kids standing around us laughed softly.

'Good,' I said. 'Then I call earth to the circle, and ask that you guard us with the strength of stone and the richness of wheat-filled fields. Come to me, earth!' I lit the green candle and was washed in the scents of a meadow – surrounded by birdsong and flowers.

'It's just so cool!' Stevie Rae said.

'So is that.' Erik's voice surprised me and when I looked at him he pointed to the circle. Confused, I followed his hand to see a beautiful silver thread of light connecting each of my four friends – the four personifications of the elements – and making a boundary of power within the candles that had already lit the circumference.

'Like it was for us alone, only it's stronger now.' Stevie Rae whispered the words, but I could tell by Erik's startled look that he'd heard her. Guess I'd have some explaining to do later, but now was definitely not the time to worry about that.

I moved quickly back to Nyx's table at the center of the circle to complete the casting. I faced the purple candle that sat on the table.

'Finally, I call spirit to our circle and ask that you join us bringing insight and truth with you, so that the Dark Daughters and Sons may be guarded by integrity. Come to me, spirit!' I lit the candle. It blazed even brighter than Shaunee's, and the space around me was filled with the scents and sounds of all of the other four elements. They filled me, too, making me feel strong, calming and steadying me, even as they energized me. With steady hands I took up the braided length of eucalyptus and sage. I lit it with the spirit candle, let it burn for a little while, and then blew it out so that the fragrant smoke billowed in waves around me. Then I faced the circle and began my speech. I had been worried about what I was going to say since Neferet had showed up and literally stolen the biggest part of what I'd planned to talk about. But now, in the middle of the circle I'd cast, filled with the power of all five of the elements, my confidence had been restored as I hastily reworded lines in my head.

I wafted the braided smudge stick around me as I walked

the circle, meeting kids' eyes and trying to make everyone feel welcome.

'Tonight I wanted to change things from the type of incense burned, to the abuse of our classmates.' I spoke slowly, letting my words and the smoke they mingled with soak into the listening group. They all knew that under the leadership of Aphrodite the incense used during Dark Daughters' rituals had been heavily laced with pot, just as well as they knew that Aphrodite had loved bleeding some poor kid they called the 'refrigerator' and 'snack bar' and mixing his or her blood into the wine everyone sipped. Neither was going to happen again as long as I had anything to do with it. 'I chose to burn eucalyptus and sage tonight for the properties the herbs contain. For centuries eucalyptus has been used by the American Indians for healing, protection, and purification, just as they used white sage to drive out negative spirits, energies, and influences. Tonight I ask the five elements to empower these herbs and magnify their energy.'

Suddenly the air around me moved, drawing the smoke from the smudge braid with it in curls and wisps, carrying it throughout the circle as if a giant's hand was wafting through the air currents. The fledglings in the circle murmured in awe, and I sent a grateful, silent prayer to Nyx, thanking her for allowing my power over the elements to manifest so clearly.

When the circle quieted again I continued. 'The full moon is a magical time when the veil between the known and the unknown is thin, and can even be lifted. That is mysterious and wonderful, but tonight I want to focus on another aspect of the full moon – that it is an excellent time to complete, or end, things. What I want to end tonight is the old negative reputation of the Dark Daughters and Sons. As of this full moon night that part of us has ended, and a new time has begun.'

I kept walking, moving around the circle in a clockwise direction. Choosing my words carefully, I said, 'From here on the Dark Daughters and Sons will be a group filled with integrity and purpose, and I believe the fledglings Nyx chose to gift with elemental affinities represent the ideals of our new group well.' I smiled at Damien. 'My friend Damien is the most authentic person I know, even when being true to himself has been a hard thing to be. He represents air well.' The wind around Damien picked up as he smiled shyly at me.

I turned to Shaunee next. 'My friend Shaunee is the most faithful person I know. If she's on your side, she's there whether you're right or wrong – and if you're wrong she'll tell you about yourself, but she won't desert you. She represents fire well.' Shaunee's mocha skin glistened as her body glowed, unburned but alight with flame.

I went to Erin. 'My friend Erin's beauty sometimes fools people into thinking she has great hair, but no brains. It's not true. She is one of the wisest people I know, and Nyx proved that she looks to the interior when she chose Erin. She represents water well.' As I walked past her I could hear the sound of waves crashing on a shore.

I stopped in front of Stevie Rae. She was looking tired, with dark circles bruising the otherwise pale skin under her eyes, which made sense. Obviously, she'd been worrying too much about me – as usual. 'My friend Stevie Rae always knows when I'm happy or sad, stressed or relaxed. She worries about me; she worries about all of her friends, sometimes she is too empathetic, and I'm glad that now she has the earth she can draw strength from. She represents earth well.'

I grinned at Stevie Rae, and she smiled back at me, blinking fast so that she wouldn't cry. Then I walked to the center of the circle where I put down the smudge braid and picked up the purple candle. 'I'm not perfect, and I'm not going to pretend to be. What I promise you is that I sincerely want what is best for the Dark Daughters and Sons, and for all of the fledglings at the House of Night.' I was getting ready to say that I *hoped* I would represent spirit well when Erik's voice rang across the circle.

'She represents spirit well!' My four friends agreed loudly, and I was pleased (and more than a little surprised) to hear several other fledglings chime in with them.

CHAPTER TWENTY-TWO

WHEN I STARTED TALKING AGAIN EVERYONE INSTANTLY quieted down. 'Each of you who believes you can uphold the ideals of the Dark Daughters and Sons, and will try your best to be authentic, faithful, wise, empathetic, and sincere – you may continue your membership in this group. But I want you to know that there will be new fledglings joining us, and they won't be judged on the way they look or who their best friends are. Make your decision, and see me or any of the other Prefects and let us know if you want to stay with the group.' I caught the eyes of some of Aphrodite's old buddies and added, 'We won't hold the past against you. It's how you act from here on that counts.' A couple of the girls looked guiltily away from me, and a few more looked like they were trying hard not to cry. I was especially glad to see Deino meet my gaze steadily and nod somberly – maybe she wasn't so 'terrible' after all.

I put down the purple candle and picked up the big ceremonial goblet I'd filled earlier with sweet red wine. 'And now let's drink in celebration of a full moon, and an end that leads to a new beginning.' As I worked my way around the circle offering the wine to each fledgling, I recited a Full Moon Ritual prayer I'd found in the old *Mystical Rites of the Crystal Moon* by Fiona, the Vampyre Poet Laureate of the early 1800s.

'Airy light of the moon
Mystery of the deep earth
Power of the flowing water
Warmth of the burning flame
In Nyx's name we call to thee!'

I focused on the words to the beautiful old poem, and sincerely hoped that tonight actually would be the beginning of something special.

'Healing of ills
Righting of wrongs
Cleansing of impurity
Desiring of truths
In Nyx's name we call to thee!'

I moved quickly around the circle, and was happy that the majority of the kids smiled at me and murmured 'Blessed be' after they sipped from the goblet. Guess no one minded that tonight's wine was absent the blood of a bullied fledgling. (I refused to think about how much I would have loved the taste of fledgling blood mixed with the wine.)

> 'Sight of the cat
> Hearing of the dolphin
> Speed of the snake
> Mystery of the phoenix
> In Nyx's name we call to thee
> and ask that with us you will blessed be!'

I drank the last of the wine and put the goblet back on the table. In reverse order, I thanked each element and sent them away as in turn Stevie Rae, Erin, Shaunee, and finally Damien blew out their candles. Then I completed the ritual by saying, 'This Full Moon Rite is ended. Merry meet and merry part and merry meet again!'

The fledglings echoed, 'Merry meet and merry part and merry meet again!'

And that was it. My first ritual as leader of the Dark Daughters was over.

I was actually feeling a little empty and almost sad – you know, kinda like the letdown you have after you've waited and waited for spring break, and then it comes and you realize you don't have anything to do now that there's no school. Well, honestly I only had about a second to feel like that before my friends converged on me, all talking at once about handprints and cement drying too soon.

'Please. Like my Twin can't call in a little water to soup that cement right up if it has the nerve to dry before we can make our handprints,' Shaunee said.

Erin nodded. 'That's what I'm here for, Twin. That and being an example of incredibly good fashion sense.'

'Both are very important, Twin.'

Damien gave a big, exaggerated eye roll.

'Y'all, let's just make the handprints and get out of here. My stomach kinda hurts and I got a killer headache,' Stevie Rae said.

I nodded in complete understanding with Stevie Rae. We'd slept so late we hadn't had time to eat anything. I was starved, too. And I'd probably get a caffeine-deprived headache myself if I didn't eat and drink something pretty soon.

'I agree with Stevie Rae. Let's hurry and make the handprints, and then we can join everyone else in the other room with the food.'

'Neferet had the cooks make a special taco bar. I stuck my head in there earlier and it really looked yummy,' Damien said.

'Well, come on then. Stop dillydallying,' Stevie Rae grumped while she practically stomped over to one of the cement squares.

'What's wrong with her?' Damien whispered.

'Clearly she's having PMS issues,' Shaunee said.

'Yeah, I noticed earlier she was looking kinda pale and bloated, but I didn't want to be mean and say anything,' Erin said.

'Let's just make the prints and eat,' I said, picking my own cement square, pleased that Erik chose the one right beside me.

'Um, I wetted some towels in the kitchen so you guys could wipe your hands when you're done,' said Jack, who was looking very cute and nervous holding an armload of damp white towels.

I smiled at him. 'That's really nice of you, Jack. Okay, let's do it!'

Close up I could tell that the cement had been poured into what looked like cardboard molds, and I figured it would be easy to tear off the cardboard once the cement had dried. I still liked Damien's idea of putting the handprints in the court-yard outside the dining hall – kinda like weird stepping stones.

The cement was definitely still wet, and there was a lot of laughing going on as we made our prints and then used twigs Jack ran out to collect (the kid was certainly handy to have around) to write our names.

While we were wiping our hands with the towels and studying our work, Erik leaned close to say, 'I'm really glad Neferet chose me for the Prefect Council.'

I kept my mouth shut and nodded. If I told him that actu-ally I had chosen him, with Damien, Stevie Rae, and the Twins agreeing, I would probably let the air right out of his sails. Neferet was a big deal. And it really wouldn't hurt anything (except my ego) to let him think that she was the one who picked him. I was just getting ready to change the subject and call everyone into the room with the food when I heard some weird sounds to my right. When I realized what the weird sounds were I felt my heart clench.

Stevie Rae was coughing.

Damien was directly to my right. Then came the Twins. Stevie Rae had chosen the block of cement farthest to the right, and closest to the entrance to the room with the food. A bunch of the kids were already eating, but about half of the group had stayed to watch us make the handprints and talk, so there were several more people between Stevie Rae and me, but I could see that she was still on her knees in front of her cement block. She must have felt my eyes on her because she sat back on her heels and looked over at me. I could hear her clear her throat. She gave me a tired smile and I saw her shrug and then mouth the words, *Frog in my throat*. And I remembered that's what she'd said during the monologue performance. She'd been coughing then, too.

Without looking at him I told Erik, 'Get Neferet. Fast!'

I stood up and started moving toward her. Stevie Rae had already made her handprint and signed it, and she was wiping her hands on a towel. Before I could get to her a wrenching cough claimed her. Her shoulders shook with it. She had the towel pressed to her mouth.

Then I smelled it, and it was like I'd slammed into an invisible wall. The scent of blood washed over me, seductive, alluring, and horrible. I stopped and closed my eyes. Maybe if I stayed very still and didn't open them I could convince myself that this was all just a bad dream, that I would wake up in a few hours, still nervous about the Full Moon Ritual, with Nala snoring peacefully on my pillow and Stevie Rae snoring just as peacefully in the bed beside me.

I felt an arm go around me, and still I didn't move.

'She needs you, Zoey.' Damien's voice was shaking only a little.

I opened my eyes then and stared at him. He was already crying. 'I don't think I can do this.'

His grip on my shoulders tightened. 'Yes, you can. You have to.'

'Zoey!' Stevie Rae sobbed.

Without another thought, I wrenched myself from Damien's arm and ran to my best friend. She was on her knees clutching the blood-soaked towel to her chest. She coughed and gagged again, and more blood sprayed from her mouth and nose.

'Get me more towels!' I snapped to Erin, who was sitting white-faced and silent beside Stevie Rae. Then I crouched in front of Stevie Rae. 'It's going to be okay. I promise. It's going to be okay.'

Stevie Rae was crying, and her tears were tinged red. She shook her head. 'It's not. It can't be. I'm dying.' Her voice was weak and gurgled as she tried to speak through the blood hemorrhaging in her lungs and throat.

'I'm staying with you. I won't let you be alone,' I said.

She grasped my hand and I was shocked by how cold hers was. 'I'm scared, Z.'

'I know, I'm scared, too. But we'll get through this together. I promise.'

Erin handed me a pile of towels. I took the blood-soaked towel from Stevie Rae's hands, then I started wiping her face and mouth with a clean one, but she started coughing again and I couldn't keep up. There was just too much blood. And now Stevie Rae was shaking so hard that she couldn't hold a towel herself. With a cry, I pulled her onto my lap and wrapped my arms around her, and like she was a child again, I began rocking her, telling her over and over that it would be all right, that I wouldn't leave her.

'Zoey, this might help.' I'd forgotten that there were other people in the room, so Damien's voice surprised me. I looked up to see that he was holding the relit green candle that represented earth. Then somehow, in the midst of my fear and despair, my instinct kicked in and I suddenly felt very calm.

'Come down here, Damien. Hold the candle close to her.'

Damien dropped to his knees, and oblivious to the growing pool of blood that surrounded us and soaked us, he pressed close to Stevie Rae, holding the candle in front of her face. I felt more than I saw Erin and Shaunee kneel on either side of me, and I drew strength from their presence.

'Stevie Rae, open your eyes, honey,' I said softly.

With a nasty, gurgling breath, Stevie Rae's eyelids fluttered open. The whites of her eyes were totally red and more pink tears leaked down her colorless cheeks, but her eyes caught on the candle, and they held.

'I call the element earth to us now.' My voice strengthened and got louder as I spoke. 'And I ask that earth be with this very special fledgling, Stevie Rae Johnson, who has been so newly gifted with an affinity for the element. Earth is our home – our provider – and earth is where we will all someday return. Tonight I ask that earth hold and comfort Stevie Rae, and make her journey home a peaceful one.'

With a rush of fragrant air we were suddenly enveloped in the scents and sounds of an orchard. I smelled apples and hay, and heard birds chirping and bees buzzing.

Stevie Rae's reddened lips tilted up. Her eyes never left the green candle, but she whispered, 'I'm not scared anymore, Z.'

Then I heard the front door burst open and Neferet was there crouched beside me. She started to move Damien and the Twins out of the way and take Stevie Rae from my arms.

My voice blasted the room with its power, and I saw even Neferet jerk back with surprise. 'No! We stay with her. She needs her element and she needs us.'

'Very well,' Neferet said. 'It's very nearly over anyway. Help me get her to drink this so that her passing will be painless.'

I was going to take the vial filled with milky liquid from her when Stevie Rae spoke with surprising clearness. 'I don't need it. Since earth came there hasn't been any pain.'

'Of course there hasn't been, child.' Neferet touched Stevie Rae's blood-smeared cheek and I felt her body relax and stop trembling completely. Then the High Priestess looked up. 'Help Zoey lift her onto the stretcher. Keep them together. Let's get her to the infirmary,' Neferet told me.

I nodded. Strong hands gripped Stevie Rae and me, and in moments I was placed on the stretcher with Stevie Rae still in my arms. Surrounded by Damien, Shaunee, Erin, and Erik, we were carried swiftly out into the night. Later, I remembered so many weird things about the short trip from the rec hall to the infirmary – how it was snowing heavily, but that it seemed none of the flakes touched us. And it seemed abnormally quiet, as if the earth were holding itself still because it was already mourning. I kept whispering to Stevie Rae, telling her that everything was okay, and that there was nothing to be scared of. I remember her leaning forward and vomiting blood over the side of the stretcher and how the scarlet drops looked against the clean white of the new-fallen snow.

Then we were inside the infirmary, and lifted off the stretcher onto a bed. Neferet gestured for my friends to move close to us. Damien crawled up beside Stevie Rae. He was still holding the lit green candle, and he lifted it so that if she opened her eyes again, Stevie Rae would see it. I drew a deep breath. The air around us was still filled with apple blossoms and birdsong.

Then Stevie Rae opened her eyes. She blinked a couple times, looking confused, then she looked up at me and smiled.

'Would you tell my mama and daddy that I love them?' I could understand her, but she sounded weak, and her voice was filled with a terrible wetness.

'Of course I will,' I said quickly.

'And do something else for me?'

'Anything.'

'You don't really have a mama or a daddy, so would you tell my mama that you're their daughter now? I think I'd worry about them less if I know y'all have each other.'

Tears were pouring down my cheeks and I had to take

several sobbing breaths before I could answer her. 'Don't worry about anything. I'll tell them.'

Her eyes fluttered and she smiled again. 'Good. Mama will make chocolate chip cookies for you.' With obvious effort, she opened her eyes again and looked around at Damien, Shaunee, and Erin. 'Y'all stick with Zoey. Don't let anything pull you apart.'

'Don't worry,' Damien whispered through his tears.

'We'll take care of her for you,' Shaunee managed to say. Erin was clutching Shaunee's hand and crying hard, but she nodded in agreement and smiled at Stevie Rae.

'Good,' Stevie Rae said. Then she closed her eyes. 'Z, I think I'm gonna sleep for a while now, 'kay?'

'Okay, honey,' I said.

Her eyelids lifted once more and she looked up at me. 'Will you stay with me?'

I hugged her closer. 'I'm not going anywhere. You just rest. We'll all be right here with you.'

''Kay . . .' she said softly.

Stevie Rae shut her eyes. She took a few more gurgling breaths. Then I felt her go completely limp in my arms and she didn't breathe again. Her lips opened just a little, as if she was smiling. Blood trickled from her mouth, her eyes, nose, and ears, but I couldn't smell it. All I could smell were the scents of the earth. Then, with an enormous rush of meadow-filled wind, the green candle went out, and my best friend died.

CHAPTER TWENTY-THREE

'ZOEY, SWEETHEART, YOU HAVE TO LET HER GO.'

Damien's voice didn't really register in my mind. I mean, I could hear his words, but it was like he was speaking a weird foreign language. I couldn't make any sense of them.

'Zoey, why don't you come with us, now?'

That was Shaunee. *Shouldn't Erin chime in?* I'd barely formed the thought when I heard, 'Yeah, Zoey, we need you to come with us.' *Oh, there's Erin.*

'She's in shock. Speak calmly to her and try to get her to release Stevie Rae's body,' Neferet said.

Stevie Rae's body. The words echoed weirdly through my

mind. I was holding on to something. I could tell that much. But my eyes were closed and I was really, really cold. I didn't want to open them, and I didn't think I'd ever get warm again.

'I have an idea.' Damien's voice bounced around inside my mind like a pinball machine. 'We don't have candles and we don't have a sacred circle, but it's not like Nyx isn't here. Let's use our elements to help her. I'll go first.'

I felt a hand grasp my upper arm, and then I heard Damien muttering something about calling air to blow about the scent of death and despair. A big wind whooshed around me, and I shivered.

'I better go next. She looks cold.' That was Shaunee. Someone else touched my arm and after some words I didn't quite catch, I felt surrounded by warmth, like I was standing very close to an open fireplace.

'My turn,' Erin said. 'I call water and ask that you wash from my friend and future High Priestess the sadness and pain she's feeling. I know all of it can't go away, but could you please take just enough from her that she can bear to go on?' Her words registered more clearly on my mind, but I still didn't want to open my eyes.

'There's still one more element in the circle.'

I was surprised to hear Erik. Part of me wanted to open my eyes so that I could look at him, but the rest of me, too much of me, refused to move.

'But Zoey always manifests spirit,' Damien said.

'Right now Zoey can't manifest anything by herself. Let's give her some help.' Two strong hands gripped my shoulders, along with the other hands that grasped places on my arms. 'I have no affinity for these things, but I do care about what happens to Zoey, and she has been gifted with an affinity for all five elements,' Erik said. 'So I, along with all of her friends, ask that the element spirit help her wake up so that she can get over the death of her best friend.'

Like an electric shock, my body was suddenly zapped, filled with an incredible sense of awareness. Against my closed eyelids I saw Stevie Rae's smiling face. It wasn't bloodstained and pale, like it had been the last time she'd smiled at me. The image I saw was a healthy, happy Stevie Rae, and she was walking into a beautifully familiar woman's arms while she laughed joyfully.

Nyx, I thought, *Stevie Rae is being embraced by the Goddess.*

And my eyes opened.

'Zoey! You're back with us!' Damien cried.

'Z, you're going to need to let go of Stevie Rae now,' Erik said somberly.

I looked from Damien to Erik. Then my eyes went to Shaunee and Erin. All four of my friends had their hands on me, and they were all crying. Then I realized what it was I was clutching in my arms. Slowly, I looked down.

Stevie Rae looked peaceful. She was too pale, and her lips were turning blue, but her eyes were closed and her face was relaxed, even though it was covered with blood. Her blood wasn't dripping from her orifices anymore, and part of my mind realized that it smelled wrong – stale, old, dead. Almost like mold.

'Z,' Erik said. 'You have to let her go.'

I met his eyes. 'But I told her I'd stay with her.' My voice sounded strange and scratchy.

'You did. You stayed with her the whole time. She's gone now, so there's nothing else you can do.'

'Please, Zoey,' Damien said.

'Neferet needs to clean her up so it's okay for her mom to see her,' Shaunee said.

'You know she wouldn't want her mom and dad to see her all covered with blood,' Erin said.

'Okay, but . . . but I don't know how to let her go.' My voice cracked and I felt fresh tears leak down my cheeks.

'I'll take her from you, Zoeybird.' Neferet held her arms out, like she was ready to receive a baby I'd been holding. She looked so sad and beautiful and strong – so familiar – that I forgot all the questions I had about her and simply nodded and slowly leaned forward. Neferet slid her arms under Stevie Rae's body and lifted her away from me. She shifted her hold on Stevie Rae, and then turned and laid her gently on the empty bed beside mine.

I looked down at myself. My new black dress was soaked with blood that was already stiffening and drying. The silver threads still tried to glitter in the gaslights of the room, but instead of the pure light they gave off before, they now sparkled with a copper hue. I couldn't keep looking at them. I had to move. I had to get out of there and get this dress off. I swung my feet over the side of the bed and tried to stand up, but the room pitched and rolled around me. Then the strong hands of my friends were back on my arms, and I felt anchored to the earth through their warmth.

'Take her back to her room. Get her out of that dress and cleaned up. Then be sure she goes to bed and is kept warm and quiet.' Neferet was talking about me like I wasn't there, but I didn't care. I didn't want to be there. I didn't want any of this. 'Give her this to drink before you put her to bed. It will help her sleep without nightmares.' I felt Neferet's soft hand on my cheek. The warmth that passed from her body to mine was a shock, and I instinctively jerked away. 'Be well, Zoeybird,' Neferet said kindly. 'I give you my word that you will recover from this.' I didn't look at her, but I knew she shifted her attention back to my friends. 'Take her to the dorm now.'

I was moving forward. Erik was on one side of me with his hand securely under my right elbow, Damien was on my left, holding me tightly, too. The Twins were close behind us. No one spoke as they led me from the room. I glanced back over my shoulder to see Stevie Rae's lifeless body on the bed. It almost looked like she was sleeping, but I knew better. I knew she was dead.

The five of us left the infirmary and walked into the snowy night. I shivered, and we paused long enough for Erik to take off his jacket and drape it around my shoulders. I liked the way it smelled, and tried to think of it and not the hushed fledglings we were passing and how as we approached each of them, whether they were alone or in groups, the kids moved off the sidewalk, bowed their heads, and silently crossed their right fists over their hearts.

We got to the dorm in what seemed like seconds. As we entered the main room the girls who were watching TV and sitting around in groups all fell totally silent. I didn't look at any of them. I just let Erik and Damien lead me to the stairs, but before we got there Aphrodite was blocking our way. I blinked hard to focus on her face. She looked tired.

'I'm sorry Stevie Rae died. I didn't want her to,' Aphrodite said.

'Don't say shit to us, you fucking hag!' Shaunee snarled. She and Erin stepped forward, looking like they wanted to beat the crap out of Aphrodite.

'No, wait,' I made myself say, and they hesitated. 'I need to talk to Aphrodite.'

My friends looked at me like I'd lost every bit of my mind, but I stepped out of the nest of arms that were holding me up and walked unsteadily a few paces away from the group. Aphrodite hesitated, and then she followed me.

'Did you know about what was going to happen to Stevie Rae?' I asked, keeping my voice low. 'Did you have a vision about her?'

Aphrodite shook her head slowly. 'No. I just had a *feeling*. I knew something terrible was going to happen tonight.'

'I get them, too,' I said softly.

'Feelings about things or people?'

I nodded.

'They're harder than my visions – not as specific. Did you have a feeling about Stevie Rae?' she asked.

'No. I was clueless, even though now I can look back and see signs that something was wrong with her.'

Aphrodite met my eyes. 'You couldn't have stopped it. You couldn't have saved her. Nyx didn't let you know it was going to happen because there was nothing you could have done.'

'How do you know? Neferet says Nyx has deserted you,' I said bluntly. I knew I was purposefully being cruel. I didn't care. I wanted everyone to hurt as much as I did.

Still looking me straight in the eyes, Aphrodite said, 'Neferet lies.' She started to walk away, but changed her mind and came back. 'And don't drink whatever she gave you,' she said. Then she left the room.

Erik, Damien, and the Twins were at my side in a blink.

'Don't listen to whatever that hag had to say,' Shaunee huffed.

'If she said something nasty about Stevie Rae, we're gonna kick her ass,' Erin said.

'No. It wasn't anything like that. She just said she was sorry, that's all.'

'Why did you want to talk to her?' Erik asked. He and Damien had ahold of me again, and now they were leading me up the stairs.

'I wanted to know if she had a vision about Stevie Rae's death,' I said.

'But Neferet has made it clear that Nyx has turned her back on Aphrodite,' Damien said.

'I wanted to ask anyway.' I was going to add that Aphrodite had been right about the accident that almost happened to my grandma, but I couldn't say anything in front of Erik. We came to the door to my room – *our* room – Stevie Rae's and mine, and I stopped. Erik opened it for me and we stepped in.

'No!' I gasped. 'They've taken her stuff! They can't do that!' Everything that was Stevie Rae was gone – from the cowboy boot lamp and the Kenny Chesney poster, to the gyrating Elvis clock. The shelves over her computer desk were empty. Her computer was gone. I knew if I looked in her closet, all of her clothes would be gone, too.

Erik put his arm around me. 'It's what they always do. Don't worry, they didn't throw away her stuff. They just moved it so that it wouldn't make you sad. If there's something of hers you want, and her family doesn't mind, they'll give it to you.'

I didn't know what to say. I didn't want Stevie Rae's *stuff*. I wanted Stevie Rae.

'Zoey, you really need to get out of those clothes and take a hot shower,' Damien said gently.

'Okay,' I said.

'While you're in the shower we'll get you something to eat,' Shaunee said.

'I'm not hungry.'

'You need to eat. We'll get you something simple, like soup. Okay?' Erin said. She looked so upset, and was so obviously trying to do something, anything, to make me feel better that I nodded. Plus, I was too tired to argue with anyone. 'Okay.'

'I'd stay, but it's past curfew and I can't be in the girls' dorm,' Erik said.

'That's okay. I understand.'

'I want to stay, too, but well, I'm not actually a girl,' Damien said. I knew he was trying to make me smile, so I made my lips move up. I imagined I looked like one of those scary, sad clowns who had a smile painted on his face along with a teardrop.

Erik hugged me, and so did Damien. Then they left.

'Do you need one of us to stay while you take a shower?' Shaunee asked.

'No, I'm fine.'

'Okay. Well . . .' Shaunee looked like she was going to cry again.

'We'll be right back.' Erin took Shaunee's hand and they left the room, closing it with a soft, final click.

I moved carefully, like someone had switched me 'on,' but had set my speed at slow. I took off my dress, bra, and panties and put them in the plastic-lined wastepaper basket that sat in the corner of our – I mean *my* – room. I closed up the plastic bag and put it by the door. I knew one of the Twins would throw it away for me. I went into the bathroom and meant to get straight into the shower, but my reflection caught me, and I stopped, staring. I had turned into a familiar stranger again. I looked horrible. I was pale, but I had bruised-looking circles under my eyes. The tattoos on my face, back, and shoulders stood out in stark, sapphire contrast to the white of my skin and the rust-colored smears of blood that covered my body. My eyes looked huge and unusually dark. I hadn't taken off my Dark Daughters' necklace. The silver of the chain and the copper of the garnets caught the light and gleamed.

'Why?' I whispered. 'Why did you let Stevie Rae die?'

I didn't really expect an answer, and none came. So I got in the shower and stood there for a very long time, letting my tears mix with the water and the blood and wash down the drain.

CHAPTER TWENTY-FOUR

WHEN I CAME OUT OF THE BATHROOM SHAUNEE AND ERIN were sitting on Stevie Rae's bed. They had a tray between them that held a bowl of soup, some crackers, and a can of brown pop, nondiet. They had been talking in low voices, but as soon as I entered the room they stopped.

I sighed and sat on my bed. 'If you guys start acting all abnormal around me I'm not going to be able to handle it.'

'Sorry,' they muttered together, looking sheepishly at each other. Then Shaunee handed me the tray. I looked at the food like I couldn't remember what to do with it.

'You need to eat so that you can take the stuff Neferet gave us to give you,' Erin said.

'Plus, it might make you feel better,' Shaunee said.

'I don't think I'll ever feel better.'

Erin's eyes filled with tears that spilled over and dripped down her cheeks. 'Don't say that, Zoey. If you never feel better that means none of us will, either.'

'You have to try, Zoey. Stevie Rae would be pissed if you didn't,' Shaunee said, sniffing through her tears.

'You're right. She would be.' I picked up the spoon and started sipping at the soup. It was chicken noodle, and it made a familiar, warm path down my throat, expanding into my body and chasing away some of the terrible chill I'd been feeling.

'And when she got pissed that accent of hers went out of control,' Shaunee said.

That made Erin and me smile.

'*Y'all be niiice*,' Erin twanged, repeating the words Stevie Rae had said to the Twins a gazillion times.

We smiled at that, and the soup began to seem easier to swallow. About halfway through the bowl, I had a sudden thought. 'They're not going to have a funeral or anything like that for her, are they?'

The Twins shook their heads. 'Nope,' Shaunee said.

'They never do,' Erin said.

'Well, Twin, I think some of the kids' parents do, but that'd be back in their hometown.'

'True, Twin,' Erin said. 'But I don't think anyone from

here is going to travel to . . .' she trailed off, thinking. 'What was the name of that little bumpkin town Stevie Rae was from?'

'Henrietta,' I said. 'Home of the Fighting Hens.'

'Fighting Hens?' the Twins said together.

I nodded. 'It drove Stevie Rae crazy. Even in her bumpkinness she wasn't okay with being a Fighting Hen.'

'Hens fight?' Shaunee asked.

Erin shrugged. 'How should I know, Twin?'

'I thought only cocks fought,' I said. We all looked at each other and said, 'Cocks!' and then burst out into laughter, which pretty soon was mixed with tears. 'Stevie Rae would have thought that was hilarious,' I said when I could catch my breath again.

'Is it really going to be okay, Zoey?' Shaunee asked.

'Is it?' Erin echoed.

'I think so,' I said.

'How?' Shaunee asked.

'I don't really know. I think all we can do is take one day at a time.'

Surprisingly, I'd finished all my soup. I did feel better – warmer, more normal. I was also unbelievably tired. The Twins must have noticed my eyelids getting heavy, because Erin took my tray. Shaunee handed me a little vial of milky liquid.

'Neferet said you should drink this, that it'll help you sleep without nightmares,' she said.

'Thanks.' I took it from her, but I didn't drink it. She and

Erin just stood there looking at me. 'I'll take it in a minute. After I go to the bathroom. Just leave my pop in case it tastes nasty.'

That seemed to satisfy them. Before they left Shaunee said, 'Zoey, can we get you anything else?'

'No, thanks though.'

'You'll call us if you need anything, right?' Erin said. 'We promised Stevie Rae . . .' Her voice broke and Shaunee finished for her, 'We promised her we'd take care of you, and we live up to our promises.'

'I'll call you,' I said.

''Kay,' they said. 'Night . . .'

'Night,' I called to the closing door.

As soon as they were gone I poured the creamy white liquid down the sink and threw away the vial.

Then I was alone. I glanced at my alarm clock, 6:00 A.M. It was amazing how much things could change in just a few hours. I tried not to, but flashes of Stevie Rae's death kept playing across my mind, like there was a horrible movie screen stuck inside my eyes. I jumped when my cell phone rang, and checked the caller ID. It was my grandma's number! Relief surged through me. I flipped the phone open and struggled not to burst into tears.

'I'm so glad you called, Grandma!'

'Little Bird, I woke from a dream about you. Is everything all right?' Her worried tone said she already knew it wasn't, which didn't surprise me. For my whole life my grandma and I had been linked.

'No. Nothing is right,' I whispered as I began to cry again. 'Grandma, Stevie Rae died tonight.'

'Oh, Zoey! I'm so terribly sorry!'

'She died in my arms, Grandma, just minutes after Nyx gifted her with an affinity for the element earth.'

'It must have been a great comfort for her that you were with her at the end.' I could hear that Grandma was crying now, too.

'We were all with her, all of my friends.'

'And Nyx must have been with her, too.'

'Yes,' my voice caught on a sob. 'I think the Goddess was, but I don't understand it, Grandma. It doesn't make any sense that Nyx would gift Stevie Rae, and then let her die.'

'Death never makes sense when it happens to the young. But I believe that your Goddess was close to Stevie Rae, even though her death happened too soon, and now she is resting peacefully with Nyx.'

'I hope so.'

'I wish I could come visit you, but with all this snow the roads out here are impossible. How about I fast and pray for Stevie Rae today?'

'Thank you, Grandma. I know she'd appreciate that.'

'And, honey, you have to move past this.'

'How, Grandma?'

'By honoring her memory by living a life she'd be proud of you for living. Live for her, too.'

'It's hard, Grandma, especially when the vamps want us to just forget about the kids who die. They're treated like speed bumps, just something to pause a little about, and then go on.'

'I don't mean to second-guess your High Priestess, or any of the other adult vampyres, but that seems shortsighted. Death is more difficult if it goes unacknowledged.'

'That's what I think. Actually, that's what Stevie Rae thought, too.' Then an idea came to me, along with a *feeling* that it was the right thing to do. 'I can change that. With or without permission, I'm going to be sure Stevie Rae's death is honored. She's going to be more than a speed bump.'

'Don't get in trouble, honey.'

'Grandma, I am the most powerful fledgling in the history of vampyres. I think I should be willing to get in a little trouble for something I feel strongly about.'

Grandma paused, then she said, 'I think you might be right about that, Zoeybird.'

'I love you, Grandma.'

'I love you, too, *u-we-tsi-a-ge-ya*.' The Cherokee word for daughter made me feel loved and safe. 'And now I want you to try to sleep. Know that I'll be praying for you, and asking the spirits of our grandmothers to watch over and comfort you.'

'Thanks, Grandma. Bye.'

'Good-bye, Zoeybird.'

I closed the phone softly. I felt better now that I'd talked to Grandma. Before it had been like there was a huge, invisible weight pressing down on my chest. Now that it had shifted some it was easier for me to breathe. I started to lie down, and Nala popped in through the kitty door, leaped up on my bed, and instantly began *me-uf-ow*-ing at me. I petted her and told her how glad I was to see her, and then glanced over at Stevie Rae's empty bed. She always laughed at Nala's grumpiness, and said she sounded like an old woman, but she had loved the cat as much as me. Tears stung my eyes and I wondered if there was a limit to how much someone could cry. Just then my cell phone chimed that I had a new text message. I rubbed my eyes clear and flipped my phone back open.

R U OK? Somethings wrong.

It was Heath. Well, at least now there could be no doubt at all that he and I were linked through an Imprint. And what the hell I was going to do about that, I didn't know.

Bad day. My best friend died. I text messaged him back.

It was so long that I didn't think he was going to respond. Then finally my phone chimed again.

My friends have died 2.

I closed my eyes. How could I have forgotten that two of Heath's friends had just recently been killed?

I'm sorry. I typed back.

Me 2. Do u want me to come see u?

The instant, powerful *yes!* that burst through my body surprised me, but I suppose it shouldn't have. It would be wonderful to find oblivion in Heath's arms . . . in the scarlet seduction of Heath's blood . . .

No. I typed hastily, my hands shaking. You have school.

Nuh uh SNOW DAY!

I smiled, and spent a sweet second or two wishing that I could return to the time when a snow day meant a mini-holiday of tramping through snow with my friends and then curling up to watch rented movies and eat delivery pizza. My phone chimed again, breaking into my past-life fantasy.

I'll make u feel btr fri

I sighed. I'd totally forgotten about promising Heath I'd meet him after the game Friday. I shouldn't meet him. I knew it. Actually, I should go to Neferet and confess everything about Heath and have her help me fix it.

Neferet lies. Aphrodite's voice whispered through my mind. No. I couldn't go to Neferet, and for more reasons than just Aphrodite's warning. Something felt wrong about Neferet. I couldn't confide in her. My phone chimed.

Zo?

I sighed. I was so tired that it was getting hard to concentrate. I started to text back no and tell Heath that I just couldn't meet him, no matter how much I'd like to. I even hit the N and the O keys. Then I stopped, back-spaced over them, and resolutely typed: OK.

What the hell. It felt as if my life was unraveling like the hem of an old skirt. I didn't want to tell Heath no, and worrying about our Imprint was just one thing too many to worry about right now.

OK! Came his quick reply.

I sighed again, shut off my phone, and sat heavily on my bed, petting Nala, staring at nothing in particular, and wishing desperately that I could turn the clock back a day . . . or maybe even a year . . . Eventually I noticed that, for whatever reason, the vamps who had cleared out Stevie Rae's stuff had forgotten the old, handmade quilt that she kept folded on the end of her bed. I put Nala on my pillow and got up, pulling the quilt from Stevie Rae's bed. Then Nala and I curled up under it.

It felt like every molecule of my body was tired, but I couldn't sleep. I guess I missed Stevie Rae's soft snores and the sense that I wasn't alone. A sadness washed over me that was so deep I thought I might drown in it.

Two soft knocks came on the door. Then it opened slowly. I half sat up to see Shaunee and Erin, both in their pajamas and slippers, clutching pillows and blankets.

'Can we sleep with you?' Erin asked.

'We didn't want to be alone,' Shaunee said.

'Yeah, and we thought you might not want to be alone, either,' Erin finished.

'You're right. I don't.' I swallowed back more tears. 'Come on in.'

They shuffled in and, with only a little hesitation, piled onto Stevie Rae's bed. Their long-haired silver-gray cat, Beelzebub, hopped up between them. Nala raised her head from my pillow to glance at him, and then, as if he were beneath her queenly notice, she curled back up and went promptly to sleep.

I was just drifting off to sleep when another soft knock came on the door. This time it didn't open, so I called, 'Who is it?'

'Me.'

Shaunee, Erin, and I blinked at each other. Then I hurried over to the door and opened it to find Damien standing in the hall wearing flannel pj's with pink bow-tied bears all over them. He looked kinda damp, and unmelted snowflakes were caught in his hair. He was carrying a sleeping bag and a pillow. I grabbed his arm and pulled him quickly into the room. His chubby tabby cat, Cameron, padded in with him.

'What are you doing, Damien? You know you're gonna get in a buttload of trouble if you get caught in here.'

'Yeah, it's way past curfew,' Erin said.

'You might be here getting ready to defile us virgins,' Shaunee said. Then she and Erin looked at each other and burst out laughing, which made me smile. It was weird to have a happy feeling in the middle of such sadness, which is probably why the Twins' laughter and my smile faded quickly.

'Stevie Rae wouldn't want us to quit being happy,' Damien said into the uncomfortable silence. Then he walked to the middle of the room and spread out his sleeping bag on the floor between the two beds. 'And I'm here because we need to stick together. *Not* because I want to defile any of you, even if all of you were still virgins, although I do appreciate your use of vocabulary.'

Erin and Shaunee snorted, but looked more amused than offended, and I made a mental note to ask them sex questions later.

'Well, I'm glad you came, but we're gonna have one heck of a time sneaking you out of here when everyone's eating

287

breakfast and rushing around before school,' I said, trying out escape plans in my head.

'Oh, you don't have to worry about that. The vamps are posting that the school's closed today due to snow. No one'll be rushing anywhere. I'll just walk out with y'all whenever.'

'Posting? You mean we'd have to wake up, get dressed, and go downstairs before we found out there wasn't any school? That sucks,' I said.

I could hear the smile in Damien's voice. 'They announce it on the local radio stations like normal schools do. But do you and Stevie Rae listen to the news while you get...' Damien trailed off, and I realized that he'd started phrasing the question as if Stevie Rae were still alive.

'No,' I said quickly, trying to cover his awkwardness. 'We used to listen to country music. It always made me hurry up and get ready quicker so I could escape from it.' My friends laughed softly. I waited until everyone was quiet again, and then I said, 'I'm not going to forget her, and I'm not going to pretend like her death doesn't mean anything to me.'

'Neither am I,' Damien said.

'Me either,' Shaunee said.

'Ditto, Twin,' Erin said.

After a while I said, 'I didn't think it could happen to a fledgling who had been given an affinity by Nyx. I – I just didn't think it could happen.'

'No one's guaranteed to make it through the Change, not even those gifted by the Goddess,' Damien said quietly.

'That just means we have to stick together,' Erin said.

'It's the only way we can get through this,' Shaunee said.

'That's what we'll do then – stick together,' I said with finality. 'And promise that if the worst happens, and some of the rest of us don't make it through, the others won't let them be forgotten.'

'Promise,' my three friends said solemnly.

We all settled down then. The room didn't feel so lonely anymore, and just before I drifted off to sleep I whispered, 'Thanks for not letting me be alone . . .' and wasn't sure if I was thanking my friends, my Goddess, or Stevie Rae.

CHAPTER TWENTY-FIVE

IT WAS SNOWING IN MY DREAM. AT FIRST I THOUGHT THAT
was cool. I mean, it really was beautiful . . . it made the world
look Disney-like and perfect, as if nothing bad could happen,
or if it did it was only temporary, because everyone knows
Disney is all about happily ever after . . .

I walked slowly, not feeling the cold. It seemed to be just
before sunrise, but it was hard to tell with the sky all snowy
and gray. I tilted my head back and looked at how the snow
clung to the thick branches of the old oaks, and made the east
wall look soft, and less imposing.

The east wall.

In my dream I hesitated when I realized where I was. Then I saw the figures, hooded and cloaked, standing in a group of four in front of the open trapdoor in the wall.

No! I told my dreaming self. *I don't want to be over here. Not so soon after Stevie Rae died. After the last two times fledglings died I saw their ghosts or spirits or undead walking bodies or whatever here. Even if I had been gifted with a weird ability to see the dead by Nyx. Enough was enough! I didn't want—*

The smallest of the cloaked figures turned around and my internal argument scattered from my mind. It was Stevie Rae! Only it wasn't. She looked too pale and thin. And there was something else about her. I stared, and my initial hesitation was overcome by a terrible need within me to understand. I mean, if it really was Stevie Rae, then I didn't need to be afraid of her. Even weirdly changed by death, she was still my best friend. Wasn't she? I couldn't help moving forward until I was standing only a few feet from the group. I held my breath, waiting for them to turn on me, but no one noticed me. In my dream world it was as though I was invisible to them. So I moved even closer, unable to take my eyes from Stevie Rae. She looked terrible – frantic – and she kept moving restlessly, shifting her eyes around her like she was extremely nervous or extremely afraid.

'We shouldn't be here. We need to leave.'

I jumped at the sound of Stevie Rae's voice. She still had her Okie accent, but nothing else was recognizable. Her tone was hard and flat, lacking all emotions except a kind of animallike nervousness.

'You're not in charge of usssss,' one of the other cloaked figures hissed, baring his teeth at Stevie Rae. Oh, ugh! It was that Elliott creature. Even though his body was weirdly hunched, he stood over her aggressively. His eyes had begun to glow a dirty red. I was afraid for her, but she didn't let him intimidate her, instead Stevie Rae bared her own teeth, her eyes blazed scarlet, and she gave an ugly snarl. Then she spat the words at him, 'Does the earth answer you? No!' She walked forward, and Elliott automatically took several steps backward. 'And until it does, you will obey me! That's what *she* said.'

The Elliott thing made an awkward, subservient bow that the two other cloaked figures mimicked. Then Stevie Rae pointed toward the open trapdoor. 'Now, we go *quickly*.' But before any of them moved I heard a familiar voice from the other side of the wall.

'Hey, do y'all know Zoey Redbird? I need to tell her I'm here and—'

Heath's voice broke off when the four creatures, with blurring speed, rushed through the door after him.

'No! Stop! What the hell are you doing?' I yelled. My heart was beating so hard that it hurt as I ran to the closing door in time to see the three of them grabbing Heath. I heard Stevie Rae say, 'He's seen us. Now he comes with us.'

'But she said no more!' Elliott yelled as he kept an iron grip on the struggling Heath.

'He's seen us!' Stevie Rae repeated. 'So he comes with us until she tells us what to do with him!'

They didn't argue with her, and with inhuman strength they dragged him away. The snow seemed to swallow his screams.

I sat bolt upright in bed, breathing hard, sweating and trembling. Nala grumbled. I looked around the room and felt momentarily panicked. I was alone! Had I just dreamed everything that had happened yesterday? I looked at Stevie Rae's empty bed, and at the lack of any of her stuff around the room. No. I hadn't dreamed it. My best friend was dead. I let the weight of the sadness settle into me, and knew I'd be carrying it around for a very long time.

But hadn't the Twins and Damien slept here? Still groggy, I rubbed my eyes and looked at my clock. It was 5:00 P.M. I must have fallen asleep some time between 6:30 and 7:00 A.M. Sheesh, I'd definitely gotten enough sleep. I got up, went to the heavily draped window, and peered out. Unbelievably, it was still snowing, and even though it was early, the gaslights were illuminating a slate-colored night and glistening with little snow haloes. Fledglings were doing typical kid stuff – building snowmen and having snow fights. I saw someone I thought was that Cassie Kramme girl who'd done so well in the monologue competition making snow angels with a couple other girls. Stevie Rae would have loved it. She would have made me wake up hours ago and had me out there with her in the thick of all of the fun (whether I wanted to be or not). Thinking about it, I didn't know whether I wanted to cry or smile.

'Z? Are you awake?' Shaunee called tentatively from the cracked door.

I motioned for her to come in. 'Where'd you guys go?'

'We've been up a couple hours. We've been watching movies. Wanta come down with us? Erik and Cole, that totally *fiiine* friend of his, are gonna come over.' Then she looked around guiltily, as if remembering that Stevie Rae was gone and sorry she'd been acting normal. Something inside me made me speak.

'Shaunee, we have to go on. We have to date and be happy and live our lives. Nothing's guaranteed, Stevie Rae's death proved that. We can't waste the time we've been given. When I said I'd make sure she was remembered, I didn't mean that we were going to be sad forever. It meant I'd remember the happiness she brought to us, and keep her smile close to my heart. Always.'

'Always,' Shaunee agreed.

'If you give me a second I'll put on some jeans and meet you guys downstairs.'

''Kay,' she said with a grin.

When Shaunee was gone, some of my happy facade faded. I'd meant what I said to her, it was just the acting out of it that was going to be hard. Plus, I was having a hard time shaking the bad dream. I knew it was just a dream, but it still bothered me. It was like I could hear the echoes of Heath's screams in the oppressive silence of my room. Moving automatically, I got dressed in my most comfortable jeans and a ginormic sweatshirt I'd bought from the school store a couple of weeks ago. Over my heart it had the silver embroidered insignia of Nyx standing with upraised hands cupping a full moon, and somehow it made me feel better. I brushed my hair and sighed at my reflection in the mirror. I looked like poo. So I spackled some concealer on the dark smudges under my eyes, added mascara and my shiny lip gloss that smelled like strawberries. Feeling more ready to face the world, I headed downstairs.

And paused at the end of the staircase. The scene was familiar, yet completely changed. Kids clustered around the flat-screen TVs. There should be talking, and there was, but it was definitely subdued. My group of friends were sitting around the TV we liked best: the Twins in their matching poofy chairs, Damien and Jack (looking very cozy) were sitting on the floor by the love seat, Erik was on the love seat, and I was surprised to see that his *fiiiine* friend, Cole, had pulled up a chair and was actually sitting between the Twins. I felt my lips twitch up. He was either very brave or very moronic. They were all chattering softly, and definitely not paying attention to *The Mummy Returns*, which was playing on TV. So, except for two things, it was a perfectly familiar scene. First, they were being way too quiet. Second, Stevie Rae should have been sitting on the love seat with her feet folded under her telling everyone to be quiet so she could hear the movie.

I swallowed back the teary, burning feeling in the back of my throat. I had to go on. *We* had to go on.

'Hi, guys,' I said, trying to sound normal.

This time there wasn't an awkward silence at my presence. Instead there was an equally awkward everyone-talking-perkily-all-at-once.

'Hi, Z!'

'Zoey!'

'Hey there, Z!'

I managed not to sigh or roll my eyes as I took my place beside Erik. He put his arm around me and squeezed, which made me feel weirdly better but guilty. Better – because he was totally sweet and hot and I was still a little amazed that he seemed to like me so much. Guilty – well, that could be summed up in one word: Heath.

'Good! Now that Z's here we can start the marathon,' Erik said.

'You mean the dorkathon,' Shaunee said with a snort.

'If it was the weekend we could call it the geekend,' Erin said.

'Let me guess.' I looked up at Erik. 'You brought the DVDs.'

'Yep I did!'

The rest of the group groaned in exaggerated pain.

'Which means we're watching *Star Wars*,' I said.

'Again,' his friend Cole muttered.

Shaunee arched one perfectly waxed brow at Cole. 'Are you saying that you're not a big *Star Wars* fan?'

He smiled at Shaunee, and even from where I was sitting I could see the flirty glimmer in his eyes. 'Watching Erik's long extended director's cut of *Star Wars* for the millionth time is not why I came over here. I am a fan, but it's not of Darth and Chewbacca.'

'Are you saying Princess Leia does it for you?' Shaunee quipped.

'No, I'm more *colorful* than that,' he said, leaning toward her.

'I'm not here because I'm a fan of *Star Wars* either,' Jack piped in, giving Damien an adoring look.

Erin giggled. 'Well, we know Princess Leia doesn't do it for you.'

'Thankfully,' Damien said.

'I wish Stevie Rae was here,' Erik said. 'She'd be all, *Y'all, you're not bein' very niiiice.*'

Erik's words made everyone shut up. I glanced at him and saw that his cheeks were getting red, like he hadn't realized exactly what he'd said till after he said it. I smiled and rested my head on his shoulder.

'You're right. Stevie Rae would be scolding us like a mama.'

'And then she'd make everyone some popcorn and tell us to share nice,' Damien said. 'Even though she should say share *nicely*.'

'I liked the way Stevie Rae messed up the English language,' Shaunee said.

'Yeah, she Okie-fied it,' Erin said.

We all smiled at each other, and I felt a small warmth begin in my chest. This is how it started – this is how we would remember Stevie Rae – with smiles and love.

'Uh, can I sit with you guys?'

I looked up to see that cute Drew Partain kid standing nervously at the edge of our group. He looked pale and sad, and his eyes were red as if he'd been crying. I remembered how he had looked at Stevie Rae, and felt a stab of sympathy for him.

'Sure!' I said warmly. 'Pull up a chair.' Then an inner prompting made me add, 'There's room over there by Erin.'

Erin's blue eyes widened a little, but she recovered quickly. 'Yeah, pull up a chair, Drew. But be warned, we're watching *Star Wars*.'

'Cool with me,' Drew said, giving Erin a hesitant smile.

'Short, but cute,' I heard Shaunee whisper to Erin, and I do believe I saw Erin's cheeks get a little pink.

'Hey, I'm going to make us some popcorn. Plus, I need my—'

'Brown pop!' Damien, the Twins, and Erik said together.

I disentangled myself from Erik's arm and went to the kitchen, feeling more lighthearted than I had since Stevie Rae began coughing. Everything would be okay. The House of Night was my home. My friends were my family. I'd follow my own advice and take one day at a time – one issue at a time. I'd figure out a way to wade through my boyfriend issues. I'd do my best to avoid Neferet (without being too obvious that I was avoiding her) until I could figure out what was going on with her and the weird nondead Elliott (who was enough to give anyone nightmares – no wonder I'd had such a terrible dream about Stevie Rae and Heath).

I put one bag of extra-butter, super-pop popcorn in each of the four microwaves and grabbed big bowls as they started popping. Maybe I should cast another private circle and ask Nyx for help understanding the gross Elliott issue. My stomach clenched as I realized that I would be minus Stevie Rae. How was I going to deal with replacing her? It made me feel sick, but it had to be done. If not now, for my private ritual, I'd have to find someone before the next Full Moon Ritual. I closed my eyes against the pain of missing Stevie Rae and the reality of going on without her. *Please show me what to do*, I prayed silently to Nyx.

'Zoey, you need to come into the living room.'

My eyes sprang open as Erik's voice startled me. The look on his face had my adrenaline surging through my body. 'What's going on?'

'Just come on.' He took my hand and we hurried out of the kitchen. 'It's the news.'

Even though the big living room was full of kids, it had gone completely silent. They were all staring at our big-screen TV, where Chera Kimiko was looking into the camera and speaking solemnly.

'*. . . police are warning the public not to panic, even though this is the third teenager to have disappeared. They are investigating, and assure Fox News that they have several viable leads.*

'*To repeat this special bulletin, a Broken Arrow teenager, another high school football player, has been reported as missing. His name is Heath Luck.*'

My knees no longer held me, and I would have fallen if Erik hadn't put his arm around my waist and helped me to the love seat. It felt like I couldn't catch my breath as I listened to Chera continue:

'*Heath's truck was found outside the House of Night, but the*

High Priestess there, Neferet, assures police that he did not enter the school grounds, and that he has not been seen by anyone there. Of course there is much speculation about these disappearances, especially since the medical examiner's report states that the cause of death of the other two abducted boys was blood loss from multiple bites and lacerations. And while it is true that vampyres do not bite when they take blood from humans, the lacerations do follow a pattern that is consistent with vampyric feeding. It is important that we remind the public that vampyres have a binding legal agreement with humans to not feed on any human being against his or her will. We'll have more on this story at ten o'clock, and of course will break as news becomes available . . .'

'Someone get me a bowl, I'm gonna be sick!' I managed to yell over the humming in my head. A bowl was thrust into my hands and I promptly puked my guts into it.

CHAPTER TWENTY-SIX

'HERE, ZOEY, IT'LL HELP IF YOU SWISH THIS AROUND IN YOUR mouth.' Blindly I took whatever Erin handed me, relieved when it was just cold water. I spit it into the nasty bowl of puke.

'Ugh, take it away,' I said, suppressing my gag reflex as I got a whiff of puke. I wanted to cover my face with my hands and burst into tears, but I knew that the entire room was looking at me, so I slowly straightened my shoulders and pushed my damp hair back behind my ears. I didn't have the luxury of dissolving into a panicked heap. My mind was already processing the things I needed to do – had to do. For

Heath. He was what was important right now, not me, and not my need for hysteria. 'I have to see Neferet,' I said resolutely and stood up, surprised at how steady my knees had become.

'I'll go with you,' Erik said.

'Thanks, but first I need to brush my teeth and put on some shoes.' (I'd just stuck on a pair of thick socks to come down and watch TV.) I smiled my thanks to Erik. 'I'll run up to my room and be right back.' I could feel the Twins getting ready to follow me. 'I'll be fine. Just give me a sec.' Then I turned and hurried up the stairs.

I didn't pause at my room, but kept going down the hall, turned right, and stopped before room number 124. I'd raised my fist, but hadn't knocked when the door opened.

'I thought it would be you.' Aphrodite gave me a cold look, but she stepped to the side. 'Come on in.'

I walked in, surprised by the pretty pastel interior of the room. I guess I'd expected it to be dark and scary, like a black widow's web.

'Do you have any mouthwash? I just puked and I've seriously grossed myself out.'

She pointed her chin at the medicine cabinet over the sink. 'In there. The glass on the sink is clean.'

I washed out my mouth, taking the opportunity to try to collect my thoughts. When I was done I turned to face her. Deciding not to waste time on bullshit, I got straight to the point. 'How can you tell if a vision is real or just a dream?'

She sat down on one of the beds and shook back her long,

perfect blond hair. 'It's a feeling in your gut. Visions are never easy or comfortable or fucking flower-draped like they are in the movies. Visions suck. At least real ones do. Basically, if it makes you feel like shit, it's probably real and not just a dream.' Her blue eyes looked me over carefully. 'So, you've been having visions?'

'I thought I had a dream last night, a nightmare actually. Today I think it was a vision.'

Aphrodite's lips turned up only slightly. 'Well, that sucks for you.'

I changed the subject. 'What's going on with Neferet?'

Aphrodite's face went carefully blank. 'What do you mean?'

'I think you know exactly what I mean. Something's off about her. I want to know what.'

'You're her fledgling. Her favorite. Her new golden girl. Do you think I'm actually going to say shit to you? I may be blond, but I'm definitely not stupid.'

'If that's the way you really feel, why did you warn me against taking the medicine she gave me?'

Aphrodite looked away. 'My first roommate died six months after she got here. I took the medicine. It – it affected me. For a long time.'

'What do you mean? How did it affect you?'

'It made me feel funny, detached. And it stopped my visions. Not permanently, just for a couple of weeks. And then it was hard for me to even remember what she looked like.' Aphrodite paused. 'Venus. Her name was Venus Davis.' Her eyes met mine again. 'She was the reason I chose Aphrodite as my new name. We were best friends and we thought it was cool.' Her eyes were filled with sadness. 'I've made myself remember Venus, and I figured you'd want to remember Stevie Rae.'

'I do. I will. Thanks.'

'You should go. It won't be good for either of us if anyone knows you've been here talking to me,' Aphrodite said.

I realized that she was probably right, and turned for the door. Her voice stopped me.

'She makes you think she's good, but she's not. Everything that's light isn't good, and everything that's darkness isn't always bad.'

Darkness does not always equate to evil, just as light does not always bring good. The words that Nyx had said to me the day I was Marked were mirrored in Aphrodite's warning.

'In other words, be careful around Neferet and don't trust her,' I said.

'Yeah, but I never said that.'

'Said what? We're not even having this conversation.' I shut the door behind me and hurried to my room where I washed my face and brushed my teeth, pulled on some shoes, and then returned to the living room.

'Ready?' Erik asked.

'We'll come, too,' Damien said, motioning to include the Twins, Jack, and Drew.

I started to tell them no, but I couldn't make the word come out. The truth was that I was glad they were here, glad they obviously felt the need to join forces around me and protect me. I'd worried for a really long time that my extra powers and my weird Goddess-chosen Mark would brand me such a freak that I wouldn't fit in, wouldn't have any friends. But the opposite seemed to be happening.

'Okay, let's go.' We headed for the door. I wasn't entirely sure what I was going to say to Neferet. All I knew was that I couldn't continue to keep my mouth shut, and that I had a terrible feeling my 'dream' had really been a vision, and that there was more to the 'spirits' I'd been seeing than ghosts. Most of all, I was afraid they'd taken Heath. What that said about what Stevie Rae had become chilled me to my core, but it didn't change the fact that Heath was missing, and that I think I knew who had taken him (if not what).

We hadn't quite made it to the door when it opened and Neferet glided into the room on a tide of snow-scented air. She was followed by Detective Marx and Detective Martin. They had blue down jackets on that were zipped to their chins. Their hats were covered with snow and their noses were red. Neferet, as usual, looked perfectly poised, perfectly groomed, perfectly in control.

'Ah, Zoey, good. This saves me from having to look for you. The two detectives have some rather bad news, and they'd also like to speak with you for a moment.'

I didn't spare a glance for Neferet, and I could feel her stiffening as I responded directly to the detectives. 'I already heard on the news that Heath's missing. If there's any way I can help, I will.'

'Could we use the library again?' Detective Marx asked.

'Of course,' Neferet said smoothly.

I started to follow Neferet and the detectives from the room, but paused to look back at Erik.

'We'll be here,' he said.

'All of us,' Damien said.

I nodded. Feeling better, I went to the library. I'd hardly entered the room when Detective Martin started questioning me.

'Zoey, can you account for your whereabouts between six thirty and eight thirty this morning?'

I nodded. 'I was upstairs in my room. Around that time I was talking on the phone to my grandma, and then Heath and I text messaged each other back and forth a few times.' I reached into my jeans pocket and pulled out my cell phone. 'I haven't even deleted the messages. You can see them if you want.'

'You don't have to give him your phone, Zoey,' Neferet said.

I made myself smile at her. 'That's okay. I don't mind.'

Detective Martin took my phone and started going through the text message files, copying onto a little pad the messages.

'Did you see Heath this morning?' Detective Marx asked.

'No. He asked if he could come see me, but I told him no.'

'This says that you were planning on seeing him Friday,' Detective Martin said.

I could feel Neferet's sharp eyes on me. I drew a deep breath. The only way I could do this would be to stick as close to the truth as I was able.

'Yeah, I was going to go out with him after the game Friday.'

'Zoey, you know it is strictly against school rules to continue to date humans from your old life.' I noticed, as if for the first time, the disgust that filled her voice when she said *humans*.

'I know. I'm sorry.' Again, I told the truth, only omitting a bloodsucking, Imprinting detail here and an I-don't-trust-you-anymore detail there. 'It's just that Heath and I had so much history between us that it was really hard to totally stop talking to him, even though I knew I had to. I thought it would be easier if we met and I told him to his face, once and for all, why we couldn't see each other. I would have told you, but I wanted to handle it on my own.'

'So, you didn't see him this morning?' Detective Marx repeated.

'No. After we were done text messaging I went to bed.'

'Can anyone substantiate that you were in your room sleeping at that time?' Detective Martin asked, handing me back my phone.

Neferet's voice was ice. 'Gentlemen, I already explained to you the terrible loss Zoey experienced just yesterday. Her roommate died. So, how she could have anyone substantiate her where-abouts at—'

'Um, excuse me, Neferet, but actually I wasn't sleeping alone. My friends Shaunee and Erin didn't want me to be by myself, so they came to my room and slept with me.' I left Damien out. No point getting the kid in trouble.

'Oh, that was very kind of them,' Neferet said gently,

switching in one breath from scary vampyre to concerned mother. I tried not to think of how *not* fooled I was by her.

'Do you have any idea where Heath might be?' I asked Detective Marx (I still liked him better of the two).

'No. His truck was found not far from the school wall, but the snow is falling so fast that any tracks he might have made have been completely covered.'

'Well, I should think that instead of wasting your time questioning my fledgling, the police would be spending time searching the gutters for the teenager,' Neferet said in an offhand tone that made me want to scream.

'Ma'am?' Marx said.

'It seems clear to me what happened. The boy was trying to see Zoey, again. It was only last month that he and that girlfriend of his climbed our wall saying they were going to break her out of the school.' Neferet waved her hand dismissively. 'He was drunk and high then, he was probably drunk and high this morning, too. The snow was too much for him and he's probably fallen into a gutter somewhere. Isn't that where drunks usually end up?'

'Ma'am, he's a teenager, not a drunk. And his parents and friends say he hasn't had a drink in a month.'

Neferet's soft laugh made it obvious how much she didn't believe him. Surprising me, Marx ignored her and studied me carefully. 'How about it, Zoey? You two dated for a couple of years, right? Can you think of where he might have gone?'

'Not out this way. If his truck was missing off Oak Grove

Road in BA I could tell you where the keg party might be.'
I didn't mean it as a joke, especially after Neferet's mean
cracks about Heath, but the detective seemed to be trying not
to smile, which suddenly made him appear kind, and even
approachable. Before I could change my mind, I blurted, 'But
I had a weird dream this morning that might not actually
have been a dream but could have been some kind of vision
about Heath.'

Into the stunned silence Neferet's voice sounded clipped
and harsh. 'Zoey, you have never before mainfested an affinity
for prophecy or visions.'

'I know.' Purposefully I made myself sound unsure and
even a little scared (the scared part wasn't exactly pretense).
'But it's just too weird that I dreamed that Heath was over
by the east wall, and that he was grabbed there.'

'What grabbed him, Zoey?' Detective Marx's voice was
urgent. He was definitely taking me seriously.

'I don't know.' Which definitely wasn't a lie. 'I do know
they weren't fledglings or vampyres. In my dream four cloaked
figures dragged him away.'

'Did you see where they went?'

'No, I woke up screaming for Heath.' I didn't have to
fake the tears that filled my eyes. 'Maybe you should search
everything around the school. Something's out there, and
something's taking kids, but it's not us.'

'Of course it's not us.' Neferet came over to me and put
her arm around me, patting my shoulder and making soft
mom sounds. 'Gentlemen, I think Zoey's had more than

enough upsetting for one day. Why don't I introduce you to Shaunee and Erin, who, I'm sure, will collaborate her alibi.'

Alibi. The word sounded chilling.

'If you remember anything else, or have any other odd dreams, please don't hesitate to contact me, anytime day or night.' Detective Marx said.

This was the second time he'd given me his card – he certainly was persistent. I took his card from him and thanked him. Then as Neferet led him from the room Detective Marx hesitated and walked back to me.

'My twin sister was Marked and Changed fifteen years ago,' he said softly. 'She and I are still close, even though she was supposed to forget her human family. So when I say you can call me anytime, and tell me anything, you can believe me. You can also trust me.'

'Detective Marx?' Neferet stood in the doorway.

'Just thanking Zoey again, and telling her how sorry I am about her roommate,' he said smoothly as he strode from the room.

I stayed where I was, trying to collect my thoughts. Marx's sister was a vampyre? Well, that really wasn't so bizarre. What was bizarre is that he still loved her. Maybe I could trust him.

The door clicked shut and I jerked in surprise. Neferet was standing with her back to it, watching me carefully.

'Did you Imprint with Heath?'

I had an instant of cold, white panic. She was going to be able to read me. I'd been fooling myself. There was no way I was any kind of a match for this High Priestess. Then I felt the brush of a gentle, impossible breeze . . . the warmth of an invisible fire . . . the freshness of a spring rain . . . the green sweetness of a fertile meadow . . . and the powerful infilling of elemental strength flowing into my spirit. With new confidence I met Neferet's eyes.

'But you said I didn't. You told me before that what happened between him and me on the wall wasn't enough to Imprint.' I made sure my voice sounded confused and upset.

Her shoulders relaxed almost imperceptibly. 'I don't think you Imprinted with him then. So, you're saying you haven't been with him since? You haven't fed from him again?'

'Again!' I let myself sound as shocked as I always felt at the disturbing, yet seductive thought of feeding on Heath. 'But I didn't really *feed* on him then, did I?'

'No, no, of course not,' Neferet reassured me. 'What you did was very minor, very minor indeed. It's just that your dream made me wonder if you'd been with your boyfriend again.'

'Ex-boyfriend,' I said almost automatically. 'No. But he's been texting and calling me a bunch lately, so I thought it would be best if I met him and tried to make him understand, once and for all, that we can't see each other anymore. I'm sorry. I should have told you, but I really did want to solve it myself. I mean, I got myself into the mess. I should be able to handle getting myself out of it.'

'Well, I do commend your sense of responsibility, but I don't think it was wise to make the detectives believe your dream might have been a vision.'

'It just seemed so real,' I said.

'I'm sure it did. Zoey, did you take the medicine I asked you to drink last night?'

'You mean that milky stuff? Yeah, Shaunee gave it to me.' And she had, but I'd poured the crap down the sink.

Neferet looked even more relaxed. 'Good. If you keep having disturbing dreams, come to me and I'll give you a stronger mixture. That should have kept the nightmares from you, but clearly I underestimated the dosage you required.'

The dosage wasn't all she'd underestimated.

I smiled. 'Thanks, Neferet. I appreciate that.'

'Well, you should return to your friends, now. They are quite protective of you, and I'm sure they're worried.'

I nodded and walked with her back to the living room, careful not to show my disgust when she hugged me in front of everyone and said good-bye with the warmth of a mom. Actually, she was exactly like a mom, specifically *my* mom, Linda Heffer. The woman who had betrayed me for a man and cared more about herself and appearances than she cared about me. The similarities between Neferet and Linda were becoming clearer and clearer.

CHAPTER TWENTY-SEVEN

WE RESETTLED IN OUR LITTLE GROUP AFTER THEY LEFT, AND didn't say much as the room got back to normal. I noticed no one changed the local station. The *Star Wars* DVD was forgotten, at least for tonight.

'Are you okay?' Erik finally asked softly. He put his arm back around me and I snuggled against him.

'Yeah, I think so.'

'Did the cops have any news about Heath?' Damien asked.

'Nothing more than what we already heard,' I said. 'Or if they do, they weren't telling me.'

'Is there anything we can do?' Shaunee asked.

I shook my head. 'Let's just watch local TV and see what the ten o'clock news says.'

They mumbled okays and everyone settled in to watch the *Will and Grace* rerun marathon while we waited for the news. I stared at the TV, and thought about Heath. Did I have a bad feeling about him? Definitely. But was it the same bad feeling I'd had about Chris Ford and Brad Higeons? No, I didn't think so. I didn't know how to explain it. My gut said Heath was in danger, but it wasn't saying that he was dead. Yet.

The more I thought about Heath, the more restless I became. By the time the late news came on I could hardly sit through the stories on the unexpected blizzard that had caused a white-out in Tulsa and the surrounding area. I fidgeted while we watched the shots of downtown and the express-ways, eerily empty and looking post-meteor-hit-or-nuclear-war-like.

There was nothing new on Heath except a grim report about how the weather was hampering search efforts.

'I have to go.' The words were out of my mouth and I was standing before my mind could remind me that I didn't have a clue where I was going or how I was going to get there.

'Go where, Z?' Erik asked.

My mind flailed around and landed on one thing – one little island of contentment in a world that had turned into stress and confusion and madness.

'I'm going to the stables.' Erik's look was as blank as everyone else's. 'Lenobia said that I could brush Persephone

314

anytime I wanted to.' I moved my shoulders. 'Brushing her makes me feel calm, and right now I could use some calm.'

'Well, okay. I like horses. Let's go groom Persephone,' Erik said.

'I need to be alone.' The words sounded so much harsher than I'd meant them that I sat back down next to him and slid my hand in his. 'I'm sorry. It's just that I need time to think, and that's something I have to do alone.'

His blue eyes looked sad, but he gave me a little smile. 'How about I walk you to the stable, and then come back here and keep an eye on the news for you till you get through thinking?'

'I'd like that.'

I hated the worried looks on my friends' faces, but I couldn't do much to reassure them. Erik and I didn't bother with coats. The stable wasn't far. The cold wouldn't get a chance to bother us.

'This snow is awesome,' Erik said after we'd walked a little way down the sidewalk. Someone had attempted to plow it because it was way less deep on the sidewalk than the surrounding grounds, but the snow was coming down so steadily that the plows couldn't keep up with it and it was already up to midcalf on us.

'I kinda remember it snowing like this when I was six or seven. It was during Christmas break and it sucked that we didn't miss any school.'

Erik grunted a vague, guylike response, and then we walked on in silence. Usually, our silences weren't awkward, but this one felt weird. I didn't know what to say – how to make it better.

Erik cleared his throat. 'You still care about him, don't you? I mean, as more than just an ex-boyfriend.'

'Yes.' Erik deserved the truth, and I was totally sick of lies.

We'd come to the stable door, and stopped in the halo of a yellow gaslight. The entryway shielded us from the worst of the snow, so it seemed like we were standing in a bubble inside a snow globe.

'And what about me?' Erik asked.

I looked up at him. 'I care about you, too. Erik, I wish I could fix this, make all of the bad stuff go away, but I can't. And I'm not going to lie to you about Heath. I think I've Imprinted him.'

I saw the surprise in Erik's eyes. 'From just that one time on the wall? Z, I was there, and you hardly tasted any of his blood at all. He just doesn't want to lose you, that's why he's so obsessed. Not that I blame him,' he added with a wry smile.

'I saw him again.'

'Huh?'

'It was just a couple days ago. I couldn't sleep, so I went to the Starbucks at Utica Square by myself. He was there putting up posters about Brad. I hadn't meant to see him, and if I'd known he was going to be there I wouldn't have gone. I promise you that, Erik.'

'But you did see him.'

I nodded.

'And you fed from him?'

'It – it just kinda happened. I tried not to, but he cut himself. On purpose. And I couldn't stop myself.' I kept my gaze squarely on his, asking him with my eyes to understand. Now that I was actually confronted with the very likely possibility that Erik and I were going to break up, I realized how much I didn't want that to happen, which definitely didn't help my confusion or my stress level because I did still care about Heath. 'I'm sorry, Erik. I didn't ask for it to happen, but it did, and now there's this thing between Heath and me, and I'm not sure what I'm going to do about it.'

He sighed deeply and brushed some snow off my hair. 'Okay, well, there's a *thing* between you and me, too. And someday, if we make it through this damn Change, we'll be alike. I won't turn into a wrinkled old man and die decades before you will. Being with me won't be something other vampyres will whisper about, and humans will hate you for. It'll be normal. It'll be right.' Then his hand was behind my neck and he was pulling me to him. He kissed me hard. He tasted cold and sweet. My arms went up around his shoulders and I kissed him back. At first I just wanted to make the hurt I was causing him go away. Then our kiss deepened, and we pressed our bodies together. I wasn't overwhelmed with blinding bloodlust for him, like what happened when I was with Heath, but I liked the way kissing Erik made me feel, all kinda warm and light-headed. Hell, the bottom line was that I liked *him*. A lot. Plus, he had a point. He and I would be right together. Heath and I would not.

The kiss ended with both of us breathing hard. I cupped Erik's cheek in my hand. 'I really am sorry.'

Erik turned his head and kissed my palm. 'We'll figure this out.'

'I hope so,' I whispered, more to myself than him. Then I stepped away from him and put my hand on the old iron door-knob. 'Thanks for walking me here. I don't know when I'll be back. You shouldn't wait for me.' I started to open the door.

'Z, if you really did Imprint with Heath you might be able to find him,' Erik said. I paused and turned back to Erik. He looked strained and unhappy, but he didn't hesitate to explain. 'While you're brushing the mare, think about Heath. Call to him. If he's able to, he'll come to you. If he's not and your Imprint is strong enough, you may be able to get an idea of where he is.'

'Thank you, Erik.'

He smiled, but he didn't look happy. 'Later, Z.' He walked away and the snow swallowed him.

The warm hay smell mixed with clean, dry horse contrasted dramatically with the cold, snowy outside. The stables were dimly lit by only a couple of soft gaslights. The horses were making sleepy, chewing noises. Some of them were blowing through their noses, which sounded a little like snoring. I looked around for Lenobia while I brushed the snow from my shirt and hair and started toward the tack room, but it was pretty obvious that except for the horses I was alone.

Good. I needed to think, and not explain what I was doing here in the middle of a snowstorm in the middle of the night.

Okay, I'd told Erik the truth about Heath and he hadn't broken up with me. Of course, depending on what happened with Heath, he might still dump me. How did those ho-ish girls go out with a dozen or so guys at the same time? Two was exhausting. Memory of Loren's sexy smile and incredible voice flashed through my guilt-filled mind. I chewed my lip as I grabbed a curry brush and a mane comb. Actually, I'd been kinda sorta seeing three guys, which was utterly insane. I decided then and there that I had enough problems without adding the weird flirting that may or may not be going on between Loren and me into the mix. Just thinking about Erik finding out that I'd shown all that skin to Loren . . . I shuddered. It made me want to dump myself. From now on I'd avoid Loren, and if I couldn't avoid him I'd treat him like any other teacher, which meant *no flirting*. Now if I could just figure out what to do with Erik and Heath.

I opened Persephone's stall and told her what a pretty, sweet girl she was as she gave me a sleepily surprised snort and lipped my face after I kissed her soft nose. She sighed and rested on three feet when I started brushing her.

Okay, no way I could figure out anything about dating Erik and Heath until Heath was safe. (I refused to consider that he might never be safe – might never be found alive.) I began to quiet the babble and clutter and confusion that was my mind. Truthfully, I hadn't needed Erik to tell me that I might be able to find Heath. That possibility was one of the many things that had been making me so restless all night. The cowardly truth was that I was afraid – afraid of what I might find and what I might not find, and afraid I wouldn't be strong enough to deal with either. Stevie Rae's death had left me broken, and I wasn't sure I was up to saving anybody.

But it wasn't like I had any choice.

So . . . thinking of Heath . . . I started by remembering what a cute kid he'd been in grade school. In third grade his hair had been lots blonder than it was now, and he'd had like a zillion cowlicks. It used to stand up all over his head like duck fluff. Third grade was when he'd first told me that he loved me and was gonna someday marry me. I'd been in second grade, and I so didn't take him seriously. I mean, even though I was almost two years younger I'd been a foot taller. He was cute, but he was also a boy, which meant he was annoying.

Okay, so he could still be annoying, but he'd grown up and filled out. Somewhere between third and eleventh grade I'd started taking him seriously. I remembered back to the first time he'd *really* kissed me, and the fluttery, excited way it made me feel. I remembered how sweet he was, and how he could make me feel beautiful, even when I had a terrible cold and my nose was bright red. And how he was an old-fashioned gentleman. Heath had been opening doors and carrying books for me since he was nine.

Then I thought about the last time I'd seen him. He'd been so sure that we belonged together and so unafraid of me that he'd cut himself and offered his blood to me. I closed my eyes and leaned against Persephone's soft flank, thinking of Heath and letting the memories of him drift past my closed lids like a movie screen. Then the images of our past changed and I got a vague sense of darkness and dampness and cold – and fear slammed into my gut. I gasped, keeping my eyes tightly closed. I wanted to focus in on him, like I had that one other time when somehow I'd seen him in his bedroom, but this connection between us was different. It was less clear, more filled with dark emotions than playful desire. I concentrated harder, and did what Erik had said to do. I called Heath.

Aloud, as well as with everything inside of me, I said, 'Heath, come to me. I'm calling you, Heath. I want you to come to me now. Wherever you are, get out of there and come to me!'

Nothing. There was no answer. No response. No sense of anything more than damp, cold fear. I called again. 'Heath! Come to me!' This time I felt a surge of frustration, followed by despair. But I didn't get an image of him. I knew he couldn't come to me, but I didn't know where he was.

Why had I been able to see him so much more easily before? How had I done it? I'd been thinking about Heath then, just like I had been now. I'd been thinking about . . .

What had I been thinking about? Then I felt my cheeks get hot as I realized what had drawn me to him before. I hadn't been thinking about how cute a kid he'd been or how pretty he made me feel. I'd been thinking about drinking his blood . . . feeding from him . . . and the red-hot bloodlust that caused.

Okay, well then . . .

I drew a deep breath and thought about Heath's blood. It tasted like liquid desire, hot and thick and electric. It made my body burst alive in places that had only begun to rouse before. And those places were starving. I wanted to drink Heath's sweet blood while he satisfied my yearning for his touch, his body, his taste—

The disjointed image I had of darkness cleared with an abruptness that was shocking. It was still dark, but that was no problem for my night vision. At first I didn't understand what I was seeing. The room was weird. It was more like a little alcove in a cave or a tunnel than a room. The walls were round and damp. There was some light, but it was coming from a dim, smoky lantern that hung from a rusted hook. Everything else was complete darkness. What I thought at first was a pile of dirty clothes moved and moaned. This time it wasn't just a threadlike feeler I was looking through. It was actually as if I was floating, and when I recognized the moan my hovering body drifted over to him.

He was curled up on a stained mattress. His hands and ankles were duct taped together and he was bleeding from several slashes on his neck and arms.

'Heath!' My voice wasn't audible, but his head snapped up as if I'd just yelled at him.

'Zoey? Is that you?' And then his eyes widened and he sat straight up, looking wildly around. 'Get out of here, Zoey! They're crazy. They'll kill you like they did Chris and Brad.' And he started to struggle, trying desperately to break the tape, even though all that was happening was he was making his already raw wrists bleed.

'Heath, stop! It's okay – I'm okay. I'm not here, not really.'

322

He stopped struggling and squinted around him like he was trying to see me.

'But I can hear you.'

'Inside your head. That's where you hear me, Heath. It's because we've Imprinted and now we're linked.'

Unexpectedly, Heath grinned. 'That's cool, Zo.'

I gave a mental eye roll. 'Okay, Heath, focus. Where are you?'

'You won't believe this, Zo, but I'm under Tulsa.'

'What does that mean, Heath?'

'Remember in Shaddox's History class? He told us about the tunnels that were dug under Tulsa in the twenties because of the un-alcohol thing.'

'Prohibition,' I said.

'Yeah, that. I'm in one of them.'

I didn't know what to say for a second. I vaguely remembered learning about the tunnels in History class, and was astounded that Heath – not exactly an excellent student – would remember at all.

As if he understood my hesitation he grinned and said, 'It was about sneaking booze. I thought it was cool.'

After another mental eye roll I said, 'Just tell me how to get there, Heath.'

He shook his head and a way too familiar stubborn look settled over his face. 'No way. They'll kill you. Go tell the cops and have them send a SWAT team or something.'

That was exactly what I wanted to do. I wanted to get Detective Marx's card out of my pocket, call him, and have him save the day.

Unfortunately, I was afraid I couldn't.

'Who is the "they"?' I asked.

'Huh?'

'The people who took you? Who are they?'

'They're not people, and they're not vampyres even though they drink blood, but they're not like you, Zo. They're—' he broke off, shuddering. 'They're something else. Something wrong.'

'Have they been drinking your blood?' The thought made me furious with such an intensity that I was having a hard time controlling my emotions. I wanted to rage at someone and shriek, *He belongs to me!* I forced myself to take several deep breaths while he answered me.

'Yeah, they have.' Heath grimaced. 'But they complain a lot about it. They say my blood doesn't taste right. I think that's the main reason I'm still alive.' Then he swallowed hard and his face got a shade paler. 'It's not like when you drink my blood, Zo. That feels good. What they do is – is disgusting. *They're* disgusting.'

'How many of them are there?' I said through gritted teeth.

'I'm not really sure. It's so dark down here and they always come in weird groups, all smushed together like they're scared of being alone. Well, except for three of them. One's named Elliott, one's called Venus – how weird is that – and the other one is called Stevie Rae.'

My stomach knotted. 'Does Stevie Rae have short, curly blond hair?'

'Yeah. She's the one that's in charge.'

Heath had just substantiated my fears. I couldn't call in the police.

'Okay, Heath. I'm going to get you out of there. Tell me how to find your tunnel.'

'Are you going to get the cops?'

'Yes,' I lied.

'Nope. You're lying.'

'I am not!'

'Zo, I can tell you're lying. I can feel it. It's that link thing.' He grinned.

'Heath. I can't get the police.'

'Then I'm not telling you where I am.'

Echoing from down one end of the tunnel came a skittering that reminded me of the sound the science experiment rats made as they scurried through the mazes we made in AP Bio. Heath's grin was gone, as was the color that had returned to his cheeks while we talked.

'Heath, we don't have time for this.' He started to shake his head no. 'Listen to me! I have special powers. Those—' I hesitated, not sure what to call the group of creatures that somehow included my dead best friend. 'Those *things* aren't going to be able to hurt me.'

Heath didn't say anything, but he didn't look convinced and the ratlike sounds were getting louder.

'You said you can tell I'm lying because of our link. It has to go both ways. You've got to be able to tell when what I say is the truth.' He looked like he was waffling, so I added, 'Think hard. You said you remembered some of that night you found me at Philbrook. I saved you that night, Heath. Not the cops. Not an adult vamp. I saved you, and I can do it again.' I was glad I sounded a lot more certain than I felt. 'Tell me where you are.'

He thought for a while, and I was getting ready to yell at him (again) when he finally said, 'You know where the old depot is downtown?'

'Yeah, you can see it from the Performing Arts Center where we went to see *Phantom* for my birthday last year, right?'

'Yeah. They took me to the basement of it. They got in through something that looks like a barred door. It's old and rusted, but it lifts right up. The tunnel starts from the drainage grates down there.'

'Good, I'll—'

'Wait, that's not all. There are lots of tunnels. They're more like caves. It's not cool like I thought they'd be from History class. They're dark and wet and disgusting. Pick the one on your right, and then keep turning to your right. I'm at the end of one of those.'

'Okay. I'll be there as soon as I can.'

'Be careful, Zo.'

'I will. You be safe.'

'I'll try.' Hissing was added to the scurrying noises. 'But you should probably hurry up.'

CHAPTER TWENTY-EIGHT

I OPENED UP MY EYES AND I WAS BACK IN THE STALL WITH Persephone. I was breathing hard and sweating, and the mare was nuzzling me and making soft, worried, nickering noises. My hands were shaking as I caressed her head and rubbed her jaw, telling her that it was going to be okay, even though I was pretty sure it wasn't.

The old downtown depot was six or seven miles away in a dark, unused part of town under a big, scary bridge that linked one part of the city to the other. It used to be majorly busy, with freight and passenger trains coming and going almost nonstop. But in the past couple decades all of the passenger traffic had stopped (I knew because my grandma had wanted to take me on a train trip for my thirteenth birthday, and we'd had to drive to Oklahoma City to catch the train there) and the freight train business had definitely dwindled. Under normal circumstances, it would only take a few minutes to zip from the House of Night to the depot.

Tonight I was not dealing with normal circumstances.

The ten o'clock news had said the roads were impassable, and that had been – I checked my watch and blinked in surprise – a couple hours ago. I couldn't drive there. I suppose I could walk, but the urgency I felt was telling me that wasn't good enough.

'Take the horse.'

Persephone and I both shied at the sound of Aphrodite's voice. She was leaning against the stall door looking pale and grim.

'You look like crap,' I said.

She almost smiled. 'Visions suck.'

'Did you see Heath?' My stomach clenched again. Aphrodite didn't have visions of happiness and light. She saw death and destruction. Always.

'Yeah.'

'And?'

'And if you don't get on that horse and get your ass to wherever he is, Heath is going to die.' She paused, meeting my eyes. 'That is, unless you don't believe me.'

'I believe you,' I said without hesitation.

'Then get the hell out of here.'

She came into the stall and handed me a bridle I hadn't noticed she'd been holding. While I put it on Persephone, Aphrodite disappeared to come back with a saddle and saddle blanket. Silently, we put the tack on Persephone, who seemed to sense our intensity because she held completely still. When she was ready I led her from the stall.

'Call your friends first,' Aphrodite said.

'Huh?'

'You can't beat those things on your own.'

'But how are they going to go with me?' My stomach hurt, I was so scared my hands were shaking, and I was having trouble understanding what the hell Aphrodite was saying.

'They can't go with you, but they can still help you.'

'Aphrodite, I don't have time for riddles. What the hell do you mean?'

'Shit, I don't know!' She looked as frustrated as I felt. 'I just know that they can help you.'

I flipped open my cell phone and, following my gut and breathing a silent prayer for guidance from Nyx, punched Shaunee's number. She answered on the first ring.

'What's up, Zoey?'

'I need you and Erin and Damien to go somewhere together and call to your elements, like you did for Stevie Rae.'

'No problem. Are you gonna meet us?'

'No. I'm going to get Heath.' To her credit, Shaunee hesitated for only a second or two, then said, 'Okay. What can we do?'

'Just be together, manifest your elements, and think about

me.' I was getting really good at sounding calm even when I thought my head might explode.

'Zoey, be careful.'

'I will. Don't worry.' Yeah, I'd worry enough for both of us.

'Erik isn't going to like this.'

'I know. Tell him . . . tell him . . . that I'll, uh, talk to him when I get back.' I had not a clue about what else to say.

'Okay, I'll tell him.'

'Thanks, Shaunee. I'll see ya,' I said and closed the phone. Then I faced Aphrodite. 'What are those creatures?'

'I don't know.'

'But you saw them in your vision?'

'Today was the second vision I had about them, though. The first time I saw the other two guys being killed by them.' Aphrodite brushed a thick strand of blond hair from her face.

Instantly I was pissed. 'And you didn't say anything about it because they're *just* human teenagers and not worth your time to save?'

Aphrodite's eyes blazed with anger. 'I told Neferet. I told her everything – about the human kids – about those *things* – everything. That's when she started saying my visions were false.'

I knew she was telling the truth, just as surely as I had begun to know that there was something dark about Neferet.

'Sorry,' I said shortly. 'I didn't know.'

'Whatever,' she said. 'You need to get out of here or your boyfriend is going to die.'

'Ex-boyfriend,' I said.

'Again I say whatever. Here, I'll give you a leg up.'

I let her hoist me into the saddle.

'Take this with you.' Aphrodite handed me a thick, plaid horse blanket. Before I could protest she said, 'It's not for you. He'll need it.'

I wrapped the blanket around me, taking comfort in its earthy, horsey smell. I followed as Aphrodite went to the rear doors of the stable and slid them apart. Frigid air and snow swirled in little mini-tornadoes into the barn, making me shiver, although it was more from nerves and apprehension than from the cold.

'Stevie Rae's one of them,' Aphrodite said.

I looked down at her, but she was staring out into the night.

'I know,' I said.

'She's not who she used to be.'

'I know,' I repeated, even though saying the words aloud hurt my heart. 'Thanks for this, Aphrodite.'

She did look up at me then and her expression was flat and unreadable. 'Don't start acting like we're friends or anything,' she said.

'Wouldn't think of it,' I said.

'I mean, we're not friends.'

'Nope, definitely not.' I was pretty sure I saw her trying not to smile.

'As long as we have that straight,' Aphrodite said. 'Oh,' she added. 'Remember to pull silence and darkness around yourself so humans will have a hard time seeing you on the way there. You don't have time to be stopped.'

'Will do. Thanks for reminding me,' I said.

'Okay, well, good luck,' Aphrodite said.

I gripped the reins, took a deep breath, and then squeezed my thighs together, clucking at Persephone to go.

I entered a world that was weirdly made of white darkness. Whiteout was definitely the right description of it. The snow had changed from big, friendly flakes to sharp little razorlike pieces of snow-ice. The wind was steady, making the snow slant sideways. I pulled the blanket over my head so that I was partially protected from the snow and leaned forward, kicking Persephone into a quick trot. *Hurry!* My mind was yelling at me. *Heath needs you!*

I cut across the parking lot and rear part of the school grounds. The few cars still at school were covered with snow, and the flickering gaslights that shined crazily off their backs made them look like june bugs on a screen door. I pressed the inside button for the gate to open. It tried to swing wide, but a snowdrift caught it and Persephone and I had barely enough room to squeeze through. I turned her to the right and stood for a moment under the cover of the oaks that framed the school grounds.

'We're silent . . . ghosts . . . no one can see us. No one can hear us.' I murmured against the whining wind, and was shocked when the area around me stilled. With a sudden thought I continued. 'Wind, be calm near me. Fire, warm my way. Water, still the snow in my path. Earth, shelter me when you can. And spirit, help me not to give in to my fear.' The words were barely out of my mouth when I saw a little flash of energy around me. Persephone snorted and she skittered a little to the side. And as she moved it was like a little bubble of serenity moved with her. Yes, it was still blizzarding and the night was still cold and frighteningly alien, but I was filled with calm and surrounded by the protection of the elements. I bowed my head and whispered, 'Thank you, Nyx, for the great gifts you have given me.' Silently I added that I hoped I deserved them.

'Let's get Heath,' I told Persephone. She swung into her ground-eating canter easily and I was amazed to see that the snow and ice seemed to fly back from her hooves as we magically blasted through the night under the watchful eye of the Goddess who was, herself, Night personified.

My journey was surprisingly fast. We cantered down Utica Street until we came to the exit to the Broken Arrow Expressway. Barricades were up with flashing lights warning that the expressway was closed. I felt myself smiling as I guided Persephone neatly around the barricades onto the utterly deserted highway. Then I gave the mare her head and she galloped downtown. I clung to her, leaning low over her neck. With the blanket streaming out behind us I imagined that I looked like the heroine in an old historical romance novel, and wished I was galloping to a naughty keg party with someone my kingly father had decided was inappropriate instead of heading into hell.

I steered Persephone to the exit that would take us to the Performing Arts Center and the old depot beyond it. I hadn't seen anyone between midtown and the highway, but now I saw occasional shufflings of street people around the bus station and noticed an occasional cop car here and there. *We're silent . . . ghosts . . . no one can see us. No one can hear us.* I kept the prayer going in my mind. No one so much as glanced in our direction. It really was as if I'd turned into a ghost, which wasn't a thought I found very comforting.

I slowed Persephone as we passed the Performing Arts Center and trotted over the wide bridge that spanned the confusing side-by-side meshing of old railroad tracks. When we reached the center of the bridge I stopped Persephone and stared down at the abandoned depot building that sat below us dark and silent. Thanks to Mrs Brown, my ex-art teacher at South Intermediate High School, I knew it used to be a beautiful art deco building that had been abandoned and eventually looted when the trains stopped running. Now it looked like something that should be in the Gotham City of the Batman Dark Night comics. (Yes, I know. I'm a dork.) It had those huge arched windows that reminded me of teeth between two towers that looked like perfectly creepy haunted castles.

'And we have to go down there,' I told Persephone. She was breathing hard from our ride, but she didn't seem particularly worried, which I hoped was a good sign. You know, animals being able to sense bad stuff and all.

We finished crossing the bridge and I found the broken little side road that led down to the depot. The track level was dark. Really dark. That shouldn't have bothered me, what with my excellent fledgling night vision, but it did. The truth was that I was totally creeped out as Persephone walked to the building and I began slowly circling it, looking for the basement entrance Heath had described.

It didn't take long to find the rusted iron grill that appeared to be an impassable barrier. I didn't let myself hesitate and think about how completely afraid I was. I got off Persephone and led her over to the covered entryway so she'd be out of the wind and protected from most of the snow. I looped her reins around a metal thingie, laid the extra blanket over her back, and spent as long as I could patting her and telling her what a brave, sweet girl she was and that I'd be back real soon. I was working toward that self-fulfilling prophecy thing, and hoped if I kept saying it, it would be true. Walking away from Persephone was hard. I guess I hadn't realized how comforting her presence had been. I could have used some of that comfort as I stood in front of the iron grill and tried to squint into the darkness beyond.

I couldn't see anything except the indistinct shape of a huge dark room. The basement of the creepy unfortunately-not-abandoned building. Great. *Heath is down there*, I reminded myself, grabbed the edge of the grill, and pulled. It opened easily, which I took to be evidence of how often it must be used. Again, great.

The basement was not as awful as I'd imagined it would be. Stripes of weak light filtered between the barred, ground-level windows and I could clearly see that homeless people must have been using the room. Actually, there was a lot of stuff left from them: big boxes, dirty blankets, even a shopping cart (Who knows how they managed to get that down there?). But, weirdly, not one homeless person was present. It was like a homeless ghost town, which was doubly weird when I considered the weather. Wouldn't tonight be the perfect night to retreat to the comparative warmth and shelter of this basement, versus trying to find someplace warm and dry on the streets or smush into the Y? And it had been snowing for days. So, realistically, this room should be packed with the people who had brought the boxes and stuff down here to begin with.

Of course if scary undead creatures had been using the basement the desertion of the homeless folks made much more sense.

Don't think about it. Find the drainage grate and then find Heath.

The grate wasn't hard to find. I just headed for the darkest, nastiest corner of the room, and there was a metal grate on the floor. Yep. Right in the corner. On the floor. Never, in a gazillion years would I have ever even considered touching the disgusting thing, let along lifting it and going down there.

Naturally, that's what I had to do.

The grate lifted as easily as the outside 'barrier' had opened, telling me (again) that I wasn't the only person/fledgling/human/creature who had come this way recently. There was an iron ladder thing that I had to climb down, probably about ten feet. Then I dropped to the floor of the tunnel. And that's exactly what it was – a big, damp sewer tunnel. Oh, and it was dark, too. Really dark. I stood there for a while letting my night vision accustom itself to the dense darkness, but I couldn't just stand there for very long. The need to find Heath was like an itch beneath my skin. It goaded me on.

'Keep to the right,' I whispered. Then I shut up because even that little sound echoed around me. I turned to the right and started to walk as quickly as I was able.

Heath had been telling the truth. There were lots of tunnels. They split off over and over again, reminding me of worm holes burrowed into the ground. At first I saw more evidence that homeless people had been down here, too. But after a few righthand turns, the boxes and scattered trash and blankets stopped. There was nothing but damp and dark. The tunnels had gone from being smooth and round and as civilized as I imagined well-made tunnels could be to absolute crap. The sides of the walls looked like they had been gouged out by very drunk Tolkien dwarfs (again, I am aware that I'm a dork). It was cold, too, but I didn't really feel it.

I kept to the right, hoping that Heath had known what he was talking about. I thought about stopping long enough to concentrate on his blood so that I could hook into our Imprint again, but the urgency I felt wouldn't let me stop. I. Had. To. Find. Heath.

I smelled them before I heard the hissing and rustling and actually saw them. It was that musty, old, wrong scent I'd noticed every time I'd seen one of them at the wall. I realized it was the smell of death, and then wondered how I didn't recognize it earlier.

Then the darkness that I'd become so accustomed to gave way to a faint, flickering light. I stopped to focus myself. *You can do this, Z. You've been Chosen by your Goddess. You kicked vampyre ghost ass. This is something you can definitely handle.*

I was still trying to 'focus' (aka, talk myself into being brave) when Heath screamed. Then there was no more time for focusing or internal pep talks. I ran toward Heath's scream. Okay, I probably should explain that vampyres are stronger and faster than humans, and even though I'm still just a fledgling, I'm a very weird fledgling. So when I say I ran – I mean I seriously moved fast – fast and silent. I found them in what must have been seconds, but felt like hours. They were in the little alcove at the end of the crude tunnel. The lantern I'd noticed before was hanging from a rusty nail, throwing their shadows grotesquely against the crudely curved walls. They had formed a half circle around Heath. He was standing on the dirty mattress and his back was pressed to the wall. Somehow he'd gotten the duct tape off his ankles, but his wrists were still securely bound together. He had a new cut on his right arm and the scent of his blood was thick and seductive.

And that was my last goad. Heath belonged to me – despite my confusion about the whole blood issue, and despite my feelings for Erik. Heath was mine and no one else was ever, *ever* going to feed from what was mine.

I burst through the circle of hissing creatures like I was a bowling ball and they were brainless pins, and moved to his side.

'Zo!' He looked deliriously happy for a split second, and then, just like a guy, he tried to push me behind him. 'Watch out! Their teeth and claws are really sharp.' He added in a whisper, 'You really didn't bring the SWAT team?'

It was easy to keep him from pushing me anywhere. I mean, he's cute and all, but he is just a human. I patted his bound hands where he clutched my arm and smiled at him, and with one slash of my thumbnail I cut through the gray tape that held his wrists. His eyes widened as he pulled his hands apart.

I grinned at him. My fear was gone. Now I was just incredibly pissed. 'What I brought is better than a SWAT team. Just stay behind me and watch.'

I pushed *Heath* to the wall and stepped in front of him as I turned to face the closing circle of . . .

Eesh! They were the most disgusting things I'd ever seen. There were probably a dozen or so of them. Their faces were white and gaunt. Their eyes glowed a dirty red. They snarled and hissed at me and I saw that their teeth were pointed and their fingernails! Ugh! Their fingernails were long and yellow and dangerous-looking.

'It'sss just a fledgling,' hissed one of them. 'The Mark doesn't make her a vampyre. It makesssss her a freak.'

I looked at the speaker. 'Elliott!'

'I wasss. I'm not the Elliott you knew anymore.' Snakelike his head wove back and forth as he spoke. Then his glowing eyes flattened and he curled his lip. 'I'll ssshow you what I mean . . .'

He started to move toward me with a feral, crouching stride. The other creatures stirred, gaining bravery from him.

'Watch out, Zo, they're coming for us,' Heath said, trying to step around in front of me.

'No they're not,' I said. I closed my eyes for just a second and centered myself, thinking of the power and warmth of flame – the way it can cleanse as well as destroy – and I thought of Shaunee. 'Come to me, flame!' My palms started to feel hot. I opened my eyes and raised my hands, which were now glowing with a brilliant yellow flame.

'Stay back, Elliott! You were a pain in the ass when you were alive, and death hasn't changed anything.' Elliott cringed back from the light I was producing. I took a step forward, ready to tell Heath to follow me so we could get the hell outta there, but her voice made me freeze.

'You're wrong, Zoey. Death has changed some things.'

The crowd of creatures parted to let Stevie Rae through.

CHAPTER TWENTY-NINE

THE FLAME IN MY PALMS SPUTTERED AND FADED AS SHOCK broke my concentration. 'Stevie Rae!' I started to take a step toward her, but the truth of her appearance hit me and I felt my body go cold and still. She looked terrible – worse than she had in the dream vision I'd had. It wasn't so much her pale thinness and the awful wrongness of the smell that clung to her that made her appear so changed. It was her expression. In life, Stevie Rae had been the kindest person I'd ever known. But now, whatever she was – dead, undead, bizarrely resurrected – she was different. Her eyes were cruel and flat. Her face devoid of any emotion except one, and that one emotion was hatred.

'Stevie Rae, what happened to you?'

'I died.' Her voice was only a twisted, malformed shadow of what it had once been. She still had her Okie twang, but the soft sweetness that had filled it was totally gone. She sounded like mean trailer trash.

'Are you a ghost?'

'A ghost?' Her laugh was a sneer. 'No, I ain't no damn ghost.'

I swallowed and felt a dizzy wash of hope. 'So you're alive?' She curled her lip in a sarcastic sneer that looked so wrong on her face it made me physically sick. 'You'd say I'm alive, but I'd say it's not that simple. Then again I'm not as *simple* as I used to be.'

Well, at least she hadn't hissed at me like that Elliott thing had. *Stevie Rae is alive.* I held tightly to that miracle, swallowed my fear and revulsion, and moving so quickly that she didn't have time to jerk away (or bite me or whatever), I grabbed her and, ignoring the horrid way she smelled, hugged her hard. 'I'm so glad you're not dead!' I whispered to her.

It was like hugging a smelly piece of stone. She didn't jerk away from me. She didn't bite me. She didn't react at all, but the creatures surrounding us did. I could hear them hissing and muttering. I let go of her and stepped back.

'Don't touch me again,' she said.

'Stevie Rae, is there someplace we can go so we can talk? I need to get Heath home, but I can come back and meet you. Or maybe you could come back to the school with me?'

'You don't understand anything, do you?'

'I understand that something bad has happened to you, but you're still my best friend, so we can figure this out.'

'Zoey, you're not going anywhere.'

'Fine,' I purposefully pretended to misunderstand her threat. 'I guess we could talk here, but, well . . .' I looked around at the grossly hissing creatures. 'It's not very private, and it's also disgusting down here.'

'Jusssst kill them!' Elliott snarled from behind Stevie Rae.

'Shut up, Elliott!' Stevie Rae and I snapped at him together. Her eyes met mine and I swear I saw a flash of something in them that was more than anger and cruelty.

'You know they can't live now that they've sssseen us,' Elliott said. The other creatures stirred restlessly, making evil little noises of agreement.

Then a girl stepped out of the pack of creatures. She obviously used to be beautiful. Even now there was an eerie, surreal allure about her. She was tall and blond, and she moved more gracefully than the others. But when I looked into her red eyes I saw only meanness.

'If you can't do it, I will. I'll take the male first. I don't mind that his blood has been tainted by Imprint. It's still warm and alive,' she said, and she seemed to dance toward Heath.

I stepped in front of him, blocking her path. 'Touch him and you die. Again,' I said.

Stevie Rae interrupted her hissing laughter.

'Get back with the others, Venus. You don't strike until I tell you to.'

Venus. The name triggered my memory. 'Venus Davis?' I said.

The pretty blonde narrowed her eyes at me. 'How do you know me, fledgling?'

'She knows a lot of stuff,' Heath said, stepping around me. He was using what I used to call his football player voice. He sounded tough and pissed and totally ready for a fight. 'And I'm about sick of all of you fucked-up creatures.'

'Why is *that* speaking?' Stevie Rae spat.

I sighed and rolled my eyes. I agreed with Heath – I was totally sick of all of this scary weirdness. It was time we got out of there, and it was also time my best friend started acting like the person I'd glimpsed hiding in her eyes. 'He isn't a *that*. He's Heath. Remember, Stevie Rae? My ex-boyfriend?'

'Zo. I am *not* your ex-boyfriend. I'm your boyfriend.'

'Heath. I told you before that this can't possibly work out between us.'

'Come on, Zo, we're Imprinted. That means it's you and me, baby!' He grinned at me as if we were in the middle of a prom instead of in the middle of a group of undead creatures that wanted to eat us.

'That was an accident, and we're gonna have to talk about it, but this is definitely not the time.'

'Oh, Zo, you know you love me.' Heath's grin didn't fade one bit.

'Heath, you are the most stubborn kid I've ever known.' He winked at me and I couldn't help smiling back at him. 'Fine. I love you.'

'What'sss happening . . .' the gross Elliott creature hissed. The rest of the horrid things that surrounded us moved restlessly, and Venus glided one step closer to Heath. I forced myself not to shiver or scream or whatever. Instead, a weird calm came over me. I looked at Stevie Rae, and suddenly knew what I needed to say. I put my hands on my hips and faced her.

'Tell him,' I said. 'Tell all of them.'

'Tell them what?' She narrowed her garnet eyes dangerously.

'Tell them what's happening here. You know. I know you do.'

Stevie Rae's face contorted, and the words sounded like they were being wrenched from her throat. *'Humanity!* They're showing their humanity.' The creatures snarled like she'd just thrown holy water on them (and please, that's such an untrue cliché about vampyres).

'Weakness! It's why we're stronger than they are.' Venus curled her lip. 'Because it's a weakness we don't have anymore.'

I ignored Venus. I ignored Elliott. Hell, I ignored them all and stared at Stevie Rae, forcing her to meet my eyes, and forcing myself not to look away or flinch as hers glowed hot and red.

'Bullshit,' I said.

'She's right,' Stevie Rae said. Her voice was cold and mean. 'When we died, so did our humanity.'

'That might be true with them, but I don't believe it's true with you,' I said.

'You don't know anything about this, Zoey,' Stevie Rae said.

'I don't have to. I know you, and I know our Goddess, and that's all I need to know.'

'She's not my Goddess anymore.'

'Really, just like your mama's not your mama anymore?' I knew I'd hit a nerve when I saw her jerk as if she were in physical pain.

'I don't have a mama. I'm not a human anymore.'

'Big f-ing deal. Technically, I'm not a human anymore, either. I'm somewhere in the middle of the Change, which makes me a little of this and a lot of that. Hell, the only one here who's still human is Heath.'

'Not that I hold your un-human-ness against you guys,' Heath said.

I sighed. 'Heath, un-human-ness isn't a word. It's inhumanity.'

'Zo, I'm not stupid. I know that. I was just coining a word.'

'Coining?' Had he really said that?

He nodded. 'I learned about it in Dickson's English class. It has to do with . . .' He paused, and I swear the creatures were even listening expectantly. '*Poetry*.'

Despite our awful situation I laughed. 'Heath, you really have been studying!'

'Told you so.' He grinned, looking completely adorable.

'Enough!' Stevie Rae's voice echoed off the round walls of the tunnel. 'I'm done with this.' She turned her back to Heath and me, ignoring us completely. 'They've seen us. They know too much. They have to die. Kill them.' And she walked away.

346

This time Heath didn't mess with trying to pull me behind him. Instead he whirled around and, completely catching me off guard, tackled me so that I landed on my butt on the disgusting mattress with an *oofh*. Then he turned to the closing circle of snarling undead creatures with his legs planted a hip's width apart and his hands balled into fists and he gave his Broken Arrow Tiger football growl.

'Bring it, freaks!'

Okay, it wasn't that I didn't appreciate Heath's machoness. But the boy was in over his cute blond head. I stood up and centered myself.

'Fire, I need you again!' This time I yelled the words with the command of a High Priestess. Flames burst into life from the palms of my hands all up and down my arms. I would have liked to have taken time to study the fire I'd called into being – it was cool that it could burn on me, and not actually burn me, but there was no time for that. 'Move, Heath.'

He looked over his shoulder at me, and his eyes got huge and round. 'Zo?'

'I'm fine. Just move!'

He jumped out of my way as, burning, I walked forward. The creatures cringed back from me, even as their hands tried to reach around me to get to Heath.

'Stop it!' I yelled. 'Back off and leave him alone. Heath and I are going to walk out of here. Now. If you try to stop us, I'm going to kill you, and I have a feeling that this time you're going to die for good.' Okay, I really, really didn't want to kill anyone. What I wanted to do was to get Heath out of there, and then find Stevie Rae and have her explain to me how fledglings who were supposed to have died could be walking around with bad attitudes, glowing eyes, and smelling like mold and dust.

From the edge of my vision I saw a movement. I turned in time to see one of the creatures launch herself at Heath. I lifted my arms and flung the fire at her as if I were throwing a ball. As she screamed and went up in flames I recognized her and had to fight hard not to be sick. It was Elizabeth No Last Name – the nice girl who had died last month. Now her burning body writhed on the floor, reeking of spoiled meat and decay, which was all that was left of her lifeless shell.

'Wind and rain! I call you,' I cried, and as the air around me began to swirl and fill with the scent of spring rain, I got a flash of Damien and Erin sitting cross-legged beside Shaunee. Their eyes were closed in concentration and they were holding votives the color of their elements. I pointed my fiery finger at Elizabeth's smoldering body and it was washed in a sudden flush of rain, then a cool breeze took the green-tinged smoke, lifting it above our heads, and carried its stench down the tunnel and out into the night.

I faced the creatures again. 'That's what I'll do to any of you who try to stop us.' I motioned for Heath to walk in front of me, and I followed him, backing away from the creatures.

They followed us. I couldn't always see them as we rewound our way through the dark tunnel, but I could hear their shuffling feet and muffled snarls. It was about then that I began to feel the exhaustion. It was like I was a cell phone that hadn't been charged in a while, and someone was talking on me too long. I let the fire that outlined by arms go out except for a flickering flame that I cupped in my right hand. No way Heath could see to walk out of here without that, and I was still backing behind him, keeping an eye out for attacking creatures. After I passed two offshoot tunnel branches I called for Heath to stop.

'We should hurry, Zo. I know you have this power thing going on, but there are a lot of them – more than what were back there. I don't know how many you can handle.' He touched my face. 'Not to be mean or anything, but you look like shit.'

I felt like poo, too, but I didn't want to mention it. 'I have an idea.' We'd just come around a curve where the tunnel had narrowed until I could touch either side of it by spreading out my arms. I walked back to the narrowest part of the curve. Heath started to follow me, but I told him, 'Stand over there,' and pointed farther down the tunnel the way we were heading. He frowned, but did as I told him.

I turned my back to Heath and concentrated. Lifting my arms, I thought of newly plowed fields and pretty Oklahoma meadows filled with uncut winter hay. I thought about the earth and how I was standing within it . . . surrounded by it . . .

'Earth! I call to you!' As I lifted my arms a vision of Stevie Rae flashed across my closed eyelids. She wasn't as she used to be – sweet-faced and concentrating hard over a glowing green candle. She was curled up in the corner of a dark tunnel.

Her face was gaunt and white and her eyes glowed scarlet. But her face wasn't an emotionless parody of herself or a cruel mask. She was weeping openly, her expression filled with despair. *It's a start*, I thought. Then, with a swift, powerful motion I lowered my arms while I commanded, 'Close!' In front and above me, pieces of dirt and rock began to fall from the ceiling. At first it was just a trickle of pebbles, but soon there was a mini-avalanche going on that quickly drowned out the pissed-off growls and hisses of the trapped creatures.

A wave of weakness crashed over me and I staggered back.

'I got ya, Zo.' Heath's strong arms were around me and I let myself rest against him for a moment. Several of his cuts had broken loose during our escape, and the ripe scent of his blood tickled against my senses.

'They're not really trapped, you know,' I said softly, trying to keep my mind off how much I wanted to lick the line of blood that was trickling down his cheek. 'We passed a couple other tunnels. I'm sure they'll be able to find their way out eventually.'

'It's okay, Zo.' Heath kept his arms wrapped around me, but he pulled back enough so that he could look into my eyes. 'I know what you need. I can feel it. If you feed from me you won't be so weak.' He smiled, and his blue eyes darkened. 'It's okay,' he repeated. 'I want you to.'

'Heath, you've been through way too much. Who knows how much blood you've already lost? My drinking more of it isn't a good idea.' I was saying no, but my voice trembled with desire.

'Are you kidding? A big, studly football jock like me? I got plenty of blood to spare,' Heath teased. Then his expression turned serious. 'For you, I have anything to spare.' While he looked into my eyes, he wiped one of his fingers down the damp red slash on his cheek and the rubbed the blood on his bottom lip. Then he bent and kissed me.

I tasted the dark sweetness of his blood and it dissolved in my mouth to send a surge of fiery pleasure and energy through my body. Heath pulled his lips from mine and guided me to the cut on his cheek. When my tongue snaked out and touched it, he moaned and pressed my hips closer to his. I closed my eyes and began to lick—

'Kill me!' Stevie Rae's broken voice shattered the spell of Heath's blood.

CHAPTER THIRTY

My face flamed with embarrassment as I pushed myself out of Heath's arms, wiping my mouth and breathing hard. Stevie Rae was standing down the tunnel just a few yards from us. Tears still rained down her cheeks and her face was twisted in despair.

'Kill me,' she repeated on a sob.

'No.' I shook my head and took a step toward her, but she backed away from me, putting up her hand as if she wanted to hold me off. I stopped and gulped some deep breaths, trying to get myself under control. 'Come back to the House of Night with me. We'll figure out how this happened. It'll be okay, Stevie Rae, I promise. All that matters is that you're alive.'

Stevie Rae had started shaking her head as I'd begun talking. 'I'm not really alive, and I can't go back there.'

'Of course you're alive. You're walking and talking.'

'I'm not me anymore. I did die, and part of me – the best part of me – is still dead, just like it is for the rest of them.' She gestured back at the cave-in.

'You're not like they are,' I said firmly.

'I'm more like them than I am like you.' Her gaze shifted from me to Heath, who was standing quietly beside me. 'You wouldn't believe the awful things that go through my mind. I could kill him without a second thought. I would have already if his blood hadn't been changed by the Imprint with you.'

'Maybe it wasn't just that, Stevie Rae. Maybe you didn't kill him because you really didn't want to,' I said.

Her eyes found mine again. 'No. I wanted to kill him. I still do.'

'The rest of them killed Brad and Chris,' Heath said. 'And that was my fault.'

'Heath, now's not the time—' I started, but he cut me off.

'No, you need to hear this, Zoey. Those things grabbed Brad and Chris because they were hanging around the House of Night, and that's my fault because I'd told them how hot you are.' He gave me an apologetic look. 'Sorry, Zo.' Then his expression hardened and he said, 'You should kill her. You should kill them all. As long as they're alive people will be in danger.'

'He's right,' Stevie Rae said.

'And how will killing you and the rest of them solve this? Won't more of you happen?' I made my mind up and closed the space between Stevie Rae and me. She looked like she wanted to take off, but my words stopped her. 'How did this happen? What made you like this?'

Her face contorted with anguish. 'I don't know how. I only know who.'

'Then *who* did this?'

She opened her mouth to answer me and then, with a movement so fast her body blurred, she was suddenly cowering against the side of the tunnel.

'She's coming!'

'What? Who?' I crouched beside her.

'Get out of here! Fast. There's probably still time for you to get away.' Then Stevie Rae reached out and took my hand in hers. Her flesh was cold, but her grip was strong. 'She'll kill you if she sees you – you and him. You know too much. She may kill you anyway, but it'll be harder for her to do if you get back to the House of Night.'

'Who are you talking about, Stevie Rae?'

'Neferet.'

The name blasted through me and even as I shook my head in denial I felt the truth of it deep within me. 'Neferet did this to you, to all of you?'

'Yes. Now get out of here, Zoey!'

I could feel her terror and I knew she was right. If Heath and I didn't leave, we would die.

354

'I'm not giving up on you, Stevie Rae. Use your element. You still have a connection with the earth, I can feel it. So use your element to stay strong. I'll come back for you, and somehow we'll figure this out – we'll make this okay. I promise.' Then I hugged her hard, and after only a little hesitation, she hugged me back.

'Let's go, Heath.' I grabbed his hand so I could guide him quickly down the darkness of the tunnel. The light in my palm had gone out when I'd called earth to me, and no way was I going to take a chance on relighting it. It might guide *her* to us. As we ran down the tunnel I heard Stevie Rae's whispered 'Please don't forget me . . .' follow us.

Heath and I ran. The surge of energy his blood had given me didn't last long, and by the time we came to the metal ladder that led up to the grate in the basement, I wanted to collapse and sleep for days. Heath was all for rushing up the ladder and into the basement, but I made him wait. Breathing heavily, I leaned against the side of the tunnel and fished my cell phone out of my pants pocket, along with Detective Marx's card. I flipped open the phone and I swear my heart didn't beat until the bars started to light up green.

'Can ya hear me now?' Heath said, grinning at me.

'Sssh!' I told him, but smiled back. Then I punched in the detective's number.

'This is Marx,' the deep voice answered on the second ring.

'Detective Marx, this is Zoey Redbird. I only have a second to talk, then I have to go. I've found Heath Luck. We're in the basement of the Tulsa Depot, and we need help.'

'Hang tight. I'll be right there!'

A noise from above made me cut off the connection and switch the phone off. I pressed my finger to my lips when Heath started to speak. Heath put his arm around me, and we tried not to breathe. Then I heard the coo-coo of a pigeon and the fluttering of wings.

'I think it's just a bird,' Heath whispered. 'I'm going to go look.'

I was too tired to argue with him, plus Marx was on his way and I was sick of the damp, nasty tunnel. 'Be careful,' I whispered back.

Heath nodded and squeezed my shoulder, then climbed up the ladder. Slowly and carefully he lifted the metal grate, sticking his head up and peering around. Pretty soon he reached down and motioned for me to climb up and take his hand. 'It's just a pigeon. Come on.'

Wearily, I climbed to him and let him pull me up into the basement. We sat in the corner by the grate for several long minutes, listening intently. Finally, I whispered, 'Let's go outside and wait for Marx there.' Heath had already started to shiver, but I remembered the blanket Aphrodite had made me bring. Plus, I'd rather take my chances with the weather than stay in the creepy basement.

'I hate it in here, too. It's like a damn tomb,' Heath said softly between chattering teeth.

Hand in hand, we walked across the basement, passing through the slatted grayish light that reflected down from the world above. We were at the iron door when I heard the distant wail of a police siren. The terrible tension in my body had just begun to relax when Neferet's voice came from the shadows.

'I should have known you would be here.'

Heath's body jerked in surprise and my hand tightened in warning on his. As I turned to face her, I was centering myself and could feel the power of the elements beginning to shimmer in the air around me. I drew a deep breath and carefully blanked my mind.

'Oh, Neferet! I'm so glad to see you!' I squeezed Heath's hand one more time before I let go of him, trying to tele-graph *play along with whatever I say* through touch. Then I ran, sobbing, into the High Priestess's arms. 'How did you find me? Did Detective Marx call you?'

I could see indecision in her eyes as Neferet smoothly disen-tangled herself from my arms. 'Detective Marx?'

'Yeah.' I sniffed and wiped my nose on my sleeve, forcing myself to beam relief and trust to her. 'That's him coming right now.' The sound of the siren was very close, and I could hear that it had been joined by at least two other cars. 'Thank you for finding me!' I gushed. 'It was so terrible. I thought that crazy street person was going to kill both of us.' I moved back to Heath's side and took his hand again. He was staring at Neferet, looking a lot like he was in shock. I realized that he was probably remembering pieces of the only other time he'd seen the High Priestess – the night the vampyre ghosts had almost killed him – and imagined his mind was too freaked out for Neferet to make much sense of what was going on inside his head. Good thing, too.

Then car doors were slamming and heavy feet were crunching through the snow.

'Zoey, Heath . . .' Neferet moved swiftly to us. She lifted her hands, which glowed with a weird, reddish light, suddenly reminding me of the undead things' eyes. Before I could run or scream or even take a breath, she grabbed our shoulders. I felt Heath go rigid as pain shot through my body. It blasted against my mind and my knees would have buckled had her hand not been like a vice, holding me up. *You will remember nothing!* The words echoed through my agony-filled mind, and then there was only darkness.

CHAPTER THIRTY-ONE

I WAS IN A BEAUTIFUL MEADOW THAT WAS IN THE MIDDLE of what looked like a dense forest. A warm, soft breeze was blowing the scent of lilacs to me. A stream ran through the meadow, its crystal water bubbled musically over smooth stones.

'Zoey? Can you hear me, Zoey?' An insistent male voice intruded on my dream.

I frowned and tried to ignore him. I didn't want to wake up, but my spirit stirred. I *needed* to wake up. I *needed* to remember. She needed me to remember.

But who was she?

'Zoey . . .' This time the voice was inside my dream and I could see my name painted against the blue of the spring sky. The voice was a woman's . . . familiar . . . magical . . . wondrous. 'Zoey . . .'

I looked around the clearing and found the Goddess sitting on the other side of the stream, gracefully perched on a smooth Oklahoma sandstone rock with her bare feet playing in the water.

'Nyx!' I cried. 'Am I dead?' My words shimmered around me.

The Goddess smiled. 'Will you ask that of me each time I visit you, Zoey Redbird?'

'No, I'm, uh, sorry.' My words were tinged pink, probably blushing like my cheeks.

'Don't be sorry, my daughter. You have done very well. I am pleased with you. Now, it is time you awakened. And also I wish to remind you that the elements can restore as well as destroy.'

I started to thank her, even though I didn't have a clue what she was talking about, but the shaking of my shoulder and a sudden blast of cold air interrupted me. I opened my eyes.

Snow swirled all around me. Detective Marx was bending over me, shaking my shoulder. Through the weird fog in my mind I found one word. 'Heath?' I croaked.

Marx jerked his chin to his right and I tilted my head to see Heath's still body being loaded into an ambulance.

'Is he . . .' I couldn't finish.

'He's fine, just banged up. He's lost a lot of blood and they've already given him something for the pain.'

'Banged up?' I was struggling to make sense of everything. 'What happened to Heath?'

'Multiple lacerations, just like those other two kids. Good thing you found him and called me before he bled to death.' He squeezed my shoulder. A paramedic tried to move Marx from my side, but he said, 'I'll handle her. She just needs to get back to the House of Night and she'll be fine.'

I saw the paramedic give me a look that clearly said *freak*, but Detective Marx's strong hands were helping me sit up and his tall body blocked my view of the muttering EMT.

'Can you walk to my car?' Marx asked.

I nodded. My body was feeling better, but my mind was still all mushy. Marx's 'car' was really a huge, all-weather truck with giant wheels and a roll bar. He helped me up into the front seat, which was warm and comfortable, but before he closed the door I suddenly remembered something else, even though the effort made my head feel like it was going to split open. 'Persephone! Is she okay?'

Marx looked confused for just a second, then he smiled. 'The mare?'

I nodded.

'She's just fine. An officer is walking her to the police stables downtown until the roads are clear enough to get a trailer back to the House of Night.' His grin widened. 'Guess you're braver than the Tulsa police force. None of them volunteered to ride her back.'

I rested my head against the seat as he threw the truck into four-wheel drive and navigated slowly through the drifts of snow away from the depot. There must have been ten cop cars, along with a fire truck and two ambulances parked with lights flashing red and blue and white against the empty, snow-curtained night.

'What happened here tonight, Zoey?'

I thought back, and had to squint my eyes against the sudden pain in my head. 'I don't remember,' I managed to say through the pounding in my temples. I could feel his sharp gaze on me. I met the detective's eyes and remembered him telling me about his twin sister, the vamp who still loved him. He'd said I could trust him, and I believed him. 'Something's wrong,' I admitted. 'My memory is messed up.'

'Okay,' he said slowly. 'Start with the last thing you can easily remember.'

'I was grooming Persephone and all of a sudden I knew where Heath was, and that he was going to die if I didn't go get him.'

'You two have Imprinted?' My surprise must have been easy to read, because he smiled and continued. 'My sister and I talk, and I've been curious about vamp stuff, especially right after she first Changed.' He shrugged as if it was no big deal for a human to know all sorts of vampyre info. 'We're twins, so we're used to sharing everything. A change of species just didn't make that much difference to us.' He glanced sideways at me again. 'You have Imprinted, haven't you?'

'Yeah, Heath and I have Imprinted. That's how I knew

362

where he was.' I left out the stuff about Aphrodite. No way did I feel up to explaining the whole her-visions-are-real-but-Neferet-has-been . . .

'Ah!' This time I gasped aloud at the agony inside my head.

'Deep, calming breaths,' Marx said, shooting me worried looks whenever he could take his eyes from the treacherous road. 'I said whatever was *easy* for you to remember.'

'No, it's okay. I'm okay. I want to do this.'

He still looked worried, but continued with his questioning. 'All right, you knew Heath was in trouble, and you knew where he was. So, why didn't you just call me and tell me to go to the depot?'

I tried to remember and pain shot through my head, but along with the pain came anger. Something had happened to my mind. *Someone* had messed with my mind. And that really pissed me off. I rubbed my temples and gritted my teeth against the pain.

'Maybe we should stop for a while.'

'No! Just let me think,' I gasped. I could remember the stables and Aphrodite. I could remember that Heath needed me, and the wild, snowy ride on Persephone to the depot basement. But when I tried to remember past the basement the agony that speared through my head became too much for me.

'Zoey!' Detective Marx's concern penetrated through my pain.

'Something has messed with my mind.' I wiped tears I hadn't realized I'd shed from my face.

'Pieces of your memory are gone.'

It didn't sound like a question, but I nodded anyway.

He was silent for a while. It seemed he was concentrating on the deserted, snow-covered road, but I thought I knew better, and his next words told me I was right.

'My sister' – he smiled and glanced at me – 'her name is Anne, warned me once that if I ever pissed off a High Priestess I would be in serious trouble because they had ways of erasing things, and what she meant by things was people and memories.' He glanced from the road to me again, and this time his smile was gone. 'So, I guess the question is: what have you done to piss off a High Priestess?'

'I don't know. I . . .' My voice trailed off as I thought about what he'd said. I didn't try to remember what had happened that night. Instead, I let my memory drift lazily backward . . . to Aphrodite and the fact that Nyx was still blessing her with visions, even though Neferet had spread the word that her visions were false . . . to the small, almost imperceptible sense of wrongness that had grown like a fungus around Neferet, until it culminated Sunday night in her undermining the decisions I'd made for the Dark Daughters . . . to the nasty scene I'd witnessed between Neferet and . . . and . . . I braced myself against the heat that was starting to throb through my head and, along with a flash of piercing pain, remembered the creature Elliott had become feeding from the High Priestess's blood.

'Stop the truck!' I yelled.

'We're almost at the school, Zoey.'

'Now! I'm going to be sick.'

We slid to the side of the empty road. I opened the door and dropped to the snowy street, staggered to the ditch, and puked up my guts into a snowbank. Detective Marx was beside me, pulling back my hair and sounding very dadlike as he told me to breathe and everything would be okay. I gulped air and finally stopped heaving. He handed me a handkerchief, one of those old-fashioned linen ones that was folded neatly into a clean square.

'Thanks.' I tried to hand it back to him after wiping my face and blowing my nose, but he smiled and said, 'Keep it.'

I stood there, just gulping air and letting the throbbing in my head go away as I stared across a field of untouched snow to some distant oaks that grew along a massive stone and brick wall. And with a start of surprise, I realized where we were.

'It's the east wall of the school,' I said.

'Yeah, I thought I'd take you the back way – give you more time to collect yourself, and maybe restore some of that memory.'

Restore . . . What was it about that word? Tentatively, I thought hard, trying to remember while I braced myself against the pain I was sure would come. But it didn't, and into my memory came the vision of a beautiful meadow, and the wise words of my Goddess . . . *the elements can restore as well as destroy*.

And then I understood what I had to do.

'Detective Marx, I need a minute here, okay?'

'Alone?' he asked.

I nodded.

'I'll be in the truck, watching you. If you need me, call.'

I smiled my thanks, but before he'd turned to go back to the truck I was walking toward the oaks. I didn't need to be under them – to actually be in the school grounds, but being near them helped me center myself. When I was close enough to see how their branches entwined like old friends, I stopped and closed my eyes.

'Wind, I call you to me and this time I ask that you blow clean any dark taint that has touched my mind.' I felt a gust of cold, like I was being battered by my own personal hurricane, but it wasn't pressing against my body. It was filling my mind. I kept my eyes tightly closed and blocked out the throbbing ache that had returned to my temples. 'Fire, I call you to me and ask that you burn from my mind any darkness that has touched it.' Heat filled my head, only it wasn't like the hot spear that I'd felt earlier. Instead it was a nice warmth, like a heating pad on a pulled muscle. 'Water, I call you to me and ask that you wash from my mind the darkness that has touched it.' Coolness flooded through the warmth, soothing what had been overheated and bringing incredible relief. 'Earth, I call you to me and ask that your nurturing strength take from my mind the darkness that has touched it.' From the bottoms of my feet, where I was connected firmly to the earth, it was as if a faucet had opened and I imagined putrid darkness running down and out of my body to be consumed by the strength and goodness of the earth. 'And, spirit, I ask that you heal what darkness has destroyed in my mind, and restore my memory!' Something snapped within me and a white-hot familiar sensation shot down my back, dropping me heavily to my knees.

'Zoey! Zoey! My God, are you okay?'

Once again Detective Marx's strong hands were shaking my shoulders and he was helping me to my feet. This time my eyes opened easily and I smiled into his kind face.

'I'm more than okay. I remember everything.'

CHAPTER THIRTY-TWO

'YOU'RE SURE THIS IS HOW IT HAS TO BE?' DETECTIVE MARX asked for what seemed like the zillionth time.

'Yep.' I nodded wearily. 'It has to be like this.' I was so damn tired I thought I could fall asleep right there in the cop's ginormic monster truck. But I knew I couldn't. The night wasn't over yet. My job wasn't over yet.

The detective sighed, and I smiled at him.

'You're just gonna have to trust me,' I said, sounding a lot like he had earlier that day.

'I don't like it,' he said.

'I know, and I'm sorry. But I've told you everything I can.'

'That some homeless kook is responsible for Heath and the other two boys?' He shook his head. 'Feels wrong to me.'

'Are you sure you're not a little bit psychic?' I smiled tiredly at him.

'If I was, I'd be able to figure out *what* feels wrong.' He shook his head again. 'Explain this – what happened to your memory?'

I'd already thought about my answer for this one. 'It was the trauma of tonight. It made me block what happened. And then my affinity for the five elements helped me to overcome the block and remember.'

'That's why you had all that pain?'

I shrugged my shoulders. 'I guess so. It's gone now anyway.'

'Look, Zoey, I'm pretty sure that there's more going on here than what you're telling me. I want you to know that you really can trust me,' he said.

'I know that.' I believed him, but I also knew that there were some secrets I couldn't share. Not with this really nice detective. Not with anyone.

'You don't have to deal with whatever it is on your own. I can help you. You're just a kid – just a teenager.' He sounded totally exasperated.

I met his eyes steadily. 'No, I'm a fledgling who is leader of the Dark Daughters and a High Priestess in training. Believe me, that's a lot more than *just a teenager*. I've given you my oath, and you know from your sister that my oath binds me. I promise I've told you everything I can, and if any more kids disappear, I believe I can find them for you.' What

I didn't say was that I wasn't one hundred percent sure how I was going to do that, but the promise felt right, and so I knew Nyx would help me keep it. Not that that would be easy. But I couldn't betray Stevie Rae's presence, which meant no one could know about the creatures, or at least not until Stevie Rae was safe.

Marx sighed again, and I could see that he was muttering to himself as he stomped around to help me down from his truck. But just before he opened the door to the main school building Marx (annoyingly) ruffled my hair and said, 'All right, we'll do this your way. Of course, it's not like I have a choice.'

He was right. He didn't have any choice.

I walked into the building before him and was instantly engulfed in the warmth of its familiar scents of incense and oil, and the soothing gaslights that flickered like eager, welcoming friends.

Speaking of . . .

'Zoey!' I heard the Twins squeal together, and then I was being smushed in the middle of them as they hugged me and cried and yelled at me for worrying them and talked nonstop about being able to feel it when I tapped into their elements. Damien was not far behind them. Then I was in Erik's strong arms as he hugged me and whispered how scared he'd been for me and how glad he was I was okay. I allowed myself to rest in his arms and return his hug. Later, I'd figure out what to do about Heath and him. Right now I was too tired, and anyway, I needed to save my strength to deal with—

'Zoey, you gave us quite a scare.'

I stepped out of Erik's arms and turned to face Neferet.

'I'm sorry. I really didn't mean to upset everyone,' I said, and it was the truth. I hadn't wanted to worry or upset or scare anyone.

'Well, I suppose there's no harm done, darling. We're all just so glad you're safely home.' She smiled at me with that wonderful mom smile of hers that seemed so full of love and light and goodness, and even though I knew what that smile hid, I felt my heart squeeze and wished desperately that I was wrong, that Neferet was as wonderful as I used to believe.

Darkness does not always equate to evil, just as light does not always bring good. The Goddess's words echoed through my mind, giving me strength.

'Well, Zoey is definitely our hero,' Detective Marx said. 'If she hadn't been tuned into that boy, she could have never called us to that depot in time to save him.'

'Yes, well, that's a little problem she and I will have to discuss later.' She gave me a stern look, but her tone told everyone there that I wasn't really in much trouble.

If only they knew.

'Detective, did you catch the person who has been taking the boys?' Neferet continued.

'No, he escaped before we arrived, but there's plenty of evidence that someone has been living in the depot, actually it looked like he was using it as some kind of headquarters. I think it'll be easy to find proof that the other two boys were killed there by someone who was trying to make it look like vampyres had taken the teenagers. And now, even though Heath doesn't remember much of anything because of the trauma, Zoey has given us a good description of the man to go by. It's just a matter of time before we catch him.'

Was I the only one who saw surprise flash through Neferet's eyes?

'That's wonderful!' Neferet said.

'Yeah.' I met the High Priestess's eyes. 'I've told Detective Marx a lot. My memory's really good.'

'I'm proud of you, Zoeybird!' Neferet came to me and put her arms around me, hugging me close. So close that only I heard her whisper into my ear, *'If you speak against me I will make sure no human or fledgling or vampyre will believe you.'*

I didn't pull away from her. I didn't react in any way. But when she let me go, I made my final move – the one I'd planned since the white-hot familiar sensation had seared the skin on my back.

'Neferet, would you please look at my back?'

My friends had been chattering among themselves, clearly giddy with the relief they'd felt since I'd called them while Detective Marx and I talked outside the school and asked them to meet me inside the main building, and to make sure Neferet was there, too. Now my weird request, which I'd been sure to ask loud and clear, shut them up. Actually, everyone in the room, including Detective Marx, was looking at me like they wondered if I'd perhaps hit my head sometime during my adventures and some of my brains had leaked out.

'It's important,' I said, and grinned at Neferet as if I were hiding a present just for her under the back of my shirt.

'Zoey, I'm not sure what—' Neferet began, her tone carefully pitched between worry and embarrassment.

I gave an exaggerated sigh. 'Jeesh, just look.' And before anyone could stop me, I turned so that my back was facing them, and lifted the bottom of my sweatshirt (being careful to keep the front of me covered).

I hadn't really been worried that I might be wrong, but the gasps and exclamations of awe and happy surprise from my friends were a relief to hear.

'Z! Your Mark has spread.' Erik laughed and tentatively touched the newly tattooed skin of my back.

'Wow, it's awesome,' Shaunee breathed.

'Totally cool,' Erin said.

'Spectacular,' Damien said. 'It's the same labyrinth pattern as your other Marks.'

'Yeah, with the rune symbols spaced between the spirals,' Erik said.

I think I was the only one who noticed that Neferet said nothing at all.

I smoothed the bottom of my shirt back down. I was seriously looking forward to getting to a mirror so that I could see what I'd only been able to feel.

'Congratulations, Zoey. I imagine this means that you continue to be special to your Goddess,' Detective Marx said.

I smiled at him. 'Thanks. Thanks for everything tonight.'

Our eyes met and he winked. Then he turned to Neferet.

'I'd better be going, ma'am. There's a lot of work left to be done tonight. Plus, I imagine Zoey is eager to get to bed. Good night, everyone.' He touched his hat, smiled at me again, and left.

'I am really tired.' I looked at Neferet. 'If it's okay, I'd like to go to bed.'

'Yes, darling,' she said smoothly. 'That would be just fine.'

'And also I'd like to stop by Nyx's Temple on the way to the dorm, if that's okay with you,' I said.

'You do have quite a bit for which you should thank Nyx. Stopping by her temple is a good idea.'

'We'll go with you, Z,' Shaunee said.

'Yeah, Nyx was with all of us tonight,' Erin said.

Damien and Erik made sounds of agreement, but I didn't look at any of my friends. I kept eye contact with Neferet and said, 'I will thank Nyx, but there's really another reason I'm going to her temple.' I didn't wait for her to question me, but continued earnestly, 'I'm going to light an earth candle for Stevie Rae. I promised her I wouldn't forget her.'

My friends were murmuring soft words of agreement, but I kept my attention focused on Neferet as I slowly and deliberately walked over to her.

'Good night, Neferet,' I said and this time I hugged her, and as I pulled her close to me I whispered, *'Humans and fledglings and vampyres don't need to believe me about you because Nyx does. This is not over between us.'*

I stepped out of Neferet's arms and turned my back on her. Together, my friends and I went outside and crossed the short distance to Nyx's Temple. It had finally stopped snowing, and the moon was peeking between wisps of clouds that looked like silken scarves. I stopped at the beautiful marble statue of the Goddess that stood before her temple.

'Here,' I said firmly.

'Z?' Erik said questioningly.

'I want to put Stevie Rae's candle out here, at Nyx's feet.'

'I'll get it for you,' Erik said. He squeezed my hand and then hurried into Nyx's Temple.

'You're right,' Shaunee said.

'Yeah, Stevie Rae would like it lit out here,' Erin said.

'It's closer to the earth,' Damien said.

'And so it's closer to Stevie Rae,' I said softly.

Erik returned and handed me the green votive and a long, ritualistic lighter. Following my instincts, I lit the candle and placed it snugly at Nyx's feet.

'I'm remembering you, Stevie Rae. Just like I promised,' I said.

'So am I,' said Damien.

'Me, too,' said Shaunee.

'Ditto,' said Erin.

'I'm remembering, too,' said Erik.

The scent of a grassy meadow suddenly swirled around Nyx's statue, making my friends smile through their tears. Before we walked away I closed my eyes and whispered a prayer that was a promise I felt deep in my soul.

I'll go back for you, Stevie Rae.

About the Authors

P. C. Cast is an award-winning fantasy and paranormal romance author, who is heavily influenced by her long-standing love of mythology. She was a teacher for many years but now concentrates on writing and public speaking full time. Her daughter, **Kristin Cast,** has won awards for her poetry and journalism as well as co-writing the *Sunday Times* and *New York Times* bestselling House of Night series.

For more information on the series visit www.pccast.net and www.houseofnightseries.co.uk

The story continues in

Chosen

Book Three of the
HOUSE OF NIGHT

P. C. Cast and Kristin Cast

Turn the page for an exciting preview . . .

CHAPTER ONE

'YEP, I HAVE A SERIOUSLY SUCKY BIRTHDAY,' I TOLD MY CAT, Nala.

(Okay, truthfully she's not so much my cat as I'm her person. You know how it is with cats: They don't really have owners, they have staff. A fact I mostly try to ignore.)

Anyway, I kept talking to the cat as if she hung on my every word, which is soooo not the case. 'It's been seventeen years of sucky December twenty-fourth birthdays. I'm totally used to it by now. No big deal.' I knew I was saying the words just to convince myself. Nala 'mee-uf-owed' at me in her grumpy-old-lady cat voice and then settled down to lick her privates, clearly showing that she understood I was full of b.s.

'Here's the deal,' I continued as I finished smudging a little liner on my eyes. (And I mean a *little* – the line-your-eyes-till-you-look-like-a-scary-raccoon is definitely not the look for me. Actually, it's not the look for anyone.) 'I'm gonna get a bunch of well-meaning presents that aren't really birthday presents – they're stuff that's Christmas themed because people always try to mush my birthday with Christmas, and that seriously doesn't work.' I met Nala's big green eyes in the mirror. 'But we're going to smile and pretend we're fine with the dorky birthmas gifts because people do not get that they can't mush a birthday into Christmas. At least not successfully.'

Nala sneezed.

'Exactly how I feel about it, but we'll be nice 'cause it's even worse when I say something. Then I get crappy gifts *and* everyone's upset and things turn all awkward.' Nala didn't look convinced, so I focused my attention on my reflection. For a second I thought I might have gone too heavy on the eyeliner, but I looked closer and realized that what was making my eyes look so huge and dark wasn't anything as ordinary as eyeliner. Even though it had been two months since I'd been Marked to become a vampyre, the sapphire-colored crescent-moon tattoo between my eyes and the elaborate filigree of interlocking lacework tattoos that framed my face still had the ability to surprise me. I traced one of the curving jewel-blue spiral lines with the tip of my finger. Then almost without conscious thought I pulled the already wide neck of my black sweater down so that it exposed my left shoulder. With a flick of my head I tossed back my long dark hair so that the unusual pattern of tattoos that began at the base of my neck and spread over my shoulder and down either side of my spine to the small of my back was visible. As always, the sight of my tattoos gave me an electric thrill that was part wonder and part fear.

'You're not like anyone else,' I whispered to my reflection. Then I cleared my throat and continued in an overly perky voice. 'And it's okay not to be like anyone else.' I rolled my eyes at myself. 'Whatever.' I looked up over my head, half surprised that it wasn't visible. I mean, I could definitely feel the ginormic dark cloud that had been following me around for the past month. 'Hell, I'm surprised it's not raining in here. And wouldn't that be just great for my hair?' I sarcastically told my reflection. Then I sighed and picked up the envelope I'd laid on my desk. *THE HEFFER FAMILY* was embossed in gold above the sparkling return address. 'Speaking of depressing . . . ,' I muttered.

Nala sneezed again.

'You're right. Might as well get it over with.' I reluctantly opened the envelope and pulled out the card. 'Ah, hell. It's worse than I thought.' There was a huge wooden cross on the front of the card. Staked to the middle of the cross (with a bloody nail) was an old time scroll-like paper. Written (in blood, of course) were the words: *He IS the reason for the season*. Inside the card was printed (in red letters): MERRY CHRISTMAS. Below that, in my mom's handwriting, it said: *I hope you're remembering your family during this blessed time of the year. Happy Birthday, Love, Mom and Dad.*

'That's so typical,' I told Nala. My stomach hurt. 'And he is not my dad.' I ripped the card in two and threw it into the wastepaper basket, then stood staring at the torn pieces. 'If my parents aren't ignoring me, they're insulting me. I like being ignored better.'

The knock on my door made me jump.

'Zoey, everyone wants to know where you are.' Damien's voice carried easily through the door.

'Hang on – I'm almost ready,' I yelled, shook myself mentally, and gave my reflection one more look, deciding, with a definitely defensive edge, to leave my shoulder bare. 'My Marks aren't like anyone else's. Might as well give the masses something to gawk at while they talk,' I muttered.

Then I sighed. I'm usually not so grumpy. But my sucky birthday, my sucky parents . . .

No. I couldn't keep lying to myself.

'Wish Stevie Rae was here,' I whispered.

And that was it, what had me withdrawing from my friends (including *boy*friends – both of them) during the past month and impersonating a large, soggy, disgusting, rain cloud. I missed my best friend and ex-roommate, who everyone had watched die a month ago, but who I knew had actually been turned into an undead creature of the night. No matter how melodramatic and bad B movie that sounded. The truth was that right now, when Stevie Rae should have been downstairs puttering around with my lame birthday details, she was actually lurking about somewhere in the old tunnels under Tulsa, conspiring with other disgusting undead creatures who were truly evil, as well as definitely bad-smelling.

'Uh, Z? You okay in there?' Damien's voice called again, interrupting my mental blahs. I scooped up a complaining Nala, turned my back on the terrible birthmas card from my 'rentals, and hurried out the door, almost running over a worried-looking Damien.

'Sorry . . . sorry . . . ,' I mumbled. He fell in step beside me, giving me quick little sideways glances.

'I've never known anyone before who was as *not* excited as you about their birthday,' Damien said.

I dropped the squirming Nala and shrugged, trying for a nonchalant smile. 'I'm just practicing for when I'm old as dirt – like thirty – and I need to lie about my age.'

Damien stopped and turned to face me. 'Okayyyy.' He dragged the word out. 'We all know that thirty-year-old vamps still look roughly twenty and definitely hot. Actually one-hundred-and-thirty-year-old vamps still look roughly twenty and definitely hot. So the whole lying about your age issue is a nonissue. What's really going on with you?'

While I hesitated, trying to figure out what I should or could say to Damien, he raised one neatly plucked brow and, in his best schoolteacher voice, said, 'You know how sensitive my people are to emotions, so you may as well just give up and tell me the truth.'

I sighed again. 'You gays are freakishly intuitive.'

'That's us: homos – the few, the proud, the hypersensitive.'

'Isn't homo a derogatory term?'

385

'Not if it's used by a homo. By the by, you're stalling and it's so not working for you.' He actually put his hand on his hip and tapped his foot.

I smiled at him, but knew that the expression didn't reach my eyes. With an intensity that surprised me, I suddenly, desperately wanted to tell Damien the truth.

'I miss Stevie Rae,' I blurted before I could stop my mouth.

He didn't hesitate. 'I know.' His eyes looked suspiciously damp.

And that was it. Like a dam had broken open inside me the words came spilling out. 'She should be here! She'd be running around like a crazy woman putting up birthday decorations and probably baking a cake all by herself.'

'A really awful cake,' Damien said with a little sniffle.

'Yeah, but it'd be one of her *mama's favorite recipes*.' I gave my best exaggerated Okie twang as I mimicked Stevie Rae's countrified voice, which made me smile through my own tears, and I thought how weird it was that now that I was letting Damien see how upset I really felt – and why I felt that way – my smile actually reached my eyes.

'And the Twins and I would have been pissed because she would have insisted we all wear those pointed birthday hats with the elastic string that pinches your chin.' He shuddered in not-so-pretended horror. 'God, they're so unattractive.'

I laughed and felt a little of the tightness in my chest begin to loosen. 'There's just something about Stevie Rae that makes me feel good.' I didn't realize that I'd used the present tense until Damien's teary smile faltered.

'Yeah, she *was* great,' he said, with an extra emphasis on the *was* while he looked at me like he was worried about my sanity.

If only he knew the whole truth. If only I could tell him.

But I couldn't. If I did it would get either Stevie Rae or me, or both of us, killed. For good this time.

So instead I grabbed my obviously worried friend's arm and started pulling him toward the stairs that would lead us down to the public rooms of the girls' dorm and my waiting friends (and their dorky presents).

'Let's go. I'm feeling the need to open presents,' I lied enthusiastically.

'Ohmygod! I can*not* wait for you to open mine!' Damien gushed. 'I shopped for it forevah!'

I smiled and nodded appropriately as Damien went on and on about his Quest for the Perfect Present. Usually he isn't so overtly gay. Not that the fabulous Damien Maslin isn't actually gay. He totally is. But he's also a tall, brown-haired, big-eyed cutie who looks like he'd be excellent boyfriend material (which he is – if you're a boy). He's not a fluttery-acting gay kid, but get the boy talking about shopping and he definitely shows some girlish tendencies. Not that I don't like that about him. I think he looks cute when he gushes about the importance of buying really good shoes, and right then his babbling was soothing. It was helping me to get ready to face the bad presents that (sadly) waited for me.

Too bad it couldn't help me face what was really bothering me.

Still talking about his Shopping Quest, Damien led me though the main room of the dorm. I waved at the various clumps of girls clustered around the pods of flat-screen TVs as we headed to the little side room that served as a computer lab and library. Damien opened the door and my friends broke into a totally off-key chorus of 'Happy Birthday to You.' I heard Nala hiss and from the edge of my vision watched her back from the doorway and trot away down the hall. *Coward*, I thought, even though I wished I could escape with her.

Song over (thankfully), my gang swarmed me.

'Happy-happy!' said the Twins together. Okay – they're not genetically twins. Erin Bates is a very white girl from Tulsa and Shaunee Cole is a lovely caramel-colored girl of Jamaican-American descent who grew up in Connecticut, but the two are so freakishly alike that skin tone and region make absolutely no difference. They're soul twins, which is way closer than mere biology.

'Happy birthday, Z,' said a deep, sexy voice I knew very, very well. I stepped out of the twin sandwich and walked into the arms of my boyfriend, Erik. Well, technically, Erik is one of my two boyfriends, but the other is Heath, a human teenager I dated before I was Marked and I'm not supposed to be dating him now, but I kinda sorta accidentally sucked his blood and now we're Imprinted and so he's my boyfriend by default. Yes, it's confusing. Yes, it makes Erik mad. Yes, I expect him to dump me any day because of it.

'Thanks,' I murmured looking up at him and getting trapped all over again in his incredible eyes. Erik is tall and hot, with Superman dark hair and incredibly blue eyes. I relaxed in his arms, a treat I hadn't allowed myself much of during the past month, and temporarily basked in his yummy smell and the sense of security I felt when I was close to him. He met my gaze and, just like in the movies, for a second everyone else went away and it was just us. When I didn't move out of his arms his smile was slow and a little surprised, which made my heart hurt. I'd been putting the kid through way too much – and he didn't even really understand why. Impulsively, I tiptoed and kissed him, much to the general merriment of my friends.

'Hey, Erik, why don't you spread some of that birthday sugar around?' Shaunee wagged her eyebrows at my grinning boyfriend.

'Yeah, sweet thang,' Erin said, and in typical twin fashion mirrored Shaunee's eye waggle. 'How about a little b-day kiss over here.'

I rolled my eyes at the Twins. 'Uh, it's not *his* birthday. You only get to kiss the birthday boy or girl.'

'Damn,' Shaunee said. 'I lurve ya, Z, but I don't want to kiss ya.'

'Just please with the same-sex kissing,' Erin said, then she grinned at Damien (who was gazing adoringly at Erik). 'I'll leave that to Damien.'

'Huh?' Damien said, clearly paying more attention to Erik's cuteness than the Twins.

'Again, we say—' Shaunee started.

'Wrong team!' and Erin finished.

Erik laughed good-naturedly, gave Damien a very guy-like punch on the arm, and said, 'Hey, if I ever decide to change teams, you'll be the first to know.' (Yet another reason why I adore him. He's mega-cool and popular, but he accepts people how they are and never gets an I'm-all-that attitude.)

'Uh, I hope I'll be the first to know if you change teams,' I said.

Erik laughed and hugged me, whispering, 'Not something you ever need to worry about,' in my ear.

While I was seriously considering sneaking another Erik kiss, a mini-whirlwind in the form of Damien's boyfriend, Jack Twist, burst into the room.

'Yea! She hasn't opened her presents yet. Happy birthday, Zoey!' Jack threw his arms around us (yes, Damien and me) and gave us a big hug.

'I told you that you needed to hurry up,' Damien said, as we untangled.

'I know, but I had to make sure it was wrapped *just right*,' Jack said. With a flourish that only a gay boy can pull off, he reached into the man purse looped over his arm and lifted out a box wrapped in red foil with a green sparkly bow on it that was so big it practically swallowed the package. 'I made the bow myself.'

'Jack's really good at crafts,' Erik said. 'He's just not good at cleaning up the crafts.'

'Sorry,' Jack said sweetly. 'I promise I'll clean up right after the party.'

Erik and Jack are roommates, further proving Erik's

coolness. He's a fifth former (in normal language that's a junior) and he's also easily the most popular guy at school. Jack is a third former (a freshman), a new kid, cute but kinda dorky, and definitely gay. Erik could have made a big deal about being stuck with a queer and could have gotten out of rooming with him, and made Jack's life hell at the House of Night. Instead he totally took him under his wing and treats him like a little brother, a treatment he extends to Damien, who has been officially going out with Jack for two point five weeks as of today. (We all know because Damien is ridiculously romantic and he celebrates the half-week anniversaries as well as the weekly ones. Yes, it makes the rest of us gag. In a nice way.)

'Hello! Speaking of presents!' Shaunee said.

'Yeah, bring that overbowed box over here to the present table and let Zoey get to opening,' Erin said.

I heard Jack whisper to Damien, 'Overbowed?' and caught Damien's *help* look, as he assured Jack, 'No, it's perfect!'

'I'll carry it over to the table and open it first.' I snatched the package from him, hurried to the table, and started to carefully extract the ginormous green sparkly bow from the red foil saying, 'I think I'm going to save this bow because it's so cool.' Damien gave me a thank-you wink. I heard Erik and Shaunee snickering and managed to kick one of them, which shut both of them up. Putting the bow aside I unwrapped and opened the little box and pulled out . . .

Oh, jeesh.

'A snow globe,' I said, trying to sound happy. 'With a

snowman inside it.' Okay, a snowman snow globe is *not* a birthday present. It's a Christmas decoration. A cheesy Christmas decoration at that.

'Yeah! Yeah! And listen to what it plays!' Jack said, practically hopping up and down in excitement as he took the globe from me and wound a knob in its base so that 'Frosty the Snowman' started tinkling out around us in painfully cheap and off-key notes.

'Thank you, Jack. It's really pretty,' I lied.

'Glad you like it,' Jack said. 'It's kinda a theme for your birthday.' Then he shot his eyes over to Erik and Damien. The three of them grinned at each other like bad little boys.

I planted a smile on my face. 'Oh, well, good. Then I'd better open the next present.'

'Mine's next!' Damien handed me a long, soft box.

Smile wedged in place, I started to open the box, though I couldn't help wishing I could turn into a cat and hiss and run from the room.